THE PLATINUM EDITION

MAY

2012

Copyright © 2011 by Cole Hart

Published by:

G Street Chronicles P.O. Box 490082 College Park, GA 30349

www.gstreetchronicles.com Fan@gstreetchronicles.com

All rights reserved. Without limiting the rights under copyright reserved above. No part of this book may be reproduced, stored in or introduced into a retrieval system, or transmitted, in any form, or by any means (electronic, mechanical, photocopying, recording, or otherwise), without prior written consent from both the author, and publisher G Street Chronicles, except brief quotes used in reviews.

This is a work of fiction. It is not meant to depict, portray or represent any particular real person. All the characters, incidents, and dialogues are the products of the author's imagination and are not to be construed as real. Any references or similarities to actual events, entities, real people, living or dead, or to real locales are intended to give the novel a sense of reality. Any similarity in other names, characters, entities, places, and incidents is entirely coincidental.

Cover Design: Oddball Dsgn

davida@oddballdsgn.com

Typesetting:

G&S Typesetting & Ebook Conversions

info@gstypesetting.com

LCN: 2011927142

ISBN: 978-0-9834311-2-1

Join us on Facebook G Street Chronicles Fan Page

MAN BE TOWNED

*This book is dedicated to my homies,*
*Scotty Mathis and Vernon Forrest.*
*RIP…*

## ACKNOWLEDGMENTS

First and foremost, I would like to thank God for sitting me down and blessing me with the gift and talent to write, create, and publish novels from prison. I'm Cole Hart, a certified author, founder and CEO of Executive Urban Authors. I wanna give a special shout out to my wife, Lopedia Hardwick. Never in my entire life have I met a woman more loyal than you. "Thanks for having my back, and continuing our personal prayers every night." Real women do real things! To my kids: Tiara, Kyhana, Shalia, Faith, Ashley, and Phil, the up-and-coming Millionaire Group CEOs. Shout out to my entire family, you know who you are. Dr. Jones, thanks for all your help and support. Author G-Five and the Million Dollar Book Review Family, good looking out on the interview. To Ben (Up the Way Magazine), Lawrence Wimbush, James Wilson, (Them New Jersey Dudes) that played a big part in my writing career. To all my incarcerated homies for dat Augusta, Atlanta, Savannah, Mac-Town, That Good Lyfe, C-Town, My Loc's ASAP. You know the Blue Print. To all my GD patna's and B-Dogs as well. Thanks for the support. To Davida Baldwin, good looking out on the book cover…great work!

# The Letter

How are you? I pray all's in God's grace 'n memories. I got your letter today, and I profusely apologize for my procrastination in writing you sooner. I would love to explore my afflictions with you, but since we're basically in the same predicament, I'll spare you the inappropriateness. Being that I'm here to encourage instead of discourage, I believe words are a very powerful tool in our existence, as well as supernaturally. And if we continue to speak good and righteous things over our situations, circumstances, as well as our futures, good things are sure to follow. Although rain sometimes falls in our lives, we eventually reestablish ourselves and move on. Because the things we wanted yesterday may just be the things we want to forget about tomorrow.

Through struggles and pains, we discover the true essence of what we are really made of. Therefore, we also create the un-abolished talent to determine and execute our own destinies. We understand the capabilities and intentions of those who constantly entertain us with words of endearment, companionship, and of course, friendship. It's complicated to decipher or to differentiate who's sincere and who's a blatant imposter.

As God tried us with fire, upon the altars and hands of the God bearers, so do the atrocities of life try the truest hearts of man! And although all else seems to evaporate and explicitly abandon us, we can rest assured that the almighty hands of God are persistent, merciful, and gracious in the storms of our lives! Nothing is impossible with God. Preferably, in today's world, especially in our daily lives, it's sometimes hard to feel God's unconditional love that evokes promises of comfort, companionship, and love in our lives. But, His existence is ever present by the mere fact that we continue to breathe His air, even right now as we speak. He continues to watch over us and still loves us today just as much as He loved us yesterday. So, we should ever be thankful to God, if just for another day. I have depleted every effort to try and figure out God's scheme of things, but it takes too much effort to waste time in doing so. I only continue to live each day in the aspirations of God's true intent and purpose for my life. I am not perfect; no one else who walked the face of the Earth besides Jesus can claim such a thing. But each day I continuously acknowledge and observe the inconsistencies of my life, and not only will I do better, but pray also that I will eventually *get* better. The preconceived notion that we, as humans, are not entitled to make mistakes—or at least be forgiven for our mistakes—depending on the levels or insensitivities of those mistakes is quite ludicrous because we've all made them, big and small. To be perfectly honest, our world as we know it has been embodied in the pure asceticism of values of unknown to the other worlds of vastness and complexities as we've known them in times past. Some people like me may interpret this as the "old school" ways vs. the "new generation," and that's exactly the effect I was trying to imply. But my interpretation is very simple: We all have troubles, whether far or great, and as long as we live, we will encounter strenuous episodes or situations. We all have a story to tell! But I want you to know and understand that with God on our side, who can be against us? Continue to pray! Although the doubt and bleariness of our faith seems to diminish as our day-to-day struggles continue, remember there is a light at the end of every dark tunnel, and no matter what anyone tries to perceive it to be, know that it's God. Be encouraged always as your friend or foe in spirit and in truth. God bless!

~ Bertram "Scarface" Owens.

*(After this page, there will be no more commercial interruption... So read and enjoy!)*

# BOOK I

*TO HAVE ULTIMATE VICTORY,*

*YOU MUST BE RUTHLESS*

# NAPOLEON BONAPARTE
# 1769-1821

# CHAPTER 1

The Fulton County Juvenile Courtroom was crawling with people: screaming children and some of the most nagging old women who would make your skin crawl. Just yap…yap…yap, all about nothing. Even though a lot of them were there to support their kids and grandkids, many of them were there to make sure justice was served against Terry Keys, the notorious thirteen-year-old alleged murderer who was beginning to make his name known throughout the Westside of Atlanta.

In a gun battle with a twenty-one-year-old, Terry Keys didn't hesitate to shoot. He was well trained by the older brothers. If you let the public tell it, the murder was drug related. It had become major news all over the city of Atlanta. Terry Keys had a young, handsome face—the schoolboy type, very innocent looking. His body frame was small and chiseled. His eyebrows were thick and dark, and he wore his hair neatly trimmed in a three-inch afro with not a hair out of place. He was dressed in a navy blue, two-piece suit, a white Polo dress shirt, and a blue tie.

Next to Terry sat his high-priced attorney, well known throughout the city. Andre Rizzi was a slick talker and casual dresser, with a reputation that spoke for itself. It was rumored he was connected with every major drug dealer, armed robber, and hit man in the city. He was known for playing golf, fishing, and eating at the most expensive restaurants with every judge and politician around Atlanta. His name alone carried more weight than a triple-beam scale.

As the proceedings started, the bailiff, a heavyset man in his mid fifties shouted, "All rise!" His voice boomed through the entire courtroom.

Everybody shuffled to their feet. As the judge climbed the steps that led to his bench, Terry Key's heart began erupting inside his chest at just the thought of knowing court was about to start. Terry allowed his eyes to follow the judge, darting with every step.

The judge was a chubby-faced white man, clean-shaven, with salt-and-pepper hair. Clad in his black robe, his suspicious blue eyes searched the courtroom. It was evident that he wanted to make sure everyone was on their feet. "You may be seated," he said. He cleared his throat and adjusted the microphone. He slowly lifted the wire-framed eyeglasses hanging around his neck and slid them on his face. His vision enhanced within a microsecond, and he pretended to be looking over some papers. It was all bullshit, though, and a mask came over his face; all this was just an act. He already knew the case, and he'd already received eight grand from the Regal & Alexander Law Firm as an early Christmas gift.

Andre Rizzi was married to the daughter of the founder of the law firm. Not to mention, Rizzi's wife was the judge's goddaughter. It was all an inside circle—Atlanta's own political secret society. This was something bigger going on than Terry Keys, and it would be years before he would be aware of the game of life; another pawn being moved around the board with the touch of a finger.

The judge finally lifted his head and allowed his eyes to focus directly on Terry Keys. "Young man, are your parents here this morning?" he asked.

There was a short silence. The fact of the matter was that Terry Keys had accepted the streets. His neighborhood, Hollywood Court, was his version of parents. His real biological mother was out there somewhere. Where? He didn't know...and actually, he didn't care. His father couldn't make it to court either. Terry's dad was thirteen years into a double life sentence for two bodies he'd caught in 1980. Terry hadn't ever seen him in person, but he'd heard some hood legends about him; enough to convince him that he got his gangsta from his daddy. It was inherited.

A middle-aged woman on the congested third pew stood up. Her hand slightly raised and fell back to her side just as quick. "I'm his grandmamma," she said. Then she added, "He stay wit' me."

The judge's eyes went to her quickly, and then he motioned his hand for the woman to come to the front of the courtroom. She went and stood before him.

When the judge motioned for Terry to come and stand next to her, he did as he was told and tried desperately hard to keep his mouth closed as much as possible; he didn't want the judge to see his gold teeth. He pressed his lips together and put on the saddest face he could muster.

"Son do you know with a crime like this, you could go to prison for the rest of your life?" the judge asked.

Terry nodded his head and in a clear whisper said, "Yes, sir." His hands and arms were pressed against his sides as if he were in the military.

"Is that what you want?" the judge asked.

"No, sir," Terry responded.

The judge looked at Terry's grandmother. Her skin was mahogany, and there were thin bags under her eyes. Her hair was made up in thick finger waves. She wore a red turtleneck sweater, white jeans, and boots. A diamond rope chain hung loosely around her neck. She stared into the judge's eyes, and he offered her the same stare. "What is your name?" he asked.

"Vickie Keys," she said.

"Miss Keys, where are you currently living right now?" asked the judge.

"Hollywood Court on Hollywood Road," she said proudly. Her eyes gleamed, and she stood even more erect and raised her head.

The judge curled his lips as if he were really impressed and began nodding his rather large head. He couldn't really respond because if he did, he wouldn't have anything positive to say about Westside Atlanta. It was 1991. The murder rate was at an all-time high, and the crack era was in full effect. The judge took a sip of water from the glass that sat to the right of him. He glanced around the courtroom again and noticed how impatient and agitated everyone looked. Sharply, his eyes cut back to Terry Keys. He asked, "Are you attending school?"

"Yes, sir," Terry responded. "I go to Usher Middle School." As he swallowed, his Adam's apple bobbled in his throat; he'd just told a straight-faced lie.

The judge picked up a fountain pen and pointed it toward Terry and narrowed his eyes. "You are still a child, son. I don't want to hear your name, nor do I want to see you in my courtroom ever again. You need to stay your tail in school and get yourself an education," the judge said. It was the quickest type of lecture that came to his head. He looked to the grandmother. "I'm giving him three years of probation with a monthly report from you."

She nodded, and a bright smile appeared across her face. She dropped her arm around her grandson's neck and pulled him to her.

The judge hit his gavel. "Next case on the docket!" he yelled.

Terry Keys and his grandmother turned and headed toward the defense table, where Andre Rizzi gave them a smile and extended his hand. Vickie shook his hand first, and Terry followed. Andre Rizzi held on to Terry's small boy hand and said, "Good luck and tell Wayne everything went well and to give me a call in the morning."

Terry Keys nodded and gave the attorney one final shake before they departed. He and his grandmother moved swiftly up the aisle and exited the courtroom. But in the midst of the many people and families, there still lurked anger and bitter feelings about the outcome. And if anyone wanted revenge, they would also be looking for war.

# CHAPTER 2

Hollywood Court, the project they called "the Horseshoe" at times, was a number one favorite spot on the Westside. It was a project known for violence, a place where the goons lurked. Often the stuff of rap songs, this was just one of them in Zone One, the Westside. Inside one of the small apartments, a notorious gunslinger and hustler by the name of Wayne sat in the kitchen in a nearly broken wooden chair. There was nearly $90K in cash scattered across the table. Some of it was still stuffed inside the Macy's shopping bag. Next to the money was a military-issued AR-15 assault rifle equipped with two loaded banana clips that were duct taped together.

Wayne was twenty-six years old and stood six-three. He was a hunk of a man with huge shoulders, a solid barrel chest, and thick, muscular legs. He wore a nappy afro but always kept a neat, sharp tape line. A thick goatee was wrapped around his lips. His hands were huge with thick, rusty-looking fingers. They were working man's hands, but unfortunately the only work he'd ever done was handling sling blades and thick-handled bush axes during his three-year bid in prison.

Wayne had only been home nine months and had taken full control of the project, earning himself a nice nest egg stash in the process. He was worth nearly $400K, and that alone had his name spreading through the heart of the city; only what was quickly becoming a household name wasn't Wayne. They called him Hollywood, dubbed from the project, a man serious about his issues and a ruthless mentality. Every major hustler had their own team of goons, certified killers who would put their lives on the line for their boss or were destined to catch a life sentence for one. And regardless of how powerful one man might be, he wouldn't stand a chance in the A trying to be a one-man army. It was simply unheard of. Hollywood knew this, and he had a hell of a clique he'd hand picked himself.

Across the table from him was his cousin and right-hand man, literally related by blood. They called him Bones. Bones was from Perry Homes, another Westside housing project known for heinous crimes, and Bones was part of that culture. He was a skinny man, dark, with slits for eyes; very evil looking. He was type that might be considered death struck, and just his presence alone had brought fear into the hearts of a lot of men. His aggressiveness and propensity for pistol play had his name circulating through Atlanta's underworld. Bones was twenty-two years old and had been shot more times than John Wayne in a Western flick—all before his eighteenth birthday. Even though he was down with Hollywood, he still had ties with his old comrades in Perry Homes, and if he was connected to them, that meant Hollywood was connected by association as well. Just three weeks prior, he'd killed a guy on South Grand in a car over an $200 debt. He left his entire face twisted and brains on the front windshield. He was honored for that, and not once was it mentioned. Bones wasn't much of a fighter, and he'd tell you that. Was that a flaw? Humph! He was beaten up a while back for bringing counterfeit money to a dice game, probably about two years ago. He always make jokes about his hand game. Just a week after the incident, he caught up with the guy, dressed in a fatigue army suit and black ski mask. He killed the guy and his mother after he saw them bringing in groceries from the trunk of an old-model Lincoln. He was always a suspect, but nobody could identify him, and the APD (Atlanta Police Department) couldn't get anything out of him. He was standing at the front door, leaning casually against the doorframe, watching all the drug traffic and normal activity outside in the Horseshoe.

Another team member they called Scooter, who was also born and raised in Hollywood Court, was just as sick in the head as he could possibly be. Scooter was nineteen years old, with a handicap: He was missing his hand and three inches of his arm. He'd been that way since he was nine years old. Scooter's father was from Jamaica. He migrated to Atlanta in the seventies and met his mother and married her, but the old rascal had a mental problem. There was something about kids that drove him crazy, especially Scooter. One day Scooter aggravated his father so bad that his daddy walked him to a fenced-in piece of commercial property over on Simpson Road, forced him to slide his hand through the fence, and let two huge Rottweilers eat off his hand. Then he rushed him to Grady Hospital, where he had to have surgery. Scooter went through physical and mental therapy. His dad had always told him never to tell anybody, or he would cut his tongue from his mouth. And Scooter kept it that way, never doing too much talking about anything. When he was twelve, his mother paid for him to take martial arts classes. By the time he was fifteen, he was strong and powerfully built, and everybody who had joked about his arm in the past was beaten badly. He broke noses and jawbones regularly in school and in his project. Then the word spread at the movies and at the skating rink, "That nigga Scooter know dat shit. Man, shawty killed his daddy." At the present moment, Scooter stood five-eleven and weighed a solid 225. He wasn't a heavy talker, not even with his crew, maybe a few words here and there. The police couldn't even get a word out of him. His father taught him that.

On the couch behind him, Fat Man was weighing up cooked ounces of cocaine from a half-kilo. The small living room table was covered with plastic sandwich bags, crack crumbs, a digital scale, and a half-fixed bottle of Moet and Chan Don on the floor between his legs. Fat Man was thirty-three, which made him the oldest in the crew. If you let him tell it, he was the wisest too. Fat Man was pretty huge. He was close to 300 pounds and stood six-three. He wasn't the slouchy slob type of fat, but the hard kind of big with a huge, solid belly and big jaws. Fat Man wasn't handsome; he had bulging eyes, a wide, flat nose, and uncombed hair. He was the happy-go-lucky type who spoke with a deep Southern drawl. He also had a no-nonsense attitude. Fat Man was from Herndon Homes, and he had an established reputation for being a known robber all over the city. Somebody from every zone in Atlanta had heard of him. Fat Man came from a big family with sisters, brothers, nieces, and nephews scattered all over the city. There wasn't a project or neighborhood he couldn't walk through, except Summer Hill.

His treachery led him to a bad experience over there when he tried to rob one of his sister's baby daddies. The cat was named Cutt Throat. Fat Man caught him down bad, slipping, in other words. They'd both been sniffing coke all night when Fat Man put the pistol in Cutt Throat's face in his own living room. He took his jewelry and two grand from his pockets. He fled the apartment, but before he'd made it out of the projects, he was robbed himself, pistol-whipped, and stabbed. Paving the way for his demise, Cutt Throat spared his life on the strength of his sister. She pleaded to Cutt Throat for Fat Man's life, and they came to an agreement: Fat Man would never show his face in Summer Hill again. They left him sprawled out in the middle of Grant Street with his head split and two stab wounds in his fat-ass stomach.

Fat Man finally lifted his head from the table and looked toward the kitchen where Hollywood and Bones were counting money. "Shawty, is there some mo' chicken in da' fridge?" He rubbed his stomach. "I'm hungry than a motha' fucka'!" shouted Fat Man. His final words came as a growl, or more like a roar from the belly of a grizzly bear. He lit up a Newport and quickly stood to his feet. His bones and joints began cracking and popping. He yawned, yelled, and stretched all at the same time.

Hollywood looked at him, staring at his huge, disgusting stomach that was now exposed. "Shawty, ain't you got no bigga' shirts?" Hollywood asked while he was still counting money, moving his lips with a jokingly grin.

That provoked Bones, who looked at Fat Man with his black face and pink lips, smiling. "My nigga say he on a diet. Fat, greedy motha' fucka' been eating all night."

Fat Man drew on his cigarette, flipped his head back, and blew a stream of smoke toward the ceiling. He bent in a casual sort of way and picked up the champagne bottle from the floor. He turned it up and took two deep swallows and held the bottle in one hand and the cigarette in the other. "Only thing I ate was yo' sista last night," said Fat Man.

Bones didn't like that; he considered it as a low blow, but he held his composer. He continued smiling and said, "You know I'm a pussy connoisseur. I analyze bitches too. But yo' sista Freda got some of the stankiest pussy in da' whole Atlanta. I mean, every nigga in Zone Three sayin' the same thing."

Fat Man's eyes squinted as he pointed his lit Newport at Bones and said, "Don't play wit' me, shawty."

Hollywood did everything in his might not to laugh, and he knew Bones would go on and on. He was always clowning and joking, and he didn't know his limit.

Bones went on, "I had to wear an oxygen mask last night 'cause da' pussy had took my homeboy breath da' night befo' and killed him in his sleep."

Fat Man was quick for his size. He stepped into the kitchen and went toward Bones.

But Bones was quicker. He stood from the table and ran around it with a silly grin over his face.

Hollywood stood, then had a serious look across his face. "We don't do dis type of shit."

Fat Man and Bones stared at one another for nearly twenty seconds. Silence hung in the air.

Scooter, in an even tone of voice and without any excitement said, "Here come shawty."

# CHAPTER 3

When Terry stepped out of the passenger's side of his grandmother's Ford Taurus, a huge smile formed across his face. It was a pleasure for him to see Scooter, his image behind the dust and worn down screen door. His grandmother switched off the engine and stepped out also. She slung the strap of her leather pocketbook over her shoulder. Then she closed the door. She looked across the top of the car at Terry without parting her lips. He was out of control, and she knew it, but there wasn't anything she could do about it but pray for him.

When he caught her stare, he asked, "Wuz wrong, gran'ma?"

She didn't answer; her body language actually spoke for itself. She turned around and began walking up the sidewalk, shaking her head and talking to herself. She lived about three apartments up.

Terry stood there, watched her for a minute, then headed toward the front door and began coming out of his jacket.

Scooter pushed the screen door open for him. The butt of a snub-nosed .44 Bulldog was bulging in his waistline. Scooter embraced Terry with one arm. "Wuz up, shawty?" Scooter asked him. His tone of voice didn't sound like he was too happy to see him, but then he was never too excited about anything except murder. His row of gold teeth sparkled at Terry.

Terry looked up at him, his face glowing like a full moon. "I beat dat shit, shawty."

"Check," was all Scooter said in response. Then his eyes went back to the activity in the Horseshoe.

Terry stepped inside the living room and dropped his jacket across the arm of a chair that didn't match the remainder of the furniture. He turned and saw Fat Man standing there with a Miss Winners chicken box in one hand and a cold piece of chicken in the other. He was chewing and talking at the same time.

"Next time you murda' a nigga, shawty, make sho ain't no witnesses around. One motha' fucka' recognize yo' face and point da finger at cha, and that'll get cha sent down da' road fo' da rest of yo' life." He held out a fat balled fist with his bulging eyes staring down at the much shorter

Terry.

Terry held his much smaller fist out to Fat Man. "I'm certified now, though, right?" Terry asked.

Fat Man's mouth was chewing, his head nodding up and down as though he was amazed at what the youngster has asked him. Then Fat Man replied, "You damn right. You officially certified in my book."

Terry then bowed his head slowly in agreement and moved into the kitchen, first scanning the ounces of cocaine on the living room table. He walked up to the table where Hollywood was sitting. Bones was standing, firing up a Newport, his hand cupped around the flames and the tip of the cigarette. Terry waited for a reaction from either one of them.

Hollywood was still counting money, only moving his lips. With his eyes on the table, never looking toward Terry, he said, "You cost me twenty-five stocks, shawty."

Terry stood there staring at Hollywood. He didn't know whether he was serious or not. He looked over at Bones.

With clouds of smoke curling around his face, Bones nodded his head with a silly-ass grin, as if to be agreeing with Hollywood.

Hollywood broke the silence. "Watcha got to say, nigga?"

Terry frowned. Only his eyebrows rose, and then he shrugged his shoulders. "I'll pay it back."

Hollywood's lips curled, forming a smile. He turned toward Terry and said, "You damn right you gon' pay me back." He put his arm around Terry's neck and drew him toward him. "It was money well spent though." Hollywood looked up to Terry. He adored him and thought of him as a little brother or nephew. The kid had a lot of potential, he thought, and he accepted the responsibility the best as he could to support him. When Hollywood came home from prison, young Terry was running the streets, stealing cars, burglarizing homes, toting stolen pistols, and selling crack. Hollywood knew his family and tried to better his situation. He took Terry under his wings the day Terry had shot all the windows out of a car parked in his grandmother's parking space. The car belonged to an insurance man, and that had drawn tremendous heat to the project. "Shawty, you made it home jus' in time too," Hollywood said. Then he added, "We was 'bout to go to Vegas without you."

"Where Vegas at?" Terry asked in a more curious tone of voice.

"Lil' nigga, Vegas on the other side of the world—where Holyfield fightin' at this weekend," Hollywood told him.

"Holyfield can't get me no money, shawty. I need to stay out here and grind in da' trap," Terry explained.

"Ain't too many young niggas yo' age get opportunities like dis. You betta' take advantage if dis shit. Dis some boss playa' shit," Hollywood said in an encouraging tone of voice.

That was all Terry needed to hear; he adored Hollywood. He couldn't help it. And besides that, he'd already started calling himself Young Hollywood. But he wouldn't reveal that right now; he'd keep that one under his hat until he felt the time was right. Hopefully somebody else would recognize it and just give him that title. If not, he would definitely earn it.

The night Terry caught his case, he'd just stepped out of a raggedy and rundown motel room. Night had fallen, and the parking lot of the Summit Inn was blazing with traffic. A female prostitute by the name of Red had just finished serving him. It was some of the best head he'd ever had in his life. He went downstairs to the parking lot, dressed in denim jeans, a Polo shirt, and the latest pair of Air Jordan tennis shoes. Just two hours earlier, he had been in possession of nearly two ounces of crack, all bagged in nicks and dimes. He exchanged that for the $2,600 he had stuffed in all four of his pockets.

The parking lot was crawling with junkies, a few men here and there, but the majority of them were females. The entire motel was nothing more than a trap and a whore stroll. Terry stood up against a parked Cutlass for a brief moment and allowed his eyes to scan the parking lot. Vehicles were coming through; prostitutes going in and out of cars. They worked the parking lot and Fulton Industrial Boulevard. Terry looked to his left and then to his right, paying good attention to his surroundings. Then his eyes focused on a guy that had just stepped from the backseat of a beige Cadillac. The guy wore a black Kangol pulled down over his eyes. Terry recognized this. He saw the guy counting money from a huge knot, as if he'd just made a big lick. He began examining the guy with cold eyes. He was dressed in a white T-shirt, creased jeans, and green-and-white Stan Smith Adidas, as well as the black Kangol. In three fractions of a second, the young goon had removed a lightweight loaded .380 from his waist and slammed a bullet into the chamber. He stood there for a moment, breathing through his nostrils like a raging bull. This would definitely be a challenge for him, considering he'd heard a couple of war stories about Kangol Black. However, he didn't really care about that. The son-of-a-bitch had sold him a dummy ounce a couple of weeks earlier made from candle wax, baking soda, yellow meal, and Orajel. Terry wanted his money back or blood. He moved with swiftness out into the middle of the paved parking lot, his gun pressed against his thigh, aiming toward the ground. Then he yelled, "Hey, Black, wuz up wit dat $700?"

Black was too slick for himself and very hip to the game. He didn't turn or flinch. He heard the voice loudly and clearly behind him, but he pretended as though he didn't hear a thing. He carefully shoved the money inside his pocket.

Terry was moving closer, inching a few steps at a time, his eyes still on his opponent. Then, in the blink of an eye, Kangol Black darted in between a primed minivan and an old square-body Maxima. Terry raised his gun and squeezed the trigger twice. The shots rang out, and the rear window of the minivan shattered in pieces. Terry was moving in the way Bones had once taught him, trying to stay low. He could still hear his voice. Terry saw Black running alongside an Astrovan and proceeded behind him. Black turned and let off nearly four rounds. He was reckless with his aiming though. That made Terry's adrenaline pump. He was moving in zigzag motion between moving cars. He aimed and fired three more rounds, flames bursting from his barrel. He saw Black stumble at first, and then he fell as if somebody had tripped him. He hit the ground and tumbled. His 9mm slipped out of his hand, and he stretched out his long, boney fingers to reach for it, but it was too late. Terry was on him. He squeezed the trigger, and the first bullet ripped through Black's throat. Black then reached for his own neck while choking on his own blood. Then Terry frowned and gave him two to the chest. Black was breathing heavily now, and his eyes were wide with fear. Terry watched the man die right at his feet. He was caught the next day eating a hot dog in front of the Do Drop Inn.

All this played around in his head on their flight to Las Vegas.

# CHAPTER 4

The strip in Las Vegas, Nevada was breathtaking. It was the hot spot; colorful lights danced from the ground to the skyline in oranges, blues, yellows, reds, and greens. Rolls Royces, Bentleys, and stretch limos were everywhere. Hollywood had the best of the best laid out for his crew. The limo they were in pulled in front of the MGM Grand Hotel and Casino. Even though their windows were tinted, they could see the movement and excitement that flooded the streets and the sidewalks. Scooter was the only one who didn't come. He changed his mind at the last minute, and that didn't give Hollywood enough time to convince him, so he allowed him to stay behind.

Bones had worn beige linen pants, a silk brown button-up shirt, and Hennessy colored Gators by Mauri.

Hollywood kept it simple; he was dressed in jeans, black Gator quarter-cut boots, a white silk T-shirt, and a huge monster link chain with a diamond fluttered H pendant. He only pulled his jewelry out for special occasions. He also wore a diamond and gold Rolex watch that sparkled like the Vegas lights.

Fat Man couldn't be convinced to dress casual, so he wore jeans, a huge crispy, white T-shirt by Polo, all-white Polo boots with black Vibram bottom, a black 6X Polo leather jacket, and a pair of dark shades to hide his bulging eyes. His fashion statement was plain and simple: the Fat Man was fresh as hell.

Terry tried his best to copy Hollywood's style. You couldn't take anything from the youngster either. He wore a blue-and-white Coogi pullover, short sleeves, dark blue jeans, and Atlanta's finest Stan Smith Adidas. Hollywood had become so attached to Terry that he bought the kid anything and everything he wanted.

The limo driver, a medium-sized Mexican dressed in a tux, opened the curbside door for the small entourage, and everybody exited one at a time, standing off with Hollywood.

Hollywood slid the driver a fifty. "Make sho you be here when the fight's over," he told him.

The Mexican grinned. "No problem," he said in perfect English.

When they got inside the casino, the loud noise from the slot machines filled the air. Crowds of people were everywhere. Heavy gamblers would lose their life savings tonight. Some poor white man would commit suicide and get read about in tomorrow morning's paper. Gambling tables were everywhere.

Fat Man said, "Shawty, you thank they skinnin' out here?"

"Shawty dees crackas don't know 'bout dat skin game," Bones said.

When they got into the main arena, the lights were down, and the boxing ring was illuminated. The crowd was going wild, throwing out loud, deafening screams and shouts. Everybody followed Hollywood down the carpeted aisle. He led them to their seats just in time to see Holyfield enter the ring.

History was in the making for Young Hollywood, and he knew he'd have something to brag about for years to come.

Bones didn't even sit down. He stood as though he was posing for a magazine with his hand positioned on his hips. He began moving his upper body side to side. Then he yelled, "Yeah, shawty! A-Town in da' house. Atlanta's own. Knock dat fuck nigga out, Holyfield." He then began laughing at himself. Then he cocked his head around at the crowd.

Fat Man pulled him down.

"Always rep where you from, shawty," Bones told him.

Terry stood with his hands on his hips the same way and said, "Yeah! Young Hollywood in da' house, a young slick A-town nigga."

"Nigga, sit yo' ass down," Hollywood said.

They were all laughing and enjoying themselves from that point on, and Terry would go strictly by Young Hollywood from there on out.

Holyfield dropped some poor white man in the third round, so they enjoyed the rest of the evening gambling.

When they got back to Atlanta, three days later, they learned that the city was taking a drastic turn for the worst. Scooter had informed them what was going on. The heavy hitters in Atlanta had run out of dope, and the robbing crews were out looking. The 1991 drought had finally kicked in full swing, and the only person who had some work was Hollywood. He was in possession of six keys of cocaine, and he'd already made up in his mind that he was going to stretch everything and break everything down.

As the days passed, Hollywood Court project was jumping like Techwood and John Hope. Cars were lined up bumper to bumper, arguments were going on among junkies, kids were playing, and Hollywood and his crew were eating good. He'd hired more neighborhood foot soldiers and supplied them with hand weapons and assault rifles. Chopper-toting teenagers were posted in windows of abandoned apartments. He had eyes and close ties to Flipper Temple, Bowen Homes, and Bankhead Court. By the time Christmas rolled around, Hollywood was worth a million dollars. Bones was six figures strong, and so was Fat Man. Scooter and Young Hollywood were in a position to cop at least two keys. During Christmas of 1991, there wasn't a child in Hollywood Court who went without a Christmas present, all thanks to Hollywood.

Late one night, Hollywood was leaning up against the fender of his new 500 Mercedes that sparkled under the lamppost. He wore a black mink, jeans, and Gators. Young Hollywood had his own short-body Cadillac. It was clean and black with chrome thirties. He was in deep conversation with a seventeen-year-old female with a pretty face and a shapely body. The December winter air was whipping and whistling through the night.

The female moved closer to Young Hollywood. "I'm cold," she whispered. Then she shivered and stuffed her hands in the pockets of her Georgetown Hoyas Starter jacket. Now directly in front of Young Hollywood, she whispered, "Hold me and keep me warm."

Just as Young Hollywood was about to wrap his arms around her, a loud whistle came from one of the watchmen. He nearly shoved the broad to the side. "Sit in the ca'," he said. He moved a few steps and stood next to Hollywood. They both had their weapons drawn and visible, though they weren't aiming at anything.

Four cars rolled up, one behind the other, a tight group, all with their parking lights on. The third car was a 500 Mercedes Benz, just like the one he'd just copped. The front passenger's window rolled down, and a female appeared behind the tinted window. Her complexion was caramel. She looked half-Asian by her slanted eyes, and her lips were done up with bright red lipstick. She removed her hair from her face with long, manicured nails. "You Hollywood?" she asked.

Bones appeared from out of nowhere, dressed in fatigues and a black wife-beater with the AR-15 slung across his shoulder. He took the show just that quick. He was walking around all four cars peeping in the windows. Then he stood in the middle of the street to block them off. He fired up a cigarette.

Hollywood focused his attention back on the beautiful female. "Who wanna know?" he asked.

"Da' Governor," she said proudly.

Hollywood knew the Governor was an old-school cat who nearly ran Atlanta, probably the biggest drug kingpin in Georgia. He supplied a lot of traps all over, but his businesses, clubs, and grocery stores had kept his name out the streets, and his face was rarely seen. *Now the question is, what does he want with me?* Hollywood thought. He stared at the female for a few seconds. Her eyes were seductive, and her face was chiseled perfectly as if she was molded. He took all this in very quickly. He was lost in thought for several more seconds.

Then he was interrupted. "Are you ready?" she asked, with her eyes penetrating into his.

Hollywood tucked his gun in his back pocket and folded his arms across his massive chest. He allowed his eyes to dart to all four cars, examining them quickly. "How far we got to go?" he asked.

"Come on, Mr. Hollywood. I know you're not scared, not with all the shit I heard about you." When she said that, she smiled also, revealing perfectly even white teeth.

The entire project was quiet. Hollywood was still thinking. "Fuck wit' dis bitch talkin' 'bout," he said to himself.

Then without warning, she opened her door, and the interior light highlighted her features. She stepped out, her hair flowing around her face, her black three-quarter-inch mink jacket stopped at her curved hips. She wore tight-fitting jeans that were wedged down into a pair of crocodile boots that came up to her knees. "I'll ride in your car with you." She was standing in his face now.

He handed her his keys. "You gots ta drive." He looked at Young Hollywood and said, "Get in."

# BOOK II

## *THE GOVERNOR*

# CHAPTER 5

James Washington was brought up with the motto: To get respect, you got to earn it. He grew up in Carver Homes in the sixties and seventies. By the time the early eighties hit, he'd been through it all, from shaking the P, to scalping Braves tickets and hijacking beer and liquor trucks. He robbed his first bank in '78 and got away clean with $75K in cash. He blessed the entire project, a majority of old ladies and kids. Carver Homes praised him. He formed a circle of men and brought them all together. He began his number-running business. Then, the second and third bank job put him on top. Corner stores began popping up throughout the entire Zone Three.

His name spread quickly. He loaned money and helped old ladies carry groceries. Indeed, he'd become a "man of respect," and some rumored he was connected with the Mafia because he'd had strong family ties in Chicago and Harlem. In '81, he was worth two million.

One day he was at one of his corner stores, draped in jewelry and a black-and-white pinstriped suit, when a bum walked up on him with a grocery cart full of junk. "Can I get a dolla?" the bum asked.

James Washington removed a knot of money from his pocket and peeled off five twenties and handed it to him.

The bum was so honored he reached out and hugged him. "Thank you, sir," he whispered. "You do more for us than the governor."

That day, he dubbed himself as "the Governor." Two weeks later, he'd opened up two skin houses with his uncles from Thomasville Heights. He invested money with a longtime friend from Jonesboro South. Then the marijuana trap of the South was born. The Feds had played defense, but not enough. He began investing in franchises such as Church's Chicken, The Beautiful, and Satterwhites. He was connected to a lot of people. Then when the crack era came, things began to change. More violent robbing crews began popping up all over the city, and he was feeling the effect. The younger generation was hungrier and thirstier for blood than for money. His gambling houses were becoming a "lick" every week; he was losing tremendous revenue. A lot of his team members were bowing down to the glass pipe, and that made it easier for the robbing crews to infiltrate his circles. A notorious crew from Eastlake Meadows was on the rise, terrorizing the city. The Governor made it his personal business to make the peace. He was forming bigger and stronger teams, but his face wasn't on the scene at all. He had captains all over Atlanta and murderous hit men on the payroll. By the time the mid eighties rolled around, he owned hotels and grocery stores and was worth well over fifteen million. He had sons and nephews by then, and they were just as ruthless as the rest of the city. Carver Homes was now being called "the War Zone" and Eastlake Meadows had become "Lil' Vietnam."

The Governor never uttered a threat to anyone. He was indeed a thinker and kept full control of his temper—that is, until the Miami Boyz came to Atlanta with intentions of taking over the city. They came strong and with force, and with cheaper dope prices. They befriended a few goons from the city.

When bodies began popping up, the Governor got involved. Both sides lost a few good men either to hell or to the jail. However, A-Town came out on top. The Governor disappeared again, but he always kept an ear to the street. When he heard about a young street entrepreneur by the name of Hollywood, he became eager to meet him. It was small and simple things that touched old school cats like the Governor. Simple things made him respect you.

On this Christmas night, the Governor was clad in a two-piece black silk Versace pajama set and matching bedroom shoes. He was in his den, reclined in an overstuffed leather chair sitting atop thick, expensive wall-to-wall carpeting. The room was decorated tastefully with antique furniture. The walls were covered in wood paneling, one of them decorated with a portrait of Martin Luther King, Jr. A portrait of the Governor and a host of kids adorned another wall. The Governor had a hard face and deep-set eyes, very evil looking at times. His mouth was wide, and he wore a full gray beard with strands of black.

He twirled a Cuban cigar around in his mouth and casually sipped Cognac from a clear glass. He was watching an old Ali vs. Foreman fight on his big-screen. The Governor was fifty-one years old, and enjoyed the majority of his time alone.

A knock came from the door behind him.

"Come in," he said in a raspy, wheezing voice.

Hollywood entered first, and Young Hollywood accompanied him. The female came in last and closed the door behind her.

The Governor stood up; he was no taller than five-eight. He extended a huge hand to Hollywood for a shake. Then he looked to Young Hollywood, who stood a mere five-five. He examined the quality of the young man and checked his eyes to see if he could hold a stare. He tried, but the Governor had an evil aura about him. It worked to his advantage. He gave his hand to Young Hollywood and said, "How y'all young playas Christmas was?"

Young Hollywood spoke first because he was shaking the man's hand at the time. "It was good."

The Governor nodded. "Y'all have a seat."

"Daddy, I'll be in the kitchen if you need me," the female said. His eye contact with her told her, *"Okay."* She left, and the Governor took a seat in his recliner chair.

"So who's the young man here?" he asked.

"Dis my lil' buddy from da' neighborhood. He like my lil' brother," Hollywood explained. His eyes shifted to Young Hollywood. "Good deeds, fine man." There was a short silence. Then Hollywood said, "So what you wanna see me about?"

The Governor lit his cigar, and the gray smoke enveloped him. He appeared calm and cool. He offered Hollywood a drink and a cigar, both of which were refused; Hollywood didn't drink or smoke. "Jus' a few things," the Governor said as smoke seeped from his lips. "First of all, I wanna thank you for spreading your wealth to them kids out there in the project."

Hollywood relaxed a little and allowed his facial muscles to loosen. He smiled, "Thank you."

"Old lady Pearl speaks highly of you," the Governor said.

Hollywood thought for a minute. All he ever did was check in the old woman from time to time to see if she needed anything from the store or if she was all right. She was eighty-six, and he was surprised she could even remember his name. He laughed, "Yeah, we call her neighborhood watch."

The Governor bowed his head in respect. "You remind me of myself a few years ago. Yo' name been ringin' bells in da' streets. Are you well protected?"

"Streetwise, I got a team," said Hollywood.

The Governor shook his head. "Naw. I mean *real* protection—police and politicians. You'll need such people in your corner. It takes money to make money. Buy yo'self a longer run. Then you get out of the game," the Governor, pointing his cigar at him. "You're definitely on the right track." He shifted his eyes to Young Hollywood. "You're a handsome young man. Knowledge and wisdom comes with time, and in order to be a good leader, you have to be a damn good follower and an experienced listener. Don't let nobody tell you different when I say this. The great men in this world weren't born great. You have to grow and earn your greatness." Then he asked, "How old are you?"

"I'll be fourteen in two months," answered Young Hollywood.

"You ready before your time. You ever played Monopoly before?" asked the Governor.

Young Hollywood nodded.

"Have you ever won?"

"Yes, sir."

"And how did you go about winning?" the Governor wanted to know.

"Depends on how many people you playing against. If I can't land on the property I need, I'll probably have to trade somebody," Young Hollywood explained.

"Have you ever played and lost because everybody teamed up against you?" asked the Governor.

"Yeah, plenty of times. That's the only way they could beat me," said Young Hollywood.

The Governor nodded and scratched his beard. He puffed on his cigar and looked back at Hollywood. "You heard what the youngster just said." The Governor had had their undivided attention now.

"Yeah," said Hollywood.

"When you are known for winning, the streets will team up on you and get you out the way…one way or another. You got your instructions, now lay your foundation. Try to buy as much property off the Monopoly board as you can. When you become a legitimate businessman, the other team will have to go back into the huddle. They got to find another defense," explained the Governor. After a long silence, the Governor asked, "Do you two trust one another?"

They both nodded.

The Governor took a swallow of Cognac and then a deep breath. "I hate to be the bearer of bad news, but yo' cousin Bones ain't right."

"Why you say dat? I trust him wit' my life," Hollywood said.

"Three reasons. One, he jus' lost close to fifty grand last week at the gambling house. Two, he's from Perry Homes. And three, he's more bloodthirsty than he is money hungry. He hasn't told you his people in Perry Homes been asking questions about you?" He paused. "You next on the chopping block."

Hollywood shook his head, and his eyes turned cold.

The Governor pointed a long, fat finger. "You better watch yo'self."

# CHAPTER 6

In his dream, Young Hollywood was strapped to a stretcher in the rear of an ambulance. His chest was filled with bullet holes. His two hundred dollar Polo Rugby shirt he'd just copped from Phipps was ruined. An IV needle was wedged in the elbow of his right arm, and he was receiving oxygen by mask. His eyes were darting from one paramedic to the other. Neither one of them was saying a word. He spoke with a muffled voice from behind the oxygen mask, "Shawty, ain't nothing wrong wit' me."

The ambulance pulled into the open-ended garage of the emergency entrance at Grady Memorial Hospital. It was more of an unloading dock for the wounded and the dead. The ambulance came to a stop. The rear doors swung open, and he was rolled out on his stretcher. Two doctors and two nurses were waiting on him. One doctor began pounding on his chest.

"I'm straight, Doc. Doc, I'm good, I'm tellin' you!"

His words were ignored. They moved him into a treatment room under bright fluorescent lights, where several surgical residents waited. They all began flexing their fingers inside of rubber gloves.

Young Hollywood was motionless for a minute until they began cutting and ripping his shirt from his upper body.

"How many times was he shot?" the doctor asked.

"The report says thirteen," a young blonde nurse answered.

"Thirteen?"

Young Hollywood's eyes darted around the room, his lips turning purple-black. On the left side of him he saw Kangol Black sipping on a can of Coca-Cola. "I'll be ready in a minute," he said and held up the can as he invited him to a long-distance toast.

Young Hollywood frowned. He was angry and felt his body turning cold as ice—no fear, no grief, no nothing but pure rage. He batted his eyes closed for a mere second, and when they popped open, Bones was standing over him.

Bones's skull and face were smashed in by large-caliber bullets. His nose was gone, and he didn't have any eyes. His chin was twisted, half hanging from his face. He managed a smile; no teeth. The he spit a used bullet fragment that landed on Young Hollywood's stomach. Bones began to laugh out load. Then he stopped. "Shawty, y'all niggas didn't have to do me like dis."

Then Young Hollywood mumbled, "You brought it on yo'self, shawty."

"Wake up, boo," a soft, tender voice whispered in his ear.

Young Hollywood looked to his right. His little lady friend was propped up on her elbow, staring at him, a beautiful sight to wake up to. She kissed him on his lips. Her name was Sasha, and she was in a class all by herself. Sasha was seventeen and more sexually experienced than Young Hollywood. He was fourteen now, and waist-deep in the game. His spending habits were up higher than ever before since he'd met Sasha. Her alluring green eyes and golden-honey skin caught him off guard. He had first set eyes on her two months ago at the Greenbriar Mall. She had worn her long jet-black hair in one thick rope braid that hung to the middle of her back. She was taller than Young Hollywood by two inches, but that was something he didn't care about. He'd fallen in love. She reached beneath the covers and massaged his soft organ until it stiffened in her hand. She went underneath, held on to him with both hands, and licked him carefully. She wanted to make sure he enjoyed the wetness from her mouth and tongue. He removed the covers; he liked to watch her. His toes curled. She went deep one time and gagged. She slowed down. Her eyes stared into his. He reached and grabbed her breast. Her small nipple was hard. She moaned. It must have turned her on because after that, she began bobbing her head up and down. Young Hollywood felt himself about to cum. His stomach muscles tightened. She swallowed and didn't come up until she'd licked him dry.

He showered and ordered room service—green pasta, shrimp, and garlic bread—and they washed everything down with tea.

Sasha stood up. Her waist was small, her hips were curved greatly, and her thighs were thick and muscular. She posed for Young Hollywood, spun around, and bent over at the waist. She made her ass cheeks jump, one side at a time. When she stood back up, she faced him and blew him a kiss. He pretended to catch it. They both laughed at that. "I'ma go take a shower," she said and then faded into the bathroom.

Young Hollywood slipped into a pair of jean shorts and punched in Hollywood's cell phone number. He didn't get an answer. Then he dialed Scooter. No answer there either.

He cradled the phone in his hand and tried thinking of Fat Man's cell number. He punched it in and got an answer on the third ring. "Wuz up, shawty?" Young Hollywood said. "Where Hollywood?"

Fat Man growled into the phone. "Shawty…where you at?"

"At the Marriott downtown," answered Young Hollywood.

"Shawty, man…Hollywood died last night in a motorcycle crash."

Those words alone could've killed Young Hollywood. The life drained out of his body. He knew this wasn't a joke 'cause real niggas don't play about anything like that.

"You still there?" Fat Man asked.

"Yeah. What I need to do?" Young Hollywood was nervous and could barely speak.

"Come to da spot," Fat Man said harshly from the other end, and then the line went dead.

Young Hollywood sat still on the edge of the bed for a minute. He dragged his head around and stared blankly at the carpet. Things were moving too fast for the young soldier now. They'd just buried Bones three months earlier, and he was the one responsible for his death. That had given him a lot to think about. Hollywood had given him the order, and that made him feel like he was doing the right thing. The plot Hollywood had given him was still special. Hollywood had told Young Hollywood to get him some hot wheels. He'd bought himself a white Camaro. That same night, Young Hollywood was to wait and hide at the Norfolk Southern Railroad Yard. It was a large area and spooky at night, but Young Hollywood knew the area well because he'd stolen from some of the railroad containers several times. He waited nearly two hours, then out of nowhere, Hollywood and Bones appeared out of the dark, both dressed in dark clothes. Hollywood had a compact .45 pressed against Bones's back.

Bones spotted Young Hollywood, and a smile spread across his face. "Ha ha ha ha ha," he began laughing.

A train horn blared from a distance.

"Shawty, you know da game fucked up when yo' own cousin wanna kill you," Bones said with his death-struck grin spreading across his face.

Hollywood lowered the .45 below his waist and pulled the trigger. The explosion was loud. The hammer shock impact hit Bones in his hip and knocked him off his feet. He fell to his back, reaching for his leg, his face balled into a mask of fury. Hollywood handed Young Hollywood the .45. "Deface him," Hollywood ordered.

Young Hollywood took the gun. "What is dat?"

Bones was surely crazy; he tried laughing at that statement too.

Hollywood folded his arms across his chest and said, "Shoot him in the face until you can't see his face no mo'."

Young Hollywood didn't ask another question. He stood over Bones and aimed directly at his face. *Boom...Boom...Boom... Boom...Boom...Boom!* He emptied the clip, and Hollywood reached in his pocket and gave him another one. By the time he finished, he was staring at a ball of blood with muscle tissue and bone fragments scattered everywhere.

When Sasha came out the shower, her hair was bundled in a towel, and she was wrapped in a thick terrycloth bathrobe. She saw Young Hollywood staring into space. He seemed stunned and out of it. She moved next to him. "Wuz wrong?" Her hand rubbed the side of his face.

"Jus' get dressed," he said, as tears fell from his eyes.

# CHAPTER 7

The "spot" was a two-story red brick home Fat Man and Hollywood had chipped in on together. It was located in the Ben Hill area, somewhere between Cascade and Campbellton Roads. They'd meet up there and sometimes cook up keys of cocaine at a time.

When Young Hollywood pulled up in front of the house, he was alone. He noticed Fat Man's Lexus and Scooter's Chevy had taken up the entire driveway. That made him frown more; he was already frustrated. He eased his Cadillac Seville up close to the curb, switched off the engine, and climbed out. He angrily slammed the door and walked across the uncut lawn. His nine bulged underneath his shirt, and his keys jingled in his hand as he climbed four levels of red brick steps. He pressed the illuminated doorbell, and then he waited; Hollywood was on his mind. *My playa patna ain't dead,* he was saying to himself. "Damn!"

He heard footsteps on the other side of the door, and then the door came open. He looked up at Fat Man through the glass storm door. Then he opened the storm door and stepped inside. The living room was completely deserted. There wasn't one piece of furniture, not even a painting on the wall. This was how it was; Hollywood didn't want anybody to be comfortable. Young Hollywood looked closely at Fat Man. There was puffiness around his bloodshot eyes. He gave a look as though he was taking it extremely hard. They touched fists, then Fat Man placed one of his huge hands on Young Hollywood's shoulder. They moved into the kitchen.

Scooter was sitting on the far end of a wooden table facing them, but his eyes were down, staring at nothing on the table. Smoke seeped from a cigarette he held pressed tightly between two fingers. His eyes were puffy and red also. He set the cigarette in the black plastic ashtray and quickly turned up a fifth of Hennessy. Some wasted alongside his mouth, and he wiped it away. As he placed the bottle back down, he made eye contact with Young Hollywood and took a seat in one of the chairs.

The house was in total silence, and not one word was whispered around the table. Nearly ten minutes passed.

Fat Man retrieved a box of Newports from his front pocket, took out a cigarette, and set the box on the table. He fired up the cigarette. "Dis some fucked-up shit here," he said. Then he added. "Pimp was a good nigga. He didn't deserve no shit like dis."

Scooter had a deadly stare in his eyes when he cut them up toward Fat Man. There was another long silence before Scooter said, "A hard pill to swallow?"

"You damn right," Fat Man replied, smoke seeping from his mouth. His stare was just as evil.

Young Hollywood's eyes darted from Scooter to Fat Man, and something just registered in his head. He said, "What about shawty money?"

"We took everything to his mama dis morning," Fat Man said as he reached across the table and thumped the ashes from his cigarette in the ashtray.

"Wuz everything? I mean—"

"Shawty, you questioning me like I'm a flaw nigga or somethin'. I ain't got no reason to take nothin' from pimp."

Young Hollywood was indeed quick and hot tempered. He removed his sixteen-shot 9mm from his waist and slammed it hard to the table.

Fat Man looked at it, and Scooter did also.

"Don't scream at me, nigga, like I'm a chump off!" Young Hollywood said.

Fat Man analyzed the situation for a moment, looked at the gun again, then looked at Scooter. The hand his cigarette was in began to tremble. Nobody knew it but him and God. He carefully reached for the Hennessy bottle, then turned it up to his lips. After two quick swallows, he said, "Shawty, you know I talk loud anyway. Miss Idella got everything. We—"

Young Hollywood interrupted in an icy tone, "Who is *we*? Who else went wit' cha?"

Scooter stood up and took the bottle from Fat Man, then threw it into the wall. It shattered, spewing liquor everywhere. "Shawty, y'all niggas need to chill wit' dis fucking shit," Scooter said. He looked at

Young Hollywood. "We took everything to his mama, pimp—900 grand and three ca's. And she got da' keys to dis house and dat other one." He slowly turned and walked away without saying another word. They knew Scooter was crazy—mentally disturbed actually.

Young Hollywood stood up from the table and tucked his gun back inside his waistline. He adjusted his shirt.

The sound of Scooter's roaring car engine came through the walls. The music was vicious, and it began vibrating the walls. Then they heard a loud *crash,* and tires squealing against the asphalt.

Fat Man got up and walked toward the door. He stepped outside on the front porch and noticed Scooter backing his Chevy against the front bumper of his raspberry-colored LS 400 Lexus. The Chevy pushed his car into the street, smashing the front end in. Scooter pulled his shift down in drive and sped off. Fat Man was stunned, and all he could do was shake his head from side to side. Deep down inside, he knew he'd have to deal with Scooter for that—just for that.

Hollywood's mother lived in Covington, Georgia, located on the outskirts of Atlanta. The neighborhood was quiet, with middleclass couples and families with houses priced at $200K to a half-million dollars. Earlier that morning, Fat Man and Scooter went to see her. They gave her three bags of money and took two sets of keys to her. She cried with them and gave them Krsipy Kreme donuts.

Nearly seven hours after they'd left, night had fallen. A car pulled up in her driveway. The streetlights illuminated three heads on the inside of the car from behind the dark tinted windows. The passenger's side front door opened, and the interior light brightened the driveway. Cutt Throat stepped out dressed in jeans, a white Polo windbreaker, and brown Polo boots. He closed the door, walked around the front of the car, and climbed a short flight of steps that led to a brick front porch covered with green indoor-outdoor carpet. He rang the doorbell and unzipped his windbreaker halfway. He removed six plastic red roses he had bought from the corner store. The Hallmark card came at a discount. For more than a minute, he stood there holding the card and roses. "Answer this door, lady," he said to himself.

A moment later, there was a soft voice asking, "Who is it?"

"Dis is Jacob, Miss Idella," he lied. "Wayne and I went to school together, and I just wanna drop these gifts off to you and offer my condolences."

There was a short silence. He figured she was looking at him through the peephole. The bolt-action locks were being removed, and then he heard the chain.

He held the roses at the top of his nose. When the door opened, Cutt Throat produced a gun at the lady's midsection. He stepped forward and pressed the gun to her stomach.

Her eyes stretched wide with fear and her mouth formed a perfect O.

"I came to pick up somethin'," was all he said. Then he forced himself all the way inside.

Fat Man was relaxing in his secluded three-bedroom condo out in Decatur. Nobody knew about this one. He was being very careful now. The living room was neatly decorated in all black furniture. The coffee table was made of white ivory and thick glass. There was a mound of fish-scale cocaine piled up on a plate. He leaned forward on the couch and positioned himself in front of it. When he dug the end of his driver's license into the cocaine and took himself two quick hits, the phone rang. He stood, wiped his nose, and walked to the mini-bar. He picked up the black cordless phone. "Hello?"

"Bout time yo' fat ass do somethin' right."

Fat Man smiled when he recognized Cutt Throat's voice. "You got it?" he asked. Then he glanced at his Rolex; it was almost twelve a.m. "Give me an address."

# CHAPTER 8

Over twelve limousines were lined up back to back on Ashby Street, and nearly 100 cars were scattered behind them. The death of Hollywood had brought out several players, minor-league hustlers, kingpins, goons, gangsters, junkies, and even a few NFL players. People were standing around on the sidewalks in separate huddles; most of them were dressed in black. Beautiful women stood around whispering and pointing. The funeral was basically a fashion show. Pimps rode through in Benzes, Cadillacs and Rolls Royces. They were at least thirty vehicles deep. They weren't attending the funeral itself but had come up with an idea that they would block all moving traffic on Ashby Street. The headlights of each car were on. They kept their cars running and parked in front of the church, and over sixty street-walking whores filed out from the cars. All of them dressed in either black dresses or black two-piece suits and six-inch heels. They each carried two red roses.

The crowds of people that hung around outside began to move in closer to see what they had going on. The whores made a line, and one by one, they began carefully organizing the roses until the last one finished. The roses spelled out: HOLLYWOOD, WE MISS U, PIMP. All the whores separated and went back to the cars, where their pimps waited. As they drove off, they bumped their horns and waved. The spectators gave them a round of applause.

Inside the church, women shed tears as the pastor was finishing his encouraging words about how fine a man Hollywood was and how it was God's calling and he was now in a better place. But the majority of the people who filled the pews and lined the walls in the church had their minds made up. To them, there wasn't a better place than Atlanta. When it was time for the viewing of the body, feet shuffling, loud cries, screaming, and hollering began before the casket was ever opened. Young Hollywood, Scooter, and Fat Man all had a seat on the front pew. They were equally dressed in tailored tuxedos and Gator shoes. They knew Hollywood wouldn't have wanted it any other way. After the body was viewed, Hollywood was buried and lowered into the ground at Lincoln Cemetery.

When the funeral was over, Fat Man hurried to his car, and before he could get inside, two goons in suits and nappy afros approached him. They caught him off guard. One of them produced a Glock and pressed it against his stomach. The move was so smooth and carefully executed that nobody else around noticed. Fat Man recognized both of them, and beads of sweat were forming on his forehead. "What dis shit 'bout?" he growled in his deep, wheezing voice, his bulging eyes darting back and forth.

"Y'all niggas killed Bones. We already know from word in da street." The guy paused and looked around. The coast was clear. "But once we find out the true facts, yo' fat ass and them two young bitch-ass niggas gon' be buried next to Hollywood."

Before Fat Man could get a word out, the guys had swiftly moved around his car and blended in with the huge crowd. He didn't have an idea about shit. From his understanding, the hit had come from Perry Homes. Then the word was he'd robbed old man Money Jay from the Bluff, and he'd put the hit out. Something was fishy in the air. The Westside cross game was like no other, and Fat Man was caught up in the crosshairs.

The next day after the funeral, Hollywood Court seemed to have changed. Everybody was breaking off into their circles. Of course, Scooter and Young Hollywood had bonded together, and they still had some power. There were a few young teen players still loyal to them. A week had gone by, neither one of them had seen or heard from Fat Man. That alone had given them both a reason to either rob and kill him or just touch him for a nice lick. They both had experience in the field. They talked about it in a motel room one night. Young Hollywood was growing up; he was thinking more now and was eager to reach the top. At this present time, he and Scooter were buying three kilos of cocaine together and some Grade-A fish scale too. They were working heavy, and they sold hard and soft. (*Hard* is another name for cooked cocaine; *soft* is the powder form.) After three months had gone by of staying down and grinding, they had stacked up close to $400K. Now, they were ready to make their own statement.

It was August, a hot and beautiful Sunday evening, when they decided to pull their new cars out. They both had copped a Lexus Sports Coupe from a dealership out in Marietta that took cash under the table. Both of them had chosen the color black, and they had the soft peanut butter interior. It was obvious that Young Hollywood was the leader; he had a lot of influence over Scooter. Scooter wasn't a thinker. He was just trained to go, and that was by any means necessary.

When they decided to hit Grant Park, Young Hollywood pulled in first with Scooter behind him. Four young goons were in Young Hollywood's short-body Cadillac; his homeboy Ghost was driving. Behind them was a Suburban filled with young hustlers that ranged in age from fifteen to twenty years old. They all were strapped, hoping some drama would kick off. Young Hollywood cruised through, and beautiful women were everywhere with fresh hairdos, tight-fitting shorts, miniskirts, and halter tops. He tapped his horn at the crowd, leaning so low they could only see the A on his fitted cap. They tried hard to see who he was. They found a nice-sized area near a tree that would fit all three cars and the SUV. They backed in and lined up one beside another.

Young Hollywood never got out of his car. He was just enjoying the cool air conditioner, smoking his own personal blunt, and shouting hard on his cell phone. He finally got out, his phone still pressed against his face. With Versace shades covering his eyes, he was dressed in Polo shorts, a Polo T-shirt and Jordans and wore a fancy-looking link chain. He sat on the hood of his Lexus and kicked it with Sasha while his crew began setting up the grill. They had brought steaks, flounder, shrimp, and an array of other stuff. Grills were smoking all through the park. "You told yo' mama?" Young Hollywood asked over the phone.

"She already knows I'm pregnant. I haven't told her about the house yet," said Sasha over the phone.

Together, Young Hollywood and Scooter had copped a house in Stone Mountain. It was a brick two-level home with a two-car garage, three bedrooms, and a nice-sized den in the basement. Young Hollywood had invited Sasha to come live with him. Scooter protested because he'd wanted his privacy, but Young Hollywood told him it would only be for a couple of months until Sasha had the baby, and then they would get another house.

"Well, you need to go ahead and let her know. Nigga don't want no drama comin' from yo' end," explained Young Hollywood.

"My mama don't be trippin' like dat," Sasha told Young Hollywood.

"Shidd!" He smiled, and then he looked up and noticed an entourage of Benzes, all black except one white one. They were the big-body 500 Sedans with gleaming rims that sparked off blinding reflections underneath the sun. Young Hollywood looked amazed. "Hold up for a second," he said into the phone. He lowered the cell phone with his mouth hanging open.

# CHAPTER 9

Scooter pulled up beside Young Hollywood just as the row of Benzes was cruising by. They all had tinted windows—dark—except for the white one. Scooter pointed with his nub at the clean white Benz. "That's Fat Man shit."

Young Hollywood was studying him now. He removed his shades as his head followed the Benz at a slow pace. "Shawty gotta get it," Young Hollywood said.

Fat Man appeared to not have noticed them., but in reality, he had seen them clearly from his peripheral vision.

Their animosity was rising; now they were hoping he would park.

Their other soldier, Ghost, walked up. He was right at five-ten with long, powerful arms and fists the size of a full roll of tissue. He had similar features of a fire-breathing dragon, and the way he always looked down his hose enhanced his ugliness. He carried a huge .357 and always wore big shirts to conceal it. Even though he kept his tool, his choice of weapon was his hands. He was extremely strong, cocky, and didn't know his own strength. He was from Bowen Homes and Bankhead. His grandmother and auntie lived in one project, and his mother and sisters lived in the other. He and Scooter came up rough together. They had fought each other several times in the past. Scooter was just too good with his hands, his nub, and his feet. "Y'all got beef wit' dat fuck nigga, Shawty?" That was the question he asked, and that was all he wanted to know.

Scooter tapped him with the nub, "In a minute."

Young Hollywood brought the phone back to his face, "I'ma call you back." He hung up. Then he looked at Ghost.

Ghost grinned and flashed six pretty gold teeth across his top front. "Shawty, I'll kill dat nigga out here right now," he growled. "I'm bored anyway."

Young Hollywood shook his head. He knew Ghost wanted to prove his loyalty and show his skills.

Ghost described himself and his skills as biting. Then he actually said it, "Dis shit biting."

"We came to chill and have fun," Young Hollywood said. "Let's smoke out and cookout."

And they did just that. They smoked, had drinks, and ate well. They were learning to enjoy themselves now and leaving the drama at a minimum unless it came to them. And the way the goons lurked in Atlanta, it damn sure was gonna come.

Inside the treatment room in Grady Memorial Hospital, Young Hollywood was glancing around the room. With his eyes focusing hard, trying to adjust to the bright overhead lights, he squinted with a deep frown, an oxygen mask laced across his face.

A tall white doctor was flexing his fingers inside the rubber gloves again. He was smiling down at Young Hollywood and began shaking his head as if to say he'd been a naughty boy. Then the white face turned to Bones's face.

A cold, delicious, angry feeling came over Young Hollywood. "Fuck you, nigga," Young Hollywood said. "I don't bar dat shit."

Bones produced a scalpel and held it tightly in his right hand. His eye sockets were hollow, and his ugly disfigured face was monstrous looking. "Here we go," Bones said. He made the incision, slicing across his ribs. The cut was deep, and a trail of blood appeared. Bones ignored that.

Young Hollywood felt the pain and grunted with his fist clenched tightly into round knuckle balls. The white of his ribs was now exposed.

"Saw," the doctor said.

A nurse handed him a small bone saw.

Young Hollywood flipped his head, and there was Kangol Black. He extended the Coca Cola can again. Then the sounds of a baby crying gave him hope. Young Hollywood smiled and threw up the peace sign as if he knew he was in a dream.

When he opened his eyes, Sasha was carefully cradling their three-month-old son and feeding him from a bottle.

Young Hollywood was fifteen now, but in reality, he felt as though he was twenty-five trapped in a teenager's body.

Sasha smiled at him. "You gotta stop screamin' in yo' sleep. You gon' scare the baby half to death," she whispered softly.

Young Hollywood worked his way up on his elbow and slowly crawled across the huge king-sized bed. He looked at his son with his smooth, deep chocolate skin that he'd taken from his daddy. His eyes were jade green, and his hair was so thick and curly. He was just adorable. He moved his tiny fingers, and Young Hollywood leaned in close so he could play with his face. "Dis my lil' nigga right here," Young Hollywood said. He was smiling and making funny goo-goo faces. He and Sasha had argued several months about what they were going to name the boy. He wanted his first name to be strictly Hollywood Keys. She wanted Terry Keys, Jr. He told her it would be, but when he signed the birth certificate, he made his first name Corleone, snatching it from the family name off the movie *The Godfather*. His middle name was Terry, and he was a junior. Sasha was mad at first, but Young Hollywood had made the name grow on her since the day he was born. The baby was very exotic looking, and they knew the Italian name fit him perfectly. "You cookin' breakfast?" he asked her.

"You might need to cook dis morning," she said.

Young Hollywood grabbed the TV remote from the nightstand and aimed it at the seventy-two-inch screen. "The only thing I'm cookin' is some keys."

Sasha grinned and said, "You so damn silly."

"You love dis silly shit though," he said as he looked at her.

"You know I do," she responded. Then she looked down at the baby; his eyes were closed. She put her finger to her lips and whispered, "Shhhh."

He pressed the mute button on the TV; he was rewinding the movie *King of New York*.

Sasha carefully laid the baby in the center of the bed. She leaned into Young Hollywood, and they kissed. "I forgot to tell you good mornin'." She climbed out of the bed and walked toward the bedroom door, her pretty round ass cheeks bouncing and peeking from underneath her T-shirt.

Young Hollywood grabbed the cordless phone from the nightstand and punched in Scooter's house number.

Scooter answered on the fourth ring with heavy sleep in his voice, "Wuz up, shawty?"

"Nigga, how you know it was me?" Young Hollywood asked, and then he realized he was talking too loud and cut his eyes down at his son.

"'Cause ain't but two people got my number. That's you and my mama. Besides, it's eight thirty in the mornin'."

Young Hollywood climbed out the bed and slipped on the silk boxers that were lying on the floor. He whispered into the phone, "You know them folks comin' to cut da grass dis mornin' and clean da carpets." Young Hollywood stood in front of a tall mahogany wood dresser. He opened the third drawer from the top and removed a small sack of weed and a Glock 17. "All right, shawty," he said. "Boy, you must've had a rough night last night."

He heard Scooter laughing. "Yeah, the twins from Magic City," he said.

Young Hollywood grinned and said surprisingly, "Bof of 'em?"

"Come on, shawty! Dis me now." Then he added, "Let me go ahead and get up. Is Sasha cookin'?"

"Yeah, right now," Young Hollywood said.

"Tell her to hold me a plate." He hung up.

Young Hollywood rolled himself a blunt, smoked half of it, took a shower, and got dressed.

# CHAPTER 10

An hour later, Scooter and Young Hollywood were sitting alone at the breakfast table. Sasha had prepared scrambled eggs and cheese, hot-ass grits, Jimmy Dean pork sausages—the round ones that had to be cut—and Eggo waffles drowned in Aunt Jemima syrup.

Young Hollywood stuffed half a sausage and a scoop of eggs in his mouth. He chewed it and tried talking at the same time. "I ordered twenty-five of dem thangs," he said to Scooter.

"At the same price?" Scooter asked.

He stood up, went to the refrigerator, and pulled out a gallon jug of orange juice. He poured himself a glass. "Nah... They dropped 'em down to eighteen-five. We can give 'em to Ghost fa twenty-fo'."

"We'll fuck wit' him fa' twenty-three," Scooter said. "We'll give him five and let him grind. He got a lot of niggas to feed." He sat back down at the table.

Young Hollywood nodded and said, "That sounds reasonable." Then he asked, "What about the studio? We still gon' fuck wit' it?"

Scooter shrugged. "Whatever you wanna do, shawty." He damn near stuffed a whole waffle in his mouth. "Dis shit good as a motha' fucka'," Scooter said. The doorbell rang.

Young Hollywood got up. "Landscaping people," he said and walked through the dining room, then the living room to answer the door.

When he opened it, there were two Mexicans dressed in coveralls standing on the front porch. Their names were embroidered on their chest pockets. "We here to do yard front and back?"

Young Hollywood nodded. He looked out into the street. Their company van was parked out there with a cage attached to the rear. Another Mexican was removing a riding lawn mower and a blower. Young Hollywood nodded his head. "I'll be in here," he said.

The Mexicans smiled and extended their hands.

Young Hollywood shook both the men's hands and closed the door, and they went to work. When Young Hollywood got back in the kitchen, Scooter was sitting at the table talking on his cell phone.

"Not right now. Probably later on."

Young Hollywood lit up a blunt from the ashtray, sat at the table, and waited for Scooter to get off the phone.

"Shawty, I need to do dis shit now," Ghost was saying from the other end. He sounded agitated and far too anxious.

"Jus' sit tight fa' a couple hours. Everything in motion now," Scooter said.

"Come on, Shawty. Don't do me like dat." Ghost was sounding as if he was about to cry.

"Shawty, you got to understand. Dis shit don't revolve around you. A nigga can't move nothin' he ain't got. It's gon' be at least two hours. And take my word, shawty, it's gon' be worth the wait.

"All right, my nigga," Ghost said. Then he paused and asked quickly, "Where Young Hollywood at?"

Scooter was becoming frustrated, and Young Hollywood noticed it. Scooter said into the phone, "He right here."

"Let me speak to him real quick," Ghost said.

Scooter gave Young Hollywood the phone, and in return, he accepted the blunt.

"Yeah? Wuz up, shawty?"

"Shawty, I got some country niggas ready to pay, and—" Ghost replied.

"Whoa...whoa, shawty." Young Hollywood interrupted him. "Not on da' phone like dat."

"Yeah, you right. Damn, my bad, shawty," Ghost said.

"Two hours, shawty." He angrily slammed the flip phone closed. Then he looked at Scooter. "What da' fuck wrong wit' dat nigga, pimp?"

Scooter passed Young Hollywood the blunt and raised his eyebrows. "Dat nigga crazy fo real." He shook his head side to side, and then a thought hit him. He slammed his nub into the wooden table. "I knew it was somethin' I fo'got to tell ya."

Young Hollywood gave him an anxious stare.

"I ran into them niggas Eight Ball and MIG the other night at the club. They was wit' Twan from da' Bluff. You know dem niggas be throwin' small concerts and shit. We can do dat too, wit' da' studio,"

Scooter said.

"You got dem niggas number?" Young Hollywood asked.

"Naw...but I got Twan hook-up, and dat nigga doin' stupid numbers on da' heroin," Scooter replied.

Young Hollywood rubbed his hands together, but before he could speak, a light knock came from the back patio door.

Scooter was the closest; he already knew who it was and he quickly answered it. He unlocked the glass door and slid it open.

The two Mexicans entered; the same two from the front door. One of them carried a large army-green canvas bag. They each shook hands with Scooter. "My friend," they said to him and moved toward the kitchen table.

Scooter closed and locked the glass door, and they all huddled around the table.

The Mexican unzipped the bag and removed each kilo of cocaine one at a time and lined them up on the table. "You wanna test?" he said.

Young Hollywood shook his head and clapped the Mexican on his shoulder. "We know you good."

Scooter turned around and opened the cabinet under the sink. He removed a large waterproof duffel bag and hoisted it upon the table in front of Young Hollywood, where he quickly unzipped it. Stacks of small face hundreds, fifties, and twenties were packaged in brown rubber bands in $1K stacks that totaled up to $462,500.

"It's all there. Wanna count?" Young Hollywood asked.

This time, the Mexican clapped Young Hollywood on his shoulders. They smiled around the table and greeted one another with friendly handshakes and brief hugs. Scooter let them out the glass patio doors. They tucked the money in the van and proceeded with manicuring the lawn and trimming the hedges. This was actually their business and cap.

Inside the house, Sasha was coming down the stairs. She was fully dressed and was carrying her son, Corleone. He was wrapped in a blue baby blanket. She went into the kitchen.

Young Hollywood and Scooter had placed the bricks back inside the canvas bag and were now debating on how fast they should move.

"I'm goin' over to my mama's house," she said. She kissed Young Hollywood and waved goodbye to Scooter.

When she left, Young Hollywood said, "Call dat nigga Ghost."

Scooter dialed his number on the cell. It rang several times before he hung it up. Three minutes later, Ghost was calling back. Scooter answered and asked, "Where you at, pimp?"

"I'm over in da' hood," Ghost said. "I'm headed to the Community Grill, finna get me somethin' to eat," he added. "You by yo'self?"

"Yeah. Y'all ready?"

"Yeah. Swing by Young Hollywood crib."

"Check." He hung up.

"Dat nigga mad?" Young Hollywood asked.

"You can tell he's hidin' it."

"Let's get some practice in while we wait."

Scooter had him in training off and on for the last eight months, teaching him Tae Kwon Do.

# CHAPTER 11

It was twenty minutes till twelve when Ghost whipped into Young Hollywood's driveway in a low-key Chevrolet Cavalier he'd borrowed from his sister. He bumped the horn once before he opened his door and stepped out. The hot summer heat was blazing, and the smell of the fresh-cut grass was in his nose. He took the winding concrete flattop that led to the red brick steps, and when he climbed to the porch, the front door was already open.

Scooter stepped aside and allowed Ghost to come in. They dapped each other.

"Wuz up, shawty?"

"Same ol' shit," Ghost said. He was definitely hiding his animosity.

Scooter closed the door and locked it. They went downstairs to the basement where Young Hollywood was working a thick Everlast punching bag with his hands and feet.

Ghost grinned, then said, "Dat bag don't hit back, shawty."

Young Hollywood stopped. He was covered in sweat and was only wearing gray sweatpants and an old pair of Reebok Classics. He looked at Ghost, his facial expression serious, "You say dat to say what?"

Scooter saw anger in Young Hollywood's eyes, and before another statement was made, he playfully tapped Ghost on both of his kneecaps and his shins. Then he spun him around him within the blink of an eye and tapped his lower spinal cord. He knew Ghost was strong and hit hard as hell; he also knew he was slow.

Young Hollywood was impressed. He watched them tussle for a minute until Ghost pager vibrated.

Ghost stopped and said, "Hold up, pimp." He unclipped his pager and read the number. A look of excitement spread across his ugly face. "Dis dem niggas, shawty," he shouted. "Five bricks can be gone right now."

Young Hollywood shouted, "Get on dis bag first. Talkin' all dat shit, let me see you work dis big motha' fucka'."

When Ghost went to the bag, he threw a flurry of punches, and every last one of them landed with a solid *thud.* His jab was incredible, and he had a right hook that would knock a basketball sixty or seventy yards if he held it in his hand and punched it. Then he stopped, bent over, and rested. With his hands on his knees, he was breathing like a bull.

"Dat motha' fucka' have punched somebody," Young Hollywood said.

Ghost nodded his head, still breathing heavily. He stood straight up. Then he turned toward the bag again and began kicking it with force. They forgot to tell him the blue leather would mess up a new pair of shoes.

A week later, the Mexicans were back again, and they went through the same routine. Things were beginning to look good. They were preparing to have a state-of-the-art studio built in an office building downtown on Peachtree until the robbing crew followed Sasha home.

Four men followed Sasha to the house. Two of them were dressed in all black, including their bulletproof vests, and the other two were dressed in army-green fatigue pants and long-sleeved jackets buttoned up to their necks. When she pulled into the two-car garage and pressed the button on the remote for the door to close, two of them slipped underneath before it was all the way down. She killed the engine to her Acura Legend. Anita Baker's voice was still crooning; it then stopped too. She finally opened the door. The two masked men removed themselves from a crouched position at the rear of the car. When she closed the door, she turned and faced them. Suddenly, her eyes widened with fear. The ski masks were enough to scare her half to death, but there were two of them, and they aimed guns at her face. "Don't say nothin'. If you scream, you'll die," one of them said to her. The other one opened the back passenger's side door and carefully removed Corleone from his car seat. He didn't cry. Sasha nearly fainted. They escorted her inside the house. Then the other two began searching the garage and the backyard.

Young Hollywood didn't have any security whatsoever. Inside the house, in his bedroom, Young Hollywood was asleep, resting well. He was in his boxers, his hair braided in neat thick rows. His bedroom door was ajar.

One of the masked men peeped inside. He was down low, nearly on his knees. He saw Young Hollywood sleeping between the cool sheets. The TV was on a cartoon channel. Tom was chasing Jerry, as usual. The guy opened the door a little further; his Glock .40 ready and aimed. The guy was a creeper. He moved swiftly and silently. The other guy was right behind him. They stood over Young Hollywood for a second or two before waking him up.

Then he heard Sasha scream, her voice echoing from downstairs. Young Hollywood rose quickly, but only to face a bright flashlight and what appeared to be a gun.

Downstairs, Sasha was bound with duct tape at her ankles. Her wrists were taped heavily also. And the worst was the odd position she was in; they had her bent over at the waist, but at least she was fully dressed though. Her waist and hands were taped to her ankles, and when she saw her three-month-old son being stuffed inside the microwave, she screamed. Her heart was rumbling, ripping inside her chest. One of the masked goons placed his hand over her mouth. The other guy closed the door on the microwave. She went crazy, but there was only so much she could do because of the position she was in.

When Young Hollywood was brought into the kitchen he saw the position they had Sasha in, and that cold, delicious feeling of anger and hatred went through every vein in his body. The goons hadn't said anything. They hadn't demanded any money or drugs. *What is going on?* Young Hollywood was standing, his eyes searching each face. Only the eyes could be seen, and he wanted to put a bullet between each and every one of them. One goon kept aiming the bright flashlight in his face with one hand and held his gun behind his back with the other. Young Hollywood examined him quickly. He thought of him as the shooter. His gun would be large back there, something that would take him out, away from his happiness within seconds. One goon was roughly binding his hands behind his back.

He didn't realize his junior was stuffed inside the microwave until the goon pressed the button and the door popped open. Young Hollywood's eyes stretched when he saw this. The flashlight wasn't facing him anymore. His eyes swept across the room, searching everyone. He swore revenge; he'd kill everybody. The goon lifted

Corleone from the microwave. He was crying, screaming from the top of his tiny lungs. The goon placed the barrel of a forty-five to the baby's mouth. Young Hollywood had tears in his eyes, and in a low, raspy drawl, he said, "I got everything, $650K."

"What about dope?" Another guy asked.

"Seven bricks. I swear, dat's it." Young Hollywood tried to conceal his anger. He dropped his head. He'd been defeated, and tears fell from his face. Then out of his peripheral vision he noticed the strangest thing. *It can't be,* he thought. But he was seeing it with his own eyes. Then a powerful blow caught him from the blind side. His jaw cracked, and he was feeling the pain before he hit the floor.

By the time Young Hollywood was released from the hospital, his fractured jaw had gone down a little. Four days passed. He was stressing hard, and when he and Sasha arrived at their home, he told her he wanted her to take the child and go live with her mother for a couple of weeks. She didn't ask any questions.

Thirty minutes after Sasha and Corleone left, Scooter arrived. They went into the kitchen and sat across the table from one another. Young Hollywood was drinking more than usual. He poured himself a huge cup of Hennessy and fired up a rolled blunt. Scooter eyed him, waiting on a command of some sort; this was war. But what Young Hollywood let roll off his tongue, Scooter couldn't believe. He took a drink and a long pull from the blunt. He said in a strange tone of voice, "It was Ghost that robbed me."

Without hesitation, Scooter asked, "How you know?"

"I seen his shoes. He had blue stains on his white Jordans. He's dead."

Scooter's eyebrows bunched together, his eyes squinting. He French-rolled the smoke, looping it through with his nose and mouth. Then he said, "Shawty, in a situation like dis, you got to know fo' a fact."

"I got all da motha' fuckin' facts I need," Young Hollywood growled. He had the heart of an entire army. He looked Scooter square into the eyes, as though he was searching for answers. His uncontrollable temper was flaring, and the liquor had him pouring sweat. "I know it was Ghost, pimp. I'ma kill him, his mama, and his kids. And if I find out who was wit' 'em, they asses dead too."

Scooter nodded and pulled on the blunt again. "Well, by all means, Ghost is a dead man on sight," Scooter said.

# CHAPTER 12

Fat Man was exquisitely tailored, and he'd turned his swagger volume up by three notches. His neck and wrists were foolishly draped in expensive jewelry. He wore five-carat sparkling diamonds in each ear, and he'd invested nearly $30K in gold and diamond teeth. The entire front and bottom row were glistening under the lights at Club 112. He was in the VIP section, where he'd leased three private booths for six months straight.

It was New Year's Eve night, and for the last few months, Fat Man and his crew had been eating really well. He and Cutt Throat, who was now his brother-in-law, had established a foolproof game plan. Fat Man had decent cocaine connects with a couple of dreads he'd met from New York. He was in the position to buy 100 bricks at $15K a piece. However, he kept his number at a minimum of fifty bricks a month because they were really a notorious robbing crew that actually sold their victims the work until they were in position to cop a large quantity. To them, a large quantity ranged anywhere from twenty to one hundred bricks. Often they'd befriended some loyal customers and help build their bank. Cutt Throat would then assemble his family in Summer Hill to do the rest. They mostly worked on out-of-towners from the Carolinas, Tennessee, and Alabama. Just a couple of weeks prior, Fat Man and Cutt Throat had cleared $700K and used all that money to go toward their up-and-coming studio and record label. Fat Man hired an attorney to handle the legal process, and they were on their way to stardom.

Tonight, the club was packed wall to wall, and Fat Man and Cutt Throat were prepared to spend every bit of at least $40K that night alone. They sat at their booth, and their goons had the other two booths occupied. The three tables were covered in bottles of champagne, mostly Cristal and Dom P. The smell of exotic marijuana filled the air, and the sounds of the loud, deafening rap music vibrated the walls and rang in the ears. The women came through in groups, and they were all beautiful with shapely bodies and exotic-looking eyes. Fat Man didn't take notice because of his powder-sniffing habit. He was looking down, untying a knot from a sandwich bag filled with chunks of fish-scale cocaine. He was fascinated, and the sight of it had his stomach flipping. He took two huge bumps from his manicured pinky nail. The coke drained within seconds, and he stood and shrugged out of his mink. A bouncer who stood nearby reached for it. Fat Man politely handed it to him, and he disappeared with it, knowing he'd get a nice tip if he took care of it.

Fat Man looked across the table at Cutt Throat. Cutt Throat was a smooth cat; he was your laidback type of guy. He wore a bald head and wood-framed Cartier shades. He was in his late thirties and had a lot of game underneath his belt. Clad in an apricot-colored suit and matching Gators, he was leaning to the side and casually smoking an expensive Cuban cigar, staring at all the fine, beautiful women who walked by. With the smoke curling around his face, he looked at Fat Man. "Bad bitches all through dis motha' fucka' tonight, shawty."

Fat Man didn't like to talk too much when he was on the cocaine, so all he did was nod his head in agreement, then slipped on a pair of tinted Cartier glasses also. They were a popular choice of eyewear in the city. Fat Man sipped Hennessy from a glass. "I don't wanna get too geeked up tonight," he said.

Then a trio of women was escorted inside the VIP by two huge, muscular bouncers and was seated two tables down. Fat Man and Cutt Throat were caught off guard by the three beautiful women. Fat Man made eye contact with one of them.

She smiled and waved and when she said, "Hey, Fat Man," his heart melted.

It made him wonder how such a beautiful lady had recognized him. He stared from behind his shades. He was impressed by her beauty alone. Playing it calm and cool, he only threw up the peace sign. He watched her sit down. Her body was gently curvy.

She whispered something to the other two women who were with her, and a second or two later, they were looking toward Fat Man and Cutt Throat.

"You gotta' fan club, pimp," Cutt Throat said. He rose from the table and with a professional swag, he carefully buttoned his jacket and eased to the next table, where his crew was sitting. He dapped them all after whispering something and came back to the table where Fat Man was sitting.

"You leavin' fo' real, shawty?" Fat Man asked. He sounded disappointed, and he'd turned his focus on the bag of cocaine. He snorted in the public eye; he didn't care who saw him. He was being reckless.

"Happy New Year, nigga," said Cutt Throat as he held out his hand.

Fat Man reached out and shook it. "Be safe, pimp," Fat Man said.

"All da time," Cutt Throat said. Then he was escorted to his car by one of the bouncers.

When he was gone, Fat Man didn't waste any time calling the female over to his table, and to his surprise, all three of them came. He was quickly revived again. He ordered more champagne and fresh buckets of ice. Good reefer was being fired up and passed around. The three women were game tight, and they all began asking Fat Man questions he found flattering. They sniffed coke with the Fat Man right in the club, and that took the cake. Five minutes passed, and he reached inside his pocket and removed $6K in hundred-dollar bills and carefully laid the cash on the table. His arrogant statement really caught them off guard. "I'm buyin' y'all tanight," he commented. And, with that said, they all left together. Fat Man couldn't refuse.

When they got outside, the parking lot was filled with expensive cars and a long row of gleaming black limousines with uniformed chauffeurs. Fat Man stood at the curb, his vision slightly blurred, but the cocaine had him alert. He watched everything from where he stood.

The tallest female of the three wore her hair in tiny micro braids. She had high cheekbones and almond-shaped eyes and a shapely body. She was dressed in leather boots with a black leather motorcycle jacket that stopped at her waist. Her name was Ayonna. She stood next to Fat Man while they waited on the valet to bring his Benz. She would ride with him, while her two girlfriends followed behind in their car.

When the Benz pulled up, Fat Man took the driver's seat, and Ayonna occupied the passenger's seat. He tipped the valet a fifty-dollar bill. Fat Man lit up a cigarette, pulled out his personal bag of cocaine, and hit it before he pulled out of the parking lot. He passed the bag to Ayonna.

She didn't really sniff cocaine, but she wanted to fit in. She needed to be with Fat Man at least for tonight anyway. She looked at him with her seductive eyes. She then dug her nail inside the bag. "Can I suck yo' dick while you drive?" she asked. Her voice was soft and steady.

That question devastated Fat Man. He laughed and revealed his pretty gold teeth. Then he pulled the gear stick into drive. A light drizzle began to come down. He shrugged his shoulders. "Dat's on you, shawty," he said.

When they pulled out of the parking lot, she'd already freed his soft penis from his pants. She came out of her boots and climbed up in her seat on her knees and dropped her head in Fat Man's lap. Her thick, soft lips played all over his penis until it began to grow. "Damn," she whispered. "I underestimated you." She was on him like a pit bull, and she had him standing at full attention.

Fat Man began to sweat and pressed the button to open the sunroof. He grunted and found himself squirming in his seat. "I ain't tryin' ta get no cum all over me."

"Don't worry, boo. I'ma swallow," she said.

Fat Man led the way to his condo in Decatur. The other two females parked next to him, and they all congregated in the quiet parking lot. The light drizzle had stopped, and the newly paved asphalt was still slick. Fat Man led the women up a flight of stairs and inside his condo. He switched on the light, and it revealed his expensive leather living room set. "Y'all make ya'self at home," he said and waved his hand dismissively in the air. He went into is bedroom and thirty minutes later, he was back, freshly showered. He was covered in a thick gray and black Polo robe with an attached hood that he wore also.

The three females were in their panties, having drinks, huddled up on the floor around the blazing fireplace. Ayonna looked up, her eyes glossy from the cocaine. She crawled over to where Fat Man stood and parted his robe. His huge stomach and hairy chest were exposed, and the scent of Versace cologne filled the air. One of the other females crawled over also. Her name was Moschino. She and Ayonna went to work on Fat Man together while the other female lay back on the floor and slid her panties to the side and began fingering herself and licking her nipples. Her eyes were penetrating into Fat Man's, and he stared back into hers.

He broke the trance. "Let's go to da bedroom," he insisted.

Inside the bedroom, the four of them crawled into the super king-sized bed until a thought ran across Fat Man's mind. He got up and moved inside the walk-in closet. He twisted the dial on a nice-sized four-foot safe hidden behind several plastic garment bags. When he opened it, he removed a Ziploc that contained nine ounces of powdered cocaine. The remainder of the contents consisted of several stacks of cash money that were rubber-banded in blocks. Fat Man didn't bother locking the safe; he trusted the women.

The following morning, Young Hollywood and Scooter went to the apartment condo complex and climbed the steps just as casual as if they lived there themselves. Scooter knocked on the door with the nub bone of his left arm. The knock was for insurance; they knew nobody was there. Scooter stepped back and raised his leg and with one powerful kick, the door flew open. He had his gun drawn, and so did Young Hollywood. Inside the apartment, they moved through the living room, to the bedroom, then to the walk-in closet. The safe was in the exact same spot where Ayonna said it would be. Scooter tried the latch, and to his surprise, it was unlocked. He opened it, and Young Hollywood removed a black trash bag from the inside of his jacket. He and Scooter switched positions, and he quickly loaded the trash bag with the stacks of money. They were gone in less than five minutes.

# CHAPTER 13

Dons and Divas Hair and Nail Salon was located in the Greenbriar Mall plaza. It was the salon in Atlanta where several ballers went to get their hair cut, their nails trimmed, and their faces shaved. The women sometimes spent as much as $250 just on their dos. The hair salon had an exquisite layout. The floor was block-tiled marble, shined to a high gloss. Chairs and booths lined the walls, along with mirrors and glass. Several rows of dim pin lights decorated the ceiling.

All the chairs were occupied with customers. Some women were getting their hairdos upgraded, and a couple of big-money hustlers were getting their nails done and haircuts. Fat Man was comfortably reclined in the third chair on the left-hand side from the glass entrance door. His barber, a nice-looking female who wore a short honey-blonde hairdo, dressed in a black plastic overcoat, went to the sink and soaked a towel in steaming hot water and politely placed it on Fat Man's fleshy face and neck. The steam relaxed him. He was due to get his hair washed and a nice haircut. He was a loud talker and really entertained the entire salon by telling them his fancy New Year's Eve story about the trio of women.

A female pimp named Stallion sat two chairs down from Fat Man. She couldn't help but smile while getting her eyebrows arched. "So, pimp, when did you realize dat da bitches were tryin' ta take you fa' ya' coke?" she asked.

Fat Man said in his wheezy voice, "Shawty, dem bitches had some of da best head in da state of Georgia. They tried ta throw me off wit' dat move, but befo' I got too caught up, I went to my closet where da safe was at and pulled out a big bag of white girl. See, I had a mirror on da inside door of the safe. When I seen 'em watchin' me, I knew somethin' was up then."

"How much you got hit fo'?" a guy asked from another chair.

Fat Man grinned. "Nothin' really," he responded. Then he added, "Let's say $10K worth of counterfeit money and $100K worth of da *Atlanta Journal Constitution*."

A few laughs erupted through the salon. Fat Man had them all going now. He talked and talked: blah, blah, blah. He continued with details on his cocaine-sniffing habit, and before he knew it, an hour had passed. What he didn't realize was that somebody in the salon also knew about the lick and called Scooter and Young Hollywood to let them know Fat Man was making a joke about the situation.

Just then, a guy came toward the salon door. He opened it with his back because he was pulling another guy in a wheelchair. Young Hollywood carefully backed into the salon. He wore a tan-colored piece of pantyhose over his face and a Falcons fitted cap down over his eyes. When he finally spun Scooter around in the wheelchair, he stood up with his neck encircled by a six-inch foam collar. He camouflaged his face with pantyhose also.

Fat Man was still talking. "I been gettin' money fo' yea's," he said.

Then, in the blink of an eye, he saw Scooter right before his eyes. Scooter raised his right hand with a short-handled ax, gripped tight as he could hold it. He swung and nailed Fat Man in the center of his forehead and left the ax there. The salon filled with deafening shouts and screams. Fat Man sat there, with his huge eyes stretched wide open and his mouth slightly parted as though he was about to plead for his life. It was too late, and Young Hollywood and Scooter had vanished and left the wheelchair in the center of the floor and the ax in the center of Fat Man's head.

"Somebody call da police!" someone shouted.

Later that night, Young Hollywood and Scooter decided to lay low for a while. They sat around Young Hollywood's den, drank, smoked reefer, and watched TV. After all, they'd committed the first murder recorded in the year 1994.

Scooter sat up on the edge of the sofa and aimed the remote control at the stereo sound system. *Southernplayalisticadillacmuzik* began filling the room. Scooter slowly bobbed his head to number twelve. The reefer had relaxed him, and OutKast just made him lose himself. He sat back on the couch, closed his eyes, and crossed his feet. "Damn, we blowed da lick, Shawty," Scooter said.

Young Hollywood was sipping on a glass of rich Hennessy and unbraiding his hair one cornrow at a time. He looked at Scooter.

"Where you think dat fat-ass nigga had his stash?"

Scooter shrugged. "Dunno, pimp. I do know dis... dat nigga Ghost been hidin' good."

Young Hollywood rubbed his hands together as if he could taste Ghost. He stared into space, trying to visualize how he could do it. Then something funny hit him. He said to Scooter, "Shawty, you crazy as fuck too."

Scooter smiled but never opened his eyes. With his head titled back, he said, "Yeah... I know." But deep down inside something was bothering Scooter—something he wished he hadn't done. He knew he couldn't change what had happened. He also knew he had to locate Ghost. Then, out of the blue, his cell phone rang. He opened his eyes and grabbed it from the glass coffee table. He flipped it open. "Yeah?"

"Yeah, boo. Dis Cat Eye. How you doin'?" Cat Eye was a well-respected and connected stripper who worked at the Gentlemen's Club. She and Scooter were good friends.

"I'm good, shawty. Wuz up?" he said.

"Yo' peoples jus' showed up," she said.

His adrenaline began pumping quickly. His eyes went to Young Hollywood, and he stood to his feet. "Who?" He asked her that question because he wanted to hear it from her mouth. He wanted to be sure. His eyes darted back and forth to Hollywood and to whatever else was spread around the den.

Then she said from the other end, "Da nigga Ghost. He just got 'bout five cats wit' 'im."

For a brief moment, Scooter stopped breathing. He looked at Young Hollywood with an ice-cold facial expression. His eyes were as deadly as a striking cobra's. He began nodding his head slowly. "Can you hold 'em there for 'bout two hours?" he asked her.

"I can try," she whispered. "You owe me too." She hung up on her end.

Scooter flipped his phone closed. "Look, shawty, dees niggas at da Gentlemen's Club right now," he said eagerly. "Now dis my call due to da fact that I invited him in our circle."

"Regardless of dat, shawty," Young Hollywood responded, "we

don't wanna rush into nothin' that we jus' put in work."

"Fuck dat shit, shawty," Scooter nearly screamed. "Dis fuck nigga put yo' baby in da microwave, nigga!"

Young Hollywood asked, "So we jus' walk up in da club and shoot da nigga on sight?"

Scooter held out his hands, palm facing down; they locked eyes with one another. "I don't get scared too easy, shawty," Scooter said.

Young Hollywood thought about that for a minute, and then he slapped the palm of Scooter's hand. "I'm wit' whatever, shawty."

"Good, we gon' go over to Hollywood Court. We gon' pick up Dave and Kelly. They'll shoot, and they certified."

"I hope so," Young Hollywood said.

# CHAPTER 14

Inside the Gentlemen's Club, Ghost and a couple of his associates had a table in the VIP section. Ghost had been out of town for the last month and had copped himself a house in Griffin, Georgia, about thirty minutes away from the city. Tonight was his first time back. He had an addiction he couldn't control, and that was called the Ass Club, and there were more here in Atlanta than hospitals. And tonight, one or the other would determine his life. Gorgeous and exotic women strolled through the club in six-inch heels and Victoria's Secret fruity lotion. Some were in thongs and matching bras. Others were in heels and fine cotton stockings and nothing else. A few more wore cropped camisoles and boy-cut shorts, and the best part about it was that they were from all walks of life.

On the stage, a dark chocolate female worked the chrome pole by slowly siding downward, upside down. Her thick legs wrapped around the pole. She reached the floor of the stage and pressed her palms flat. She then did an acrobatic move and flipped herself upon her feet. Now standing in an upright position, she began walking the length of the stage with long, seductive strides and with every step, she dropped four quarters from her vagina. Money was being thrown up on the stage.

"Give me some change!" one guy shouted. He was waving a hundred-dollar bill from the sideline.

She walked over to him and stood in front of him, her dark nipples hard and erect. Her shaved vagina and the rest of her body were oily-skinny. She worked her muscles and allowed three quarters to drop.

He caught them in his hand, and with a smile, he tucked the hundred-dollar bill in her garter belt.

She blew him a kiss and thanked him by turning around and bending over to make her cheeks spread and bounce. She looked back at him, her ass jumping like Jell-O, and it continued to move in such fashion as she slowly rose up.

The crowd went wild, and the DJ shouted, "Give it up for Africa!"

Outside in the parking lot, Young Hollywood was behind the wheel of a black SS Monte Carlo with a souped-up engine and a stolen tag. Scooter was in the passenger's seat next to him. He was clad in all black, and his choice of weapon was two Glock 40s. One was tucked in his waist, and the other he held in his gloved right hand. Young Hollywood backed into a parking space between a Lexus GS and a Honda Accord. He switched off the engine, and from where they were parked, they could see the entrance to the club. He had an AR-15 lying on the floor in the backseat. The other half of their team, Dave and Kelly, had a Grand Am parked around the corner from the club, and they patrolled the parking lot on foot, moving carefully between cars until they were ready to go inside the club.

Back inside the club, Ghost had two females dancing for him. They were both pretty and had well-shaped bodies. They kissed one another, squeezed one another's nipples, and rubbed one another's asses inside the VIP room. He spent a grand for the action. This was how he'd been accustomed to the entertainment life. *You get what you pay for.* Ghost wore an all black waist-length mink jacket, starched denim jeans, and black Air Force Ones on his feet. He called for the waitress, a tall, slender woman with a bright smile. "Get me a sixty-piece chicken wing wit' extra sauce," he said, and gave her a hundred-dollar bill. "Bring a six-pack of Coronas on ice, too, and some breadsticks. Keep da change."

She walked off, and as she was leaving, Ghost studied the red string bikini lost between her round ass cheeks. He looked at one of his partners, who sat at the table next to him. "Da waitress bitch in high rank," he said.

The guy nodded. His eyes swept across the room until they found a tall red female dressed in red lingerie with floral embroidery and lace. The guy tapped Ghost to get his attention, and his eyes found her too. Then she disappeared from their view.

Ghost stood up with his mink jacket zipped up to his neck to hide his bulletproof vest underneath. He walked across the club and into the bathroom. He found an empty stall and unzipped his jacket and then removed it. He hung it over the hook latch to take a leak. The vest felt uncomfortable, and he tried to adjust it. He'd even thought about taking it off and wiping himself down. His T-shirt underneath was soaked, and he could feel the cotton fabric clinging to his skin. He shook himself off and flushed the toilet. Then, he rolled off a few sheets of tissue and stuffed it in his back pocket. He adjusted his vest again and quickly slipped into the mink jacket and zipped it back up. He went out and made his way to the sink. Marijuana smoke was in the air, coming from the end stall. Ghost washed his hands. The bathroom maître'd had an array of cologne, cigars, cigarettes, peppermint, and candy. Ghost gave him a ten and took a Black & Mild cigar from the tray and a handful of mints. He then removed the paper from the cigar, and the bathroom maître'd lit it up for him. The sweet aroma filled the air, and the smoke circulated above his head.

When he walked through the bathroom door, he was facing two guys with their caps leaning on their heads. He recognized Dave's ill-twisted face and Kelly's long neck, but it was too late for anything. Ghost stood and raised his arm across his face when he saw the guns in their hands. The first three shots that hit him sent him backwards; the next four pinned him against the wall. He dropped to his knees with a *thud.* Another shot rang out, and that one went through his jaw. He fell flat on his face.

Outside in the parking lot, Young Hollywood and Scooter saw the front door burst open, and several people were struggling to get out. Panic showed across the majority of their faces.

"You thank they got 'em?" Young Hollywood asked.

Scooter's eyes were glued to the front door. "More than likely," he whispered.

Two police cars pulled into the parking lot, their blue lights flashing like crazy. An ambulance followed moments later, and then they saw Dave slowly emerging from the crowd and running as if he were an innocent bystander. He came to the driver's side window. "We got dat nigga, shawty," he said. "I lost Kelly. Man y'all niggas get out of here." He jogged off into the night.

Young Hollywood started the engine.

Scooter held out his nub and said, "Slow down, pimp. We gotta make sho dis nigga dead."

Another ambulance rolled up, followed by another Fulton County Sheriff car. They all rushed inside.

Scooter picked up his cell phone and punched in Cat Eyes's

number.

"Hello," she answered.

"Wuz goin' on in there?"

"A lot of shit!" she screamed. "They got one dude."

Scooter's eyebrows bunched together, and he asked suspiciously. "Who is *they*?"

"The police. They caught one dude," she repeated.

"What about the other dude?" Scooter asked.

"Oh he ain't dead. They puttin' him on the stretcher now. He had on a bulletproof vest," she replied.

Without another word, Scooter hung up the phone and looked over at Young Hollywood. "Shawty, da nigga ain't dead. He had on a vest, shawty. And they got Kelly."

"How da' fuck they got Kelly?"

Scooter shrugged. He didn't care about Kelly; all he cared about was Ghost. He wanted to make him a ghost. He looked across the parking lot and saw a stretcher being rolled out. He strained his eyes and craned his neck. He knew it was Ghost being loaded into the rear of the ambulance. "Motha' fucka'," he whispered.

# CHAPTER 15

The ambulance took off, the red lights blazing as it muscled its way out through Ellis Street. Cars and trucks were pulling over, clearing the path. The siren was roaring, and a light drizzle had begun to fall. The paramedic behind the wheel had called in. The fastest way to Grady Memorial Hospital was to catch South Eighty-five. The ambulance was heading that way.

In the rear of the ambulance, Ghost was covered in blood. His mink was cut off of him. His vest was still tightly strapped. He wouldn't let them remove it. He told them he'd lose his strength; his face was drenched with sweat. The lady paramedic kept wiping his face. A wad of bloody gauze was taped to his jaw. His eyes were dark and anxious, with a touch of coldness.

The lady patted his face with a cold rag. "Calm down," she whispered. She tried placing an oxygen mask over his face.

He jerked his head from side to side. He was a stubborn something, a mean son-of- a-bitch. He could feel the bullets burning his insides, and when he noticed the ambulance was beginning to slow down, he knew he was near the hospital.

Then a small glass window that separated the rear of the ambulance from the front slid open. The driver said in a panicky voice to the paramedic and the passenger, "We're being forced to pull over." He called in the emergency over the CB, and then he pulled over to the side of Eighty-five.

Ghost managed to grip the lady's hand, his eyes wide. "They... want me... dead," he whispered, "Please he'p... me."

The ambulance finally stopped.

The lady's eyes were in pain and pierced with sheer terror. "Who is it?" she asked.

"Young Hollywood... Scooter," he replied.

From the outside they heard banging on the rear doors. "Open dis shit!" a voice yelled.

"Don't! They gon' kill me," Ghost pleaded.

Outside, Young Hollywood had the SS blocking the ambulance.

The car was running. His eyes were moving rapidly and fiercely. He knew they didn't have much time to do this.

Scooter went from the rear of the ambulance to the driver's side. He tucked the Glock underneath his armpit and opened the door. "Cut dis shit off," Scooter demanded.

The driver switched off the ambulance.

Time was running short. He pointed the Glock at the driver. "Get out!" he shouted, "And unlock dis back door."

The driver got out.

Scooter guided him around to the rear, twisting his collar. "Make 'em open it, or I'll shoot yo' ass," Scooter shouted, sweat pouring from his face.

Sirens were wailing from a distance.

"Hurry up, shawty!" Young Hollywood shouted.

When the rear doors opened, Scooter pulled the stretcher out. He looked at the two frightened paramedics. "Run, run, fast as you can!" Scooter yelled.

They took off in the darkness up Eighty-five.

Scooter snatched Ghost and shoved the barrel of the Glock in his mouth. "You bad business, pimp," Scooter said. Then he gave him six face shots.

Ghost's head erupted. Bone and brain fragments splattered everywhere.

Scooter jumped into the passenger's seat, and they sped off. But then a problem occurred. There was a roadblock up ahead, and it would be extremely dangerous for them to go backwards. They bailed out on foot and separated, crashing the car into the gray concrete wall. Somewhere above, a black helicopter flashed a long bright light, and the police saw a running figure under the night-vision heat sensor.

When Kelly was escorted into the interrogation room, he had a tired look on his face. He was exhausted, and his lips were busted. The Gentlemen's Club bouncers got a hold of him when he got caught up in the crowd. Two homicide detectives, one white and one a huge black guy, forced Kelly into a wooden chair and locked themselves inside the small room with him. They both stood before him, leaning against a wooden table. Kelly's hands were cuffed in front, and he held a blood-stained washcloth pressed against his mouth. His red-veined eyes darted from one detective to the other. He was nervous and needed a cigarette.

The black detective, whose name was Young, folded his arms across his chest and stared directly into Kelly's eyes. "Now, due to the fact that you were caught at the scene of the crime with the murder weapon and in front of a host of witnesses, to save your ass, you need to tell me somethin'," he said in a tough, persuasive tone of voice.

Kelly sat patiently. He slightly shrugged his shoulders as if he didn't have a care in the world, then he said in a muffled voice, "Come on, Bishop. You know me, and you know I ain't killed nobody, pimp."

Bishop was Detective Young's first name, and because Kelly had had run-ins with him before, he knew it and used it. Young used to patrol the Westside Zone One area before he made detective. In his patrol car days, he terrorized every area on Hollywood and Simpson Roads. He'd been shot at several times in Techwood, and he finally killed an armed teenager in John Hope one night in the late eighties. He was promoted a couple of months later. Bishop Young flashed a grin and sucked his teeth more than once, and the sound was annoying. He removed a pack of Newports from his inside jacket pocket. He tapped the pack in the palm of his hand, packing the cigarettes for better freshness. He unwrapped the plastic and the paper, removed two singles, and lit one up; the other one was tucked behind his ear. "Are you familiar with the name James Mosley?" he asked Kelly. Streams of smoke were seeping from his mouth.

Kelly shook his head smoothly and replied, "No."

Bishop Young gave an impressive look, curling his lips downward. He removed the cigarette from the groove of his ear and lit it up from the one he was smoking. When he held it out to Kelly, he said, "James Mosley killed his daddy a few years ago in Rachael Walk Apartments. You remember Jamaican Jack from Hollywood Court, right?"

Kelly placed the cigarette between his lips and pulled on it long and hard. He filled his lungs, exhaled, and asked, "Don't nobody know who killed Jamaican Jack?"

Bishop Young replied, "I believe your friend Scooter knows. At least he told me that just as well as he told me that you and he went inside the Gentlemen's Club to kill Ghost."

Kelly began to panic. His eyes widened just a little, and he asked nervously, "Scooter? Where he come in dis at?"

The white detective, who had been standing quietly, finally decided to speak for the first time. "We caught Scooter about an hour ago, fleeing from the scene of the crime where he hijacked the ambulance on South Eighty-five and killed Ghost. He said you paid him, a murder for hire."

"Man, I don't even know shawty."

"And that's it? You know you can save yourself now," the white detective said. "This is your chance to get your get-out-of-jail card."

Kelly pulled on his cigarette again. He was thinking long and hard now. Minutes passed, and no one had uttered a word. Kelly began to sweat, and then his mind frame changed all of a sudden. "Who else ya'll got?" he asked.

"Who else we need?"

Kelly smiled.

# BOOK III

# CHAPTER 16

Sasha was in the center of a king-sized bed in a hotel room downtown, on her knees. Her thick, glossy ass was spread, and a guy name Frank was behind her, entering her roughly with his long penis. His huge, ugly hands gripped her small waist. He pulled her to him, and he slammed into her; their thrusts meeting in unison. She moaned in a whispered melody, desperately trying to suppress the wounded animal sounds.

Another guy was in front of her. He was sitting down where the pillows were. He, too, was naked. A mat of hair covered his chest and stomach. He wore a thick link chain around his neck and a diamond-encrusted Jesus pendant. His stiff, thick penis was standing full erect because Sasha had her thick lips wrapped around it. She held him with one hand and tried desperately hard to balance herself. "Shiiiit," she managed to say. She stopped briefly from sucking the guy in front of her. She removed him from her mouth and looked back at the guy, Frank, behind her.

Frank was grinding slowly now, pulling his long, hard organ out far enough to allow only the head to be wrapped around her thick, juicy vagina lips. Then he moved back inside of her in long anticipated strokes.

She arched her back more and spread her knees further apart. "Damn, you fuck good, nigga," she whispered. "Slap my ass," she demanded.

Frank's hands were small, but he had long, boney fingers. He slapped Sasha on her yellow butt cheek.

She moaned and then filled her mouth with the other guy's penis. She sucked him until he came. Thick hunks erupted, and it was all over her face. That turned her on even more. She slammed back into Frank roughly, meeting his driving thrust until she began to sweat. Her entire body was covered in small beads of sweat. Frank growled and let out a loud drawl, and then he went limp and fell on the bed next to her. She looked the other guy in his eyes, "Give me a bump," she asked, not knowing his name. He reached over on the wooden nightstand where a glass ashtray was filled with cocaine and heroine, a combined mixture known as *speedball*. She relaxed a little and rested her head on his thigh. She kissed the tip of his penis with precaution, as if she were pecking a sleeping baby on the lips. The guy filled his pinky fingernail with the speedball and held it out to her nostril; she sniffed, and then he said, "I'm Juan."

"Yeah right," she said cheerfully. Then she rubbed her nose. She could feel the cocaine and the bitter-tasting heroin draining into her throat. A chill ran through her body, but in a few minutes the drugs had relaxed her all over. Ten minutes later, she was mounted on Juan's stiff penis, riding him as if he was a horse and she was the jockey. This sex session went on until eight o'clock the following morning. Juan and Frank left her room and gave her a measly hundred-dollar bill that contained two grams of speedball. By ten a.m., Sasha had showered and dressed and pulled her hair into a tight ponytail. She had been up two days, using her body and looks as her main asset. And since it had been two years since Young Hollywood had been locked up in the Fulton County Jail on Rice Street, she'd been going through living hell. Sasha was an all-out whore now that she was in and out of a relationship with a young pimp cat that called himself Debonair.

Sasha and Debonair met a year earlier when she was dancing at Magic City. Debonair saw her one time and couldn't resist her beauty and her well-shaped body. That night he gave her $500; the next night he came back and gave her another $500 and his cell phone number. The following night, he didn't show up, and that sparked her curiosity about him. She tried calling him for three days in a row but never got an answer. Then she began asking some of the other girls around the club about Debonair. Some responded by calling him a fake-ass wannabe pimp, and others spoke of him with great respect. They said he had inherited his pimping skills from his daddy and uncles, and the whole family was getting good money with massage parlors and expensive escort services. This impressed Sasha even more. She had his features tattooed on her memory chip. She could see his long, thick, wavy hair, his thick eyebrows and long eyelashes. Debonair was tall, six-five, and yellow, almost like herself. He kept a clean-trimmed goatee, and his face was chiseled sharply. But the icing on the cake was that he drove a Mercedes Benz 600 sedan, cocaine white with white leather interior and wood-grain finish.

Those old memories made her moist between her legs, and as she sat up in the lonely hotel room, she decided to call him. She didn't get an answer.

Ten minutes later, her phone rang. "Hello. Did somebody call here for Debonair?" a female's voice asked from the other end.

"Yeah, this is Sasha. Can you tell him I called?"

"Hold on."

She could hear talking in the background. Women were laughing at something, and she prayed she wasn't the joke. While she was holding on, she politely unfolded the hundred-dollar bill and took her two quick bumps of the speedball.

Nearly ten minutes passed, and finally his voice came through the phone. "Well, well, well," he said. "You know this is money week. I'm assuming you've finally come to your senses," he said with pure confidence.

Sasha was lost for words for a moment and then she asked, "Will you come get me?"

"Have you come to your senses?" he asked her. There was power behind his words.

Sasha paused and closed her eyes for a brief moment. She thought about her house she once had, the mortgage she couldn't keep up, and the cars Young Hollywood left behind. She pawned the titles for money and spent it all on nothing. At least she'd have a place to stay with Debonair. She'd burnt major bridges. Her family had disowned her, and the worst thing in the world she did was give up her son, putting Corleone up for adoption. That was all she had left. Her mother hated her for that. She'd gotten rid of everything, including her soul. Sasha allowed all of this to play around in her head. Sometimes it hurt and made her heart ache like hell, but now she was caught up in the trenches of Atlanta's own ruthless and treacherous underworld. Her eyes wandered across the room. The bathroom door was ajar. There was a pair of electric-blue stilettos parked in the corner. She licked her cracking lips and shook her head violently for a brief moment. Then she pushed those ugly memories away from her head. "Yeah," she finally said, "I've come to my senses."

Now there was a short silence from Debonair's end. She felt his power again. "Good, I'ma send one of my people there to come get you."

Her eyes glistened with excitement, and she nervously fumbled with a cigarette. "Why can't you come?" she asked in a worried tone of voice. She grabbed a book of matches, struck one, and then fired up the generic brand. The harsh taste went excellent with her dope.

"Because I'm in Houston," he replied.

She let out a thin line of smoke. "The restaurant?"

"Naw, bitch. Texas. Now stop asking them dumb-ass questions," he growled. "Now where you at?"

She told him, and he hung up. She sat there, staring at her young, sultry body in the mirror.

# CHAPTER 17

An hour later, a knock came from the outside Sasha's room door. Sasha had dozed off but woke up quickly at the sound. She got up from the bed, crossed the floor, and answered the door. The female that stood on the other side was tall and dark chocolate with almond-shaped eyes. She wore her haircut low, almost like a boy, but she was cute with the style. She was dressed in tight-fitting Khaki Capris, a white halter top, and an all-white Air Force Ones. "You Sasha?" she asked. Her eyes examined her.

Sasha nodded her head and replied, "Yeah."

The girl extended her hand. "I'm Paulette. Debonair sent me to come get you. You got everything packed up?" She spoke in a professional tone of voice and never removed her eyes from Sasha.

"I got two big suitcases. Will you grab one of them fo' me?" Sasha asked.

Paulette stepped inside the room. The stale odor of sex and cigarettes was in the air. She stood near the front door and scanned the messy room. There were dirty dishes and glasses from room service scattered across the dinette table. Little plastic liquor bottles from the mini-bar were on the floor. Her eyes paused at two condom wrappers.

Sasha came toward her with a huge suitcase and sat it down at her feet.

Paulette stared at Sasha's ass as she walked away across the room. "You know, Debonair don't allow us to live in filth. He's real strict about us being clean and keepin' our personal hygiene up. We got our own personal doctor that gives all the girls monthly checkups and physicals," Paulette proclaimed.

Sasha grabbed the other suitcase and moved toward the door. "I don't normally live like this. Jus' had a rough night last night," she said.

Paulette flashed a grin and picked up the suitcase; her teeth were pearly white and even. They began walking out the door, and Paulette asked, "How many?"

"How many what?" Sasha responded.

"How many niggas you fuck last night?"

Reluctantly, she answered, "Jus' two."

When they stepped off the elevator on the lobby floor, Paulette asked her if she had a tab with the hotel. Sasha wanted to leave without paying, but Paulette told her they conducted business on a professional level. Paulette went to the front desk and left $130 with the concierge. Forty minutes later, Paulette pulled into the driveway of a house out in Buckhead, a private and secluded area. She and Sasha stepped out of the car and walked up a flight of red brick steps. Paulette rang the doorbell, and within minutes, the front door opened.

A short Chinese man dressed in slacks and a button-down dress shirt stood before them. He wore wire-framed glasses and appeared to be in his mid-forties. He stepped to the side and allowed the ladies to come in. He introduced himself to Sasha as Chung Li and proudly noted that he was the Debonairs' family doctor.

Paulette found a seat in the living room while Chung Li took Sasha to the back room and checked her for any STDs and to see if she was pregnant. He also took blood samples and gave her a physical.

The process took a little less than an hour, and when Sasha appeared back into the living room, she gave Paulette a suspicious smile. Paulette stood up and kissed Chung Li on his cheek.

Chung Li had had an overwhelming smile spread across his face and continued to nod his head uncontrollably. "She's good," he said.

Sasha grinned at that comment.

When they were outside and in the car, Paulette started the engine and looked over at Sasha and asked, "How was it?"

"I have neva' had my pussy ate like dat befo'," Sasha replied.

Paulette pulled the gear stick into reverse and began backing out of the driveway. "Well, you ain't had me yet," Paulette said cunningly.

Sasha sucked her teeth and responded, "I hear you talkin'."

Across town, Paulette whipped her Honda Accord into the deep paved driveway of a huge, four-bedroom house on Nisky Lake Drive. The house was two stories, red brick with a three-car garage. There were plenty of parking spaces. When Paulette killed the engine, she touched Sasha's hand. "Look, here's the deal. It's seven bitches that stay here in this house, and you're counted in also. The majority of everybody get along very well with one another. If you get a bitchy attitude, you might as well leave it here in the car. Don't take it inside. Is that understood?"

Sasha nodded. "I'm cool."

"Also, all of us are considered family, and when a new family member is brought home, each of us greets the new members with a kiss. Some may peck your lips, and others may shove their tongue down your throat. I just thought I'd give you a heads up on that so you won't jump on the defensive end."

Sasha nodded again. "I can work wit' it." She stared at Paulette with a look in her eyes as if she wanted to ask several questions, and really she did, especially about Debonair. Paulette seemed cool. Her demeanor told Sasha she was someone she could share secrets with. However, she was still a stranger to her, and she wouldn't let it get too far out of control. She did have some common sense.

When they stepped out of the car, Paulette removed one suitcase from the backseat, and Sasha grabbed the other. She was already beginning to feel nervous as they approached the front door. Paulette sat the suitcase down and inserted a key inside the lock. Then she slowly twisted the door handle and pushed the door open.

The first female who greeted Sasha was Asian-American. She was beautiful and well shaped. Her skin was the color of golden honey, and she carried a smile that was breathtaking. Paulette allowed Sasha to enter first. Sasha stepped into the tiled foyer and sat her suitcase down. The Asian girl hugged her first. Her perfume smelled fruity, and Sasha loved the way she smelled.

"I'm Amber," the Asian girl chirped happily.

"I'm Sasha."

Amber smiled. "It's nice to meet you. Are you here to stay?"

Sasha cut her eyes at Paulette, and Paulette gave her a nod of approval. Sasha looked back at Amber. "Yes, I want to," she answered.

Amber leaned in and placed her lips on Sasha's, and they kissed. Their tongues were twirling and twisting around one another. Sasha's heart began to pump hard inside her chest. She could feel her nipples getting hard. Finally, they separated from each other.

Another female stepped forward. "I'm Cherry," she said proudly.

Cherry wore a long T-shirt. She was short, nearly five feet tall, with a pretty face and nice-sized breasts. She tiptoed on her pretty feet and kissed Sasha on her lips. "Nice to meet you," she said and stepped out of line.

The next female who stepped up to Sasha was an exotic-looking white girl with ocean-blue eyes and jet-black hair. She had a tan and a perfectly round apple bottom. She was dressed in a white T-shirt and lace panties and focused her attention on a cherry lollipop she was slowly sucking. She carefully removed it from her mouth and offered it to Sasha. Sasha parted her lips, and the girl inserted it inside of Sasha's mouth and toyed around with it between Sasha's lips. Then, she removed it from Sasha's mouth and sucked on it herself. Sasha stood there briefly for a moment. Some of this was new to her, and she just prayed she'd fit in.

# CHAPTER 18

The IV needle wedged in Young Hollywood's arm was aggravating him like hell. He was being wheeled into the treatment room again, and the bright fluorescent lights forced him to squint. Three of the surgical residents stood around his hospital bed. Young Hollywood removed the plastic mask he was receiving oxygen from. "I don't need no assistance," he said. His eyes began searching the faces of the people who were beginning to surround him. All the faces were white, and none of them looked familiar.

Then suddenly the door came open, and Fat Man walked in, dressed in a white overcoat. The ax was still wedged deep in the center of his forehead. Dried blood was running down his face and eyes. He was stuffing his hands inside of rubber gloves. When he got to Young Hollywood, he stopped and stood over him. His face and eyes were covered in blood as well.

Young Hollywood looked up at him. "What da' fuck you want?" he asked calmly. "I didn't kill you."

"Yeah, but you was dere," Fat Man said in his deep Southern drawl. "And you know dat shit was fucked up."

"You had it comin'," Young Hollywood said. He then folded his hands across his chest and said, "You jus' crossed one too many niggas."

"Yeah, but I had a lot of shit goin' on. I had a lot to live fo'."

Young Hollywood laughed aloud. Then he stopped and shrugged his shoulders. "You gotta take da good wit' da bad, Fat Man," Young Hollywood said. "If you feel you did what was right, then you shouldn't even be in my dream. Niggas like you don't deserve no second chances."

With that said, Fat Man faded away before his eyes, and when Young Hollywood opened his eyes, he saw Scooter standing in the center of the cell floor they shared together on Rice Street. They were on the seventh floor; seven south. They had been there for over two years. Scooter had let his hair grow into a long, wild, bushy afro, and so had Young Hollywood.

Scooter beamed in on Young Hollywood when his eyes opened. "Shawty, you been talkin' in yo' sleep like a motha' fucka'. Who da hell you was dreamin' 'bout?"

Young Hollywood sat up. His long, thick afro was flat on the right side. He used his fingers and rubbed his eyes, trying desperately to remove the sleep. Then he stared at the floor, massaged his temples, and within two seconds, he cut his eyes up at Scooter. "Shawty..." He sounded tired, and his voice drifted off. He didn't like talking to anyone about his dreams. That was his secret, and he wouldn't share them. So he decided to talk to Scooter about something else. He actually flashed a grin. "We got two weeks befo' we go to trial. My punk-ass bitch done lost all my shit, and I got to go face court wit' a fuckin' state-appointed attorney."

"When da last time you talked to shawty?" Scooter asked with a concerned look spreading across his face.

Young Hollywood shrugged and replied, "It's been about a month." He pounded his fist into his hand. "Pimp, I swear to God, if I ever catch up wit' dat bitch, I'ma beat her ta death."

"I thought she was dancin' at Magic," Scooter commented.

"She was da last time I spoke wit' her mama, but since then, she done changed her phone number. I don't know where my son at or nothin'." He paused and took a deep breath. "Dis shit got me stressin', Shawty." His eyes were beginning to moisten.

Scooter recognized the emotional side in his young partner and clapped his hand against his shoulder. "Look at me, pimp," Scooter said in a demanding voice.

Young Hollywood raised his head. His heart was aching with pain, and the results showed all over his face; he wiped his eyes with the back of his hand, stood to his feet, and faced Scooter as if a surge of energy had shot through his body.

Scooter stared him directly into his eyes and pointed his finger toward his face. "We both came up hard in da game, shawty, and you know dat. Me? I'm a soldier to da heart—a man amongst men first and foremost. You got da same ambition and mentality. I know where yo' heart at, pimp, and I damn sho feel yo' pain. But you also got to understand, when you live in da fast lane without pumpin' yo' brakes at all, you bound to have a wreck." Scooter raised his arms around and stared around the small two-man cell. "Look around you. See dis shit?"

Young Hollywood looked around. Then his eyes went back to Scooter. "Yeah," he responded.

Scooter took a deep breath and said, "Dis is our results of a wreck, a big accident dat was bound ta happen. So right now, it is what it is, pimp. Them suckas dead. We livin' and breathin' jus' as good as any motha' fucka' on da street. And as long as you got it in yo' heart to be real wit' yo'self, real shit happen. Don't worry about dat bitch, my nigga. Get dat ho' out yo' system and focus on what's ahead. You break now, dem crackers win."

Young Hollywood stood in silence for a moment. He felt paralyzed, and he was finding it hard to continue their conversation with such deep sadness written all over his face.

Scooter threw his handless arm around his neck. "It's gon' be all right, Shawty. You young. Yo' life ain't even started yet, and you're a vet already."

They were leaving their cell and walking out into the range when Young Hollywood asked, "A vet? What is dat?"

Scooter grinned. "A vet is short fo' veteran. It really means you're a very experienced person that served in a certain position. So in our position, we are both known and recognized fa our work all over the city. We A-Town Veterans, and don't let nobody else tell you different. Check dat."

# CHAPTER 19

The first day of trial, Scooter was dressed in a three-piece gray suit, a crisp white dress shirt, and a dark gray tie. His attorney was sitting next to him; he was casually dressed as well, clad in a dark, expensive suit and Vibram-bottom dress shoes. His name was William Beauchamp, and he had an impressive track record for his aggressiveness in all Fulton County courtrooms. The fee he was charging Scoter was $75K, and that had wiped him out completely. Young Hollywood and his attorney sat next to them at their own defense table, both well dressed and handsome. Each table was covered with stacks of paper. The jury box was filled with twelve concerned-looking jurors.

The judge had finally stepped into the courtroom, and a chubby-faced bailiff yelled, "All rise!"

The entire courtroom stood as the judge climbed the steps that led to his bench, and when he got in position, he told the court to be seated. Everyone sat and the courtroom was silent. The judge was scanning through a few papers, flipping a sheet at a time. He finally stopped and cleared his throat into the microphone placed near his face. Then he positioned himself in his seat and spoke into the microphone, "Ladies and gentleman of the jury, I need you to please stand and raise your right hands."

All the jurors quickly shuffled to their feet and raised their right hands in unison.

The judge continued, "You shall well and truly try the issue formed upon this Bill of Indictment between the State of Georgia and Terry Keys and James Mosley, who are charged with the offences of murder for hire, felony murder, malice murder, hijacking a motor vehicle, hijacking a government motor vehicle, two counts of aggravated assault, possession of a weapon during the commission of a crime, and a true verdict, given according to the evidence, so help you God."

They all nodded and mouthed *"Yes"* and *"I do"* in silence.

The judge said, "Thank you. You may be seated." The judge then looked down his nose at the prosecutor's table. The state attorney was dressed in a fancy beige suit; he was a black guy in his mid forties who was desperately trying to fight for a judge position. His name was Richard Myers, and the prisoners in the Fulton County jail referred to him as Michael Myers: Jason, in other words. He was known for his heavy conviction rate, and if he had to, he'd put the knife through your back. Nobody wanted to face him. He offered high cop-out pleas: football numbers. He was the worst of the worst, and he didn't have any understanding at all.

"Mr. Myers, would you like to present your opening statement?" the judge asked politely.

Richard Myers calmly uncrossed his legs. He stood up and unbuttoned his jacket and moved to the center of the floor. He faced the jury box and scanned the several easy-looking faces. He cleared his throat. The entire courtroom seemed quiet enough to hear a needle drop on a carpeted floor. "Good morning, ladies and gentlemen," he said.

"Good morning," they all chirped back in unison.

"First of all—and correct me if I'm wrong—an ambulance is made to help save lives and transport people to hospitals, correct?"

They all nodded.

He went on. "This morning, we have a murder case that's rather bizarre and heinous. This is one of the worst cases Atlanta has heard of, if not the worst. However, I will not spend the whole morning giving you details. I will let the evidence and the witnesses do the talking. Today, this Monday morning, we'll start with facts, not fiction. Once again, you, the jury, will decide for yourselves if these two men here deserve to be set free or be sent to prison."

The third day of the trial, Kelly was called to the witness stand by the state attorney. He stood from the rear of the courtroom. He wore jeans and a Polo dress shirt. His hair was neatly cut, and he was freshly shaved. When he got to the witness stand, he was told to raise his right hand. He did.

"Do you swear to tell the truth, the whole truth, and nothing but the truth, so help you God?"

"I do."

"You may be seated," the bailiff told him.

Kelly sat down and adjusted his seat and the microphone. He

scanned the entire courtroom and saw a few faces he recognized from their neighborhood. A lot of friends and family members from Hollywood Court were in the crowd. He didn't feel any remorse.

The prosecutor rose. Today, he was in a three-piece gray pinstriped suit and tie. He took the floor. "For the record, sir, would you please state your name?"

Kelly leaned into the microphone and said loudly and clearly, "Kelly Anderson."

"And Mr. Anderson, where are you from?" Richard Myers asked.

"I'm from Hollywood Court projects."

"Good. Now, do you see any of your associates in this courtroom this morning, people you grew up with in Hollywood Court?"

"Yes."

"Can you point them out this morning by their street names?"

Kelly pointed his finger at Young Hollywood first. "Dat's Young Hollywood right there." Then he shifted his finger to Scooter. "And dat's Scooter."

Scooter and Young Hollywood both sat with gleaming eyes fixed directly on Kelly's face. Then Scooter stood with a calmness resting over his face and body. He said, "Your Honor, fo' da record, he's a bitch, and he's a dead man."

The courtroom went haywire and the judge hammered his gavel.

The last day of trial, they were both found guilty on all charges and sentenced to three consecutive life sentences plus seventy-five years. Time to be served was at the Georgia State Correctional Facility. At this point, the only thing Young Hollywood had on his mind was how in the hell was he going to get out of it; his plan would take years.

# CHAPTER 20

Sasha walked Metropolitan at night. A light drizzle of rain was beginning to fall, and the streets were slick wet. Cars passed by, and the tires hissed against the asphalt. Tonight she wore jeans, a Versace T-shirt, and a pair of small Air Jordans on her feet. Her hair was pinned up, and the minor touches of make-up she wore enhanced her beauty.

Sasha strolled further up past Chocolate City, her healthy legs chopping like scissors. Females walked the streets on both sides. Some were barely dressed, and some wore real hooker clothing, like thongs under short leather skirts and T-shirts tied in a knot without a bra, their hard nipples pressing against the cotton material. Women were everywhere, marching this way and that way. Some were revealing their vaginas as cars passed.

All Sasha had to do was walk, and if a trick saw her fine ass walking from the back, he would have to stop. Finally she stopped just as a forest-green Lexus sports coupe was cruising by. She made eye contact with the driver of the car. It was a white guy, she noticed, and he continued to watch her as he passed. Then he slowly eased to the side of the street with his caution lights blinking. Sasha hurried toward the Lexus, nearly jogging. This was something she had to do. The other whores out there were ruthless, and the majority of them would debo the customers. When she got to the passenger side of the Lexus, she heard the automatic locks *click,* and she opened the door and got in. The leather seat was comfortable as hell. Her entire body began to relax as if a burden had been lifted off of her. She looked at the driver. He had a square chin and a hawk-like nose. His eyes were gray, and his hair was jet black and combed to the back. "Hey," Sasha said as she flashed a grin.

"Hello," he shot back. He extended his hand, and Sasha took it.

"I'm Strawberry," she lied smoothly, her beautiful, luminous eyes zoning in on him.

He was caught by surprise. He actually felt his heartbeat beginning to speed up. The trick was lost for words, and Sasha made him nervous.

He shifted his long stare away from her and finally built his nerves up to say something. "Where to?" was all he could manage.

"It all depends," Sasha said in her most seductive tone of voice.

"On what?"

"On you."

Her voice and her smile made him blush. His face was turning tickle pink. The trick looked ahead. Bright headlights were speeding past. "I need at least three hours with you."

Sasha put on her best performance. She allowed her face muscles to relax and put on her sad face. "So that's all?"

The trick had eased the Lexus out into traffic, wedging in between a Honda Civic and a Cadillac Deville. "Is $500 good for three hours?"

Sasha reached across the console and rubbed between his legs. "You like head?"

He nodded like a child. A bright smile spread across his face, and he revealed an even row of white teeth.

She started unfastening his pants, and he eased further into his seat. He began flipping his eyes from her to the road. She had him out now, in her hand, his pink penis pulsating in her hand. She leaned across and wrapped her mouth around him. She deep-throated him and then slowly brought her mouth up to the base. She popped him out of her mouth like a Blow Pop. Then she looked at him. "You wanna taste my strawberry shortcake?"

He nodded his head, out of control this time. There wasn't a doubt in Sasha's head that she had herself a real sucker.

Four hours later, Sasha was spread across a king-sized bed inside a suite at a luxury hotel in Marietta. They were on the tenth floor. The white guy had spent $300 on the room, $200 on champagne, and another $200 on Sasha for a gram of heroin. She already had her cake, and so far, she'd milked him for $1,500 cash for herself.

While they lay in the bed, he played with her hair; twirling it around his fingers. "Will I be able to see you twice a week?" he asked her.

"That depends on you, baby. You know my man will be expecting me to be working."

"I don't have a problem paying for your time," he said. Then he held up her hair and eased his tongue in her ear.

She tensed up and made a teasing sound with her mouth. "That do something to me," she whispered. She closed her eyes and eased up against him. "You make my pussy so wet."

"I wish I could spend the rest of my life with you." He went down between her legs. He couldn't resist the strawberry shortcake.

Sasha spread her legs slowly.

The trick licked her carefully, starting with her clit. It was fat and looked swollen. Her vagina was soaking wet, and the way he licked her down there made her feel so good. She came two minutes later. Her body was quivering, and her hands were all over him.

She asked, "Is Allen your real name?"

"Yes. What reason would I have to lie?" He massaged her firm breasts and twirled her nipples between his forefingers and thumbs. Allen took a deep breath. "Don't you want a better life?' I mean, you're too pretty to be running the streets."

"I deserve better," Sasha said, "but I made a commitment to my man to stay loyal. I gave him my word."

"Is this man of yours a pimp?"

"That title is out the door. He's an entrepreneur, very well established."

"Maybe I should speak with him about you."

"Let's not rush into things. You don't know me that good anyway."

Allen sighed, and a long, deep breath followed. Then he rested his head on Sasha's chest until he fell asleep.

Sasha didn't return to the house until the following morning. She reported to Paulette, who told her Debonair was mad as hell and that she could get beaten up real bad. But when Sasha told Paulette that she'd made $6K in one night, the whole situation changed.

# CHAPTER 21

Six months had passed since Young Hollywood had been sentenced. He'd been transferred to Lee Arendale State Prison in Alto, Georgia, but everybody just labeled the place just plain ol' "Alto." Alto was located in northern Georgia near the Tennessee line in an area surrounded by huge mountains. It was built to house prisoners between the ages of seventeen and twenty-one, and it was considered the second most notorious prison in the state. The White Elephant was number one and would stay that way for years to come, but Alto was the Gladiator School and when they said, "Kill or be killed," that was exactly what they meant.

It was a cold winter morning, and the yard was crawling with young gangstas from every city in Georgia. Atlanta was deep, but so were Savannah, Augusta, Macon, Columbus, and Albany. Every city rolled in big cliques, and nine times out of ten, nearly everybody was strapped with either knives made from lawnmower blades or huge combination locks in socks, tucked in their waists for easy access.

Young Hollywood walked the yard with forty other cats, all from Atlanta. This was his first week on the yard, and his face was fresh. His choice of weapon was a six-inch piece of steel with a needlepoint tip. The handle was made of boot string and duct tape finger grips. Young Hollywood linked up with a couple of guys who were from Perry Homes projects. They had all heard of Young Hollywood and what he was doing on the streets. Now he was in a totally different field. A test of his creditability was sure to come, and his own homeboys would be the ones to test him.

Later that night, Young Hollywood went into the open shower, where there were at least ten other guys. The shower area was steamed up, and the water was hot. Young Hollywood was wrapped in a beige beach towel. He carried his soap dish, rag, and a clean pair of boxers. He found himself an available showerhead between two guys who were showering and holding a good conversation about the Los Angeles Lakers. They talked around Young Hollywood as if he wasn't there. When Young Hollywood removed his towel, suddenly from out of nowhere somebody whistled. He didn't know whether it was targeted at him or not, so he didn't say anything; that was his cue, and he missed it. The shower began to empty and minutes later, Young Hollywood and some other guy were in there alone. Young Hollywood had taken notice that the guy had his back to him.

He stood six-two and appeared to be very muscular. When he turned around and faced Young Hollywood, he had a full hard-on and was masturbating with one hand and washing with the other. His eyes were beady, and he used them to stare directly at Young Hollywood's eyes. "Where you from?" the freak asked. He needed Young Hollywood to answer his question without asking him anything.

Young Hollywood knew in his head what was going on, but he didn't allow it to show on his face, neither did he question the situation. "From Atlanta," he replied.

The guy began moving toward Young Hollywood. He had gotten the response he wanted, and he was still stroking himself. "I'm from Atlanta too," the freak said. He got closer to Young Hollywood. His eyes were searching his entire body. "You cute too."

Young Hollywood smiled, but deep down inside, he was burning hotter than hell. He cut his water off and grabbed his towel; inside the thick terrycloth was his ice pick. He clutched it firmly in his hand as he pretended to dry off. Young Hollywood didn't bother getting dressed. He went to work on the muscle freak with strong, aggressive swings. He poked the guy in the neck first, three times before the blood began to gush out.

The guy reached out to grab Young Hollywood. He tried gripping him around his waist.

Young Hollywood took flight with face stabbings, and the big freak yelled out in pain. He took out his eyes, and when he fell, Young Hollywood fell on top of him. He was sticking, stabbing, and pounding his fist like it was going out of style.

The freak was pronounced dead at 2:45 a.m.

The next morning, Young Hollywood was transferred to Reidsville, also known as the White Elephant.

When Young Hollywood arrived at Reidsville Georgia State Penitentiary, he was led straight to SMU, the lockdown units in L, M, and K buildings. Then they moved him to another section of the prison in a cell-house dormitory. He lived there fifteen months before he was involved in an assault on an officer. From there, he went to lockdown, where he would remain for the next few years.

# Chapter 22

Young Hollywood was in dorm E-1, a lockdown unit. He shared his cell with his alter-ego. He'd become accustomed to working out on an everyday basis. He had too much time on his hands and had prepared himself mentally to accept that he wouldn't be getting out. Besides, he'd caught another twenty years for the murder of the big freak when he was in Alto. He pled guilty, and the state ran the time in with what he had.

Inside his cell, he had a steel toilet and sink, a small area for a mattress, and a desk. The floors were made of concrete, and the entire front wall was constructed of steel bars. Everybody who walked by could see inside his cell unless he hung up sheets or blankets and used them as curtains.

One night, as Young Hollywood was lying on his back, with his hands folded behind his head, he stared at the ceiling and began listening carefully to some of the other prisoners who were housed in E-1.

One convict yelled from down the range, "Good mornin', ladies and gentlemen. I say ladies because some of y'all are bitches. You know who you are. Welcome aboard the White Elephant, the morgue really, if you ain't careful."

Several guys began laughing.

"Hammer, it's too early fa dat shit dis morning!" another guy yelled. But he had humor in his voice.

Young Hollywood sat up in his bed. The name Hammer registered in his head, and he became curious. He slipped his feet into a pair of shower shoes and tuned his ears in.

"Too early? Naw, it ain't too early. We jus' in time," the man referred to as Hammer replied.

Young Hollywood realized the voice was closer to him than he thought. He walked to the front of his cell and gripped the bars with both hands. It didn't take him long to build up his nerves. It wasn't that he was scared or anything, but he really wasn't into meeting any new friends. He yelled out, "You the Hammer from Atlanta?"

The entire dormitory fell silent. Young Hollywood didn't know what was going on. He was new and didn't realize he was in violation, and something as simple as interrupting a conversation could get you killed—or at least nearly killed.

"Who da fuck is you, askin' 'bout Hammer?" the voice came from the cell right next door.

"I'm Young Hollywood, Zone One, Hollywood Court."

"When you get here?" Hammer asked.

"Night befo' last," Young Hollywood responded.

"Yeah, dis Hammer from da A. You musta heard about me out there."

"Dat all depends," Young Hollywood interrupted.

"On what?" Hammer asked.

"On if you know a lady name Ruth Ann Keys."

"Nah. Neva' heard of her, shawty." There was a short pause, and then Hammer said. "But since you jus' got here, I'ma pull yo' coat on how shit is runnin' down here. I'll get at you later on tonight."

Later that night, Hammer sent a kite to Young Hollywood's cell. Young Hollywood got it and unfolded it. He began reading silently to himself. The letter read: "What's up, bro'? This Hammer. I don't discuss my business on the airwaves. You don't do that down here. Now, about the lady you asked me about, Ruth Ann. Where do you know her from? Get back at me soon and give me the business."

Young Hollywood sat down at his desk and began writing on his notepad: "Wuz up, big homie? The lady Ruth Ann is my mama. My name is Terry Keys, and she told me I have a daddy, but he in prison. All I know is his name was suppose to be Hammer. I'm just trying to see if it's you or not. Did you get locked up in 1980?" He folded the letter and sent it next door.

Fifteen minutes later, another one was dropped in his cell. He got it and unfolded it and he began reading: "You know, it's funny how things happen. I was just telling one of my comrades the other day about your mama. We had an eight-month relationship, and you wasn't born yet. I did get locked up in the '80s. I killed two guys at the red light on Simpson Road, and your mama went crazy. She did as much as she could at the time, but I never woulda thought in a million years that I'd meet you in prison. How much time do you have, and how long have you been locked up?"

Young Hollywood wrote: "I fell in '96. Me and my partner caught three life sentences plus seventy-five years. I caught another twenty years 'cause I killed a nigga in Alto. I don't feel no remorse about shit, except that I left my only son out there. His mama fucked up all my money and everything. I don't have no outside support."

Hammer wrote back: "Have you been working on your case? You know there are loopholes in every case, especially in Georgia. We are under a fucked-up system. I came in with two life sentences myself, but I represented myself and got my shit overturned. I pled guilty to a straight twenty-year sentence. I'll be out in two more years. I know you don't know me good enough to believe in me, but in here you got to trust somebody. This shit fo' real down here, and niggas will try to kill you if you look at them wrong. I'ma get back at you in the mornin'. Peace up."

Young Hollywood and Hammer wrote back and forth to one another faithfully during the following months. Hammer pulled his coattail on so many different things concerning life and surviving in Reidsville. Young Hollywood shared his entire life story with Hammer and also put Hammer up on game as to what was going on in the streets. He told him about how the rap game was taking over the streets of Atlanta, and there were several millions dollars to be made. Young Hollywood told Hammer about the Governor, and Hammer said he had never heard of him, but he really did know him, even though he'd never heard of the name.

# CHAPTER 23

Hammer's birth name was Rufus Hayes. He wasn't an old man, but at the age of forty-two, he was pushing it. Hammer wasn't a big guy. He stood five-nine and was as strong as two men; very powerfully built, though a simple-looking man. Hammer was more of a joking type of guy. He didn't walk around mean mugging all day either. He wore his hair cut low, tempered with thick waves. He was a shade darker than Young Hollywood, but they shared resembling features.

Hammer grew up in Atlanta the hard way with very few family members, and he was the only child. His parents died years back, and he took that to heart. When he was on the streets in the seventies, he'd become a household name. If you needed somebody killed, you got Hammer. If you needed somebody robbed, you got Hammer. Beat up? You called Hammer. Bank jobs? Hammer. Plain and simple, Hammer didn't play with anybody, and people always told him he took things too serious. He simply felt everything is personal business, and that's just the way shit is.

In the eighteen and a half years Hammer had been incarcerated, he'd taken college courses in business and earned a bachelor's degree in psychology. He taught himself not to speed and to be aware of his surroundings. He had a bad habit of simply playing on people's intelligence and often practiced his skills on other prisoners. On the outside, he seemed like a normal convict, but on the inside, he was a walking nuclear bomb. He was respected on the streets and in the system as well. He shared his life with his son, told him things only God knew about. They became close in just a few months, and loyalty was the number one key between them both. The only thing Hammer hadn't learned to do was love.

Even though Sasha had Debonair as her pimp, she still managed a way to continue to see Allen without Debonair knowing. Allen had secretly purchased a two-bedroom apartment in Cobb County and had it fully furnished just for him and her. The apartment was neatly decorated for Sasha's taste. There was a leather green circular sofa that nearly took up the entire living room floor. A wood-grain and leather mini-bar sat in one corner, and Chinese screens and panels were set up where they were needed. A big-screen TV and a stereo system accompanied the remainder of the furniture.

In the bedroom, a huge oak king-sized bed had taken up a lot of space. A chest of drawers was to the left side of the room. Mirrors covered the majority of the ceiling, basically over the bed.

Sasha had candles burning, strawberry scented at that, and the room smelled so good. Sasha was lying across the bed in nothing but a huge T-shirt that swallowed her. On the bed with her were an ashtray, a half-smoked blunt, and a Bic lighter. She flipped the TV to a news segment, and as it played, she fired up the blunt and French-rolled the smoke.

Then a knock came from the door. It didn't really scare her, but she knew Allen had his own key, and nobody else knew her in the complex, so that made a wave of nervousness wash over her. A curious expression appeared across her face. She stubbed the blunt out again and left it in the ashtray. Sasha climbed out of bed and walked into the living room. She took light steps just in case it was someone she didn't need to see. When she made it to the door, she looked through the peephole. Her heart fell into her stomach when she saw Debonair standing on the other side. In her head, something was telling her to open it. Then again, something was telling her not to. Then again, she didn't really trust her own judgment. That was one of her flaws. Sasha unlocked the door and then opened it. She stared up at Debonair. His facial expression was emotionless; she was never able to read him. She wished she could, but it seemed a stone-cold blank expression was one of his main assets.

"Can you have company?" he asked her.

She stepped to the side and opened the door further.

Debonair stepped inside and stood at the door next to her. He crossed his arms at the wrist in front of him. He was dressed in white linen pants and a matching pullover shirt. He wore Hennessy-colored Gator shoes on his feet.

Sasha looked up in his eyes and he stared down into hers. His presence was known, and the sight of him frightened her. She finally swallowed and parted her lips. "What's wrong?"

Debonair ignored her. His demeanor was strong and powerful, but with the quietness and his eager stare, Sasha was beginning to panic.

When she tried to make a quick dash toward the door, he gripped her by the collar of her shirt and snatched her like a ragdoll. He threw her to the floor and slammed the door shut. Just as she tried to scream, he knelt down next to her and covered her mouth with one hand and gripped a handful of her hair with the other. He said in a whisper between clenched teeth, "Bitch, if you scream or even attempt to, I'ma break yo' motha' fuckin' neck." The fear in her eyes told him she would obey his command. He pulled her from the floor. "Get dressed," he said and guided her into the bedroom where her clothes were. A few minutes later she was dressed, and he walked her outside and guided her to a waiting car.

It didn't take thirty minutes for Debonair to make it to the destination where he wanted to take her. He pulled the car into the garage of a two-story house made of red brick and trimmed with yellow paint. He guided Sasha into the house through the utility room. Inside, he took her upstairs to one of the three bedrooms and forcefully shoved her onto the bed. "Get naked," he said calmly and began removing his gator-skin belt from the loops.

Sasha stripped down to only a hot pink thong and a pair of Polo footies. She stood before Debonair with a worried look across her face.

Debonair moved across the room and sat down on a brown leather ottoman to begin unlacing his shoes, and then he carefully removed them. He stood again and took off his pants. He folded them neatly and sat them at the foot of the bed. Then he removed his shirt and did the same thing with it.

Sasha rolled her thong down her hips and stepped out of it one foot at a time. She climbed into bed on her hands and knees. She knew Debonair was soft and that he couldn't resist her. He allowed her to remove his penis from his silk boxers. She eased it through the pee hole and inserted it in her mouth.

Debonair relaxed a little and reached on the nightstand and grabbed a fresh Cuban cigar and a lighter. He tore off the end with his teeth and spat it on the floor.

His penis was standing at full attention now and Sasha treated it as a precious jewel. Her tongue licked around the head and the full length.

He fired up the cigar. The smoke twirled around his face. He pulled on it until the burning end was bright red. Then, on an impulse, he clutched a handful of Sasha's hair and yanked her head backwards. It all happened so fast. He pressed the hot cigar against her face. Her skin began frying, and she screamed out in agony. Debonair burnt her again and again on her lips, face, neck, breasts, and stomach. Sasha had nearly passed out from the pain and the smell of her own burning flesh creeping into her nose.

# CHAPTER 24

Time was moving incredibly quick. Hammer and Young Hollywood were still side by side. They prepared their business plans together and studied for hours at a time. Hammer taught Young Hollywood never to argue, always to just take action. And that was something Young Hollywood had already been doing. Hammer just taught him finesse. They played chess with one another through the bars. Hammer prepared meals, especially the famous Georgia prison meal called "hot pockets," a meal that's made from Ramen Noodles, beef and cheese sticks, chopped onions, bell peppers, and any flavor of potato chips or crackers; topped off with squeeze of cheese and hot sauce or homemade honey mustard. Prepared the right way, the meal was good.

Young Hollywood and Hammer even shared their workouts. They were doing 2,500 crunches, 2,000 push-ups, and 1,000 squats and calf raises. Hammer also worked out with extremely heavy water bags and sometimes jogged in place for two hours straight. Hammer was in the best of shape and had every right to be. He only had one year left before it was time for him to be released, and you could bet your bottom dollar he would do what he had to do. Nothing or nobody was gonna stop him from doing it.

There wasn't too much Sasha could do but turn tricks. Her face was destroyed, and she had picked up a lot of weight. She was fat, in other words. She'd become a full-fledged heroin user. She wasn't on the needle, but sniffing was just as bad. She was still working the streets of Atlanta, in and out of cars every day, all day. Debonair still had her under his fingers, but she didn't live with Paulette and the rest of the girls. That was because Debonair wanted to humiliate her. He had her staying in a raggedy rooming house on Simpson Road. She had one bedroom and shared a bathroom with four other junkies. Sasha slept on a mattress on the floor. Her room had a suitcase full of clothes in one corner. When her door opened, she didn't bother to look up.

A guy stepped inside her room. He appeared to be a junkie himself. "Wake up, bitch." He tossed a ten-dollar bill on the floor. "Let me get some head real quick."

Sasha opened her eyes and saw the ten-dollar bill on the floor. Her eyes went back to the junkie. She was in a deep nod herself. Her eyes closed, then opened again. "No deal," she whispered. "I can't even buy me a sack wit' dat."

Without hesitation, the guy moved to the balled-up ten-dollar bill and picked it up from the floor. "Bitch, you ain't all dat, acting like yo' head jus' sho nuff da best in da city."

"Man, get out my room," she said, holding a sharp razor blade in her hand. She stood up, and the guy left without saying a word. It had been close to a year since Debonair had burned her face and body with the cigar. Since then, she'd basically lost her mind, but she wasn't crazy enough to leave Debonair because she knew he would kill her. She carried her knife just in case she ever had to face situations like that again. When Sasha went out into the hallway, she faced off with a female junkie who was smoking crack from a glass pipe. Sasha passed her and went to the bathroom. She knocked on the door and waited for someone to answer from the inside. No one did.

She walked inside, locked the door behind her, and stood in front of the mirror and stared at her reflection. The cigar burns had healed, but the circular, puffy scars were still there and very noticeable. Sasha touched her cheeks on each side. She was disappointed with herself. She never would have thought in all her life she would be in a situation like this. *What would it have been like if Young Hollywood was still here?* Her eyes became watery, and a tear rolled down her cheek. She opened the medicine cabinet. There were over ten different bottles of pills. She didn't bother reading any labels; the warnings didn't concern her. She turned on the cold water in the sink and cupped her hands together under the running water. She then splashed it into her face. Sasha had made up her mind. She didn't want to live any longer. She began opening several bottles of pills and pouring them into the palm of her hand. She started popping them three at a time, all different ones. Fifteen minutes passed, and Sasha was sitting on the floor. Her eyelids had become heavy. She'd taken over seventy pills. Then she slowly tilted over.

A week had passed, and the worst possible thing happened to Sasha;

she was still alive. Lying in her bed at Grady Memorial Hospital, she finally began to get some rest. She was in a white gown that somebody had bought her. Her hair had been combed and pulled to the back in a tight ponytail. She was there surrounded by complete quietness. Her breathing was heavy, but she was in good shape. Through blurred vision, she noticed several colorful balloons and a vase filled with roses.

Then the oddest thing happened: Paulette appeared at the side of her bed. She reached out and touched the side of Sasha's face. "How you feelin'?" Paulette asked her.

"Like shit," Sasha responded, her voice cracking.

"I got a message for you from Debonair," Paulette said as she began unfolding a small piece of paper. She handed the paper to Sasha.

Sasha held the paper in her hand and began reading it to herself: "Yeah, bitch, I see you tried to get away from me. I pimp hard, and you know this. It don't make a difference if you killed yourself or not, you still won't be able to get away from this pimpin'. When you get out that damn hospital, you need to come see me, because you cost me money. You know you got to hit the track. It's pimps in hell too, ho. Always remember that, bitch. And thank Paulette for that gown, flowers, and balloons." Sasha handed Paulette the letter, closed her eyes, and cried silently on the inside. Then, without warning, she broke all the way down and cried like a baby.

Paulette rubbed the side of her face again. "It'll get better, baby girl," Paulette whispered. She leaned down and kissed Sasha's forehead. She wanted to kiss her lips, but they looked too disgusting. Paulette hugged her. "Don't cry," she said as she held her in her arms. "Don't cry."

# BOOK IV

# CHAPTER 25

It took Hammer over twelve hours to arrive in Atlanta on his Greyhound trip from Reidsville, Georgia. When he got there, the only thing he could do was stare at the city in shock. Atlanta had grown tremendously. Skyscrapers were high in the sky, and the entire city was dancing with lights. When Hammer stepped off the bus, he caught the first available cab in sight. He hopped in the backseat.

"Where you headin'?" the driver asked.

"The closest check-cashing spot," Hammer said. Hammer was a top-notch hustler when he was in prison. He'd sold marijuana and cocaine and had all the money he earned sent to his books. He had a check worth $6,400.

When the taxi driver pulled out into traffic, it was nearly eleven thirty p.m. An hour later, he had checked in at the Marriott Hotel downtown, rented a suite for three days. Hammer soaked for three straight hours in the hot Jacuzzi with bubbling water. It was a good way for him to ease his mind. When he finished, he lay out across the huge, comfortable bed in a pair of boxers and got a good night's rest. He was up at six, and drinking coffee downstairs in the lobby, still dressed in his state-issued khaki pants, dress shirt, and hard-bottom shoes. Hammer stared around, examining his surroundings with untrusting eyes. Unfamiliar people chattered nonchalantly. This was the real world, and Hammer knew it, but the problem was the way he would deal with it. The man was downright ruthless in his mind, body, and soul. Young Hollywood had explained to him in detail about how much money could be made in the music industry. Only Hammer pronounced it in the streets. His ruthless state of mind made him think differently than normal civilians. Hammer would sometimes ask himself questions that would put him in a live-or-die situation. He was just an odd person like that—a heavy risk-taker who was too bold for himself, let alone someone else.

A lady in a two-piece pantsuit and high heels, with flowing hair and hazel eyes passed by. She flashed a grin at Hammer and waved when she saw him staring. She went to the elevator and waited for its arrival. The doors of the first elevator parted open. Two white couples emerged, and the lady went inside.

Before the doors could close, Hammer caught them and stepped inside. On the twelfth floor, the doors opened, and Hammer stepped out with the strange woman. He held her hand firmly while casually leading her; more like guiding her, down the carpeted corridor. They laughed all the way to his suite.

Inside, Hammer sat the young lady down on the sofa in the living room area.

She crossed her legs and tried very hard to keep from staring at Hammer. She smiled. "Sooo, Mr. Hayes," she said, "what trades did you take up while you were incarcerated?" She tried her best to sound seductive.

Hammer caught it, too, but he wasn't interested. Hammer removed a chair from the dining table. He sat it on the other side of the coffee table and sat down and faced her. He crossed his legs and prepared himself mentally as if he was in a job interview. Hammer stared at her, hard into her eyes. "My main priority is getting myself situated. I'll be a very rich man soon, and I'm looking for someone more of your caliber, a business wife bound by trust and loyalty only, nothing out of the ordinary."

"You sound very convincing, Mr. Hayes, but you've got to understand, coming home from prison and trying to keep up with the Joneses is the quick route back in. Slow down and think for a minute."

Hammer held his composure. His eyes were alluring, but this strange lady that sat before him didn't know how dangerous he really was. He finally allowed a grin to break across his face. "I've been incarcerated twenty straight years, Miss Day, so I've had ample enough time to prepare myself. All I'm asking from you is that you would handle my paperwork and meetings and things of that sort. I'm very dedicated to getting this started." There was a long pause. Then he asked. "Will you help me?"

Miss Day shrugged her shoulders. "I don't see why not," she said firmly. Then she stood. "Do you have a cell phone?" she asked.

Hammer stood and pointed a finer. "Good question. Remember, I just came home yesterday. Give me a number or card to contact you. I'll call you six days from now."

Miss Day retrieved a business card from her leather purse and held it out to Hammer.

He took it and scanned it over. "Are you living here in Atlanta?"

She nodded. "Yes. I'm here at the hotel, attending a real estate seminar."

"Good. I'll keep that in mind. Do you remember what we are bonded by?"

"Trust and loyalty."

Hammer extended his hand.

She shook it and felt his powerful grip.

"Be looking for my call in six days."

When Miss Day left the room, Hammer removed a folded piece of paper from his pocket. There were a few numbers scribbled on it. He picked up the phone and dialed.

An older man's voice picked up on the other end. "Hello?"

"May I speak with Vincent please?"

"Who's callin'?" the old man asked from the other end.

"This Hamma."

Excitement rose in the voice from the other end. "What damn Hamma?"

"It ain't MC. I can damn sho tell you that."

"Where the hell are you?"

"I'm downtown."

"Where at downtown?"

"A shelter."

"Don't bullshit me, nigga."

Hammer smiled, and his eyes were filled with excitement. Then he said, "The Marriott."

"I'll be there in about two hours."

Hammer allowed his smile to fade away. The jokes were over just that fast. "You keep it quiet about me. Leave my enemies asleep."

"Leave 'em 'sleep, huh? Now that's a funny one. What's your room number?"

Hammer told him. They talked about five more minutes, and then they hung up. Hammer kicked off his shoes and removed his dress shirt. He walked across the floor; the thick carpet felt good underneath his feet. Hammer stared at the thick drapes that hung over the window. The drawstring was to his left. He pulled it, and the drapes parted slightly, just enough for a streak of sunlight to peek in. He pulled it again, and they parted all the way. He opened the sliding glass door, and fresh air rushed him. He stepped outside onto the balcony. Four cushioned chairs surrounded an iron table with a glass top. He took a seat, kicked his feet up on the table, and crossed them. With several slow breaths, he finally titled his head back, closed his eyes, and relaxed.

# CHAPTER 26

Vincent was a big man. He stood an even six feet and weighed nearly 300 pounds. He had had a huge neck covered with layers of fat. His stomach was huge, the hard kind of fat. He was in his late forties with a short salt-and-pepper haircut. Vincent stepped down from the passenger's seat of a cocaine-white Escalade with a huge duffel bag slung across his shoulders and neck.

The driver stepped down as well. He was a hunk of a man himself. He was six-four ,and they called him Little Vincent; Vincent was his father.

They got out and walked across the parking lot and went into the lobby and rode the elevator up to Hammer's room.

When the knock came from the outside of Hammer's door, he stood to his feet with confidence. He went to the door and unlocked and opened it all in one swift movement.

Vincent handed his son the duffel bag and nearly bear-hugged Hammer. They embraced one another and clapped each other's backs. Vincent pulled away, and a smile spread across his fat face. "It's good to see you. They said you died in prison."

Hammer stepped aside and allowed Vincent and his son to come inside. "What did they say I died from?"

"Some shit..." He cut himself off because he realized he'd said a curse word. He tapped the side of his head. "Say you got burned up in yo' cell down in Reidsville."

"Right plan, wrong man," Hammer said with a smile. Then he looked at Little Vincent and sized him up, and his smile faded somewhat away. "Who this you brought with you?"

Vincent turned around and pulled his son forward. He introduced Hammer to his son and vice versa. Hammer and Vincent chatted for the next two hours. Then the two of them sat across the dining table from each other. Vincent unzipped the duffel bag and removed $35K in cash. The money was bundled and separated in thousand-dollar stacks, all neatly wrapped in beige rubber bands. "Got you thirty-five grand right here," Vincent said. Then he removed a cache of weapons set in foam cutouts, along with their silencers.

Hammer removed one of the guns and carefully examined it. He caressed it and adored it even more. "Where you get the silencers from?"

"It's all who you know out here now. Everything has changed. Snitchin' is at an all-time high. It's a lot of money out here to be made though. The young cats call assault rifles choppers now, and they want it to be known that they will use them. It's still a lot of old playas out here too. The majority of them—or shall I say us—we prefer the bodies to disappear completely."

Hammer was taking all of it in. He leaned back in his chair, and his facial expression changed a little. Then he removed one of the silencers and twirled it around in his left hand. "Those days are far behind me now. I'm more interested in starting my own record label and gettin' into this studio shit."

Then the son spoke up. "You dealin' wit' da rap game?"

Hammer looked at him. "Yeah, I plan to. They say it's a lot of money with it."

"Yeah, it is, but it's just like dealin' wit' da streets."

"I'm sure I'll be able to deal with it. I'm good at dealing with situations. Ask yo' daddy about me." Hammer waved his hand dismissively. "That's not even a problem. Right now I need to find out about a young lady named Sasha Alexander."

The young Vincent stared at Hammer. "Pimp, you trickin', or how you know her?"

"She my son's baby mama. Do you know her?" He stared with intense eyes. Then he sat the silencer back into the foam cutout and brought the chair back down to all four legs. Hammer stood up and folded his arms across his chest. His eyes never left the son. "I'm assuming you know her," Hammer said.

"Yeah, I know her. I haven't seen shawty in a couple months though. Last I heard, she was fuckin' wit' Debonair."

"Debonair? Who is he?" Hammer was becoming more interested now. His eyes never left the son.

"Debonair rankin' number three in top pimpin'. His daddy and uncles run all the big escort services. You know Debonair, the one burned Sasha's face and shit. Dat girl use to be pretty as hell."

"Where you think I can find her at?" Hammer asked anxiously.

"Any major ho' stroll…Stewart, Cleveland Avenues."

"You know Stewart ain't Stewart name no mo'. It's been changed to Metropolitan," Vincent said. Then he added, "Why don't you let me give you a tour of the city? You need clothes and all."

Hammer smiled without saying a word. His mind was somewhere else. Then he said, "Get me two young kids around eighteen. They gotta be tough but willing to listen. Give them a grand a piece and have them find Sasha for me." He went to a drawer in the nightstand and removed a folded envelope. From it, he took out an old photo of Sasha and her son Corleone. He gave the photo to the young Vincent. "I got to find this girl."

"And do what to her?" Vincent asked. Now he had a curious stare in his eyes. His look was more of a question.

"She got my grandson somewhere. I just need to talk to her." He paused. "Until then, I'll enjoy this lovely hotel and their room service. You know, I lived in a cell on twenty-three-hour lockdown for fourteen years, just me by myself."

"You don't wanna see your old neighborhood?"

Hammer went to the window and opened the curtain. The skyline of downtown Atlanta was clearly visible. "This is my neighborhood, the whole fucking A-Town." He took a deep breath. "When I show my face, niggas gon' show respect." That said, he walked over to Vincent and gave him another hug and then kissed his cheek. He did the same thing with the son.

Downstairs in the parking lot, Vincent and his son loaded inside the Escalade. They started the engine. Vincent stared blankly out into nowhere, and his son noticed. He strapped his seatbelt and asked, "Wuz up, Daddy?"

"That's a crazy son-of-a-bitch. He got a good heart though. And let's just be thankful that he's on our team," Vincent commented.

"Is he that serious?" Little Vincent asked.

There was a short silence. Then Vincent looked at him like he couldn't believe he'd asked such a foolish question and said, "You'll see." He let out a deep breath. "I gotta feelin' we all gon' see. Hamma's back in town."

# CHAPTER 27

The next night, Sasha drove an old beat-up Grand Prix through the bluff. Her left headlamp had blown, and that made her nervous because she was already in violation by not having any insurance. She pulled the car in front of a house that was half-burnt. Four guys were standing in the front yard. Two of them were dressed in camouflage, and the other two wore dark denim jeans and long black T-shirts. Sasha rolled down her window.

One of the hustlers approached. He leaned down in the window. "Wuz up, shawty?" he asked.

Sasha looked at him. Her hair was made up with extra-long weave, and she wore too much make-up; her skin looked plastic. "I'm sick, baby," she said. "Can I get one on my face? At least until I go turn a couple of tricks."

The guy stared at Sasha again, this time harder. He held up a finger to tell her to hold on. He went back to the yard where the other three guys were huddled. "What dat girl name was Mo said?"

One of the other guys dug a piece of paper from his pocket, and by the time he could read the name Sasha Alexander, she had pulled off. One of the young guys that wore the green fatigues spoke into a two-way Nextel. A slight chirping sound cracked. "Stop dat bitch in dat red Grand Prix!"

Sasha had nearly made it to the corner of Simpson Road when a long, old-model Lincoln Town Car pulled out of a dark driveway and blocked off the street. The Lincoln was dented badly, and all the windows were broken out. The Grand Prix came to a screeching halt, and the closer Sasha got to it, the vision came to her eyes that there was nobody behind the wheel. The car was used to block off anybody who came through the bluff and tried to rob or snatch a sack. Sasha looked around the dark street and noticed two guys dressed in dark clothing, heavily armed. Her eyes were wide with fear as she stared down the barrel of a mini-assault rifle.

"Cut da ca' off," one guy said. He shoved the barrel of the assault rifle in her face.

She turned off the engine, placed her hands on the steering wheel, and looked straight ahead. She knew how the bluff was. They had a reputation that was respected. From her peripheral vision, she noticed three younger kids lined up next to one another, pushing the Lincoln back into the yard.

One of the armed guys stepped closer to the window. Sasha noticed that his breath was laced with alcohol. "Step out," he demanded.

Nervously, she did, her hands shaking like a leaf on a tree in the wind.

Hammer was downstairs in the hotel fitness center on a crunch machine. He was soaked in sweat and dressed in a white wife-beater and gray sweatpants and Nikes. He had done a little shopping at a downtown sporting goods store earlier during the day. He moved to a squat machine. His upper shoulders pressed against thick black pads.

The words, "Mr. Hayes, report to the front desk. You have a call," came across the intercom in the gym.

Hammer went to the front desk.

The concierge greeted him with a smile. Then she handed him the phone.

"Hello?"

"Hey, sir," the voice said from the other end. "I found the shoes you is lookin' fo'. Do you need me to bring them up?"

"Give me your number, and I'll call you right back," Hammer replied. When Hammer got the number, he tipped the concierge a twenty and went upstairs to his room. He went inside and dialed the number he was given.

The guy answered from the other end on the first ring.

"Do you have her with you?" Hammer asked.

"Yeah, shawty right here in da backseat."

"Let me speak to her."

There was a short pause, and then a shaky female voice answered, "Hello?" It was Sasha.

"Do you have a son by the name of Corleone Terry Keys?" Hammer asked.

"Nope." She sounded sassy.

"Listen at me. My son is Terry, Young Hollywood," he said calmly.

"Are you Sasha Alexander?"

There was a long pause, and then she said, "Yes. I'm Sasha."

Hammer was relieved, though she didn't know it. "Can I talk to you tonight on a positive level?" he asked.

"I guess," Sasha responded.

"Good. Put the guy you with on the phone." A moment later Hammer said, "Yeah, bring her to my room."

By the time Sasha and the two young goons arrived at Hammer's suite, he'd showered and groomed himself. When the knock came at the door, he casually opened it and greeted the three of them. "I need to talk to her in private," he said to the two goons. Then he peeled off twenty crisp hundred-dollar bills and handed them ten a piece. They smiled gratefully, and their eyes gleamed with excitement. "You can wait in the parking lot for her. When she comes down, ya'll make sho she get home safely."

"Well, I hope it don't be long," Sasha spoke out, "'cause I got to go to work."

Hammer turned and looked at her. He held up an index finger and slightly cocked his head to one side.

She read in his eyes and also the tightness of his facial muscles that he was a serious man. That provoked her into obeying. She folded her arms across her chest and turned away from them.

Hammer looked at the two again, his eyes darting from one to the other. "Do we have everything understood?"

They both nodded.

Hammer escorted them out into the hallway. He closed the door as they left. Then he turned to Sasha and said calmly, "Have a seat."

She took the chair, her eyes down at the ground.

Hammer sat at the dining table across the room. "Look up. Don't look at the ground unless you're watching your step," he said. Then he asked, "You got something to tell me?"

"No," Her eyes moved up to his.

"Obviously you do."

"Why you say dat?"

"Where is Corleone? And don't lie to me."

"He at auntie house in Virginia."

"Let's go see him." Hammer went on, "You lying, Sasha." Hammer stood up. His eyes had turned to slits. He jumped over to Sasha so quick that she never saw him move. She jumped and covered her face, but she didn't scream. He stood over her. His face was in a fury, and then he caught hold of himself. He reached and grabbed her hand. She slowly turned and looked up at him "Stand up!" he insisted. She stood, and Hammer pulled her into his powerful arms.

Sasha was in tears, and she wasn't trying to hold them back. "I'm sorry," she cried. "I'm so sorry."

Hammer rocked her side to side and held her firmly. "It's gonna be all right. Shhh." He was whispering in her ear.

"I'm sorry," she continued.

"Where is he, baby?"

Sasha cried even harder. Her lips and hands were trembling, and her heart rate had increased. She desperately tried to calm herself. Then she wiped tears from her eyes.

Hammer could smell her body odor, and that was something he disapproved of. He would give it to her in the raw too.

"I…I gave him up," she finally said.

Hammer closed his eyes and tightened his grip on her. He took a deep breath. "Do you have an option to get him back?"

"I don't think so."

"We'll get him back," he said. Hammer pulled away from her and stared into her eyes. "Who is Debonair?"

"Jus' a friend. Nobody special."

"Is he your pimp?"

She felt defeated again and nodded her head.

"Is he the one that burned your face?"

Another nod.

"Do you want a better life?"

"Yes," and the way she sounded, it was believable.

"Where can I find Debonair?" he asked her calmly as possible.

Fear jumped into her eyes. "I don't know about dat," she said.

Hammer noticed this. He stared hard into her eyes. "You and my son had a relationship together. You have a child together, which is my grandchild. Everything falls on me because I put my word on it. Now everything I need, you will do it. Is that understood?"

Without one single word she nodded her head.

# CHAPTER 28

The next evening, Paulette, Amber, and Cherry were huddled together in front of a huge flat-screen TV watching an erotic triple-X tape. Paulette wore small shorts and a colorful tank top. She had cotton balls stuffed between each of her toes as she painted her nails red. Amber was next to her. A rolled blunt was pressed between two of her fingers, and she couldn't wait to light it. Her other hand was used to play around with Cherry's clit.

A knock came from the front door, and Paulette stood quickly and raced on the ball of her heels to the door to answer it. She looked through the peephole. A pizza deliveryman was standing on the porch with a huge insulated pizza bag in his hand. Paulette turned her head toward the den. "Who ordered pizza?"

There was a short silence. Then one of the girls yelled, "We didn't, but we can use it."

Paulette grinned and even she thought about the pizza. Her stomach growled. She looked through the peephole again and saw an eye looking at her. She squinted, and then there was a blinding flash. The 9mm bullet ripped through the door and into her eye socket. She spun around. Two more bullets followed. Chips of split wood flung from the door, but not one shot was heard. Paulette hit the floor, blood seeping from her face, spoiling the thick white carpet that laid her to rest. Then two powerful kicks from the outside of the door nearly took it off the hinges.

When Hammer entered, Amber and Cherry were just coming around the corner; they saw Paulette lying face down and the gun that Hammer had pointed at them. They froze, their eyes stretched wide with fear.

Hammer was quick, kind of like a cheetah. "Get down! Not a word," he whispered. The Pizza Hut cap was pulled down over his eyes.

Amber and Cherry got down on the floor.

Hammer hitched up his pants and squatted down next to the girls. "Where is Debonair?" he asked calmly. He didn't sound excited or anything. His cold eyes were like truth serum.

"We can call him," Amber said. Tears were rolling down her cheeks, and she was shaking like a leaf on a tree.

Hammer wore a cheap pair of leather gloves and casually rubbed the back of his hand across Amber's face. "Where is your phone?" he asked, and then he moved swiftly across the floor to the front door. He closed it back and tried the best he could to put it back into place. He covered the bloodstains with a throw rug.

Nearly two hours passed. When Debonair pulled into the driveway in his convertible Benz, he picked up his cell phone and punched in the house number.

Amber answered on the first ring. Her voice was full of energy. "Where you at?"

Debonair looked long and hard at the front of the house. He had a deep gut feeling that something wasn't right. He cradled the phone, and then he killed the headlights. The front of the house fell dark. "Open the door," he said. Debonair then reached under the seat and grabbed his Glock and stuffed it in his waistline. He saw Amber standing in the door. Debonair switched off the engine and removed the keys from the ignition. He stepped outside and gently closed the car door; you never slam a Benz door. He walked toward the house, and the closer he got, the clearer his vision became. He could see Amber, her face covered in white cream, her head wrapped in a towel, and her body covered in a robe. When Debonair climbed the red brick steps and approached the door, he looked at Amber. He could only see her eyes. Debonair crossed the threshold and stopped directly in front of her, and he looked down at her.

She closed the door behind him.

Hammer revealed himself by speaking to Debonair. "I've been dying to meet you," he said in his deepest voice. He sounded more masculine than ever.

Debonair was shocked. That surely caught him off guard and even made him choke up. When he saw the weapon in Hammer's hand, a look jumped into his eyes, as if he wanted to try something.

Hammer pressed the barrel of the silencer in his midsection and slapped him across his face with the other hand. Blood flung from his mouth. Hammer gripped him around his throat and pressed him against the wall. Debonair couldn't believe the strength he had. Hammer moved the gun up to Debonair's forehead. "You can comply with me and live or go against me and die."

"Comply," Debonair whispered. He could barely talk, and even as a man himself, the presence of whomever this was behind this white mudpack had him extremely nervous.

Hammer guided Debonair to the dining room and then felt around his waist. The lump was on his left side. Hammer removed the Glock and tucked it in his own waist.

Inside the dining room, Debonair stopped in his tracks when he saw Paulette sitting at the table, her shirt covered in blood and her eye covered with tape. Amber was sitting at the table next to her. The cordless phone was taped to the side of her face, and her hands were duct taped behind her back. Cherry was in the same position: taped to the dining room chair, hands bound, and her mouth gagged.

"Comply?"

Debonair nodded.

Hammer showed him to his seat, and he sat next to him. Debonair stared at Paulette, who was very dead. Her open eye was looking straight ahead. He had never seen anything like it, and he was actually scared to death.

The following morning, Hammer was up bright and early. He ordered room service to his hotel suite: scrambled eggs, a well-done sirloin steak with sautéed onions and bell peppers, two slices of toasted wheat bread, and a grapefruit sliced in two halves. He sat at the table sipping freshly squeezed orange juice and reading an article from the Metro section of the *AJC*. It read: "Four bodies were found dead early this morning in the Ben Hill area. The victims are presumed to have been burned to death, though the bodies have not been identified. The Atlanta Police Department is seeking leads. If you have any information or would like to report a missing person, please call 1-800-700-HELP..."

Hammer went to the Sports section and read an article on the Falcons and folded the entire newspaper. He set it aside and stared across the length of the table, where he had stacked and lined up one $170K in neat stacks. The table was a sea of green and white, funded by Debonair. Hammer buttered a slice of toast, bit into it, and chewed carefully on a small piece of steak. It had been four days since Hammer had been home, and he hadn't yet talked to his son, but he'd already decided he wouldn't contact him until he could produce what he promised he would. Hammer picked up the phone and dialed Sasha's room number; he had paid for a suite next door to him.

She answered, "Hello?"

"Are you resting?" he asked her.

"I'm tryin'. My stomach's crampin'."

"You got any methadone?"

"Jus' enough. I don't wanna get hooked on dis shit. What time did you get back?"

"Just know everything is all right. Now you got to hold up your end of the deal. Right now you just get yo'self some rest, and I'll see you this evening."

"Okay." She hung up.

Satisfied, Hammer hung up, grabbed the steak knife and fork, and began slicing bite-sized squares of the meat. He bit into one, closed his eyes, and savored the floor. Hammer thought to himself, *It feels real good to be home. Just what the motha'fuckin' city ordered.*

# CHAPTER 29

Young Hollywood stirred in his bunk and woke up when breakfast trays were being served. According to his watch, it was five thirty in the morning, and that meant the trays were late.

"Chow call!" an officer's voice rang out from somewhere down the range.

Young Hollywood flipped back his covers. His eyes were squinting against the light. He slowly swung his legs out of bed and eased his feet into a pair of Nike slides. When he stood up, he stretched and yawned. His face was unshaved, and his mouth had that bitter early-morning taste.

When the officers got to his cell, they slid him his tray.

Young Hollywood removed the top. On the tray were watery oatmeal and raisins, scrambled eggs, two slices of bologna, and two muffins. This meal always disgusted him; he actually hated it. He removed the two pieces of meat and left the remainder there. He was still half-asleep when a light turned on in his head, something very important. Young Hollywood took the tray again and set it on the floor next to his bed. He grabbed his hand mirror and went to the bars. He used it to look both ways. Both officers were long gone down the range. Young Hollywood went back to his tray. He removed the top again and moved the now-cold oatmeal from the big rectangle slot. Underneath was an ounce of mid-grade marijuana, taped to the tray in plastic. When he removed the marijuana, he went to the sink and rinsed off the remainder of oatmeal and quickly dried it off with tissue. Young Hollywood went to his desk and sat down. He tore open the bag and removed a small bud. He broke it down and pulled out a rolling paper and rolled it up.

When Young Hollywood fired up the joint, the scent took over the air. Ten minutes later, Young Hollywood was feeling so good he decided to clean up his cell. He plugged in his radio and hooked up his CD player to it. He popped in a CD called *I'm Serious* by T.I. Young Hollywood knew him personally from middle school and referred to him as Lil' Cliff. Just two days earlier, Young Hollywood and some other guy down the range had had a verbal altercation concerning T.I. Young Hollywood had to laugh at the situation himself as he played the scene back in his head.

The morning started off good for Young Hollywood. He woke up early and went to a medical call-out to get some foot cream. The nurses were as nice as ladies could be in Reidsville. It was still the hardest prison in Georgia and the most respected. When Young Hollywood was escorted back to his lockdown cell, he immediately slid in his *I'm Serious* CD and began working out with extreme push-ups. He sometimes recited the verses out loud as he worked out. "These niggas robbin' me. I pray to God it's nothin' but a robbery. I gave them all I had, so they pulled the lick off flawlessly. They yellin', fussin', cussin'..." He took a breather and began counting the push-ups. The song continued to play, and he continued to bob his head. "Dumpin' seven, and they all in me, on my fallin' knees..." He was breathing hard now, and he was nearly at 130 straight. "Seen my whole life flash before my eyes... I'm out of here... all my life smoked a lot of weed, drank a lot of beer, sold a lot of keys..."

"Damn, nigga, get off shawty dick!" a guy yelled from down the range.

Young Hollywood bounced to his feet. He killed the music and went to the bars. "Who you talkin' to?" He was breathing heavy, and his chest was rising and falling. His eyes had turned bloodshot red, and his face was in a mask of fury. His hands gripped tightly around the bars.

"Nigga, I'm talkin' to whoever dat is dat keep rappin' dat bullshit T.I."

Young Hollywood's eyes glistened with excitement. His mouth became watery, and he was so angry he was blowing up like a dead body. "So obviously, you jus' another fuck nigga hatin' on shawty, or is it me you don't like?"

"Bitch, nigga, dat go fa whoever. You know who dis is. Killa Black."

Young Hollywood had heard about Killa Black. He had a helluva reputation in Atlanta and in prison, bodies stacked on top of bodies. He also had a special technique where he burned up a couple of guys in their cells. Hammer had spoken highly about him and warned Young

Hollywood about his treachery.

Young Hollywood was still gripping the bars. He was lost in thought for a minute or two, and then he said calmly. "You know what, shawty? You right."

"I know I'm right. Y'all niggas be screamin' shawty name like he certified. He ain't flipped a brick, and you ain't either."

"I'm finished talkin', pimp." He went to his bed and sat down. Sweat was pouring from his face. His heart was racing faster than normal. Killa Black was going on and on with nonstop disrespectful comments concerning Young Hollywood and T.I. He began thinking to himself. He needed to get at Killa Black. He wanted that mouth. Then he began taking deep breaths to calm himself down.

Ten minutes later, the library orderly came through with a metal rolling cart filled with novels ad religious material. The guy that was pushing the cart stood an even six feet. He was slim, with huge hands. His eyes were opaque and deadly looking, but he appeared to be smooth and very easygoing.

When the cart rolled near Young Hollywood, he jumped to his feet. "Scarface!" he called out, and the sound of his voice was filled with excitement.

Scarface paused in front of his cell. His stare was as deadly as a king cobra's. His eyes never left Young Hollywood. "Wuz up?"

Young Hollywood's eyebrows bunched together, and he lowered his voice. He eased close to Scarface, close enough to clearly see the ugly scar that ran from his ear to his cheekbone. "You know me, right?"

Scarface was silent. He wasn't much for small talk. He ignored Young Hollywood.

"Anyway, my daddy jus' went home," he whispered. "He told me if I ever needed anything to get at you."

"I'm listenin'," Scarface finally spoke, his lips barely parted.

"How much will you charge to burn a nigga up fo' me?"

Scarface stepped away from the cell and pretended to be looking at a few books. "I don't think we got James Patterson's *Kiss the Girls*." He removed a hardback from the cart.

An officer walked by, making his usual rounds, but he passed without a word.

Scarface went back to the cell. "Who you talkin' 'bout?" he whispered. His deadly stare was turning anxious.

"Dat nigga Killa Black." Young Hollywood nearly growled the name between clenched teeth.

Scarface thought about it for a small moment and then asked. "You want 'im dead or jus' fucked up?"

"Nah, don't kill 'im. I just want him fucked up."

Scarface folded his arms across his chest. "Have $400 sent to my books, and get me an ounce of reefer."

"Good. I got $400 cash right now. I only got a half-ounce of reefer left, but I can give you my word. You get it did today, and in two weeks, I'll have a grand sent to you as a bonus. I'll talk to Hamma dis week and explain everything to him. You got my word."

Scarface began thinking again, weighing out options, and his palms began to sweat. Then he grinned down on his teeth and leaned closer to Young Hollywood. "Personally, I don't get involved in other niggas' problems. You know how da rules go. Yo' city, yo' problem. Give me da cash now. Send me the reefer through the orderly show from Savannah."

"Check dat." Young Hollywood moved to the rear of his cell and removed a small white envelope from a manila one. He went back to the bars and slipped Scarface the money.

Scarface gave him a bow of the head, a way of showing respect, then slowly moved down the range.

Young Hollywood pressed play on his CD player again. This time he turned the volume up to ten, and the whole E-1 could hear T.I.

Down the range, Killa Black yelled out, "Fuck, nigga you still—" He stopped and began screaming, yelling at the top of his lungs. "Help! Heeellp. He burnin' me up! Somebody help me."

Young Hollywood sat on his bunk and stared out into space for a second or two. He killed the music altogether and said proudly. "I guess you can say I took dat personally. Fuck nigga." He raised his hand up to his forehead, two fingers pressed together. "I salute you, pussy nigga." Then he thought about something Hollywood had told him back when he was thirteen years old: *"Money well spent."*

# CHAPTER 30

Inside an expensive clothing store downtown, Hammer stood on a four-inch wooden platform in front of a wall mirror. He was being tailored in three-piece suits and ties and expensive dress shirts. Gold cufflinks were, a must and Gator dress shoes would accent his attire. Sasha had told him what he would look good in, and the Italian manager of the store would bring him up to standard.

When he was finished shopping for himself, they went to an elegant clothing store for women. He let Sasha shop for herself. She bought leather boots, heels, jeans, blouses, a couple of dress suits here and there, and a few purses. Everything was name brand, the majority *Dolce & Gabbana*, Prada, Coogi sweat suits, and tiny, colorful Nikes for women. Hammer wanted the best for Sasha. He wanted her to feel needed, to feel like a woman again, and it was all for a good reason. He had something very important for her to do. She was a piece to his puzzle, basically just another pawn on the chessboard.

When they were finished shopping, Hammer took her to a private doctor downtown. When she was thoroughly examined physically and mentally, she was set up by the private doctor to be seen once a week for support and help with her drug habit.

Back at the hotel, Hammer sat Sasha down at the dining room table. He sat across from her. She looked into his striking eyes, and he said in a soft-spoken, very polite voice. "Are you comfortable around me?"

She grinned. "Yes, sir. Why do you ask that?" She sounded serious and very convincing.

Hammer was faster than a New York minute. He thought quick and took action even faster. He carefully placed his elbows on the high-glossed tabletop. He then wedged his fingers between one another and leaned in toward her. Her grin faded, but she never took her eyes away form him. He said. "I gave Terry my word that I'd find you and make sure you're well taken care of. That goes for my grandson as well. I told him I would not contact him until I have you both. Neither one of us was aware of your problems. Me personally, I don't like problems, but my concern is to make sure he's not wanting for nothing while he's in prison. That'll be your position. Is that understood?"

She nodded her head.

"I want the best fa' you and I want the best fa' my grandson. Above all, I need my son home. Is that understood?"

She nodded again.

"From this day forward, you'll have no more ties or connects with any old friends or associates. They'll only hold you back. I'm your family now. Is that understood?"

She nodded again, and then she asked a question of her own. "So you are gon' help me get Corleone back?"

"All you have to do is what I say." He stood quickly and made Sasha nervous. He went inside his inside jacket pocket and removed a Cuban cigar that was given to him in one of the stores. "Today I want you to find a plastic surgeon that can fix your face."

She smiled again, and then her eyes widened. "Fo' real?" Happiness was in her voice.

"I stand on my word. Now go handle yo' business, and I'll call you later on tonight."

Sasha got up and went to her own suite.

When she was gone, Hammer got on the phone and called Vincent.

"I'm glad you called." Vincent said.

"Yeah. What's the business?" Hammer asked.

"Somebody wanna see you."

"Who?"

"Da Governor."

"Who the fuck is the Governor?" Hammer asked. "And how the fuck do he know me?"

"You gotta be jokin', right. You don't know who da' Governor is?"

"If I did, I wouldn't be asking."

"Man, you mean to tell me you don't remember James Washington from Carver Homes?"

Hammer thought for a second. *James Washington.* He thought harder. *Carver Homes.* He thought even harder. Then he remembered a bank robbery job he went on with a dude from Carver Homes. He remembered that guy J.W. as a son-of-a-bitch. "J.W.? Yeah, that motha' fucka' owe me."

"You'll have a chance to discuss that with him."

"How did he find out I'm out?" Hammer sipped on a warm bottle of orange juice. His eyes turned into thin slits.

"Ain't no tellin'. You know da Governor is well connected. Listen, I'll be there to get you tonight at nine thirty. Be ready." Vincent hung up.

Hammer hung up also. Then he showered and dressed in a new suit he'd just bought from Neiman Marcus.

Next door, Sasha soaked in soothing bath water. The water was hot and very relaxing. She'd spent over $200 at Bath and Body Works. As she relaxed, she thought about her son, hoping he hadn't been adopted yet. If he was still at the home, he would be easier to get back. She washed her body carefully, not missing anywhere. She never would have thought her life would change so drastically. She also knew Young Hollywood would never love her again, not after what she did. She would try her best to make him happy though. When she got out of the Jacuzzi, she toweled herself dry in front of the mirror. She was still fat and looked disgusting. "I got to lose some of this weight," she said to her reflection.

After she dried off, she lotioned her body and lit up the entire room with the exotic scent. She covered herself in the hotel robe. Then she called downstairs to the front desk and inquired about a personal trainer. Then she tried finding a surgeon. She was ready to get herself back together.

# CHAPTER 31

Vincent and Hammer rode in an expensive Mercedes-Benz S600 V-12 Coupe. The Atlanta highway was busy with traffic, and they listened to Marvin Gaye on the stereo system, each of the two lost in their own thoughts. Hammer watched the passing headlights and checked the rearview mirror. Twenty minutes later, Vincent turned into a well-lit gated community Northwest of Atlanta and cruised down a long, winding driveway that led them to a mansion. In the driveway were a black Bentley Azure, two black Lincolns with tinted windows, and a host of other cars. Two Ferraris were ducked off in two of the four garages.

"J.W. got his weight up fa' real huh?"

Vincent switched off the engine, looked over at Hammer, and said, "Yeah, and this ain't even his place. It's worth three million."

"Who stay here?" Hammer asked.

"Two of his sons and their wives and kids. He got property spread all over. He's stayin' here 'cause he's gettin' old, and his family got to keep a close eye on him." Vincent leaned on the horn and gave two bumps.

One of the two French doors swung open, and a guy stood there in the door.

Vincent and Hammer got out; Hammer followed Vincent's lead, but he was more next to him than behind him. Hammer examined the house, and he was more than impressed with the three levels. They climbed the brick steps that led to the porch.

Vincent shook the hand of the man waiting at the door. "Mike, how you doin'?" he said to the guy.

"I'm good."

Vincent nodded. "This is Hamma."

Hammer extended his hand out to the guy named Mike. Hammer's handshake was so powerful, it made Mike look at him as though he wasn't human.

"Good to meet you," Mike said.

When they walked inside, Hammer was even more impressed.

The living room was made up in all white—marble floors, expensive double-stuffed white furniture, and three crystal chandeliers that hung from the ceiling in one row.

The Governor appeared from a side door. He was in black pajamas and a black velour smoking jacket. He made eye contact with Hammer at fifteen feet apart. They stared at each other for a few seconds.

Hammer said, "If I had my hamma, I'd shoot you."

"It wouldn't be the first time," the Governor said in a cracked voice. He sounded weak, but he managed a smile.

Hammer did the same, and they both began moving toward one another; they embraced. Hammer held the older man in his arms. He could feel his weakness. The Governor's skin was beginning to sag a little. They separated, and the Governor showed Hammer to a seat. Vincent sat, and so did Mike.

The Governor looked at Mike. "Get me cigars and champagne," he said.

Mike got up and went somewhere in another room.

"That your son?" Hammer asked.

"Jus' a friend of the family."

Hammer nodded, his head and eyes searching the room. Then they froze on the Governor. "My twenty years in prison, I've been hearing about the Governor. Great stories too. And you've gotten real fat out here while a lot of guys starved."

Mike came back with a beautiful female in a peach dress in tow. She carried crystal champagne glasses. Mike carried a box of Hanna Cubans and a bottle of champagne that couldn't be pronounced. Everything was placed on the marble table between the three of them, and then he took off again.

The Governor looked Hammer in his eyes. They shared the same cold, evil stare. From one killer to another, the Governor popped the top on the champagne. He half-filled the three glasses. The Governor picked up the glass closest to him. "Welcome back."

"Don't disrespect me, J.W. Respond to my last statement."

The Governor grinned. "J.W. I ain't been called that since—"

Hammer cut him off. His hand motioned side to side in front of him. "Give me the business." His voice was demanding.

"Okay. You want the business? You drifted off away from me after the last bank job. You took two team playas with you, but you really didn't trust them like we trusted each other. You know them guys were killers also, Hammer." The Governor wet his throat, his fierce eyes still on Hammer. "Then you followed yo' first mind. You killed the only two soldiers that could link us together."

"You think I don't know you sent the hit?"

"I knew you knew. I also knew you were so arrogant that you sent every penny or piece of dollar that I sent you. You sent it back. I'm a man of my word, Hammer, and you know this."

"And I am too," Hammer responded.

This time he sipped champagne from his glass. He frowned from the bitter taste and set the glass back down. "Well, I damn sho can tell you this. The streets need a motha' fucka' like you. Now what do you have planned?"

"A-Town."

"A-Town what?" the Governor asked.

"A-Town records."

"Come on now, Hamma. It's a million and one things to do in Atlanta ta' get rich. The music industry is overcrowded."

"So you mean to tell me ain't no more room?" he said and pointed both hands at himself. "I can't do what I want in my own city?"

"Things have changed, Hammer. The rules have changed, and the playas."

"Listen at me, J.W. I got a son that's in prison. He's serving three consecutive life sentences plus an additional ninety-five years. To the outside world, he's a menace to society, and he'll never be released from prison. I think otherwise. The rap music thing is his idea. I gave him my word that I'd handle everything for him."

The Governor listened carefully. He rubbed his hand across his face and let out a small whistle. "That's a lot of time. Who he killed, the president?"

"Nah, jus' some nothing-ass nigga. You remember the case about the guys pulling over the ambulance on eighty-five and holding the two paramedics hostage?"

"Yeah, big case, all over Fox Five and CNN. That was your son?"

the Governor asked.

Hammer nodded.

"Like father, like son," the Governor said. Then he looked at Vincent. "What the streets lookin' like?"

"Everything is still smooth so far. I got word on a new crew that call themselves BMF. They're heavyweight. I heard they over in Fourth Ward. Say they do good business, and they got a couple artists under their label."

The Governor looked back at Hammer. "I'ma open your account with $6000K. I heard you're staying in a hotel. You need to get out of there. I got an empty penthouse in Buckhead. Are you afraid of heights?"

Hammer shook his head.

"Good. It's on the twenty-third floor."

"Is it mines to keep?"

"However long it takes fo' you to get on your feet. I'm sho you'll get tired of it after a year anyway." The Governor took a long pause and fired up his cigar.

"Them motha' fuckas' bad fa' your health," Hammer said.

The Governor let out a stream of smoke. "You remember our motto?"

Hammer smiled. "Real niggas do what they want to."

"Exactly. Now is there anything else you need?"

Hammer thought for a minute. He didn't really want anyone else in his personal business, but at the same time, he didn't want to hurt any more people, so he said, "I got a grandson I haven't seen before. His mother put him up for adoption, and I want custody of him."

"And you gonna take care of him?"

"Damn right," Hammer responded.

When the Governor called for Mike, he appeared and stood in the middle of the floor. The Governor looked at him. "You still connected with the girl from DFACS?"

He nodded. "Yeah, she's the director."

The Governor looked at Hammer. "Wuz the name?"

"Corleone Terry Keys Jr.," Hammer said, and then he asked, "Can we get him this week?"

"Just relax, Hammer. Get settled in at the apartment so you can have a legit address just in case we may have to go that route."

"Well, it could be that route or mine. That boy belongs with his family, and I'ma get him one way or another," he said, and he meant every word of that.

# CHAPTER 32

The next day, Hammer took Sasha downstairs to the inside gym. They worked out together. He wanted her to focus on exercising and getting in a good sweat. When he got back to his room, he made a phone call, and a soft voice answered from the other end.

"Yes?"

"May I speak with Miss Day please?"

"This is her. Who's calling?"

Hammer stood and walked to the window. He drew the string on the curtain and overlooked the city. "This is Mr. Hayes."

"Well, stranger, are you aware that you're a day late."

"Better late than never," he replied.

"Are you still at the hotel?"

"For the moment. That's what I needed to talk to you about."

"Well maybe we should talk face to face. Let's say we have dinner tonight together. No restaurants either—room service."

"That sounds good and very interesting, but at the moment, I have several issues and a lot of business to handle. I need you to set up an appointment with the best interior decorator in Atlanta."

"And what are we decorating?" she asked.

"A spacious penthouse in Buckhead."

"Humph. Big things huh?" she replied.

"Yeah, if that's what you wanna call it. You get on that for me and contact me here at the hotel," Hammer insisted.

"I'll get on that right now. Is it all right if I deliver the message personally?"

Hammer smiled. "That'll work."

The Brown family consisted of a lady in her mid forties by the name of Sarah. Sarah worked eight hours a day at a local dry cleaners. She was chubby with a round, cute face and bad feet. Her husband, a short, stout man in his late forties, was very mean and sometimes aggressive when he wanted to be. His name was plain old Joe, and he'd been working construction off and on for the last ten years. He was a heavy drinker and smoked two packs of Kools a day.

They lived in a two-bedroom rundown house in College Park, and in the last three months, Corleone Terry Keys had been living with this disgusting couple and was going through pure hell. He was five years old now. He had his own bedroom, and that was his world. Joe couldn't have kids, and that was why he hated them. One day, they were both going on and on about the bills, and Sarah came up with a bright idea to adopt a child from the agency so they could receive the nice check that came with it.

Sarah was the one who chose Corleone. "He's so cute," she said months ago. His face had been tattooed on her memory ever since. She had to have him and wouldn't let him go for anything. She was literally in love with him.

Inside Corleone's bedroom, he was lying down on his stomach watching cartoons when Sarah entered. She'd just gotten off work, and as a matter of fact, she came home an hour early so she could have some personal time alone with Corleone.

He looked up at her when she entered. His hands were propped under his chin. He actually smiled when he saw the McDonald's bag she carried.

"Hey, baby. Mama's home." She said cheerfully and then she handed him the bag. "I want you to hurry up and eat 'cause you get to take yo' bath befo' yo' daddy comes home."

"He ain't my daddy," Corleone responded.

Sarah's face saddened. She sat on the bed next to him and ran her fingers through his soft, curly hair while he unwrapped the hamburger. Then she slowly rubbed his back and said, "I know you don't like him, baby. Jus' hold on fo' me, okay?"

Corleone held the burger with both hands, and his eyes cut up to Sarah as he was biting into it. Ketchup and mustard ran down the side of his mouth.

"Look at you! You makin' a big mess," Sarah said. She stood up and began undressing, first her shirt and then her bra. Her huge round breasts were exposed, her nipples long and black. Then she carefully wiggled out of her pants. Her womanly odor hit the air. She wore white bloomer underwear. She sat back down on the bed next to Corleone, who was still chomping away on his burger. Sarah snuggled up close

to her son. She leaned back on the bed and slowly moved her panties to one side and twirled a nipple between two fingers. Then, just as she was getting ready to penetrate herself, the phone rang from the next room. "Shit," she said and stood up. Before she left the room, she instructed Corleone to hurry up and eat. When she got to the living room, she grabbed the phone. "Hello?"

"May I speak with Mr. or Mrs. Brown?" the caller asked.

"This is Mrs. Brown."

"Do you have legal custody of Corleone Terry Keys?"

A curious look appeared across her face. "I surly do."

"Okay listen at me good. It's been a big mistake, but it can all be taken care of. We're offering a one-time deal of \$50K to return him back to the home of his grandfather—"

Sarah hung up in the caller's face. The phone conversation had gone in one ear and out the other. When she went back to Corleone's bedroom, he was nearly finished with his hamburger. She smiled. "Look at my baby." This time, she hooked her thumbs under the edge of her panties and rolled them down her wide hips. She stepped out of them and left them in the middle of the floor. Corleone looked at her as she inserted a finger into her vagina. "You wanna take a bath with Mama?"

He stuffed two small fries into his mouth and stared up at Sarah with green, anxious eyes, his small mouth chewing vigorously. Then he shook his head "No."

Sarah's eyes turned cold, and that old kindhearted smile she had faded away. "You got to take a bath with me befo' Joe comes home." She raised her voice and knocked the small pack of fries from his hand.

Corleone gave her the most evil look she'd ever seen.

"Now take off yo' clothes," she demanded.

No more than thirty minutes later, Mike called the director of DFACS. He knew the female personally and always helped her out when she needed it. He sat behind a cherry oak desk dressed in a linen shirt, jeans, and dress shoes. He was on hold listening to the boring music that played in his ears.

"Michael."

"Yes?"

"Okay. Corleone Terry Keys Jr. was returned to us yesterday. I got all the paperwork fixed up where his grandfather signed for him today under the name of Rufus Hayes. Is that correct?" she asked from the other end.

"All that sounds good, straight down to the T."

"You owe me," she said.

He responded, "I got a special gift fa' you. Just be patient."

"You know what I want. Don't play crazy."

Mike smiled. "I'll see you this weekend." He hung up the phone and quickly punched in a cell phone number. Somebody answered from the other end, a guy with a deep Southern voice. Mike explained the situation in detail from the untraceable phone. The last statement he made was that the bodies were not to be found.

# CHAPTER 33

Joe pulled up in the gravel and dirt driveway of his home in an old-model 1500 pickup truck with a cement mixer attached to the rear. Joe puffed out of control on a Kool cigarette. He then took a swallow of liquor from a plastic container. Next, he checked the rearview mirror to see if the gap on his bald spot had grown any wider. Everything was still in place, and he batted his eyes closed for a mere second or two. He switched off the engine, stepped down from the truck, closed the door, and walked across the uncut brown lawn that led to the front door. He slid his key into the lock and roughly turned the door handle at the same time. When he stepped inside, he saw a huge lump rolled up in cheap oriental carpet they had for the living room floor. Joe felt a stirring of panic erupt in his stomach and chest. His eyes began to bulge. "Sarah?" he called out.

Then an older-looking guy appeared from the kitchen, dressed in a dark suit and Gators. He had a small-caliber pistol pointed at Joe, and he said in the calmest tone of voice, "She's wrapped up right now." Then he pointed toward the floor at the rolled-up carpet.

A wave of nausea ran through Joe and a bewildered look was all over his face. He asked with a deep sadness in his voice, "What cha do to her?"

The man replied, "Killed her, the same thang I'ma do to you." The stranger raised the pistol and squeezed off two rounds.

The bullets ripped through Joe's chest. He dropped his keys and cigarette and began clutching his chest. When he dropped to his knees, the stranger put another bullet between his eyes. Joe's head flipped back with a yank, and then he fell face forward.

The man looked out the front window. A white service van was pulling up to the front door. The rear door swung open. Two goons stepped out dressed in overalls and Falcons fitted caps pulled down over their eyes. They came to clean up the mess.

Hammer was all relaxed. He was soaking in the Jacuzzi in a pair of swimming trunks reading a book about starting a record label. Some things were making a lot of sense to him, and some were not. However, he would still use his own theory. He always had a better way: his way. He laid the book down and leaned his head back and relaxed. The hot water massaged his muscles. He closed his eyes for twenty minutes. He was thinking hard about Young Hollywood. He thought to himself, *He won't suffer in prison like I did, and he won't do twenty years. I'ma do everything in my power to move him, and that's on my life.* He pushed himself out of the water and began toweling himself dry when a loud knock came at the door. He wrapped himself in a terrycloth robe and went to the door. He saw Vincent through the peephole and opened the door. When he did, he laid eyes on his grandson for the first time in his life.

Corleone stared up at Hammer, his jade-green, exotic eyes penetrating his grandfather. "Who are you?" Corleone asked. His hand gripped tightly around two of Vincent's fingers.

All this was new to Hammer. A cheerful smile spread across his face, and he knelt down. "My name is Rufus. Do you know your daddy's name?"

"My real daddy's name is Terry Keys. He's in jail," Corleone said.

"Well, I'm your daddy's daddy. That makes me your grandfather."

Corleone let loose of Vincent's fingers. "I wanna talk to my daddy," Corleone said.

Hammer reached out for him.

Corleone was hesitant for a moment. He then looked up at Vincent.

Vincent smiled and tilted his head toward Hammer.

Corleone went to Hammer as Hammer stood and picked him up in his arms. "I don't wanna stay wit' dat lady no mo'," he said.

Hammer brought him into the room. "You won't stay with nobody but me, and that's a promise."

"You got any toys?" Corleone asked.

Hammer laughed and said, "We'll get some today."

# CHAPTER 34

Hammer and Corleone arrived at the penthouse. The doors separated, and they were now facing a pair of bone-white doors that were at least ten feet wide and twelve feet high. The designs wee handcrafted and carved. A huge brass lion's head frowned angrily at Corleone.

"Look, Granddaddy. A lion." he pointed. Hammer had him dressed in a red and white Coogi two-piece and all white Jordans.

"Yeah, lions are the king of the jungle," he said while inserting the pen key into the lock. He punched in a six-digit security code on a brass keypad.

"But this is not a jungle. This is Atlanta," Corleone said.

"You right again, but Atlanta also has a lion's den," Hammer said as he opened the door. He was holding Corleone's hand, and they both entered together. This was Hammer's first time seeing the penthouse since it had its makeover, and Corleone didn't have a clue about the world he'd have in his own spacious bedroom. Hammer closed the door, and Corleone took off running across the wide spacious floor that was covered from wall to wall in black marble with gold-colored veins. The entire living room was tailored just the way Hammer ordered. There was a black and brass baby grand piano situated in the far left corner. A billiards table sat in the center of the floor. It was painted black with a black felt top and brass lions' heads for feet. The right wall was occupied with an octagon-shaped bar, stocked with just about any kind of alcohol and wine he could think of.

Corleone stood at one of the huge gothic windows and said, "Look, Granddaddy. The ca's are so small!"

Hammer went up to the window and stood next to his grandson. He placed his hand on his shoulder and said, "This is where we will be staying until yo' daddy comes home."

"Well, when will dat be?" Corleone asked.

"Hopefully soon. I'ma do whatever it takes to get him home," Hammer replied.

"Well, can't we go see him, Granddaddy?"

"In due time," Hammer said, and then he drew the boy closer to him. "You wanna see your new bedroom?" Hammer asked.

Corleone began jumping up and down. "Which way?" A bright smile was turning across his face, and even Hammer himself was excited. He and Corleone ran across the marble floor and up three steps into a hallway lined with black-and-white photos of Martin Luther King Jr. in several different events. There was a double set of French doors to the right. Hammer turned both brass knobs at the same time and pushed both doors wide open. The room was painted blue with glow-in-the-dark stars spread around the ceiling and walls. There was a king-sized bed sitting in the corner, a mahogany dresser, and an array of toys. He had his own forty-two-inch screen TV and a Playstation 2 hooked up to it with every game that came with it. Corleone even had his own personal computer with Internet hookup, and a stereo set in another corner. Corleone walked slowly through his room. He was scanning everything, allowing the tips of his fingers to rub along it as though he was window shopping.

Hammer noticed this and said, "Everything in this room belongs to you."

"Everythang?"

"It's *everything*, not *everythang*. I want you to start pronouncing your words correctly."

"Okay, Granddaddy." Corleone ran and dived on the bed, just as happy as he could be.

When Hammer went into his personal office, he sat comfortably in his oak desk. He picked up the phone and dialed the operator. "Give me First Bank of America please," Hammer requested.

"First Bank of America. This is Susan. How may I help you?"

"I would like to speak with the chief loan officer."

"He's in a meeting right now. Would you like to leave your name and number? I'll see to it that he gets back to you."

"That'll work," Hammer said. Then he gave her all of the information and included his Buckhead address. That was guaranteed insurance, and he knew it. Hammer was trying to get a loan for a million dollars, and he was sure to get it. Ten minutes later, the phone rang, and Hammer answered. He simply said, "Yes?"

"You have a collect call from an inmate at Georgia State Prison."

Hammer smiled and pressed the five before the operator could finish. When Young Hollywood's voice came through the phone, Hammer leaned back in his chair. "Well, well, well! Long time," Hammer said.

"Wuz up on yo' end, pimp? Is big shit poppin' or what?"

"Something like that. I got somebody here that's been waiting to talk to you." Hammer stood and went to his office door. With the cordless phone in his hand he called out, "Corleone!" He could hear his tiny feet slapping against the floor. Hammer handed the phone to the boy.

"Who is it, Granddaddy?" Corleone asked.

"It's your daddy. Talk to him."

Corleone put the phone against his face. "Daddy?"

"Hey, wuz up, boy?" Young Hollywood said.

"Nothin'. I got a Playstation 2 and a computer and a great big bed and a lot of toys and clothes. My granddaddy say he want me to go to a private school."

"That's good. You make sho you listen to yo' granddaddy and stay on top of yo' square."

"What is my square?"

Hammer laughed and shook his head. His arms folded across his chest, and he was enjoying himself to death listening to his grandson ask several questions over the phone. Young Hollywood asked questions and answered them for a minute, and then Corleone gave Hammer back the phone." He wanna talk to you, Granddaddy?"

Hammer took the phone and put it to his ear.

"I see you got things in motion," Young Hollywood said.

"So far, I'm preparing my strategy."

"Have you built a team yet?"

"I'm working on everything as we speak. I'll send you some pictures of Corleone and myself. Are you all right in there?" Hammer asked. "I'll send you a couple dollars, but in the meantime, I want you to hold your head up because I got something very important for you. Make sure you stay sucka free, and keep them lame-ass niggas out your face."

"Yeah I can do that," he said, and then he added, "You know I had to deal wit' dat nigga Killa Black."

"That's a small problem if you dealt with it. It is what it is. Other than that, I'm working on getting' you out and getting' things as comfortable as possible while you in there," he said and then he added, "I got a lot of legwork to do. I wanted to ask you this before I did it. What do you think about me having your grandmother move in with me to watch Corleone?"

"It sounds like a good idea, but Grandma ain't gon' wanna leave Hollywood Court."

"Let me worry about that," Hammer said and checked his watch.

"Call me tomorrow."

"Check."

*Click.*

# CHAPTER 35

A month had passed since Sasha had been through facial surgery. She was beautiful once again, and she'd begun getting her body in shape. Last week, Hammer had provided her money to purchase herself a two-bedroom apartment and a brand new car. It was a small Acura, and she looked good in it. Sasha had her hair cut low and wore it in a style like Toni Braxton. When she got dressed that morning, she stepped into a pair of snug-fitting black jeans, a white Sean John short sleeved, and all-black leather Air Force Ones.

When she got in her car, the clock on the dashboard read 7:23. It took her fifteen minutes to get to work from where she lived, and when she pulled her Acura into the parking lot of Phillips State Prison, she had her mind set and focused on one thing: *Do whatever Hammer wants me to do.* For the time being, she had to work as an officer-in-training. When she switched off her engine, she stepped out of the car and said to herself, "Here we go."

Inside the prison, Sasha congregated with several more cadets in black and white uniforms. All together there were twelve females and two males. Sasha had the prettiest face among them all, but there were four other girls who ranked with her. The cadets were divided into groups of five, and each group was led by a sergeant or someone of higher rank. Sasha was in a group of all women, and she did not crack a smile nor pay attention to any of the inmates who whistled and shared their comments. The group toured the compound. They walked the yard, the dining hall, and a few dorms. Sasha was eager to learn, and she wasn't self-conscious about anything. She knew she had to perform, and she soaked up everything that came across her path.

She befriended another female by the name of Angel. Angel was petite and pretty and didn't have a car because she couldn't afford it. Sasha gave her a ride home.

After Sasha dropped her off, she went to her own place, and the first thing she did was call Hammer to give him an update on her first day.

He explained to her that the prisoners would come at her from every angle and direction with conversation and game. "Don't break weak, fold, or bend for nothing. You're not hurting fo' nothing. If you need anything, let me know," Hammer insisted.

"Okay," she said cheerfully, and then she asked, "How is Corleone?"

"He's doing fine. He'll be enrolled in a private arts and drama school here in Atlanta. Don't worry about him, okay?"

A tear rolled down her cheek. "When will I be able to see him?"

"Don't worry about him, Sasha. Stay focused on your career right now. We got a lot of work to do."

She wiped her face with the back of her hand and took a deep breath. After accepting Hammer's advice, she quickly got off the phone, went to the computer, and studied a college course she was taking. After a few hours, she ate, showered and went to sleep.

The next morning, she and Angel rode together. Sasha told her she could depend on her for a ride until she got herself together. Sasha knew Angel was down on her luck and desperately needed the job to come through for her. Somewhere down the line, Sasha would make her work for the gas money and the time she spent driving her to and from work. When Sasha pulled into the prison parking lot, she killed the engine and looked Angel in her eyes with a long, gazing stare that spelled out, *"I wanna taste you."*

"Why you lookin' at me like that?" Angel asked, smiling.

"I wanna cook fo' you tonight." Then she leaned over and kissed Angel passionately on her lips.

Angel was caught by surprise, but she didn't resist. She actually reached over the console and slid her hand between Sasha's legs.

Sasha grabbed Angel's hand and guided it to where she wanted it.

"We can't be doin' dis out here in da parkin' lot," Angel said.

Later that night, Sasha and Angel sucked, licked, and tasted one another for three hours. Sasha had her right where she wanted her.

Angel was lying flat across the bed with her legs spread eagerly. "My pussy sore," Angel whispered.

"You jus' got to get used to me," Sasha said. Then she buried her face in between her legs again. Angel's clit was tender and red, and Sasha went for it with her tongue. She licked around it in circles first and watched Angel's eyes roll to the back of her head. She moaned and began shivering. While Angel's eyes were glued to the ceiling,

Sasha hooked her arms under Angel's thighs and pulled her to the edge of the bed. She kissed her vagina and then tongued it as though she was kissing another set of lips. When Angel screamed out that she was cumming, Sasha began nibbling on her. Then she stood and stepped back to wait for Angel's reaction.

"Come here, Sasha. Don't stop," she begged. She began touching herself with one hand and reaching for Sasha with the other.

When Sasha went back to her, she politely lay down on top of her, clit to clit, lips to lips, and nipples to nipples. Sasha got in her ear and whispered, "Do you wanna move in wit' me?"

"If you want me to," Angel replied.

"That ain't what I asked you." Sasha looked her square in her eyes.

"Yes I want to."

"Are you willing to dedicate yo'self to me and nobody but me?"

"I got a boyfriend," Angel said.

"If he was any good or if he loved you, you wouldn't be struggling like this. From this day forward, you my bitch. I'ma take care of you. Is that understood?"

Angel nodded. Her lustful eyes were staring directly into Sasha's.

"Oh... you scared to talk now? Angel, I don't want you fallin' weak fo' none of them niggas at that prison. That's including the officers too. When we finish training and get in our blue suits, we'll have another mission complete. Now, are you sure you're gonna ride with me?"

Angel grabbed Sasha's face and held it between her hands. "Sasha, don't jus' be tellin' me this." She parted her lips, inviting Sasha's tongue and lips to take hers.

Sasha leaned into her, and their tongues wrapped around each other's. Their heartbeats were in unison with one another. "Jus' do what I need you to do, okay?"

"Okay," Angel whispered, and then she came again.

# CHAPTER 36

For the next couple weeks, Hammer stayed swamped in paperwork. The million-dollar loan he had asked for was given to him with no problem. He also had a paid lawyer to handle all his legal issues. Hammer possessed the gift of gab. He could speak at any level and basically converse about anything. He'd found a location for his record label and his quarter-million-dollar studio in a high-rise building downtown on West Peachtree Street. The building was made of steel with a glass front.

Altogether, he was paying $25K a month for rental fees. Hammer didn't care about the money; all that was minor to him. He always thought big, and the picture he had envisioned would stay there until he could bring it into existence.

Sitting across the table from his attorney and financial advisor, Hammer's eyes were scanning a few legal papers before signing. He looked up at his attorney and said, "I want my shit incorporated—everything."

"No problem," his attorney said.

Hammer looked at his financial advisor. "Can I depend on you?"

His advisor replied, "On legal advice? Yes."

"That's all I'm interested in. Are you a high-risk investor?"

"My portfolio speaks for itself, Mr. Hayes. I've been in this business for twenty years, and I'm very experienced."

Hammer nodded. "I'ma take your word on this, Mr. Graham, but I have big plans to become a mega-millionaire in the next couple of years, and you are a key factor on my team." With that, Hammer stood and extended his hand for a shake. "Dinner on me next week," he said before he left.

When Hammer arrived back at the penthouse, there were two phone messages left for him. He pressed the button to listen to them.

The first one was Sasha. "Hello, Mr. Hayes. This is Sasha, and I was calling to let you know we have another team playa'. She's cool far as I know. I got her staying with me until further notice, and both of us did get hired at the prison. Talk to you later, and thanks for everything."

He pressed the stop button, and the machine went to the next message.

"Hey, Hamma, dis Vincent. All I know is that there's a welcome home party being arranged for you and the new birth of A-Town Records. This yo' chance to meet a lot of big dawgs. Call me later on. I believe the Governor is responsible. You ain't heard it from me though. Call me when you get this message."

Hammer just shook his head in disbelief. Things were moving for him now, and he knew it would get much better. He wouldn't stop until it did. The house phone rang, and he answered it. "Yes?"

"Hello, stranger," a female voice said from the other end.

Hammer didn't catch the voice, and a touch of curiosity arose inside of him. With his eyebrows bunching together, he finally asked, "Who is this?"

"This is Nicole Terry, your interior decorator. We really didn't get a chance to meet, and I was wondering if we could have dinner."

"My interior decorator? I tell you what. I got a lot of things going on right now, and my time is valuable. Can you convince me?"

"Well, my pussy gets uncontrollably wet, I've never been with a black man before, and I'm an interesting woman."

"Where do you live?"

"In Gwinnett, four bedrooms and twenty acres of land, my own estate and ranch. Do you ride horses?"

"If I can pull a million out of his ass," Hammer replied.

"Maybe you need to give me a day. Let me show you some better things in life from my point of view."

"How long will it take you to come get me?"

"Are you serious? I mean, I could be there in like an hour."

Hammer couldn't control his grin. He knew where this would lead, and he was already thinking heavily about the opportunity that came with it. The benefits would be out the roof. Hammer checked his watch; it was a little past one o'clock. He spoke back into his phone, "Will this be worth my while?"

"I can promise you it will," she said.

Hammer thought for a second and responded, "I'll be waiting in the lobby." When Hammer hung up, he took a quick hot shower and dressed. Then he checked himself in the wall mirror. He was clean shaven and dressed to impress. Downstairs in the lobby, Hammer found a seat in a comfortable chair and waited. He crossed his legs.

Fifteen minutes later, an aqua-blue Aston Martin pulled up in front.

Hammer could see the striking white woman behind the steering wheel from where he sat. Her hair was long and auburn, flowing past her shoulders, blowing underneath the air conditioner. She wore big black Gucci shades on her eyes and what appeared to be a silk designer scarf around her neck. Hammer stood from his chair and made his way through the brass double-doors and out onto the sidewalk. He moved around to the passenger's door and opened it and got in.

Nicole looked at him from behind her tinted shades. She wore a nearly see-through white dress, and her nipples were growing hard at just the sight of Hammer. "You smell great. What are you wearing?" she asked while pulling out into traffic.

Hammer shrugged his shoulders. "I thought that was you. What are you wearing?"

Nicole pulled up her dress and showed him her shaved, meaty vagina, and then she smiled and said, "Nothing."

Hammer laughed, and then he began examining Nicole. Her skin was evenly tan, and her mouth was rich and soft looking. Nicole was forty-eight years old and didn't look a day past twenty five. When Hammer saw the meaty flesh between her legs, his penis began rising through his dress pants.

She noticed this as well; the long, hard organ growing down the length of his inner thigh. "Is that real? Can I touch it?" She sounded so excited she could barely drive. Then she showed Hammer her vagina again. "See? It's wet already."

Hammer looked again. He couldn't believe it. She was creaming all over herself. He reached over and touched it, and when he pulled his fingers back, there was a long string of pre-cum attached to them. "It's been a long time," Hammer whispered. Then he withdrew himself from her altogether and leaned back in his seat. "Don't say another word until we get to our destination." He tried hard to focus on something else. Then he asked, "Is this your ca'?"

"Yes, for Tuesday. Wait until you see what I got for the rest of the week," she added.

They rode the rest of the way in silence.

# CHAPTER 37

The home of Nicole Terry looked like a movie set, something right off of *Cribs*. Her estate was set far back from the main street. They drove quietly down a long, winding, paved driveway lined with pine trees on both sides. Hammer gazed out the window across a long stretch of green pastures and noticed three white houses. There was a stable beyond that for a herd of horses. A sloping hill led to a forest on the other side. There were flowerbeds and beautiful green hedges that had been neatly manicured.

Nicole whipped her $100K car around the side of her house as though she was driving a Cutlass or something more on that level. She parked in front of one of the five garages and slammed the shaft in park. She looked at Hammer with a more anxious look on her face than a kid at an ice cream parlor. "I live in this big old place all by myself. My housekeeper lives in the guesthouse out back, and my horse trainer is here from eight to eight. I have an indoor swimming pool if you'd like to go swimming." She took a deep breath and rubbed her hands together. "What would you like to see first?" she asked.

"If you can fuck or not, because like I said, my time is very valuable."

"Why do you have to be so angry?" she inquired.

Hammer folded his arms across his chest and looked at Nicole with a smirk across his face. "Would you believe I just did twenty years in prison, and I've been out almost a month, and I got a lot of shit to do? My main priority is to free my son. He's serving three life sentences plus an additional ninety-five years," he said, delivering his speech.

Nicole sat quietly and listened like an obedient little child. She finally removed her shades. Her eyes were slanted, an exotic shade of blue-green. She said, "Let me help you then." She reached over and tugged at Hammer's zipper on his pants and within a few seconds, she had freed his penis and had her mouth and lips wrapped around him. She held him with both hands while Hammer reclined in his seat. He closed his eyes and allowed his fingers to run through her hair while she sucked him up. "My first chocolate dick," she mumbled.

"My first white bitch," he shot back. He jerked, nearly about to cum.

She noticed this also and began moving her mouth faster and faster. Hammer grunted and began shoving her head until her lips were at his scrotum. She swallowed without gagging one time. Hammer was so impressed with her he had to take another look at her.

"Good?" she asked. Then she wiped the corner of her mouth with the back of her hand.

"So far," he responded.

Inside her home, she led Hammer to her huge master bedroom that was tastefully decorated with expensive everything. Nicole stripped Hammer of his clothes and quickly undressed herself and lay flat out on the edge of the bed. She grabbed Hammer by his long, stiff penis and guided him to her. "Oh my God!" she cried out when the head parted her fat vagina lips. He entered her deeper, and the sensational feeling was out of this world. Her muscles grabbed onto him and squeezed him firm and tight. Hammer couldn't believe how hot and wet she was. She yelled out, "I'm cumming! I'm cumming, damn it. Shit!" She flung her head side to side while rotating her hips at the same time. She wrapped around him, gripped his butt checks, and cried out, "Go deeper. Hurt me, Daddy."

Hammer was long stroking and pounding harder and harder, and Nicole was screaming louder and louder. Hammer fucked her to sleep an hour later.

By the time she woke up, she saw Hammer through the glass wall that separated her room from the adjourning gym. He was running full speed on an expensive treadmill, covered with glossy sweat.

Nicole got up. She wrapped the satin sheet around herself, walked to the glass door, and opened it. She stood there leaning against the doorframe. "Do you want something to eat?"

Hammer didn't respond. He didn't even look back. His muscular legs were still pumping, his bare feet slapping against the thick leather belt.

"Mr. Hayes."

Hammer hated to be disturbed during his workout. This was something Nicole didn't know, but she'd soon learn. When Hammer didn't respond, she walked away and prayed she didn't blow it. Nicole was lonely, with no kids or husband. She had her home and property, which were worth nearly three and a half million dollars. Her interior decorator business was bringing her somewhere between $750K to $1.5 million a year. She was impressed with Hammer. She had designed his entire penthouse from the creation of his mind. She loved his swagger. He moved with confidence, something she hadn't ever seen in a black man before. Now that he'd sexed her and fucked up her world forever, she would become a piece to his game.

Ten minutes later, Nicole had her housekeeper prepare evening dinner: peppered flounder with stuffed bell peppers and Cajun rice.

She went to the shower that was joined with her bedroom. It was laced in pink marble with white veins. The shower was the size of a small bedroom. Nicole removed the satin sheet from her shoulders. Her breast was full and rose pink, and her round bottom jiggled as she walked under the water. Then other sprouts of water began flushing from the walls. She closed her eyes and wrapped her arms around herself.

Hammer crept in from the back and moved her hair from her neck and ear. He kissed her neck and nibbled on her earlobe. She relaxed in his powerful arms. Her heart began pounding with every touch. He toyed with her nipples. She reached behind herself and gripped his penis. It began growing in her hands. She bent over at the waist and gripped her ankles. "Fuck my ass, but go slow," she said.

After they ate, they went horseback riding along the trail at a slow trot. Hammer found himself amused at her way of life, but still, he was addicted to the hustle—the thrill of being a gangsta. He was mentally and physically ready to do whatever the fuck he wanted to. He was becoming versatile, preparing himself for the best of both worlds. They trotted, nearly walking, next to one another along the edge of a trail. This was all her property. Hammer examined the scenery. *I could live someplace like this.* It was peaceful and quiet, away from the normal world and nosey neighbors.

"What are you thinking about?" she asked him.

He snapped away from his thoughts and looked toward her. The sun enhanced her beauty. She brushed the hair from her face. She was dressed like a Polo jockey. He was really impressed. *Money's a motha' fucka', but bein' rich is a different story.* Then he said, "Life in general."

# CHAPTER 38

It was nearly nightfall when Hammer stepped off the elevator on his penthouse floor. He looked at the frowning lions. *The king of the jungle,* he thought to himself. He inserted his pen key and pressed in his security code. He opened the door and entered, and out of nowhere, Corleone ran and jumped in his arms.

"Granddaddy! Where you been?" he shouted.

Hammer shifted his grandson to one arm and closed the door with the other one. He kissed Corleone on his forehead. "Your granddaddy been working," he said and moved toward the high-back leather sofa and sat down. He placed Corleone on his knee. "Have you been giving your grandmother any problems?"

"No," Corleone replied.

"Where is she?" Hammer asked. He grabbed both of his tiny hands and brought them up to his face.

Corleone smiled and covered Hammer's eyes with both hands. "She in da kitchen. She fixin' me a cake," he said happily. Then he jumped down from Hammer's knee. "I gotta go, Granddaddy. She needs my help."

Hammer leaned toward Corleone. "Give me a hug."

Corleone wrapped his arms around Hammer's neck. "Love ya', Granddaddy." He released his neck and took off running, and all Hammer could do was shake his head. As long as Corleone was all right, he was all right.

He picked up the phone and dialed Vincent's number.

Vincent answered, "Wuz up, shawty?"

"I'm ready to see the city now," he said seriously.

"Give me an hour."

Hammer hung up and went into his room and straight into the walk-in closet. He changed into a suit in order to conceal his pistol and shoulder holster. Hammer tried to think ahead. His plans were nearly mapped out for the rest of the year. He was now ready to build himself a team of a few good men, and he wanted some of his old enemies to be a part of that team.

Hammer went into the spacious kitchen and found Vickie and Corleone preparing a red velvet cake. She was in her late fifties but in good health. She wore her salt-and-pepper hair pulled back in a tight ponytail. Her skin sagged a little, but nothing too out of place. Hammer didn't trust too many people with his grandson, but Vicki was his great grandmother by blood, and to him it couldn't get any better. In his book, that was certified.

Night had fallen. The streets were filled with night crawlers, goons, and human goblins. Hammer rode in the passenger's seat next to Vincent. They cruised through the West End through the Muslim community, one of the most notorious hoods in Atlanta. Vincent pulled up to the curb at the corner of Lucille and Holiness. He then parked his Benz and looked at Hammer.

Hammer didn't pay attention to Vincent staring at him. His eyes were heavily focused on the busy streets. Bums were posted on corners begging for money. Hammer opened his door and stepped out. The streets were buzzing with activity, and cars cruised by with blazing headlights. Andre 3000's voice was crooning from an A-frame house across the street. The front porch was crowded with young guys with dreads, saggy jeans, and extra long T-shirts. Hammer leaned down and peeped his head in the car. He said to Vincent, "When the last time you saw him?"

Vincent shrugged. "It's been at least five years," he said. Then he pointed out the front windshield. "That's his house though." His finger aimed at a tall wooden house, four houses down from the house where the kids were with the dreads.

Hammer's head shifted in that direction. The light was on in the front room. "Give me a minute." Hammer closed the door and ran swiftly across the street. He ran up the steps and onto the wooden front porch. The door came open before he could knock. The lights in the front room were out now. Hammer noticed this and realized he was being watched.

Two guys appeared from each side of the porch. One of them held a mini-assault rifle aimed at Hammer's midsection. A red beam danced across his face and neck from the other side. That guy held a massive handgun with both hands.

The guy who stood behind the screen door appeared to be shorter than five-five and black as night. He was so dark that Hammer could only see the whites of his eyes. "Who you want?" the man asked from behind the screen, his voice growling.

"I'm lookin' for Diamond," Hammer said.

"I am Diamond."

"You can't be the Diamond I'm looking for."

"Who da fuck is you, nigga?" Diamond growled again.

Then the metallic coil action of a weapon being loaded and cocked sounded off in his ears.

Hammer wasn't stupid. "I'm Hamma," he said. "Diamond know me as Rufus."

The guy at the door disappeared from Hammer's sight, and in less than two minutes, he was back, and he pushed the screen door back and allowed Hammer to come in. When Hammer entered, the guy Diamond whistled, and his crew faded into the night. That was their signal to retreat back into their places. Diamond led Hammer into the kitchen, where the light was bright. He stared at the older Diamond—the real one. The older man sat at the raggedy wooden table; an assault rifle was in his hand. Hammer stared at it. He had never seen such a weapon up close and personal. That alone impressed him. He stared up into the older man's eyes.

Diamond, who was now fifty-two years old, had a head full of nappy gray hair and a full beard. He stared back at Hammer. "Last I heard, you got killed in prison. They say you got burned up in yo' cell. And you wanna know what I said when I heard it?"

Hammer didn't respond. He just looked at him.

Diamond went on, "I knew somebody would finally take him, and I be damn if you ain't still livin'."

"The good die fast," Hammer responded coldly.

Diamond looked Hammer over, and then he looked at his nephew who stood behind him. He waved his hand dismissively at the nephew, who then disappeared into another room of the house. "Have a seat," he told Hammer.

"I'm good. I don't have long. I just came to let you know that my old beef with you is settled, and I need some assistance."

Diamond had a heavy sparkle in his eyes. He stared into Hammer's, and neither one of them broke their stare. He smiled at Hammer grimly.

Hammer still watched him intently, and his intelligent look was more powerful than ever.

Diamond asked, "Assist you in what?"

"Building a powerful team. You know, the Bulls didn't win the rings without a powerful team."

"And who is Michael Jordan?"

"The whole damn team. Your position, you gotta build a strong four-man team of nothing but certified killers. I'll fund what you need, and I'll meet and talk with no one but you. Your crew must be certified and loyal to no one but you. Can you handle that?"

"Damn right! Wuz in it fa' me?"

"You'll be a millionaire in two years."

Before the night was over Hammer had recruited three known killers from all over Atlanta and told each of them," You'll be a millionaire."

# CHAPTER 39

Sasha dressed quickly. She wore her blue pants extra tight. Her small bikini-cut panties were cutting into her heart-shaped ass cheeks. She strapped on a small girdle that covered her stomach only. She was still a little chubby around her waist, and she hated that too. A lot of women did. After that, she strapped on her bra and her creased blue button-up shirt.

Angel came into the room. She'd already gotten dressed, and she was ready and eager to get to work. Angel looked her up and down. "I see you got on them tight-ass pants. Who you tryin' to catch?"

Sasha eyed her through the dresser mirror; Angel was standing behind her. "The warden," Sasha said, and she was dead serious.

"They say he don't even get down like dat." Angel walked up close to the mirror and began lining her sensual lips with a thin black line.

Sasha tucked in her shirt, and then she moved up to the rear of Angel and placed her hands on her hips. She slid her wet tongue inside Angel's ear.

Angel tensed up a little and closed her eyes.

Then Sasha whispered, "The right situation, baby, and any nigga will break. Believe me, I know." She looked at her watch. It was 5:40.

"I jus' don't see it. Hell naw. No deal. I jus' thought about they said he was fuckin' dat captain bitch."

"Well, if it take me to go through that bitch to get to him, a bitch gotta do what a bitch gotta do," Sasha commented.

"Do she like pussy too?" Angel asked curiously. She turned and faced Sasha.

"I don't know, but I'll assume she do due to the fact that she got a pretty face and a fat ass and that fucked-up attitude."

Angel laughed, and then they left for work.

When Sasha and Angel got to the prison, they split up and went to their own posts. Sasha worked the dorm, basically the control. She pressed buttons and kept up with the count. She noticed so many different types of men, and she was examining them all. She saw a guy that stood five-eleven with smooth chocolate skin, and he was in good shape too. They made eye contact. He was handsome, she thought, but she was out fishing for a prize far greater. Hammer had instructed her to try to get under the warden, if she could, and she would damn sure give it everything she had. Her eyes still followed the guy until he disappeared.

A voice came across her radio. "All units stand by for the warden's inspection."

Sasha pressed a button on the switchboard and spoke into a microphone. "Stand by for inspection." Her voice boomed throughout the entire dorm. Five minutes later, the dorm was live and full of activity. The prisoners were moving around like ants, trying to get prepared for inspection. Then, no more than twenty minutes later, the warden came through the door leading the crowd of six, sergeants and up. He stood six-two with handsome features. His muscular tone was concealed by a three-piece suit, Stacy Adams, and matching tie. She examined him quickly and didn't need binoculars to see how close he and the captain lady were. As she walked next to him she could see they were nearly the same height. Her gold bars sparkled on her collar. Sasha nearly lost it when she found her turning up her nose. She had to accept that the captain was a looker, as though she came out of a magazine. She had porn star features and walked with long strides. Her bottom was so round and her waist so small that even she couldn't keep her eyes away from her.

When the inspection team entered the dorm, the prisoners yelled out, "Sir, good mornin', sir! Ma'am, good mornin', ma'am."

No one acknowledged Sasha.

When she and Angel got to the apartment, she was mad as hell. She picked up the phone and called Hammer's private number.

He answered on the third ring. "Hello?"

"Hey, Mr. Hayes," Sasha said. She was agitated, and it was clear in her voice.

"How you doing, Sasha? What's going on?"

"Man, I don't think I'll be able to get at pimp," she said, sounding agitated.

"Tell me what's wrong."

"He fuckin' wit' dis captain broad, and she got his ass wide open.

He won't even look my way." A light touch of jealousy was rising in her voice.

There was silence on the line between the two. Hammer was thinking seriously, long and hard. He finally asked, "Give me an overall rating of her from one to ten."

"Physical appearance, she's a ten. She got a fucked-up attitude though."

"Them be the best ones," he said. Then added, "I tell you what... let her know that she's been invited to a private and prestigious party. Women must wear evening gowns. Let her know you'll be picking her up by limousine."

"I'm invited too?" A surprising glow spread across her face.

"Of course. She's your guest. Tell your other friend to come also. This should be interesting."

"What if she's not interested?"

"I'm sure you can convince her. Stop acting like you green or something."

"I'm jus' new to dis part of the game."

"It's still the same game, Sasha. It all depends on how bad you wanna win. Motha' fuckas' don't make it to the top on the strength of nothing. If you don't want it, you won't get it."

She thought about his words long and hard. He was fuel to her fire, her motivation. She finally said. "I want it. I wanna win."

"Good, because that's the only way you gonna get it. Now get yourself situated, and I'll see you this weekend."

"Okay."

*Click.*

The next day, Sasha caught the female captain in the parking lot. *"Hey, bitch. Bring yo' punk ass here."* Those were the words Sasha wanted to say. Instead, she approached the captain just as she was about to climb up into her solid black Range Rover. "Excuse me, Captain Reeves."

The captain turned around, and she gave Sasha a look as if she didn't want to be bothered. She was nearly frowning. Her face twisted around her mouth. "Yeah?" Her keys were jiggling in her hand.

Sasha could've slapped the taste from her mouth at the sound of her voice. She caught hold of herself and said, "I don't know if you're interested or not, and I may be wrong for what I did, but I spoke to my uncle on your behalf."

"On my behalf? Concerning what?" the captain asked.

"He needs somebody to search for talent and beautiful women like yourself. I told him about you and that you was very business minded. Please don't make me look bad, because there'll be a lot of important people there, and if—"

The captain cut her off. "You're talking too fast. Important people where?"

"He invited you to the party, formal wear only. Please at least meet him."

Captain Reeves smiled. Her teeth were even and white. "Are you going also?" Captain Reeves's eyes studied Sasha briefly, and then she turned toward the SUV and scribbled her number on a piece of paper and handed it to Sasha. "Call me."

And that was exactly what Sasha needed.

# CHAPTER 40

Hammer, Vincent, the Governor, and four hired goons rode together in the rear of a plush white double-stretched Navigator. Expensive cognac and champagne was being passed around. The Governor was dressed in an all-white, tailor-made tuxedo and shoes handcrafted from the tail of an alligator. He puffed casually on a Cuban cigar, sitting with his legs crossed.

Hammer was dressed the same: white-on-white tuxedo and handcrafted gator shoes, silk tie, and gold cuff links.

Everyone else had to wear black tuxedos or black gowns, something the Governor had come up with.

The gathering was held at an elegant and spacious ballroom out in Buckhead. When they arrived at the front entrance, there were over twenty sleek limousines lining both sides of the streets, and every last one of them had their own uniformed chauffeurs. Hammer glared out the window. He was impressed. There was even a red carpet that stretched from the curb to the front entrance. Huge muscular men in black tuxedos lined the carpet on each side. A crowd of women and men played the background. When they finally came to a halt, Hammer looked over at the Governor. His face was surrounded by a cloud of smoke, and the ten-carat diamond ring sparkling from his pinky finger nearly blinded him. He said, "You know I don't like surprises, so what should I expect?"

The Governor removed the cigar from his mouth. "Plenty of women, plenty of money, and a lot of well-connected people." Hammer nodded, and then he looked to Vincent. "What about you, Vincent? Don't surprise me."

Vincent stared at Hammer, and a grin spread across his face. "Do I look like I'd surprise you?"

By now the chauffeur had parked. He got out and was standing at the rear door. When he opened it, the four casually dressed goons stepped out first, followed by Vincent. Hammer saw him shaking hands with a lot of people as he strolled the red carpet that led him inside the double-doors.

The Governor and Hammer climbed out, one behind the other. The people applauded them. There was something serious about Hammer, and the look he carried on his face was self-explanatory. There were rumors in the air about Hammer. Some said he was one of the most feared men in Atlanta. Some said he took a fall for the Governor and did twenty years on his head. But in all actuality, Vincent and the Governor were the only two people alive that knew Hammer and his capabilities. But now he was a thinker, and nobody knew what he was thinking.

When they entered the doors that led to the wide, spacious area where the party was being held, nearly 200 people turned their attention toward Hammer and the Governor. Loud, thunderous hand-clapping erupted throughout the building. The Governor even stopped himself and turned toward Hammer and began clapping.

Hammer tried hard to control his grin, and then he went ahead and accepted his position as if he was a Don or something. He unbuttoned his double-breasted jacket and placed his hand on his waist and looked out over the crowd. There was sea of people bunched together in expensive tuxedos and backless gowns. The Governor had hired the Atlanta Symphony to play live music—nothing was too much for the old-school gangstas and hustlers. Hammer worked his way through the crowd, and the Governor was now following him. "Go to the stage," the Governor said. Hammer went to the stage. There were two huge suede high-back chairs with brass lion heads for feet and hand rests. Both chairs were sitting next to one another. The Governor took the chair on the right, and Hammer automatically knew the one on the left belonged to him. Huge black banners stretched from wall to wall that read: "Welcome Home, Gangsta."

It was something else. Hammer crossed his legs and stared out into the overwhelming audience. Beautiful, sophisticated women were everywhere.

The Governor leaned over toward Hammer and whispered, "See the lady there?" He pointed, and Hammer's eyes followed his finger.

There was a seductive-looking woman standing nearly six-two in heels and a black suede evening gown. She noticed the Governor and Hammer looking her way. She smiled and bowed her head toward them.

They both waved, and the Governor said, "She's an active citizen here in da city. She donates a quarter-million every year to charity. She graduated with honors from Spelman, and she's strictly business."

"Where do you know her from?" Hammer asked while watching her.

"She works for me."

"That figures. Lots of motha' fuckas' work for you." Hammer's eyes scanned the crowd. He saw Sasha. She was indeed beautiful, and the other two women who were with her were too. He noticed them chatting with two NFL players.

"You say that to say what?" the Governor asked. "I'm very thankful for everything you've done for me, but you got to understand me J.W. I got to do me the way I wanna do it, not the way you want me to do it."

"I know you are your own man, but you got to understand me, Hamma. It don't take much to get caught up in dis city."

"You've been living a miserable life, J.W., as if you was the one serving twenty years in a cage." Hammer paused briefly. Then he added, "I'm itching for action. I live for this shit. Maybe it is personal. Who's to say? Nothing against you though... and I'm sure you know that." Hammer looked the Governor square in his eyes and then held out a clenched fist.

The Governor did the same, and they touched fists.

"I respect you, J.W., and I'm very loyal to you. However, I don't want my situations to hinder you or involve you in no kind of way."

"And you say this to say what?"

Hammer whispered, "I'm still that killer—that savage beast you knew back then."

The Governor just shook his head in disgust. He took a deep breath. "Hamma, what you fail to realize is there's several niggas here in Atlanta with the same mentality. Bodies be popping up all over this motha' fucka' every day."

There was a long pause. Then Hammer said, "Well, now it's fixing to be bodies disappearing all over this motha' fucka' until I get what I need, and I don't think I got to explain that to you."

Hammer looked out into the crowd again and saw Diamond dressed in a black three-piece suit, a black tie, and black shirt. There were four guys with him. Three of them were very mean looking, and the last one would be considered a pretty boy. They were all dressed in black suits and hard-bottom shoes.

Diamond made eye contact with Hammer, but neither one waved or uttered a word. Diamond was basically letting it be known that he was there, and this was his clique.

Hammer sat back, relaxed in his chair, and when the Governor didn't respond to Hammer and Diamond making eye contact, he knew he was getting old.

Captain Reeves was escorted to a rented limousine driven by one of Hammer's associates. They called him Iron Head. He was a short, slender man in his mid forties with opaque eyes and a deadly, untrusting grin. He was clean shaven and dressed in a chauffeur uniform. His eyes swept across the rear parking lot as he patiently waited at the rear door of the limousine. Iron Head opened the rear door for Hammer, and he climbed in and sat next to the beautiful captain. Hammer held out his hand, and she politely shook it. She was indeed very pretty, but Hammer wasn't interested.

When Iron Head climbed in behind the wheel, he pressed the button to lower the panel that separated the driver from the passenger. He looked back at Hammer for directions.

"Get on the expressway. I got a ranch house out in Gwinnett County."

Iron Head nodded and turned back toward the front and started the limousine.

Hammer looked at Captain Reeves, and before she knew it, he'd removed a silenced .380 from the mini-bar. He shot her twice in the head and didn't even ruin his white tuxedo.

# BOOK V

# CHAPTER 41

An entire year had passed. It was now 2001, and Hammer's name had spread throughout Atlanta as the most powerful and notorious killer the city had ever seen. Just in the last eight months alone, Hammer had signed a male R&B group, two female solo artists, and three ferocious rappers, all from Atlanta. So far, only one guy had refused to sign with his label, and that was because he was already signed with another clique of dope boys. Their entire crew had been missing for four months now. Everybody suspected Hammer and his A-Town Record Company to be responsible for their disappearance.

What did Hammer care about such foolish allegations? He was plugged in with people in high places now, and those people—judges, politicians, district attorneys, and so forth—were all getting a piece of the pie. But out of all the people he was connected with, he couldn't find one attorney in Atlanta to take his son's case. However, he paid a quarter-million to an expensive team of lawyers out of New York to take it. He knew Young Hollywood would have to sit for a while. He'd prepared himself for at least ten to twenty years. Hopefully he wouldn't have to do that long, but however long he would have to do, Hammer would make sure he did it at ease, with nothing to want for and anything he needed.

One morning, he sat behind a huge cherry oak desk in his high-back leather swivel in his downtown office. Across from him was a poorly dressed guy from Africa that had only been in the United States for two years. His name was Kangoma. He stood six-three and wore a four-inch sandy-red nappy afro. Kangoma had jet-black skin and naturally red veiny eyes. Hammer had only known him for four months. Hammer caught him in a restaurant parking lot going through huge trash dumpsters. Kangoma had a wife and son who were still overseas in Africa, and in Atlanta, he lived in the streets. He was recognized first by one of Hammer's associates called Poi Boi. Poi Boi jacked up Kangoma by his shirt and shoved the barrel of a fifty-caliber Desert Eagle under his chin because he tried to get close to Hammer in the parking lot. Hammer decided it was only a minor problem. He spoke with Kangoma that night and learned that he was from Africa. He was pleased to hear his story and gave the African his number. And now, here they were, face to face.

Kangoma spread his huge hands. "Please, Mr. Hamma, I need a job."

Hammer eyed him suspiciously, examining his very movement. If he'd had a nerve twitch, Hammer would know about it. "Kangoma, have you ever killed before?" Hammer asked.

"In my country? Yes. United States? No."

Hammer placed his hand, a balled fist under his chin. Kangoma had his undivided attention now. He allowed his stare to penetrate into his. Hammer's creative mind was working in overwhelming speed, and the plan he'd just formulated in his head could only come from the mind of a genius. "What would it take for you to go back and forth to Africa as you please?"

"First, I would want to get my family... here in da United States."

"That's not the issue. As a matter of fact, that's not a problem at all. Let's say I get all this done. You'll have your own house, and your wife will earn an income."

Kangoma smiled. "Who will I have to kill?"

Hammer had to laugh at that statement himself. "As of now, nobody, but what I would like for you to do is, after we get your passport and paperwork handled, I'ma need for you to get familiar with someone that has good quality heroin."

"Heroin?" Kangoma said. He could feel his skin crawling. He wouldn't have to search far once he got back home. He could actually feel his life about to change. "How would we get it back?"

"As of now, all you do is find the resources. I'll find the money in U.S. currency."

"But Mr. Hamma, there are other Africans here from my country. They know so much about this."

"I prefer to do things my way," Hammer said in a tone of voice as if to say he would always have the final word. And he did.

Another two months passed, and Hammer had Kangoma ready and set to go get his family. Hammer had purchased a nice three-bedroom brick house in the Ben Hill area. Kangoma owned his own car now.

He drove himself to the airport in a brand new Lincoln. He parked in the parking lot and jumped out and removed a three-piece luggage set from the trunk, along with an additional $20K. With that type of money in Africa, he could be a very rich man, but he would be loyal to Hammer by any means necessary. When he boarded his plane, the first thing he did was pull out his phone and call Hammer to confirm his position

The only response Hammer gave him was, "Take your time. I'll see you in a month."

They'd already discussed their business and their strategy. Hammer didn't have to trust Kangoma. He dealt with him and saved him already because that was the proper thing to do. He was only preparing for the future.

There was a meeting being held at one of the skyboxes in the Georgia Dome. Hammer chose the spot because he had privacy and also because Corleone wanted to see Mike Vick play. Corleone stood at the glass that overlooked the jammed dome. He wore his red and black Vick jersey, baggy jeans, and black Air Force Ones. He wore his hair in long dreads and was so caught up in the game he wasn't even thinking about his granddaddy and his clique behind him.

Altogether, there was Hammer, Poi Boi, Iron Head, Dave, and some new guy that Hammer had never met until that day. He went by the name Six Nine because that was his height.

Hammer sat in silence and checked his watch. Diamond was supposed to be there. He was about to remove his cell phone from his pocket when the door came open. Diamond entered and apologized for being late. He took the first available seat and crossed his legs. Hammer cleared his throat and looked at Poi Boi and Dave. They were the ones responsible for the meeting, so Hammer needed to hear what they had to say.

Poi Boi looked at Six Nine. "Explain in detail, word for word, what you told me and Dave."

Six Nine didn't have a worried look across his face. Actually, he was more anxious than anything. Six Nine had a small mouth and a hawk-like nose with a long, square chin. He looked straight at Hammer and instantly recognized the cold stillness of a killer. He caught the same vibe from Poi Boi, Diamond, Iron Head, and Dave. Everybody was patiently waiting. Six Nine felt his palms beginning to sweat, and he rubbed them together to get hold of himself. His eyes darted one more quick time, and then he said. "Y'all don't really know me, but they call me Six Nine. Anyway, I be over at the truck stop on Bankhead on da regular, and since I been there, I been noticing that every Thursday, two Mexicans be coming through and swapping trucks. Shawty, I been peepin' da move fa' da last three months, and I know they either got a shit load of reefer or a ton of coke one." He slammed a huge fist into his open hand. "Man I know dis lick would put a nigga in high rank. All I need is 'bout 200 bands."

Hammer squinted, this time with a confused look. "Bands? Explain that to me," he said.

Corleone turned around, screaming and shouting, "Touchdown, Granddaddy!"

The stadium was in an uproar. Iron Head stood first and moved to the huge gothic window. "Mike Vick, stand strong, young nigga."

Six Nine leaned up. He pinched the bridge of his hawk-like nose. "Bands, as in rubber bands. We call a grand one band. You get ten bands, that really mean ten stacks."

Hammer said in a low, raspy drawl. "And you want 200 bands?"

Six Nine's adrenaline began pumping. He rubbed his hands together once again. He nodded his head up and down. He was captivated because he knew he could make it happen with the help he needed.

"Today is Sunday," Hammer said. "We'll set everything up for Thursday."

Six Nine had his own arrogance and killer instinct. His eyes darted around the room, and he studied Hammer's eyes again. They stared into one another for several seconds.

Hammer didn't trust him.

HAPTER 42

he stopped at the threshold of the door and scanned the crowded room of people. Laughter was in the air. Kids were screaming with joy, happy to see their incarcerated loved ones. Young Hollywood stood still with a long platinum link chain with a diamond-encrusted cross hanging from his neck. He saw Hammer waving his hand in the air about twenty tables back. Young Hollywood smiled and moved in that direction.

Corleone was making his way toward his daddy at the same time. He was casually dressed in tailored tan pants, small and cute Mauri Gators, a linen shirt, and his jet-black locks were hanging around the collar of his cream-colored mink jacket. When he got to Young Hollywood, he nearly jumped up into his arms. "Hey, Daddy!" he shouted cheerfully.

Young Hollywood kissed his son on his cheek. "Wuz up, gangsta?" he said. He grabbed Corleone's hand, and they went to the table where Hammer was sitting.

Hammer was also casually dressed. He wore a black mink, jeans, and black Mauri Gators. He embraced his son and held him tight. "You lookin' good," Hammer said.

They separated. Young Hollywood stared him up and down. He cut his eyes toward his son and said, "We can tell who got da money." A smile spread across his lips. They all sat down in hard plastic chairs surrounding a small round table. Corleone went to his daddy and bounced upon his thigh. He began wiggling out of his jacket. Hammer took it and laid it across the back of the chair. Corleone went to sleep five minutes later, and Young Hollywood held on to him like a precious jewel.

Hammer whispered, "Shit lookin' good in the city." He twisted the top from a bottled spring water and took a quick sip, just enough to wet his throat.

"Yeah. What them lawyers talkin' 'bout?"

Hammer shrugged out of his mink. He was feeling exhilarated. He cut his eyes at a Coke bottle-shaped woman who was staring in their direction as she walked by. He looked back at Young Hollywood and said, "I got to play a conservative game with these crackas. I'm in a rush, but they'll never know. I'm expecting you to pull at least ten years to give shit time to die down, you know."

Young Hollywood nodded. He wasn't feeling the ten-year ordeal, but he didn't have any other choice. "What the hell?"

Hammer continued, "In the next six to eight months, be prepared to get transferred."

Young Hollywood frowned, and his eyes turned cold. "Transfer? I ain't tryin' to go nowhere but home from here."

"If you don't like the move, you can always come back," Hammer responded. He took a sip from his bottled water again. "But I know once you get there, you're gonna be satisfied. Trust me."

"Well, you need to tell me what da business is now so I can go ahead and make a decision on dis shit."

"Don't question my judgment," Hammer said. Then he changed the subject. "You read the *AJC* metro section last Friday?"

"Yeah," Young Hollywood answered with excitement.

"The article about the drug heist and the five Mexicans who were found shot to death?"

Young Hollywood nodded.

"We caught a half-ton of coke on that lick." He was whispering again.

"A half-ton? Not literally, right?"

"You damn right, literally—1,000 pounds of cocaine. Also, I plugged in with an African guy. I'm trying to get in on the heroin too. And when you come home, I'm retiring."

Young Hollywood smiled; his gold teeth sparkled underneath the bright lights in the visitation room. "You know I'ma jack-of-all-trades anyway," he said and then he asked, "At this moment, what is the net worth of A-Town Records Incorporated?"

"Legal money's $7.3 million. By the end of next year, those numbers will triple, and in about three years, we'll be worth well over $100 million."

"I'm impressed," he said, and he was seriously anxious for it too.

Nicole Terry was lying out beside her inside the swimming pool in a one-piece Burberry swimsuit sipping on a fruity daiquiri mixed with

Courvoisier XO Imperial. Her nails were painted bright red. Her gently curved body was still and vulnerable. Staring out into the sparkling blue water, she slowly batted her eyes closed. Hammer was on her mind and nothing more. Anything else would blur her vision. "Why won't he call me?" She asked herself that question nearly three times a day when she didn't hear from him. She could feel his rough, thick fingers crawling around her soft shoulders and down to her breasts. The more she thought about him, the wetter she got. Nicole took a sip from her straw and touched her inch-thick clit through her Burberry swimsuit.

In the driveway, Hammer pulled up in a steel-colored Rolls Royce. Diamond was in the passenger's seat next to him. He pressed a button on his console, and the middle garage door began to open. Hammer cruised on into the garage.

Diamond stared around in amazement at the wide, spacious area. "Who shit is dis?" he asked.

Hammer killed the engine and then carefully looked at Diamond. "This my hideout." He winked. Hammer removed his cell phone from his pocket and punched in Nicole's house number.

"What took you so long to call me?"

"I'm out in the garage. I brought company with me also. Is everything set up?"

"Of course, honey," she said. "You don't have to tell me anything twice."

Hammer nodded to himself. He was satisfied at this point. When he got inside, he introduced Nicole and Diamond to one another. They shook hands, and then the three of them sat down at a round marble table. No food or drinks were offered. Hammer knew this wouldn't take long, and he was ready to get right down to business. He looked hard at Nicole, as if to tell her to get on with it.

She caught the hint and said cheerfully, "It's all arranged, honey. If your friend can have the horses shipped from Nigeria to Europe, I can have them shipped here to the United States within a week."

"And you do understand we'll have to put these horses to sleep once we get them here?" He was speaking as calmly as possible because he knew women sometimes have the tendency to let their emotions conflict with reality. She was an animal breeder and loved horses, but Hammer really didn't care for her or about her damn horses. Millions flashed before his eyes.

"I'm devastated." She placed her hand on her chest.

For the next thirty minutes, Hammer gave her the business. His conversation was thrilling, and she ate up every word of it. He didn't tell her the horses would be trafficking six kilos of heroin; he knew she'd had a disturbing sense of what was going on. Hopefully she wouldn't get out of line. Anyway, Hammer was a master at persuasion. He'd already made up in his mind that if she'd ever go against him or his word, he would bury her on her own property with the four other corpses that were out there.

# CHAPTER 43

Six Nine bounced out the backseat of a yellow cab in the parking lot of the most exotic car dealerships in the entire Atlanta area. He wore a Retro Atlanta Hawks jersey, a matching New Era fitted cap, baggy jeans, and sneakers. Around his neck was the strap of a Louis Vuitton leather duffel with nearly $50K in cash stuffed inside Ziploc bags. He pushed through the glass double-doors and stepped onto a marble floor, where a long row of foreign cars were displayed on the showroom floor.

An Italian-looking guy stepped forward with his black hair brushed to the back. Expensive jewelry sparkled from his neck, fingers, and wrist. He looked up at Six Nine with an extended hand. "How can I help you this evening?"

Six Nine shook the guy's hand and held it while he stared around the showroom. "I'm lookin' fo' somethin' real foolish, pimp."

"Sports or luxury?" the salesman asked.

"Real foolish, pimp," he said again anxiously. "I'm used to talkin' numbers. I got $48K in cash right now. I need somethin' foolish." He was nearly demanding now. His breath was laced with reefer and alcohol, and then his eyes went to something real expensive and flashy. In his words, foolish. He couldn't take his eyes away from the yellow Ferrari. That was it, and he wanted it so bad that it made his skin crawl. He pointed his long index finger toward the Ferrari and insisted, "I want that."

The Italian flipped his head back at the quarter-million-dollar machine. "Phew," he said. Then he added, "There's a waiting list." Three weeks later, Six Nine had purchased the Ferrari with a hefty down payment and nearly a year's worth of payments. Six Nine gunned the expensive machinery down Campbellton Road, where several groups of broads were huddled up with different types of hairdos. Some wore candy-pink weave. Others wore colorful wigs and long black weave, and nearly every last one of them had a Coca-Cola bottle figure. Six Nine whipped up in front of a candy-red Hummer sitting high on chrome rims. Three guys and four made-up girls had the SUV surrounded. When Six Nine parked his Ferrari in the middle of Campbellton in broad daylight, he knew he would turn heads and gain the attention he wanted. Without saying one word to anyone, he stepped out and left the car running. He was geared up in baggy jeans, and a camouflage bulletproof jacket with nothing over it but a huge platinum link. He slung a Bushmaster Carbon 15 over his shoulder and stepped to one of the half-naked ghetto models with a twisted blunt between his lips. "Anybody got a light?" he asked. His eyes scanning the crowd. The girl produced a Bic lighter. He leaned down toward her, and she lit the blunt for him. He gave her a twenty-dollar bill, and she jumped in his car and toured Atlanta with him. Later that night, he found himself in Magic City, Nickies, Blue Flames, Strokers, the World Bar, and ESPN. His spending habit had grown overnight. He spent twenty thousand on a rose gold and diamond grill. He was sniffing coke by the ounces and smoking the most expensive weed that money could buy.

Two weeks later, he was down to $12K in cash, a Ferrari, a crying-ass baby mama, and a fucked-p attitude. He sat in the living room of a two-bedroom apartment on a leather sofa, dressed in silk smiley-face printed boxers. He had a pile of nearly fifteen grams of cocaine in a small saucer. Six Nine stared up into space. The huge-screen TV was showing highlights of Kobe Bryant on ESPN, pasteurizing some unknown poor guy with a tremendous dunk. Next to him on the sofa was his Calico 9mm. On the right was a pistol-grip AK with a 100-round drum inserted underneath. At his feet were a blue pit bull puppy and four boxes of ammunition. His cell phone rang, and when he checked the number, it was the person he'd been waiting to hear from. He finally took a deep breath and fired up a Newport. "Wuz up, OG?" Six Nine said into the phone.

"Man, listen to me. I need to see you face to face."

"Who da fuck is dis?" the deep voice growled from the other end.

Six Nine's face drew into a frown. "Nigga, dis Six Nine," he said with authority.

"Nigga, you sound like you got some animosity toward dis way."

Six Nine sucked on his cigarette and blew double streams of smoke from his nostrils. He hated to bite his tongue, and he would never bow down to any man, but he knew how to play the game. He finally mumbled, nearly below his breath, "You right, pimp. My bad."

"Now who would you like to speak to?" the voice asked from the other end.

"Poi Boi."

"Speakin'."

Six Nine rolled his eyes. He had a real bitchy attitude at times. "Can you arrange a meetin' wit' me and Hamma?"

Two hours later, Six Nine was being escorted into the office of Hammer's studio. The room was dominated by a monolithic marble-slab table and color photos of the artist that was under his label. Six Nine was escorted by a short, cute chick with deep dimples, dressed in a Prada sweat suit. Once he got inside the huge office, he was shown a seat. The lady left, and five minutes later, Hammer, Poi Boi, Dave, and Iron Head came in single file. They all gave Six Nine a hand or a slap on the back.

Iron Head was the last one in. He closed the door and stood there. Arms folded across his chest. He watched Six Nine like a hawk. Iron Head was a connoisseur for smelling bad vibes. He felt it in his bones, and the glare Six Nine had in his eyes didn't impress him either.

"What's the problem, Six Nine?" Hammer asked him with a confident look across his face.

Six nine took a deep breath. His eyes darted around the room to everyone in his sight. "I wanna know if I can take dat offer you laid on da table fa' me a couple weeks ago."

"Why didn't you take it then?" Hammer asked cautiously. "I was speed-ballin', shawty," Six Nine replied. He dropped his head as if he'd been detected.

Hammer studied him carefully. He asked, "How much money do you have left?"

A long silence fell over the room. "'Bout $15K... but you know I'ma go get it. Jus' let me borrow 'bout five bricks so I can bounce back."

Hammer unbuttoned his Armani blazer and placed his hands on his waist. "Fools don't deserve money. You told me out your own mouth, your own words that you just wanted $200K, and I took it upon myself to give you an additional $200K. Altogether you had 400 bands, as you call it. And now you telling me you've fucked up nearly a half-million in less than a month."

Six Nine just stared in silence.

Then Hammer said, "My hands are tied. When you get your head on straight, come back and see me."

Six Nine stood quickly and towered over everybody in the room.

Iron Head had already drawn his pistol, but it was out of sight. "Man, I jus' turned y'all niggas on to a million-dollar lick, and a nigga can't even get a small loan to bounce back." His face was twisted into a mask of fury, and saliva was foaming in the corner of his mouth.

"See yourself out," Hammer said as he left the room.

Six Nine couldn't believe what he was hearing. He stood there for a moment with his eyes scanning everyone in the room, as if to be saying, *"Y'all motha'fuckas' gon' remember me."*

# CHAPTER 44

The very next morning, Six Nine was parked across the street from a small bank in a stolen cab. The driver was nearly beaten to death, duck taped, and gagged. He was stuffed in the trunk, with two broken ribs and a cracked jaw. The pain was excruciating when he tried to yell. Six Nine watched the bank from a shopping center parking lot in Clayton County. His eyes were averted, geeked up on cocaine, marijuana, and promethazine-codeine cough syrup.

Customers were in and out of the bank, and pedestrians were coming and going. Six Nine studied all activity. He wouldn't turn back now. No way. He was dressed in baggy denim jeans and wore a protective vest underneath a tall black T-shirt.

Inside the bank, there were six women at six different stations. People were transferring money, and some were trying to get loans. At the front door was an older white guy in a police uniform, the only bank security personnel.

Six Nine entered, dressed in dark clothing with a Pepé Le Pew mask over his face. He moved gracefully, just like the confident skunk from the cartoon. He swung one time and landed a left on the old security man's jaw. He fell to the floor and was out cold. Six Nine laid the entire bank down. "I came to kill anybody dat wanna be a hero dis mornin'." He waved his pistol-grip AK in the faces of the innocent people. Then he removed a trash bag from his waist. "You try to give me a bag wit' dye, yo' ass gon' die." Before he left, he stopped at the door and faced the bank. "Remember my face, Pepé Le Pew," and in the blink of an eye he was gone.

Later that night, Six Nine was at his kitchen table in his small two-bedroom apartment with $51,427 lined up in neat stacks across the table. His personal drink was Hawaiian Punch and promethazine cough syrup. He sipped from his huge cup and fired up a Newport. The smoke lingered in the air, and his eyelids began growing heavy. He began staring out into nowhere and talking to himself. "Niggas thank Six Nine can't get no money. I'ma bread winner fa' real. Fuck niggas ain't fuckin' wit' Six Nine from motha' fuckin' Herndon Homes. Zone

One fo' real." He was losing it. He took a sniff of coke, and seconds later, he was high. He pulled on his cigarette and sipped from his cup.

Six Nine stayed in hiding until the next weekend, and when he finally showed his face, he appeared in the parking lot valet service. His Ferrari was a real eye-catcher. He wore a canary-yellow three-quarter-inch mink, a black two-piece suit, and canary-yellow gator shoes. His neck and wrist were covered with foolish platinum and diamond pieces.

He was posted in front of Lennox Square Mall, where other hustlers, celebrities, athletes, and groupies hung out. Six Nine knew he would stick out like a sore thumb. That was what he wanted; he was scouting a real big fish. His appetite for money and fame was enormous, and he was getting bolder by the minute.

When three SUVs pulled up and stopped at the valet, nearly twenty guys poured out. The majority of them wore dreads and huge chunks, and they all wore the latest fashion clothing. Six Nine noticed that their license plates were read Columbia, South Carolina, and that made it even better. Out-of-towners were more valuable. They were so caught up in the glitz and glamour that they didn't see the real truth. Just like today. Six Nine was driving around Atlanta in quarter-million-dollar car. His appearance alone made him look like a self-made millionaire and then some.

One of the cats who jumped out of the first SUV walked up to Six Nine. He stood six feet with a neatly trimmed beard and goatee. A sparkling Rolex watch was peeping from underneath his leather jacket. He looked up at Six Nine and said, "Wuz up, homie?"

Six Nine leaned against his Ferrari. He folded his hands at his waist and allowed his eyes to meet the stranger's eyes that stood before him. Six Nine extended his hand and replied, "Wuz up, pimp?"

The guy introduced himself as Boss Hawg. He and Six Nine chatted for nearly an hour. Boss Hawg explained to Six Nine about his situation with the drug economy. He told him it was a drought in Carolina coming from his New York connect.

Then Six Nine said, "Yeah, shit fucked up because of the Trade Center bombin'. Prices up everywhere."

"Can you give me some prices?" Boss Hawg asked.

Six Nine spread his hands, and with total silence he shook his head side to side. Silence hung in the air between the two of them. Then an overwhelming idea hit Six Nine, and he asked, "How long y'all gon' be in da city?"

The guy flipped his wrist, checked his Rolex. It was seven thirty p.m. Boss Hawg looked up at Six Nine and responded, "We was gonna hit one of da strip clubs."

"My name Six Nine. I'll be yo' tour guide tanight. How many of yo' people comin' with you?"

Boss Hawg looked around. His crew was scattered around, some talking to passing women, others chatting nonchalantly amongst themselves, and the rest of them staring at Six Nine and his Ferrari as if he was an NBA player. "I know fifteen," he finally said.

The first club Six Nine took them to was called Strokers, and they were led straight to the VIP section by two huge NFL-size security guards with no-nonsense looks on their faces. They had three huge tables already set with champagne in buckets of ice, all courtesy of the manager. Six Nine was nearly broke again; camouflaging himself as a street millionaire was very cunning.

Over fifty half-naked models paraded around in two-piece mini-dresses. Some were in panties and stilettos, skirted thongs, and painted-on bikinis. Three 6 Mafia and UGK were bumping from the speakers throughout the club. The song "Sippin' On Some Syrup" was the smash hit, and just as sure, Six Nine had himself a personal bottle of the promethazine-codeine cough syrup. He and Boss Hawg had separated from the huge crew and grabbed a corner table. Boss Hawg wanted Moet and Chandon. Six Nine ordered fifteen women for the crew, a pack of Newports, and Hawaiian Punch to go with his syrup.

Twenty minutes into the club, Six Nine was feeling real groovy and cool as a motha' fucka', if you let him tell it. "Check game, pimp. Two things I don't get down wit' is niggas tryin' set niggas up fa' da jack, and niggas tryin' set niggas up fa' da Feds," Six Nine said. "I don't roll like dat,"

Boss Hawg responded in a convincing tone of voice. "I can give you my mama's phone number and address and my own separate number and address. Dat's how I do business." He touched his chest with both hands.

Six Nine pulled his cigarette long and hard, as if he had to think about the situation. It was all a hoax though. He French-rolled the thick cigarette smoke and then exhaled a long, thin stream from his small mouth. Then he said, "My people won't even answer da phone unless you buyin' fifteen or betta."

Boss Hawg tilted his head a little. "Phew." He let that escape his mouth first, and then he scratched his head. "Fifteen or betta'? Let's jus' say I only have enough money fo' ten."

Six Nine had to come out of his mink. He called a naked female in six-inch heels over. He draped the coat over her shoulders and then patted his leg for her to sit down. Then she began playing with her vagina and rotating her hips.

Boss Hawg had his eyes glued to her. "My people serious. These niggas connected fa' real. Fifteen bricks, you can get 'em fa' sixteen-five a piece. You buy twenty, you pay fifteen, plus you get five on yo' face ta seventeen-five a piece. That's how they operate, and to top everything off, you get a half-brick of coke just for curiosity." The smoke was seeping from his mouth as he spoke.

Boss Hawg's eyes widened as he said, "Man, I know you ain't serious about dat."

Six Nine kept a serious face, his eyes fixed on Boss Hawg. "You gonna get da half-brick tanight on da strength. If you come back to shop, cool. If you don't, it's still cool. Dat's jus' how we do business," and he meant every word of that.

# CHAPTER 45

Nearly two weeks later, the shipment came in. Hammer and Kangoma rode together in the front seat of a white Dooley truck with a huge silver Goose Neck horse trailer attached to the rear. They rode in complete silence up the long, winding driveway that led to Nicole's stables and ranch. It was the middle of November, and the cold weather was in full effect.

Hammer parked the truck. He looked over at Kangoma and asked, "You ready?"

Kangoma nodded. He was dressed in jeans, boots, and a red and black lumber jacket with matching hat.

He and Hammer stepped down from the Dooley. Hammer was dressed down for the occasion, in jeans, a fatigue jacket, and a new pair of steel-toed boots. They moved around to the rear of the house trailer. There were three horses in the rear; all three of them were beautiful with shiny gloss coats. A white guy appeared from the side door of the barn; he was handsome and well built. Hammer knew him as the horse trainer. "Are these the three that have to be put to sleep?" he asked.

His eyes darted from Hammer to Kangoma.

Hammer nodded.

The trainer unlocked the rear trailer, then opened the steel door. He quickly guided the first horse out and politely walked him over to the barn. No more than an hour later, all three horses were quietly and sound asleep in their separate stalls. Night had fallen, and the sky was decorated with bright stars that illuminated the twenty-acre estate. Hammer ordered the trainer to leave and gave him an additional $1,000 tip. Then he and Kangoma went to work. First, they changed into surgical scrubs. Then they lined thick plastic sheets around the barn where the horses were.

Kangoma made the first incision with a sharp surgical blade; he cut the first horse at the bottom of its stomach. The thick, dark blood poured out like motor oil. Kangoma went deeper with the blade, until his entire forearm was lost inside the horse. He was covered in the thick blood himself. He didn't care though. When he got to the horse's intestines, he sliced there also, a four- to six-inch slit. He forced his hand inside and felt around, and then his hand grasped something in the shape of a long roll of tissue. Kangoma removed it and sat it down on the small pile of hay. Then he removed three more.

Hours had passed, and Hammer was at the kitchen table now. Figures were flipping around inside his head, but he didn't want to go through the process himself of cutting the heroin. He knew the right chemist could do it for him. The heroin was so powerful that Kangoma and Hammer both had to wear oxygen mask just to breath.

When Six Nine's cell phone rang, he didn't budge. It was eight o'clock in the morning, and the rain was coming down heavy outside. Six Nine was staying in Decatur with two twins on Flat Shoals. The apartment was neatly decorated with leather furniture and African art pieces. Six Nine was satisfied because both twins knew how to cook, and they had the best Dome in Georgia. When he did move, he swatted his hand across his face. His eyes opened slowly, and his head hurt like hell. The ultimate hangover was on his back, and he was damn near afraid he couldn't shake it. His eyes wandered around the room for a minute. The TV was off, and the blinds on the windows were slightly parted. Six Nine sat up and yawned. Then he realized he was in the huge, comfortable king-sized bed alone. He finally swung his legs out of bed and stood up. When he stretched his hands out, they nearly touched the ceiling. He looked at his watch, and it read 8:10. "Damn!" he said to himself. He then stripped himself naked and bounced in the shower. Twenty minutes later, he paraded around the small apartment with a thick blue terrycloth towel wrapped around his lower body. He lit up a cigarette and started his day off with a small joint of purple haze marijuana. The smoke filled the living room, and Six Nine was beginning to come to life. He grabbed his cell phone and searched through it for any missed calls. He recognized a couple of them and disregarded them as well. Then there was one with an out-of-state area code. He stared at it for a moment while puffing on his cigarette, and then he dialed the number.

A voice answered from the other end.

"Yeah? Who dis?" Six Nine asked. He didn't recognize the voice.

"Dis Boss Hawg, pimp. Wuz goin on?"

Six Nine's eyes widened so far that they nearly popped from their sockets. He stood to his feet, and a slight smile spread across his face. "Damn, shawty, you got missin' on a nigga, din't ya?" Six Nine went into the kitchen and removed a Michelob from the fridge.

"Nah. I ran into a lil' problem, man, but everything good as can be on my end."

Dollar signs flashed in Six Nine's eyes. "When you comin' to the city?" Six Nine asked.

"I'm here. Got in last night. Is everything still good on your end?" Boss Hawg inquired.

"Well I'm glad. When can I see you?"

Boss Hawg sounded happy and anxious. He couldn't help but trust the words that Six Nine spit at him because he'd given him a half-key of cocaine just to show his gratitude. Now that was real.

Six Nine thought for a second or two. Then he said, "I'ma come pick you up solo. Me and you, nobody else. I'll call you in about two hours."

"Befo' you go, listen... I brought my wife and my kids, and I don't really wanna leave them here in the room," Boss Hawg said.

"So what is you tryin' to do?" Six Nine asked. Before Boss Hawg could answer, Six Nine cut him off. "Enough of dis phone shit. I'ma call you in forty minutes." Six Nine hung up his cell, got dressed in less than ten minutes, and was out the door, strapped with twenty dummy bricks of cocaine.

# CHAPTER 46

Six Nine was sharp and with poise. This morning he wore Pelle Pelle jeans, a wife-beater, a black leather Pelle Pelle jacket, and a New Era Falcons cap smothering down over his afro. Behind the wheel of his Ferrari, he sped through Atlanta with a suspended driver's license, a Heckler & Koch .40 caliber, and twenty dummy bricks of cocaine sealed in plastic, duct tapped, and stuffed in a waterproof duffel bag.

When he arrived at the hotel downtown, he already had Boss Hawg on the cell phone. Six Nine saw him coming through the lobby with a rolling piece of luggage and another small duffel slung across his shoulder. When he got outside, Six Nine stepped out and greeted Boss Hawg with a clap and a friendly hug. Six Nine popped the hood of the Ferrari, and when Boss Hawg loaded the property inside, he scooted around to the driver's side and got in. The passenger's side was still locked. Boss Hawg gripped the door handle, and within seconds, Six Nine had the Ferrari tires burning on the asphalt. He sped off and left Boss Hawg looking stupid.

Six Nine's adrenaline level had risen. His eyes darted back and forth from the front window pane to all three rearview mirrors. He changed gears like a professional racecar driver, screeching the tires on the asphalt and watching Boss Hawg's image slowly disappearing into the tall skyscrapers of downtown. He'd been swallowed and eaten as if he was in a lion's den. The correct word for him would be prey, and with a $320K loss. The only thing he could do now was pray.

Night fell again, and Six Nine was climbing to the top once again. He was back at the twins' apartment with a fat-rolled blunt of kush and ten bottles of champagne lined up on the glass coffee table. The twin sisters were naked and rubbing on one another's bodies and sharing the same cherry flavor Blow Pop. Six Nine had his money spread out across the living room floor. This he admired as he relaxed in the leather recliner. Staring at his world, Six Nine actually did things his way. He lived for dreams, and he wouldn't be able to cope with society if nothing was going on. The thrill of getting money made his flesh crawl.

Early the next morning, he entered another bank right around the corner from the apartment complex in Decatur. This time, he caught the bank manager entering the vault with a stack of papers and a happy-go-lucky secretary who actually grinned at the Pepé Le Pew mask. Six Nine got away clean with $270K and not one problem at all. When he finally settled down and took notes from the news anchorwoman from the television, he decided to make an important phone call. He dialed Hammer's number, but he didn't get an answer. However, he did leave a message.

Corleone was having the time of his life. Hammer and a few of his friends had put together enough money for his entire school to go to Disney World. He was down in Orlando, Florida with a group of great kids that appreciated everything Corleone's grandfather did and was doing.

Hammer had his eyes on a bigger prize, and he wanted to do bigger things as well. He stood out on his balcony, which was surrounded by tinted sheets of the glass and a well-designed roof. There was also a fireplace built inside the wall that could be seen from his bedroom and from his balcony. He admired the city skyline. It gave him energy and sometimes made him feel stronger than he actually was. He was older and wiser but still stuck in his ways, and that alone made other men hate him. He was envied more than he knew. He didn't care about any of it though. Hammer sat in his stony silence, programming mental plan. He was barefoot and wore a pair of gray Sean John sweats rolled up to his knees. He turned at the sound of a female voice.

"Telephone!" yelled Corleone's great grandmother. She extended the cordless out to him.

Hammer walked across the carpeted floor and got the phone.

The old lady went ahead about her business.

"Hello?" Hammer said.

"Yeah. Wuz up, lame?" Six Nine barked from the other end.

Hammer hung up the phone in his face.

The following evening, Hammer and Nicole Terry were having dinner at an exclusive restaurant down the street from his penthouse when he received a call from Sasha. "How you doin?" he asked happily.

"I'm good. I just wanted to share some good news with you," she responded.

"I'm listening," Hammer said.

"I got the position. They promoted me."

He smiled with satisfaction, like the happiest customer in a Super Walmart with the last deal. "I'm proud of you. We'll find you a house close by the prison, and I'll arrange the move." His eyes met Nicole's. She was madly in love with him, and it seemed as though he was falling for her as well.

Sasha said, "Do he know?"

"I thought I'd surprise him. I really didn't wanna speak too fast, in case I couldn't get it done. That makes your face value go down. So that mean when you say something, you better damn mean it," Hammer said.

"You right," she responded

"How you looking on funds?" he asked.

"For the moment, I'm good. I do wanna do some shopping before I go down to that country town."

"Come see me tomorrow," Hammer said.

They exchanged goodbyes and hung up the phone.

The table that separated Hammer and Nicole was round and covered with an expensive linen cloth. There were two candles with brass holders. The candle flames flickered in his eyes as he stared at it.

"What's the problem?" Nicole asked.

Hammer didn't respond.

Then Nicole said, "Maybe you'll fly to Australia with me this weekend. We can leave on Friday, and we'll be back Monday night."

"I'm not in position to leave right now," Hammer said.

"Enough of the bullshit, Rufus. You need a break. It's only two days. Trust me, you'll love it." She took a deep breath and then a swallow from her champagne glass and sat it back on the table. Her eyes met his again, this time more intently. "It's more in the world than Atlanta."

Hammer couldn't do nothing but laugh.

# CHAPTER 47

As the days passed, the north Georgia weather turned colder, and Christmas approached. Six Nine just couldn't resist showing his face, even though his name was beginning to ring throughout the city for robbing, stealing, killing, and kidnapping—not to mention that Hammer was looking for him. Nevertheless, he didn't care about that. He drove a leased Maserati that he was determined to buy through the hoods and projects. It was three thirty in the evening when he pulled up on Dill Avenue. It was cloudy, and an earlier rain shower was just drying up. He pulled the Maserati in front of a wooden house with green and white chipped paint. Across the street was a clique of females in the latest fashionable clothing and colorful wigs and lipstick. He saw them passing blunts around their circle. Six Nine bounced out in jeans, Polo boots, and a soft leather jacket with his vest underneath. He set his pistol-grip AK on the roof of the car. Careful enough not to ruin the paint, he lit himself a Newport and threw up the deuces at the clique of females.

One of the girls yelled out, "Damn, nigga! You can holla at a real bitch."

He was going toward his auntie's house now with a cigarette in one hand and the K in the other.

Another female yelled out, "Yeah, nigga! You ain't nothing but some cut anyway."

Even he had to laugh at that. When he got to the porch, a little boy came from around the side of the house. "Uncle Mitch, my mama ain't home."

"You feed my dogs?" Six Nine asked, cigarette smoke streaming from his nostrils.

The young boy's eyes wandered to the weapon Six Nine held. Kids at his age were fascinated with guns. Two more boys pulled up on bicycles and did hook slides.

Six Nine stared at them briefly then cut his eyes back to his nephew. "Nigga, did you feed my dogs?" he asked again.

"Man, I jus' came home," the little boy said. He rolled his eyes at

Six Nine and walked to the street where his friends waited for him. He hopped on the handlebars of one of the bikes, and they rode off to God-knows-where.

Six Nine walked inside the house. The living room smelled of funk and stale cigarettes. He took at the raggedy hallway and made his way to the kitchen and removed half a bag of dog food from the bottom counter. He stood up and set it on top of the counter, pulled on his cigarette, and dumped the ashes in the sink. The back door was in the kitchen that led to the backyard. Six Nine went through it. He immediately saw his three huge pit bulls. Two of them were blue, and the other was a brindle with Jeep and Carver blood. They had separate doghouses, and each one was collared to a huge chain that rotated around a spike inserted into the ground. Six Nine found their bowls and began filling them up when he heard the cars pulling up.

Back in front of the house, two SUVs and two old-model Chevys pulled up. Over a dozen men spilled out in front of the house, dressed in black fatigues, ski masks, and heavily armed. They lined up in front of the house in a semicircle, and within seconds, they were firing their weapons, all aiming at the house. The sound was unbearable, and the house was starting to look like Swiss cheese. Glass and wood chips were flying everywhere. Before the goons left, they firebombed the Maserati and left it burning in the front of the house, and over 800 shell casings were found and left behind.

Six Nine hopped a four-foot chain-link fence. He could hear and feel the high-caliber bullets whizzing pass him. He ran with long strides, pumping his legs as fast as they would carry him. His adrenaline was pumping out of control. He went across a neighbor's yard and hopped up on the hood of a parked Chevy Blazer, then onto the roof and across another fence. He'd gotten away this time, and now he was actually getting it through his thick skull that Hammer wasn't someone to play with.

Two nights later, Six Nine was up to something else. Another gorgeous plan formulated inside his head. He followed the wife of one of Hammer's associates in a Toyota Avalon. The lady's name was Brenda, and her husband was Diamond. She drove a candy apple-red Mercedes Benz C-Class. He followed behind her dressed in a bob-cut wig, tremendous lipstick, jeans boots, and a black T-shirt. He tapped her rear bumper.

Brenda looked at Six Nine through the rearview. They were at a traffic light on Cascade, exiting the Kroger Plaza. When Brenda got out Six Nine filled her upper body with .45 slugs. She fell to the asphalt, and Six Nine was gone.

Back at his hideout, he stalked the window like a retreating soldier. The curtain was slightly parted, and he carried a different AR slung across his shoulder. This one was spray-painted black with a 100-round drum. There was a Newport hanging from his mouth. His eyes were continuously dancing around the dark parking lot. He knew Hammer was thirsty for him now. *He probably got a million-dollar price tag on my head,* he thought. Six Nine moved away from the window and pulled on his cigarette as he made his way to the cushioned sofa. He took a seat, and his eyes went to the door. He'd barricaded it with the dining room table and weight set and bench. He set his cigarette in the ashtray and turned up a one-liter plastic bottle of Evian water. The AK was resting across his lap now. "Maybe I'll take a vacation," he said to himself, and then an overwhelming thought came to his head. He actually began smiling to himself. He reached under the sofa and retrieved a kitchen plate filled with nearly sixty grams of powered cocaine. He set the AK on the sofa next to him, then dipped a playing card in the cocaine, and within thirty minutes he'd made five grams disappear.

Back at the window, peeping and sweating good, he came out of his shirt. Another hour had passed, and fifteen grams were gone. By the time the sun rose, he had gone through nearly twenty grams. He was watching the kids load onto a school bus from the window. Then he saw the strangest thing: two black, old-model Lincolns with suicide doors easing through the parking lot. Six Nine nodded his head up and down. He slowly rubbed his hands together. He knew they were there for him. He picked up his Kevlar vest from the floor and slid it over his head. He knew it was useless because the caliber of weapons they would be shooting would rip him apart anyway; it was just a psychological thing.

Both of the Lincolns parked next to one another.

He quickly armed himself with the AK, turned it to the side, and eased the action back. "I got 101 rounds fo' y'all fuck niggas. Come get it!" His eyes were glistening with fluid. He got off on situations like this. He continued to watch both cars. Nobody had exited either of them. He stroked the side of the AK, his breath laced with a stale cigarette taste. Then suddenly he noticed seven little girls all dressed in identical clothing: khaki pants, cute little shoes, and burgundy sweaters with yellow V-neck strips. They all loaded into both of the Lincolns and exited the parking lot just as casually as they had entered. They weren't there for him. Six Nine breathed a little easier, he was still geeked up. His nose began running, and he wiped it with the back of his hand. When he left the window, he went into one of the two bedrooms. Inside the closet, he took out a four-foot nylon duffel bag and lifted it to the bed. He unzipped it with one long yank. The first four kilos he removed were real, squared perfectly and neatly duct taped. He began pulling out forty more. They all looked the same, but these weren't real. He took a black magic marker and wrote out "Afghanistan" in neat Arabic letters on each one of them.

The following morning, Six Nine was behind the wheel of an all-white service van. He cruised a couple of streets where he knew homeless people hung out. He pulled in front of the Circle K gas station on Riverdale Road. He remembered that there was a bum Mexican panhandler the last time he was here. Six Nine parked the van and swung his long frame out. His hair was hanging long and bushy. He examined the parking lot carefully, hoping he wouldn't slip up. He saw the Mexican standing near the payphones. When Six Nine approached him, he looked him over. Two of his top teeth were missing. His hair was long and stringy, and his beard was long and shabby. Beyond that, he had the look that Six Nine was looking for. "You speak English, *amigo*?" he asked.

The Mexican nodded.

"You wanna make some motha' fuckin' money?"

"Ohhh yeah! Lot of money. Si."

"Come on and get in dat van right there." Six Nine pointed toward it.

The Mexican walked to the van with a spray bottle and rag in his hand. Six Nine walked into the store and came out with a carton of

Newports and a huge two-liter bottle of Hawaiian Punch. He bounced up in the driver's seat.

The Mexican was on the passenger's side. He looked at Six Nine, "What kind of work?" he asked.

Six Nine started the van. He didn't answer. Instead, he pulled out into the flowing early-morning traffic. "What dey call you, '*migo*?"

The Mexican growled, "You answer my question."

Six Nine snapped. "It's easy work, *'migo*. Jus' cool out. You gon' get paid to look good. You gon' be my Cuban connect from Miami, I'ma make you rich. I'ma call you Montana. Dat's yo motha' fucking name."

By six o'clock the same evening, Six Nine had taken his Mexican friend to a dentist out in Stone Mountain. He'd paid to have two false teeth put in his mouth and had his teeth cleaned for him also. They checked into an expensive suite on one of the twenty-five floors at the Renaissance Atlanta Hotel downtown. Six Nine had spent nearly seven grand on the Mexican on just one day. *What do I care? This is gonna be fun.* Six Nine paid for one suite. When they got inside, the first thing Six Nine said was "Get yourself a shower, *'migo*."

The Mexican nodded without another word. He walked across the spacious floor and into the marble-floor bathroom. Six Nine had given him an electric razor and Dial soap and body lice spray. The clean underwear was mandatory. Later that night, Six Nine prepped the Mexican. He'd given him game and major conversation. They sat at the dining room table in their suite. They ordered room service: lobster tail, rice, steak and sautéed onions cooked in a savory gravy. Six Nine looked at the Mexican. He was clean shaven now and had his hair pulled back in a neat and tight ponytail. Six Nine had loaned him his expensive gold Cuban link. He'd bought him a huge gold pinky ring with a ten-carat cubic zirconium diamond that sparkled at every turn.

"You look like money, '*migo*."

The Mexican began nodding his head. "Call me Montana."

Six Nine nodded in agreement and stuffed a fork filled with rice in his mouth. Then he began studied the Mexican again. He was trying to picture him in expensive attire such as a button-up silk shirt, jeans, and a pair of cheap gator point boots. "Wherever we go, I do da talking. You don't speak no English unless a nigga say he buyin' ten bricks or betta."

"I got chu, my friend," the Mexican responded with excitement in his eyes.

In the course of three weeks, Six Nine and his Mexican friend had toured Georgia. They went to Athens, Augusta, Macon, Savannah, Albany, Columbus, and Valdosta, Georgia. They tricked their competitors, luring them in with the Ferrari and eye trickery, something Six Nine had surely mastered. Their last stop was Memphis, Tennessee; they only had eight dummy bricks and one real one left. They sold them all with no problem. Inside a small motel room in downtown Memphis, Six Nine and Montana counted out their earnings. They had over $100K. The Mexican was happy until Six Nine pulled out a razor-sharp hunting knife, sliced the Mexican's throat, and stabbed him several times. He removed the chain from his neck and rinsed it off in the bathroom sink. And just like that, he was on his way back to Atlanta without a care in the world.

On Christmas day, Six Nine decided to show his face around the city again. He was stunting hard too. Today, he drove a brand new glossy black Ferrari with red leather interior. He had the top dropped in the dead cold winter. He was covered in a full-length mink coat and an expensive mink hat that covered his ears. He drove down Simpson Road and through his project, chunking the deuces at his competition. He was one arrogant son-of-a-bitch.

Later on that same night, tragedy struck for the infamous Six Nine. He was gunning his Ferrari down Martin Luther King and was held up by a traffic light when two cars pulled up. He peeped the hit coming from his rearview and pressed the gas into oncoming traffic. The goons rattled the car, caused it to flip, and left him for dead.

At Grady Hospital, Six Nine had been shot twice, nothing serious. There was a deep gash across his forehead that had to be sewn up. His left arm was broken and was now in a cast. He tried to leave the hospital on his own, and the Fulton County Homicide Department gave him a visit. His DNA sample matched the ones of an unsolved home invasion and four murders from 1999. He was arrested there in Grady, handcuffed, and soon to be transferred to Rice Street's Fulton County Jail.

# BOOK VI

# CHAPTER 48

Young Hollywood was still on twenty-three-hour-a-day lockdown. He paraded around his cell in a Hanes tee, ankle socks, and sweaty boxer briefs. He now wore a thick rose gold Cuban link around his neck and a four-inch cross, encrusted with expensive diamonds.

He was in the middle of a workout when an officer came down the range and paused at his cell. The officer, a huge white guy with a round, hard belly, stared down at Young Hollywood.

Young Hollywood stood to his feet. His body was covered in sweat, and drops fell to the floor from his neck and face. "You lost something?" Young Hollywood asked. He moved to the bars and gripped them, only inches away from the officer's face, close enough to smell sour cream-and-onion potato chips on his breath.

The officer finally said, "Pack it up. You're transferring."

Young Hollywood stared into the eyes of the officer, just to see if he was serious or not. It had to be true though. The tone in his voice was too calm, disturbing even. Young Hollywood didn't want to leave Reidsville because it was rumored to be the hardest and the realist penitentiary in the state of Georgia. Young Hollywood finally flipped his wrist and checked the time on his watch. It read 11:15 p.m., and the only thing he could do was shake his head. He was disgusted as hell, but it was one of the many plans Hammer had in store for him.

Two hours later, he packed and was loaded with nearly $1,000 in hygiene and commissary, a CD player, a fan, and a big radio. When his cage door finally opened, two officers shackled and cuffed him, and two other officers loaded his property onto a cart.

"Y'all niggas stay!" Young Hollywood shouted throughout the entire dorm. "Yeah, dis Young Hollywood pimpin', and I'm leavin' dis spot."

"Where you goin', shawty?" another voice rang out. Young Hollywood recognized the voice; it was his younger homeboy from Carver Homes. They gave him the name Mad Max because he was crazy as hell, literally. The Mental Health Ward was on Level Three.

Young Hollywood was out on the range now. "They won't tell me where I'm goin', shawty. Jus' make sho you stay out of trouble."

"Check dat, pimp. Stay up though."

"And to y'all niggas dat I don't fuck wit', rest in peace fuck nigga."

Hours later, they arrived in Jackson, Georgia. Jackson State Prison was famous for three things. It was the worst diagnostic prison; it housed over 250 prisoners on death row. And it was the meet and switch stop for all major transfers on Tuesdays and Thursdays of the week. Young Hollywood rode in the back of the bus, shackled from head to toe, along with forty other convicts who were leaving Reidsville.

It was Tuesday, the middle of May 2002, and the sun was becoming overwhelmingly hot. When the Reidsville transfer bus finally made its way into the huge prison facility, they parked. The parking lot was a wide stretch of paved blacktop. It was now full of men from nearly every county jail and prisons from all over Georgia. Young Hollywood scanned the parking lot from his window seat. He saw guys coming from county jails, swapping their new tennies for a pack of Buglers roll cigarettes. A lot of old prisoners who hadn't seen friends in years were waiting. Forty yards away, two prisoners were going toe to toe with blows, and within seconds, Young Hollywood saw a guy drop flat to his face while the other guy stood over him, looking down at him. A few officers rushed the scene and cuffed the unknown guy. *Impressive*, he thought.

When it was time for Young Hollywood to come forward to be unchained, he moved swiftly, almost with an elegant grace. Swagger temperature rose to 2,000 when he stepped off the bus.

The officer pulled his file from a plastic milk crate. He opened it, looked at his face, and then at the picture in his file. It was a match. "Terry Keys, you goin' to Macon State Prison," the officer said. Another officer removed his belly chain.

Young Hollywood hadn't been so free in nearly four to five years. He hauled his property from the rear of the bus and set it down on the hot blacktop. Twenty minutes later, he was escorted to a parked white sixteen-passenger van, where a few other prisoners waited to be chained and shackled and loaded into the van and hauled off like livestock. Young Hollywood didn't care about none of that though. There were bigger things at stake for him, and knowing his daddy, the stakes were definitely high. Altogether there were nine prisoners chained and loaded on the bus. The transfer officers were saying something about waiting on the Valdosta State Prison bus since it had broken down an hour ago. After an hour and fifteen minutes, the Valdosta bus came creeping through the parking lot until it found its parking space.

Young Hollywood stood from his seat and slowly moved toward the front of the van. "Lemme use da bathroom befo' we leave."

The officers were standing at the side doors. One of the officers motioned for him to come down. He did and made small steps across the parking lot when he heard someone yell out his name.

"Hollywood! Wuz up, shawty?"

Young Hollywood looked around, then scanned the window of the Valdosta bus; he saw several heads and body figures.

Then the voice yelled out again, "Shawty, dis Scooter. Wuz up?"

Young Hollywood gave a squint, and broad smile spread across his face. When he began moving toward the bus, another officer—this time a huge down-South redneck—pointed his hand and yelled, "No visitors! Go where you goin'."

"Crackas out here trippin', pimp!" Young Hollywood shouted. "What camp you goin' to?"

"Macon State!" Scooter yelled back.

Young Hollywood smiled again. "Nigga, me too. I'ma use dis bathroom and I'ma see you in a minute."

"Check dat, shawty." Excitement was in his voice as well.

When they arrived at Macon State Prison, Young Hollywood and Scooter caught up on old times and shared their prison experiences. When they got through intake, the team went through their property carefully. They checked every letter, spot, crack, and crevice where contraband could be hidden. Young Hollywood and Scooter were both placed on the east side. Young Hollywood went to Dorm E-1 and Scooter went to D-2. He wouldn't be there long though.

Young Hollywood was assigned to a two-man cell downstairs in Number 120. The dorm held ninety-six men, and it was hot as hell inside. He dragged his property to the cell and set it down in the middle of the floor. He left it there, and then he went to the phone.

"Phones ain't on brah," an older guy said while fixing a cup of coffee at the water fountain.

Young Hollywood looked at the guy, the receiver still cradled in his hand. He slowly hung up. "What time they come on?" Young Hollywood asked.

"Fo' thirdy." The stranger held up a steaming cup of coffee and examined the smoke. Then he walked off without another word.

Young Hollywood watched him for moment; his eyes followed the old guy until he went upstairs to the top range and disappeared into a cell. Young Hollywood noticed a few guys watching him. He wasn't used to this type of environment just yet. He took a quick sip of water and eased back across the glossy concrete floor. Back inside his cell, he began unpacking his property. He had at least sixty packs of Newports and twenty packs of Black & Mild cigars. He searched through several bottles of squeeze cheese until he found the one he was looking for. When he got it, he popped the top and squeezed all the cheese out into the toilet until he found his marijuana wrapped nice and tight. He smoked a joint, and then a knock came from the door. His froze eyes wide. He told himself to calm down, and when he opened the door, he saw it was Scooter.

# CHAPTER 49

"How da hell you get over here?" Young Hollywood asked.

Scooter came into the cell with his nose in the air. "I jus' caught LT and told them I had problems in dis dorm wit' a nigga from another camp and said I'd chill if I could move to E-1," Scooter said.

Young Hollywood examined him more thoroughly. He took a real good look at his longtime friend. He didn't quite look the same. *Maybe he's worried about something. The time's probably getting to him.* "Wuz up, pimp. You a'ight?" Young Hollywood asked him. His eyes were searching Scooter's as though he was looking for something, like the wrong answer.

"I'm good, shawty," Scooter said, as he looked around the cell. "Where yo' cell-mate?" Scooter asked.

Young Hollywood shrugged and responded, "Who you askin'? Probably on detail or something. I hope he ain't no monkey-ass nigga."

Scooter laughed at that, then he said. "If he is, I'll get rid of him."

"What cell you in?" Young Hollywood was more serious now. His eyes narrowed.

"Upstairs in 214," Scooter responded quickly and moved toward the cell door and cracked it a little. He was looking out into the dorm area where blue chairs were lined behind one another in front of two TVs. "Man, I damn sho didn't wanna come here." Then he turned back toward Young Hollywood. "How da fuck bof us come here on da same day anyway?"

"Well…yu know my old man got a lot of pull out there on them streets."

Scooter's face was in question, his head slightly tilted to the side. Then he asked, "What daddy? Hollywood Court raised you."

"Shawty ain't tell you I hooked up with Hamma when I was down in da bottom?"

"Hit man Hamma?"

Young Hollywood nodded.

Scooter snapped his fingers, and an excited look spread across his face. "Shawty, I been hearin' niggas comin to da joint talking bout a nigga named Hamma. He was in da double XL too?"

"Yeah. You know we own A-Town Records, and we got da streets on smash," Young Hollywood proclaimed.

"Naw. Dem BMF niggas got shit on smash out there. I heard they got big-ass billboards out there."

"You'll see. I'm the one responsible for you transferring down here," Young Hollywood said.

They talked for nearly another hour, and by the time the four-o'clock count came around, Young Hollywood had told Scooter the entire layout, except for what he didn't know.

The following morning, Young Hollywood and Scooter were up early. It was still dark outside when they went to breakfast. When they got inside the dining hall, everything was in disarray. Prisoners were standing against the wall. Some of them were holding their trays, while others were just watching everybody else.

Checking the scenery, Scooter's eyes found a long-distance stranger sitting at a square table on the other side of the dining hall. He saw Scooter, too, but he pretended he didn't. The guy's face and eyes fell back to the plate. He didn't know what would come next.

Scooter followed the line until he got his tray from the window. He whispered to Young Hollywood, "If I go to da hole, send me something."

Young Hollywood whispered back, "If you go to da hole, let it be fo' something."

He said that with such seriousness in his voice that Scooter had to stop and take a look and him. He nodded his head as if to say *"Okay."* Then he turned around and slapped the guy in his face with the tray. But Scooter didn't stop there. He was still quick and strong. He gripped the guy around his throat, and at that moment, two other guys rushed Scooter. One of them had a knife. Young Hollywood stood back as if he didn't have anything to do with it. Then all hell broke loose.

It wasn't until two days later that Young Hollywood began to realize what was really going on. Young Hollywood and Scooter were both in the hole. This was the J-building, on the west side of the prison. The two shared a cell together, and they were both still asleep when the inspection team came around.

Something told Scooter to get up. He listened to the voice that whispered in his head. He flipped the sheet back and slid from his bunk. When he stood up, he took a look at Young Hollywood. He was out cold, his mouth partly open. Scooter tapped his hand and whispered, "Get up, shawty. Fuck-ass inspection team comin' 'round."

Young Hollywood opened his eyes, and a murderous stare came from them. He only stared at Scooter for a brief second, and then his head fell back to the pillow. A loud, disturbing knock came from the door, and Scooter stared in that direction. Young Hollywood rose again and looked through the window.

There were several officers, captains, LTs, and wardens looking in. They were all nearly screaming in unison, "Get up!"

"Y'all get dressed and get ready for inspection! " one officer shouted.

"What's da motha' fuckin' problem?" a huge cert team officer asked.

Scooter grinned and shouted, "Suit up, fuck nigga." He held up his right hand and shot them a finger.

Then, a beautiful yellow female's face appeared in the small window. "Do we have a problem?" she asked.

Young Hollywood recognized the voice, and he squinted hard, trying to make the face. His heart damn near skipped a beat when he saw Sasha. He hopped down from the top bunk and went toward the door. "Excuse me," he said. Then he asked, "Who are you?"

"I'm the Deputy Warden of Care and Treatment."

Young Hollywood and Scooter both stared at her in complete, total silence. Neither one of them could believe their eyes.

Then she said, "Now get this cell straight and get dressed."

They both began straightening up their bunks and dressing quickly as possible. When the officers left their cell, Sasha was still standing there, her exotic eyes penetrating Young Hollywood. It'd been years since they'd seen one another. The anger and hatred was there, and she could see it in him, even as he tried to conceal his emotions. She moved away from the window and closed the flap.

Scooter turned to him and asked, "Shawty, how in da fuck did she make warden?" He was grinning ear to ear, but he was serious.

Young Hollywood folded his arms across his chest; he was lost in thought, in a world of his own. The question Scooter had asked was simply ignored. Still gazing at the door, he could hear her heels clicking against the concrete, but the sounds were fading away. Young Hollywood was still standing in the middle of the floor. He finally looked Scooter dead square in his eyes. "Dis doesn't go no farther than me and you, pimp." He pointed his finger at Scooter. "The old man had dis shit in the makin' da whole time." He smiled and displayed both rows of gold teeth. "Shawty, we 'bout ta lock dis whole motha' fuckin' camp down," Young Hollywood said.

"Yeah. Da ARS, You know I'm with it."

"What da fuck is da ARS?" Young Hollywood asked.

"Atlanta Revenue Service. These niggas got to pay their taxes."

Young Hollywood laughed and shook his head.

Three days later, they were released from the hole and placed back in population. They were separated again on the same side, just different dorms. Young Hollywood rolled his property into Dorm F-2. This dorm was live and buzzing with activity. An overcrowded skin game was going on at one table. A huge poker game was at another table. On the top range, there were at least twenty prisoners leaning on the rail, all staring down into the center floor. Once again, Young Hollywood didn't recognize a face.

Then somebody yelled out, "Lil' Terry!"

Young Hollywood looked around and saw an old associate who went by the name of Boogaloo. There was a tattoo wrapped around his entire neck that said "Zone One." The letters were deeply engraved in cursive letters and very noticeable. He walked up to Young Hollywood and extended his hand. Young Hollywood gripped his hand, and then they patted one another on the back. "Wuz up wit' chu, shawty?" Boogaloo asked.

"Some ol' shit, pimp. Still fightin' dees crackas, tryin' ta get my case overturned," Young Hollywood answered.

"Dat's wuz up." Boogaloo said. He quickly examined Young Hollywood from head to toe, his gold chain, watch, and the store items that he had had in his bag. Boogaloo looked back at Young Hollywood. "Shawty fuck wit' me on a pack of dem cigarettes."

"Let me get myself situated first," Young Hollywood said. Then he began studying the guy Boogaloo. *Where do I really know dis nigga from?* He asked himself. His stare was more anxious now as the freshness of his memory of Boogaloo came back to him. They were in the sixth and seventh grade together. He remembered the lies Boogaloo used to tell the class about how he used to do this and do that. He swore he was related to Run-DMC and Jam Master Jay. Young Hollywood grinned and asked, "You still be lyin'?"

Boogaloo frowned, and his facial expression filled with a mask of confusion. "Where all da slick hatin' comin' from, shawty?" he asked. He held his hand out as if to be saying, *"Hold on, pimp."* Then he added, "Nigga, we from dat city. We don't lollagag like dat."

He was cut short from his conversation when the officers came in from the sally port and began yelling, "Count time! Count time!"

# CHAPTER 50

The paparazzi rolled deep. They pulled up in front of A-Town Records and Studio in three vans, four cars, and one SUV Excursion. The rain was thick hours ago, but the hot sun had dried the majority of everything up. Hammer removed himself from the backseat of a gray Maybach and stepped out in a gray pinstriped suit and a fedora, puffing on a Cuban cigar. He had four certified goons rolling with him as well. They all climbed from the Maybach and stood around him as if he was the President of the United Fucking States.

The paparazzi rushed in, armed to the T with expensive camcorders and 35mm cameras. Flash bulbs began flashing, and nearly one dozen camcorders were aiming at Hammer. "Excuse me, Mr. Hayes. Is it true that A-Town Records has surpassed all the other major record labels in sales and has grossed more than $100 million in the last year?" one reporter asked.

Hammer removed his cigar from his mouth and let out a thin line of smoke directly at one of the cameras. "It ain't what you do, it's how you do it," he responded.

Another man in the mob asked, "Is it also true that if you meet an artist and he does not wish to sign with your label, you'll have him killed?"

Hammer smiled and walked into the glass doors of the studio, leaving his security team to block any unnecessary traffic. Inside the marble-floor lobby, Hammer bypassed several beautiful women who waited in a seating area in a group of bunched-up leather chairs. All this was becoming common now. Beautiful women flocked to the music industry by the thousands. The money was easier to obtain, and the rumored jacket-title that the rap game wore on its back was called the legal dope game. And when Frank White, the King of New York made the statement, "If a nickel bag is sold in the park, I want in," Hammer was on the same type of shit—only a little smarter though.

He moved toward one of the three elevators and was greeted by a handsome bellboy that appeared to be Italian and African-American. He wore a suit and tie and Gators on his feet. Hammer had nearly every male who worked for him in alligator-skin shoes. He had a thing for the reptile. The bellboy pressed a button, and the doors slid open. Hammer stepped inside, and so did he. They rode to Hammer's office floor, and when they exited, they were greeted well. Hammer was greeted with a standing ovation by his co-workers and staff. Nearly thirty people stood before him with loud cheering and clapping.

He removed his hat while his half of Cuban cigar was still smoking. He removed it from his mouth and held it between two pressed fingers. "What's the commotion about?" he said. His serious tone of voice and deadly eyes scanned the entire audience, and they caught on very quick.

The clapping stopped and the entire room fell silent. A tall woman in heels and with jet-black flowing hair stepped forward, and a bright smile spread evenly across her face. She looked at Hammer and handed him a piece of paper.

He took it, unfolded it, and began reading it to himself. A few seconds later, he raised his eyes at the lady and the staff. "So... I've been nominated to get the key to the city," he said. Then he walked off and paused at his office door. He turned and said to his staff. "How in the fuck the mayor gonna give a gangsta the key to the city?" Inside his office, he got behind his desk and leafed through a stack of papers that set before him, and then he came out of his jacket and shirt and removed his tie.

The phone rang and he answered it.

"You have a collect call from an inmate at a Georgia State Prison."

Hammer pressed the five to accept the call. "How you doin'?" Hammer asked.

"Still coolin'," Young Hollywood said and then asked, "You responsible for this move?"

Hammer nodded, even though his son couldn't see the nod. He responded, "Of course."

"Well, I'm good then. How Corleone doin'?" Young Hollywood inquired.

"Excellent. The best private school money can buy, and on top of that, he has a roll in a *Romeo and Juliet* play in a couple of months at the Fox Theater."

"Dat's wuz up." Then Young Hollywood asked, "Who he playin, Romeo?"

"I don't actually know for a fact. I do know it's a big event, basically for the kids though."

"Good business, good business. So what about dis end?"

"Whatever you need to talk to your people about, she's there strictly for you at your disposal." There was a short pause, and then Hammer said, "Now you do know that you also have to play your position. She dedicated to you and you only. This should keep you and hold you for a while until these lawyers get ready."

"All that is understandable," Young Hollywood commented.

Hammer spun around in his leather swivel and faced a huge life-sized portrait of Martin and Coretta King. He said to Young Hollywood, "Try your best to chill, no violence. Just get money, eat good, and have some fun."

"That shouldn't be too hard. Listen, when is you comin' to see me?" Young Hollywood asked.

"Probably next weekend," Hammer said.

"Check dat. I'll call you later dis week." Immediately after Young Hollywood's comment, the line went dead.

# CHAPTER 51

The first day Young Hollywood reported to the deputy warden's office, Sasha gave him the best head he'd had since he was twelve. It was her gift to him. Inside her office, the walls were covered with wood paneling. She had a huge, expensive oak desk decorated with African art pieces and an upgraded computer. Young Hollywood sat on the opposite side of the desk facing her. He always knew he'd see her again; he just thought it would be under different circumstances. He'd envisioned himself coming home from a long stretch and with long money to match. His conversation would be very short for a broad when he stepped into Magic City. The women would flock to him, and he would swagger check himself. There, he would see Sasha, his baby mama, the one he loved and cared for, the one that ran off on him.

She had put their son up for adoption, and that made his chest burn like hell. He wanted to question the situation about his money and his son, but he had given Hammer his word, and he wouldn't break that.

Now, sitting in the warden's office starring eye to eye with his ex was something unheard of. She finally broke the silence. "I know it's a lot of things goin' on in your head, questions you wanna ask and stuff like that. We'll get around to that, even though yo' dad told us not to talk about the past."

Young Hollywood just nodded his head, his eyes still focused in on her. "I can see good from my peripheral vision," Young Hollywood said.

"And what that suppose' to mean?" Sasha asked.

Young Hollywood stood up. "Get my OMS schedule printed out, and make me yo' orderly. I wanna start Monday, and I'll bring you a list of everything I need." He left her office without another word.

Sasha's eyes followed Young Hollywood as he disappeared from her office. She sat in silence for a moment, her elbows on the desk and the tip of her fingers pressed together. A vivid vision in her mind flashed to the good times they had and the beautiful son they created together.

Then there was the downfall of things: the robbery and the great loss of the street money that they had. She thought about her drug addiction and how she placed their son in a home and left him there without ever returning to see him. She punished herself for that, and deep down inside, she was hurting like hell. Now, with Hammer placing her in a position to straighten up her face, she would do just that.

When the following Monday came around, Young Hollywood reported to detail at six thirty in the morning. He knew he couldn't move like he wanted to, not yet anyway. He was slick and smoother than a bottle of Courvoisier XO Imperial, his mind as sharp as a razor.

He saw the head warden, a huge black guy in a tan suit. David Middleton was his name; he stood with a cigarette in his mouth, his eyes fixed on Young Hollywood. They met another gaze.

Young Hollywood was holding a broom in one hand and a plastic dust pan in the other. He walked up to the warden. "Good morning, sir."

The warden pulled on his cigarette, the smoke curling around his face. "Good mornin'," he responded back, and then he allowed his eyes to search Young Hollywood's nametag on his shirt. "Terry Keys, what prison did you come from?"

"Reidsville," Young Hollywood replied.

"Hard heads be at Reidsville. What you do to get there?"

Without hesitation, he responded, "Truthfully, a guy tried to rape me in Alto, and I offed 'im." The words came as deadly venom.

The warden dropped his half-cigarette to the ground and crushed it underneath his Stacy Adams. He looked Young Hollywood square in his eyes. "A man has to earn his respect and keep it." Without another word, he threw a hand up in the air and turned away from him and walked off.

Young Hollywood went inside Sasha's office; she was speaking to a sergeant about a grievance that had been filed against him. Young Hollywood grabbed a spray bottle and a cleaning rag. He began wiping. Pretending to be cleaning the waiting area, he wiped off tables and table legs. His eyes scanned the area, the wall shelves. There was a volume of red encyclopedias covering the first two shelves. Young Hollywood was thinking about a potential hiding spot.

Five minutes, later the sergeant came out of the office. He walked past Young Hollywood. They made eye contact, and neither one of them thought anything of it. Young Hollywood turned and looked at Sasha through the open blinds. She saw him and waved for him to come in. He walked through the door and closed it behind him.

He sat down on the leather sofa and dropped a folded piece of paper on top of her computer. She took it and hid it somewhere. Once again, their eyes gazed into one another's. Then, out of the blue, Young Hollywood said, "You got an extra cell phone?"

"I got an untraceable one for you. What else do you have on this paper that you need?"

"Fa starters, I need a pound of reefer."

"Don't be stupid. You and your daddy are millionaires. Why would—"

Young Hollywood was leaning deep in the sofa, and he whispered in the coolest tone of voice, "Bitch, never in yo' life do you question my authority or challenge my expertise."

Her beautiful green eyes glistened with excitement for some apparent reason. She actually saw that he still had power. His voice was demanding, and she loved that. She asked him, "What else?"

"Patron, my main thing is to help some of these other niggas eat, especially Scooter. He fucked up, too, you know."

"I'm not concerned about Scooter, and I really can't believe you still fuckin' wit' 'im anyway," Sasha said.

Young Hollywood shuffled to his feet, picked up his chemical bottle and cleaning rag, and stood before her. "Im'a take my break early today," he said. Then he asked, "Wuz fo' lunch?"

"You tell me. You the Don." A small grin spread across her lips. Young Hollywood stared at her, and she put on her most seductive look. He clenched his throbbing penis through his state pants. Her eyes followed. She stared at his print, and then she playfully flicked her tongue. He finally said, "Lobster tails covered in butter, cheese sticks, steak, and baked potatoes. I need a large lemonade too." Then he left her office.

It was nearly four hours later when Young Hollywood reported back to detail. The front entrance to the Deputy Warden of Care and Treatment's office was blocked off. He taped a sign on the door that read: WET WAX. DO NOT ENTER. He barricaded the front door with two brooms crossing one another. Then he actually poured fresh wax on the shiny tile floor and spread it evenly with a clean dust mop. Young Hollywood moved quickly.

Sasha was in her office, the blinds pulled closed. When Young Hollywood entered, she had the food laid out on a small table in Styrofoam trays. "Lock the door," she said and began stepping out of her cream-colored linen pants.

Young Hollywood turned and locked the door, and then he sat down on the sofa. He removed a meaty lobster tail from one of the trays. The butter was hot and in a small microwavable container by itself. He dipped it and sat back on the sofa in a very cool, relaxed manner.

Sasha was standing before him in fine cotton stockings, the fabric clinging to her legs like a second skin. Her vagina was neatly shaved and exposed. She moved toward him, still in her heels and a white blouse that she was now coming out of. When she got to Young Hollywood, she dropped to her knees before him, he spread his legs. She unbuttoned his pants and removed his rock-hard penis. She held it with both hands and used her tongue to playfully lick the full length of him. He tensed up a little and then relaxed. She filled her mouth with his penis, slowly deep-throating and slowly back up. He bit into the tasteful lobster tail, his eyes still on her.

She eased her left hand underneath the cushioned pillow next to him and came out with a small cell phone. She handed it to him, her soft, wet mouth still on his glossy black penis. She treated him with soft, gentle touches. Young Hollywood looked at the phone and flipped it open. Something told him to call Hammer. He followed his first mind; that was a habit he'd trained himself to do.

Hammer answered on the first ring. "Hello?"

Young Hollywood smiled at himself. This was the life, the high life, seriously. "Wuz up, OG?" he said to Hammer.

"I see you doin' good," Hammer said.

Young Hollywood looked down at Sasha; she was slobbering uncontrollably on his penis. He was being served like a true playa' should, even under these circumstances. He dipped the last piece of meaty lobster tail in the butter and stuffed it inside his mouth, chewed, and swallowed. "Yeah, I'm maintainin'. Jus' respresentin' da city, Daddy. Jus' representin' da city." He grabbed the back of Sasha's head and guided her in a slow rhythm, then slowly closed his eyes.

# CHAPTER 52

There were 25 floors, 479 rooms, and 23 suites at the Renaissance Atlanta Hotel downtown. Six Nine had a dramatic view of the city skyline from one of the presidential suites. He sat in front of the window in a comfortable lavender chair. He wore a Gucci printed smoking jacket with matching pajamas and slippers.

In his left hand, he held a rolled-up blunt of purple kush, and in his right he held a champagne glass filled with Hawaiian Punch and promethazine-codeine cough syrup. He'd come quite some distance in the past couple of months. His name was ringing like school bells in the city now. He laughed at that. It was a laugh that he held on the inside though; he didn't need too many people to see his happy side. He took a long, slow drag from the rolled blunt; the smoke enveloped him as he casually sipped from his champagne glass. Then he said in a low, whispering tone of voice. "I put fear in dees bitch-ass niggas. Yeah, big fear. Suckas stand down." He pulled the blunt again. "Fuck niggas runnin' 'round here disguising theyself as gangstas. Dat shit don't work wit' Six Nine."

Then a knock came from the door, a loud, thunderous one at that. Six Nine was shaken out of his deep, peaceful sleep and met the dangerous eyes of a comrade he'd befriended since his stay at the Fulton County Jail. He was on Rice Street, housed on the seventh floor with some of the worst criminals in the United States, due to the fact that Atlanta was the hub for major illegal activities. The guy who woke Six Nine was Louse Cannon, LC for short. LC and Six Nine clicked with one another after they fought knuckle to knuckle on more than four separate occasions, and each one of them had still possessed both top and bottom of their rose gold teeth. LC stood an even six feet, and wore his head clean shaven. He'd been awaiting trial on a double murder for the last six months, but he'd been stranded on Rice Street for the last three years with no money or any outside support. He now needed a miracle.

Six Nine looked up at him from his bunk. "Wuz up, shawty?" he asked, still trying to shake himself away from his dream.

"Dat nigga China Man jus' came through the door."

Six Nine really shook himself awake now. He looked up at LC, his face expression serious. "Fa real, shawty?" he asked, then he swung his legs out of bed. Excitement flashed from his eyes.

"Shawty, da nigga jus' drug his mattress in. He out there on da flo' right now." LC spread his humungous hands. Then he moved back to the cell door and pushed it wide open.

Six Nine pulled up next to him, and both of them looked downstairs from the top range. China Man was standing in the middle of the floor dapping cats and talking with a bunch of nobodies. Truthfully, Six Nine and LC had bonded so close and shared so many stories together. Nothing else mattered, except that the other two comrades who were also on the floor with them. Six Nine united his crew for a reason, and they all were formed right there on the seventh floor.

Lil' Willie, a notorious robber who emerged from a project called Capital Homes, came to the cell, standing five-four with wild dreadlocks hanging loosely everywhere. Lil' Willie had made a name for himself out in the streets of Atlanta also. He was only twenty-two years old but he had a quarter-million dollars at the age of fifteen. He had the heart and ambition to get rich, and where he lacked, Six Nine made up for it. He looked up to Six Nine like a big brother, and Six Nine respected the little motha' fucka' gangsta.

Six Nine inserted two fingers in his mouth and whistled. Half the dorm turned their head in his direction. That was when he and China Man made eye contact. Six Nine waved him up. China Man threw up a finger indicating him to hold on. That made him furious, but he tried hard not to show it. China Man continued talking to his audience, peons really. Six Nine kept his eyes on him

Lil' Willie yelled out, "Fuck you, pussy-ass nigga." He had a problem controlling his temper, and he'd been like that the majority of his life with enough heart to keep five men alive. How could he be stopped?

China man looked up, and so did his audience. He pointed his finger at himself. "You talking to me?" he asked. He didn't seem angry or anything by his words.

Then, from China Man's blindside, a huge fist smashed into his jaw. His knees wobbled, and then his legs collapsed from underneath him. When he hit the ground, the crowd scattered, and only one person was standing over him, staring down at him watching him sleep like a baby, blood seeping from his mouth. The guy that had just dropped China Man to the floor was named Angelo; they called him Big Low for short. He stood five-ten with wide, massive shoulders and huge arms. He was in his early thirties, with dark skin, thick lips, and long, crusty fingers. He looked up at the top range at Six Nine. "Wat' cha want me to do wit' 'im, shawty?" he asked in a deep Southern drawl.

Six Nine stared only for a few seconds, and then he said, "Bring his pussy ass up to da room."

Big Low lifted him from the concrete floor. China man was lightweight. He didn't weigh more than 165. Big Low snatched him up on his shoulder and went toward the stairs with him. He carried him like two Hefty trash bags.

Inside the cell, Six Nine was at the stainless steel sink brushing his teeth and tongue. By the time he started washing his face, Big Low was entering the cell with China Man draped over his shoulder. LC and Lil' Willie were playing casino on the bed. Everybody stopped doing what they were into. Big Low dropped China Man in the center of the floor. Lil' Willie stood over him, leaned down, and slapped him back to his senses. The sound rang out, and China Man batted his eyes open and stared around in a daze, stunned and unaware of his surrounding. His eyes went to Big Low, Lil' Willie, LC, and finally Six Nine when he knelt down over him.

"You got to be da stupidest nigga in da world." Six Nine twisted China Man's shirt in a tight ball, clenching it in his fist. He drew him closer to him. Then he said in a calm manner, "Word on da streets is dat you got dem bricks."

China Man took a deep breath, and his chest rose and fell. His slanted eyes staring in pure anger, and then he said, "Yeah, I fuck wit' dem. Shit dry on my end right now."

"I need money anyway," Six Nine said. "And dis what we gonna do. We gonna take you downstairs and get on dis phone. You gon' call whoeva you need to and let 'em know dat somebody gonna come buy and pick dat money up."

"How much money you talkin?" China Man asked, even though he felt kind of leery about the situation. He knew he couldn't be getting robbed inside the county jail.

"All of it." Six Nine smiled and flashed his gold teeth, serious as a heart attack. China Man might have been the first person in history to be kidnapped and held for ransom money in a damn county jail.

Nearly six hours later, Lil' Willie got on the phone and called his nineteen-year-old sister to confirm the situation about the money, which she was sent to pick it up from China Man's girlfriend. When he hung up the phone, he turned to Six Nine with a smile on his face. "She said it's two trash bags full of money," he said, his eyes wide with excitement.

Six Nine saluted his team and said calmly, "Dat should be enough to get y'all niggas on da turf. Bond fare, lawya fare, and then we'll introduce da city to the Black Cartel."

# CHAPTER 53

Young Hollywood was a chain-gang celebrity. He really didn't like all the publicity, but since it was available, why not enjoy it? Nearly three weeks had passed, and he was deeply situated. He had Scooter flipping a pound of reefer every week. They had the camp flooded with x-pills and prepaid cellular phones. The money was coming in loads, and Scooter was having the time of his life. Despite being in prison, he was living good.

Young Hollywood was kicked back in his cell contemplating his next move. Then his cell phone rang—or rather vibrated. He laid the book down and checked the number before answering. It was a 404 area code, but he didn't recognize the number. He answered it anyway. "Yeah, who dis?" he said.

"Yeah, nigga…I know what cha did last summa," the voice said from the other end. He tried to disguise his voice, and that made whoever it was sound like he was talking through a funnel.

Young Hollywood sat up and swung his legs out of bed. He slipped his feet into a comfortable pair of bedroom shoes and stood up, the phone still pressed against his face. "Getting too much money to play games, pimp," he said, and then threw another oyster into his mouth.

A knock came from the door. He turned and looked through the glass and noticed Boogaloo standing on the other side with a cell phone pressed against his face. "I'm getting money, too, shawty," he said into the phone.

Young Hollywood closed his phone and stuffed it in his pocket. He moved toward the door and pressed the button to let Boogaloo in.

He stepped inside and closed the door behind him. "Damn, pimp. You don't fuck' wit' niggas from da city no mo'?"

Young Hollywood walked over to his bunk and sat down, removed his feet from his slippers and lay back down with his hands propped behind his head. His eyes focused dead on Boogaloo. He said in the calmest tone of voice, "Shawty, you must think I'm something to play wit'."

Boogaloo stared at him long and hard, and when he finally realized that Young Hollywood was serious as a cancer victim in his last stages, he removed the phone from his face. "Nigga, you jus' take shit too serious." He slipped his own cell phone inside his pocket, moved to the rear of the cell, sat down on the desk stool, and faced Young Hollywood.

Young Hollywood didn't bother to face him. He continued to look forward, gazing at the door. "I'm getting wiser. My mind is more developed, and I'm focusin' on some bigga shit," Young Hollywood said.

Boogaloo pulled a pack of Bugler from his sock and lit up a rolled cigarette. He squinted against the smoke and quickly let out a long steam from his mouth. "So you gettin' wiser. Where you learnin' your knowledge from?"

"Suckas, lames, fuck niggas." There was a slight tone of aggression in his voice, and then he sat up and faced Boogaloo, his eyes deadlier than Botulinus toxin. "They keep me on my toes."

Boogaloo noticed this also, and when he stood up, Young Hollywood did also and slapped him across his face so hard he spun to his right and came back quick with right jab. Young Hollywood blocked it and wrapped up Boogaloo's arm with a powerful twist, then pressed his fist hard against Boogaloo's nose. He felt the thin bone and gristle collapsing underneath his powerful blow. Boogaloo let out a yelp as blood gushed from his nose and stained Young Hollywood's clothes and cell floor. Young Hollywood removed Boogaloo's phone from his pocket and shoved him out into the dormitory.

Boogaloo was on the other side of the door looking in, his face covered in blood. "Dat's fucked up, shawty," he said as he smeared blood on the window. "I'm real nigga, pimp. You gon' see."

"Get da fuck away from my cell," Young Hollywood growled. He pointed a finger. His teeth gripped tightly together.

Boogaloo went to the front of the dorm, his face swollen and was hurting like hell. He knocked on the window, and the officer in the control saw how bad he was bleeding. He pressed a button and allowed Boogaloo to enter the sally port. By now, the floor officers were coming to his aid. Boogaloo brushed passed them. "I'm goin' to medical." He then snatched his shirt off and held it to his face. Red bloodstains trailed him as he went.

Two days later, Boogaloo returned back to the same dorm, and after being interrogated by the cert team and a few LTs about cell phones and drugs, he was released from the hole. They weren't concerned about his broken nose. Both of his eyes had turned black and purple. Boogaloo dragged his property into Cell 242. His roommate was an older white guy who was covered with tattoos and wore his head clean shaved. He didn't bother to look Boogaloo's way nor attempt to help him with his property.

A knock come at the door. Boogaloo turned around and stared dead into Young Hollywood's eyes. Again, he gave a cold stare. That was him though: serious about his issues and with a swag deadlier than a team of Navy SEALs. He entered the cell without being invited. Boogaloo had a lot of heart himself, but deep down inside he knew he couldn't match the man that stood before him. He extended a balled fist, and Young Hollywood dapped him.

"I heard them folks was askin' questions," Young Hollywood said.

"Yeah. They mentioned Scooter's name. You didn't come up though," Boogaloo said.

Young Hollywood nodded slowly, his hands crossed in front of him. He actually liked Boogaloo now that he'd put him in his place, and the best part about it was that he'd kept his mouth closed.

However, the next day after Scooter got word of the situation, he paid the Gangsta Desiples two ounces and a phone to have Boogaloo beat with baseball bats out in the yard. Young Hollywood didn't know about this. As they say, what are friends for?

# CHAPTER 54

It was two weeks before Christmas, and the winter of 1999 was extremely cold in Atlanta. Six Nine and two other associates were parked in the parking lot of a rundown set of apartments on Campbellton Road called Cascade Pines. The night air was thin, and the three goons were staring at one apartment in general. They were equipped with two short-stocked AK-47s that could be easily concealed under a waist-length leather jacket.

Six Nine cracked his window from the backseat and allowed the smoke to seep away from his lit Newport. He watched the upstairs apartment window from the rear of the four-door boxed Chevy. He carried a Glock .40 in his waist and another one sitting across his lap. He wore latex gloves on his hands, and he was extremely high on cocaine. His eyes stretched even wider when he saw a silhouette, a figure from behind the curtain. He tapped the front passenger on his shoulder and said in a very aggressive tone of voice, "Somebody in da house, shawty." He said it like that and meant every word of it, as if someone had told him there wasn't' anyone inside.

Six Nine tightened his belt with the cigarette clenched between his lips, still smoking. He tucked this other Glock in his waistline. Then he adjusted his brown leather Polo jacket. He opened the rear door. Six Nine removed his cigarette from his mouth as he was swinging his long legs from the car. "I'm goin' in," he said. "Y'all niggas can sit here if you want to." He was out of the car.

The passenger in the front seat looked at the driver. Their stare lasted only three seconds. The passenger tucked the AK-47 underneath his black three-quarter-length jacket. He got out and followed Six Nine. He moved casually, climbing the stairs one step at a time. Moments later, he was on Six Nine's heels while Six Nine was still smoking on the same cigarette from the car. He knocked on the door lightly with the barrel of the Glock. Within seconds, he heard the thumping of footsteps on the other side of the door. He calmly drew on his cigarette without using his hands. Music was bumping somewhere in the background, a tune that would be tattooed on his memory chip forever.

"Who is it?" a squeaky woman's voice asked from the inside.

Six Nine looked to his associate. He actually smiled and thought to himself, *The bitch must be stupid.* Six Nine transformed as if a beast of some sort had come out of him. He stepped back, raised his leg, and with a powerful kick, he tore the wood from the seal of the door. He then rammed it all the way in with his shoulder.

The female on the inside of the apartment screamed out in horrifying pain. When they entered the apartment, Six Nine raised his gun at the female who was running desperately toward the rear bedroom. "Bookie!" she yelled out. Her words trailed off when Six Nine let three powerful rounds loose at her. They slammed into her back, all three. That flipped her to the floor in the hallway.

Six Nine ran over and looked down at her. Her hand was still twitching. He put two more to the base of her skull. Then she was motionless.

His associate removed his AK, his eyes covered with a Yankees fitted cap for a disguise. He began checking the kitchen cabinets while Six Nine entered the first bedroom to the left. A human-sized lump was under the bedspread, and he snatched it back, with his Glock .40 aimed and cocked.

It was a buck-naked midget woman with gold teeth and green contact lenses. "Please don't shoot me," she begged for her life.

Six Nine let a bullet disappear through her forehead. Her head snapped back, and she slumped to the bed. Then several shots rang out from the other bedroom through the walls. Sheetrock began flying. Fine white dust was hanging in the air. Six Nine moved back into the hallway, his eyes even wider now than a few minutes ago. His adrenaline was flowing more now than ever before.

Several more shots rang out, and then in a split second, a guy appeared in the hallway. He aimed some type of mini-machine gun with an infrared beam dancing all over the place.

Six Nine was quick on the trigger. He gunned the guy down without warning, and then he ran toward him, moved across him and into the bedroom where he noticed another guy hanging out the window with a canvas duffel bag.

He jumped out after he made eye contact with Six Nine. He heard a couple more shots and thought to himself, *It must be Dennis.* He looked downstairs through the shattered window. He saw the guy limping with the duffel bag. Then he jumped out of the window himself—one, maybe two stories wasn't a long jump for a guy who was six-nine. When he hit the ground, he aimed his Glock, and it clicked. He tucked it and then removed his other one and aimed it at the limping guy who carried the duffel bag. When Six Nine shot him, he snatched the bag before he hit the ground.

Inside the cell on Rice Street where Six Nine, Lil' Willie, LC, and Big Low were all gathered, everybody sat in silence, listening to Six Nine give his testimony, his true story about what had him trapped on

the seventh floor.

Lil' Willie, the youngest of the bunch looked at Six Nine with a moment of silence, and then he drained a Styrofoam cup and chewed on a small piece of ice. He finally said, "Shawty, if you telling da truth, you ain't suppose to tell us nothing." He crushed the ice between words.

Six Nine looked at Lil' Willie long and hard, and then his eyes drifted to LC and then Big Low. They all looked at Six Nine, staring at their leader, listening with clear ears. "I have been known to kill a couple niggas for no reason at all." He paused and shrugged his shoulders. "And it be like dat sometimes." His eyes darted to each and every one of them, waiting for a response or a show of any sign of weakness. To his surprise, they were thirsty for more. Six Nine wedged his fingers together and continued on with his conversation. "From here on, we are the fo' heads of our cartel. We are each other's strength. We will neva turn our backs on one another fo' nothing unless death divide us, and eventually, it will. But fa da meantime, we'll enjoy dis shit." He paused, leaned forward with elbows resting on his knees, and said, "I got a plan that'll get us all rich ten times over. But I'ma need y'all three on da street to pull it off. Now all three of y'all got bonds. A few weeks ago, we didn't have the money, but now we do. First da money dat we took from dat sissy-ass nigga China Man. That'll get all three of y'all good lawyas. When y'all get on da street, I'ma turn y'all on to my million-dolla streak. Second, y'all gonna build a strong team of soldiers. Niggas from Atlanta only! No outsiders. Nothin' but Grady babies. And I mean dat."

"How many niggas you talkin bout?" LC asked.

Six Nine thought for a second and replied, "At least forty."

221

Cole Hart

"Forty Niggas?' Lil' Willie said. "Fuck we gon' do wit' forty niggas?"

Six Nine smiled, flashing his expensive gold grill. "Take over da fuckin' city. What else?" And he meant it.

# CHAPTER 55

Hammer drove his glossy Black Phantom through Summer Hill projects while talking and laughing on his cell phone. Corleone sat in the passenger's seat, cramming his neck to see the flashy cars, wet with exotic paint and big shiny chrome rims. Beautiful hood stars were everywhere. Some wore candy-pink weave, others wore platinum lace bob-cut wigs. Corleone was taking it all in as his tiny eyes scanned the streets.

Hammer took notice of him out of the corner of his eye. "Hold for a second," he said into his cell phone, and then he moved it away from his face, looked toward Corleone, and said, "What's the matter?"

Corleone snapped his neck and spun his head back toward his grandfather. His eyes were in question.

Hammer pulled the Phantom to the side of the street. The name on the sign read "Frazier." It was nearing dark, and the activity was coming more to life by the minutes. He stopped the Phantom. Crews of hustlas were huddled on a porch across the street from him. They knew who he was because he was respected all over the city. He'd developed into a household name.

"Bored," Corleone finally said.

Hammer laughed, switched off the engine, and opened the door.

Corleone opened his also and climbed out of the passenger's seat and closed the door behind him.

Hammer spoke back into the phone, "Let me call you back a lil' later."

It was a woman on the other end, and she said in the sexiest tone of voice, "Why darling?"

Hammer flipped his phone closed and politely placed it inside his pocket. He eased to the back door and opened it and removed a plastic bag with two Styrofoam trays filled with macaroni and cheese, snap beans cooked with turkey, steaming white rice, and gravy. The cube steaks were cooked well done and tender.

Corleone came to his granddaddy's side. "I can carry the drinks," he said in a cheerful tone of voice.

Hammer handed him two Styrofoam cups in paper containers. "You got?"

Corleone sucked his teeth and replied, "Dis light, Granddaddy."

When they walked up to the front porch of the apartment, a stout older lady with a snow-white afro and two open-faced gold teeth greeted them at the door. She walked slumped over at the waist and had a bad nervous problem. She pushed the storm door open. Corleone stepped inside first, and she kissed his cheek. Then she hugged Hammer as he held her tight with one arm, the food in the other. "Bless yo' heart, baby," she said into his ear. She grabbed his hand and guided him through the living room and into the first bedroom. She swung the door open, and in the corner of the room, a salt-n-pepper-haired man was sitting in a wheelchair facing the window. Hammer cleared his throat. Corleone did the same thing, imitating his granddaddy. The man in the wheelchair spun himself around and faced his longtime friend. The old lady tapped Hammer's shoulder and took the bag from his hand. He okayed it with a smile and nod. She removed Corleone from the room as well.

The door closed, and Hammer took a seat in a comfortable chair. He crossed his legs and stared at the man in the wheelchair. He was of a light complexion with freckles all over his face. He wore a shiny gold rope around his neck. He stared at Hammer, then he removed the blanket, and to no surprise his legs were missing, clean from his body. He hopped out of the wheelchair and bounced to the floor with a loud *thump* and walked around on his hands. Red was his name, independent and still angry with himself. He moved to a table, pressed his strength on one hand, and removed a chessboard and pieces that were carefully situated in a small wooden suitcase.

Hammer studied him, the old gangster who had once wreaked havoc all over the city in the late eighties and early part of the nineties. His life changed in the course of a weekend when he and three other associates were ambushed on a reverse robbery. His associates were killed instantly. They held Red for ransom money and chopped off both his legs. He was left in the trunk of a Cutlass to bleed to death. How he survived was something he never told anyone, not even Hammer.

Hammer set up the table.

Red was back in his wheelchair and rolling toward Hammer. When they got face to face with one another, Red reached out his hand.

Hammer shook it.

"Good to see you," Red said, his eyes darting back and forth. He began placing his chess pieces in place.

Hammer situated his also, and then he asked, "How you feelin'?"

Red moved a piece on his side of the board and answered, "The same way I was feelin' dis time last week."

Hammer's eyes were on the board now because he had to watch Red's half-slick ass. Hammer moved a piece and said, "Ain't no reason to have an attitude. I'm on yo' side."

Red cut his eyes up to Hammer's and then studied rooks and pawns. Hammer knew something was on the old gangsta's mind.

Red moved.

Hammer moved.

Red moved again and said, "I heard you got a death threat."

Hammer moved and replied, "Yeah. Nothin' serious though. These niggas 'round ain't nothin' but a joke. They can talk it, but ain't nobody walkin' it."

Red nodded his head; it was his turn to move. He did, and then he responded, "You can't underestimate some of these young fools. Lot of 'em don't know the meaning of respect and loyalty. New breed of niggas out here now."

"Will they go to the extreme though?" Hammer asked, and then he moved. "They just not built like that, Red."

"Dat's yo' theory, Hammer. When the last time you checked out Fox Five News?"

Hammer laughed, and then his smile faded. "Seriously, I'm captivated by the new era, but you give these niggas too much fuckin' credit." His eyes turned cold and he insisted, "In order fa a motha' fucka' to have ultimate victory, you must be ruthless."

There was a long silence.

"Once again, Hammer, don't take this city fa granted." He moved, and in a low tone, he said, "Checkmate."

"Humph. Just that easy huh?" Hammer folded his arms and asked.

"Jus' dat easy," Red replied.

Hammer stood, walked to the window, and looked out where he'd parked his Phantom. Kids were playing and riding bicycles. Young hustlers stood in huddles, plotting on another lick or something of that sort. This made Hammer think. Then his cell phone rang. He removed it from his pocket and answered, "Hello?"

"Hey, this Sasha. I need to see you in person."

He exchanged a few more words with her, and then he hung up. He looked back at Red.

Red said, "Those young niggas did dis to me remember." He pointed at his lower body.

# CHAPTER 56

A small two-bedroom apartment was crowded with goons in the living room area, nearly twenty of them, ranging from age fifteen to twenty one years old. They were ill tempered, hungry for money and fame, and were willing to do anything to get it. This was Lil' Willie's team, trained to go on his command only. He loved the respect and loyalty they'd shown toward him. Since he'd been released from the county jail, he'd made a tremendous turn in his life. Once a coke sniffer, heavy drinker, and unlimited kush marijuana smoker, he was now focused, with a killer ambition and a strong team behind him. He just couldn't be stopped.

He emerged from one of the bedrooms with a finesse type of swagger. A Ruger revolver with an infrared beam hung from his leather shoulder holster. In his hand he carried bottled spring water and a DVD. Inside the living room area, it smelled of cigarettes and purple haze marijuana. He fanned his hand in the air and went straight to the DVD player and inserted the disc. A wide projector screen was set up in the corner, and the lights were cut off and curtain closed. The room was nearly dark.

Lil' Willie cleared his throat, got the team of goons' attention, and the room became totally silent. His eyes searched the crowd, and then he spotted a young guy with dreads laughing under his breath. Lil' Willie pointed to him. The young guy's face straightened all the way up. He made eye contact with Lil' Willie, who crunched his finger telling him to come to him. The young guy stood. He had deep, hollow eyes, and his face was slowly turning into a frown. He walked up to Lil' Willie and towered over him.

A dangerous look flashed over Lil' Willie's face. "Who da fuck you muggin', shawty?" His head cocked to one side, the words rolled off his tongue like Botulinus toxin.

The young sixteen-year-old dread tried his best to get himself together. Then he said, "Nobody."

Lil' Willie nodded as if he was impressed. He tapped the young goon on his shoulder and asked, "You know how to use a choppa?"

The young goon grinned, his smile bright. "Real good choppa skills on deck."

In the corner was a Russian-made AK with a 100-round drum attached. Lil' Willie pointed to it. "Get dat," he demanded.

The young, eager goon moved toward the corner and retrieved the AK

"Stay there," Lil' Willie said. He pointed a straight finger.

He stood there with a confused look across his face.

"Now, with both hands, raise the AK up over yo' head."

He did.

"Now jog in place, and don't let it down. If you let it down, you'll let me down. Then I'll be forced to use defense against you." He pointed to his forehead and said, "Use yo' fuckin' brain." He turned toward the DVD player and pressed a button. He then took the remote control and took a seat in a front row of folding chairs. The movie *Heat* popped on the screen. He pressed the button and went to the armored truck scene. "Y'all niggas pay attention," was all he said.

The room turned dark except for the flashing from the projector screen. Lil' Willie skipped scenes and went to the bank robbery scene.

"Dis wuz up." A voice came from the crowd. "Study da shit, nigga. We got to do dis shit."

LC had only been released from the county jail three days now, and in those three days, all he did was focus on his plan and goals, and that was to assemble his own ruthless team—a team strictly designed to scope out major drug dealers, kingpins, and celebrities. To do this, he had to look the part. Six Nine had taught him that: the finesse game, the trick of the eye.

He had enough time to have it tattooed on his memory forever while staying inside his small bedroom in his auntie's Summer Hill apartment. From the upstairs window, he parted the curtain and scanned the street activity. It was buzzing, live as usual. However, LC was definitely on some other shit. He finally sat down on the edge of his bed and rubbed his hand across his bald head. His mind was working, ticking like a second hand on an expensive wristwatch.

A small flat-screen TV was positioned on the dresser top. He wasn't in the mood to watch it, but he needed to a kill a little time. The remote sat beside him, He grabbed it and pressed the power button. The local show *Atlanta Homes* was on, and that caught LC's attention. The first red brick home he saw was a six-bedroom. It had a three-car garage and a million-dollar price tag. He was impressed; he wanted something flashy and expensive like that. Then the phone rang. He moved with quickness and removed the cordless phones from the stand. "Hello."

"Wuz up, shawty?" Six Nine said from the other end. "First thang in da morning, soon as Greenbrier open up, you need to be there. Go to the World Foot Locker. Buy yo'self three pair Js, the same color and size. When you go to the counter, it's gon' be a white bitch there. She da manager. She gon' ask you wuz yo' favorite position, and you gon' say, 'Six Nine'."

LC grinned and said to himself, "The thought of this guy." "When you say dat she gonna ring up the shoes and she gon give you another bag. A quarter million cash gon be in there, shawty. You already know what to do."

With a serious tone of voice, LC said, "I got cha, pimp, and dat's on everythang."

"I'll call you back in three days. You should be situated by then. Make sho you watch out fa them suckas, shawty."

"I'm on it," he said. Then he asked, "You need anythang?"

"Jus fa you to handle business."

"It's done."

Then the line went dead.

# CHAPTER 57

The following morning, the mall hadn't even opened yet, and LC waited patiently in the backseat of a taxicab. The driver of the cab was an older black guy who chewed tobacco and spit nasty-looking spit out the window. Garth Brooks was playing on the radio, and the country singer was driving LC crazy. *This guy's twisted,* he thought. "Can you cut dat shit down or off or somethin?" LC yelled out, his frown spread angrily across his face.

The driver cut his eyes to LC in the rearview mirror.

He stared back at the driver long and hard. He was itching to remove his pistol from his waistline and put his country-music-loving brain fragments across the front window. He checked his watch and caught a grip of himself. It was five minutes till nine. More cars began filling the parking lot, and it seemed as if the early-morning sun was shining directly in the back window. He frowned and tried to block the rays with his hand.

The driver finally decided to shut off the radio. Garth Brooks's voice was gone like the wind and they sat in total silence.

Thirty minutes later, LC exited the mall with three large shopping bags. Two Nike shoeboxes were stuffed with a quarter-million dollars in cash. LC bounced back in the rear seat of the cab and closed the door. "Back to Summa Hill," he said causally. He was smiling to himself like the devil's advocate.

The driver looked at him long and hard in the rearview mirror.

LC caught him staring instead of pulling off, and he asked, "What is yo motha' fuckin' problem?" His mouth was slightly twisted and parted, revealing his glistening gold teeth.

As a matter of fact, his look was so deadly that the driver became so terrified that his hands began twitching nervously. He started the engine, gave LC a wave through the mirror and a half-ass grin to follow.

When LC arrived back at his auntie's apartment, he stepped out with his Foot Locker bags. He eased to the front driver's side window and handed the driver a folded crisp one-hundred-dollar bill. The driver nodded his thanks. He began easing the cab off, and LC just shook his head side to side as he walked up to the front door of the apartment.

Inside, he went straight upstairs to his bedroom and locked the hollow door behind. He went to bed, not even caring about the tennis shoes. The two boxes of money were removed from the plastic Foot Locker bags. Duct tape was lined around the boxes like a cross. He pulled a single-edge razor from the top of his dresser that was wedged inside the size fourteen shoeboxes and flipped the tops off the both of them. Stacks of one-hundred-dollar bills lined the top of the boxes in neat, even rows, tightly wrapped in thick, beige rubber bands. LC's mouth watered as if he were eating three different flavors of Jolly Ranchers. He rubbed his hands together before he began finger fucking it. He slowly removed three thick stacks and peeled them back just enough so the money could roll off his thumb.

Then he got on the phone and called up three certified headhunters who all lived right around the corner on Crew Street. It didn't take them long to get there. The three associates arrived with dreads and bloodshot eyes, so black they looked purple, and they were hungrier than a Cuban refugee. The trio was all related.

LC took them upstairs and revealed his hand without warning. He showed them the money and talked with them for hours about their position and what they had to do. They needed guns, but they wouldn't buy them.

Two pawnshops were raided the same night. They stole weapons, army fatigues, Kevlar bulletproof bodysuits, and all the jewelry they could move. The next morning, LC and Big Low arrived at an exotic car dealership in a rental car with a duffel bag full of money. Inside they went, directly to the showroom floor. LC wanted the aqua-blue Aston Martin, and Big Low had his eyes set on a glossy black Maserati, four doors. They both leased for $2,500 a piece a month. *No problem,* they thought, and paid up for four months in advance and drove them both off the lot.

From there they followed each other through congested traffic across town. They slipped in and out of Lenox Mall in less than an hour and capped a few pieces of clothing—expensive shit too. When you ride foreign and you're from the hood, there's a good chance that you'll be wearing French- and Italian-made attire that other peers can't even pronounce.

LC drove with pure confidence, as if it were something he was already used to. He leaned slightly to the left, his hand casually clutching the steering wheel. The glossy aqua-blue paint on the expensive machine was sparkling under the sun. LC caught Big Low in his rearview mirror. His black-on-black New Era cap was slightly tilted to the left, and he was bobbing his head out of control as if he were listening to the hardest rap song out.

That made LC switch on his radio with the press of a button that was located on the steering wheel. He went to 107.5, and a hard, thunderous beat with a touch of other musical instruments came pouring through the speakers. Some guy they called Mossberg was flowing over the beat with a deep Southern drawl that made their skin crawl. LC was instantly hyped, and his adrenaline began pumping in his veins. The song was called "Tour de City," and LC grinned when he mentioned Summer Hill. When the song went off the radio, the DJ praised Mossberg and announced that he'd just signed a six-figure deal with A-Town Records. When he heard that, LC's entire demeanor changed. He picked up his cell phone just as he was coming to a red light. He dialed Big Low's number in his car. "You jus' heard dat new nigga on da radio?" he asked Big Low.

"Hell yeah. Shawty givin' it to da ass too," Big Low roared back through the phone.

The light turned green, and LC followed the traffic. He spoke back into his cell phone, "He jus' signed a deal wit' dat nigga who Six Nine beefin' wit'."

"You damn sho right, A-Town Records," Big Low said. He didn't sound like he liked Mossberg anymore, and whoever Six Nine's enemies were, they were also enemies with the entire Black Cartel.

# CHAPTER 58

Hammer sat next to the oval-shaped swimming pool in a Ralph Lauren home leather armchair with brass nail heads. The African sat next to him in an identical chair. Corleone came off the diving board and waved his hand in the air at his granddaddy before hitting the water. Hammer never ignored his grandson; even if he was in the middle of a conversation, he'd somehow still acknowledged him. Hammer waved. "I see you," he said, and then turned his attention back to Kangoma, the African. "I'm through with the heroin as of now. You've made good money, I've made good money. You got your family, and your wife has her own business. You'd break her head if you were to go to the federal penitentiary for the rest of your life," Hammer whispered.

A middle-aged lady dressed to be a professional housekeeper appeared from a sliding glass door with a silver tray that held filled champagne glasses and Bolivar cigars, snips, and a fancy lighter. She set their glasses on a small marble table between them.

Hammer got his cigar and snipped the end and twirled it between his lips before lighting it up.

The African did the same. He lit up and then said, "I got more family and friends over there. They still need my help."

"I want—no, not want, but *need*—you to take a year to eighteen months off. If heat gets on you, it gets on me. I'm the entire chess board... for both sides."

Kangoma pulled his cigar. He looked out across the pool.

Corleone was making laps.

Hammer was looking in the same direction. He yelled out, "how many?"

Corleone yelled out, "This fo', Granddaddy." He sounded winded, but he continued stroking the water and flopping his feet.

Hammer stared out into the water, lost in thought, and then he said to the African, "By then my son should be home."

Later that night, Hammer made sure Corleone was tucked in and comfortable. He sat on the bed next to his grandson and casually rubbed his face with the back of his hand.

His dreamy, exotic eyes were batting, nearly about to close. "Tell me a story," Corleone said.

Hammer twisted his mouth and responded, "You know them all already."

Corleone shook his head and said, "Not 'bout my daddy."

Hammer pinched his cheeks with both hands. "Soon to come," he said, then added, "Now take yo' butt to sleep." Hammer stood up and kissed Corleone on the forehead.

Corleone looked at him and whispered, "I got a girlfriend."

"Only one?" Hammer asked sharply.

He nodded with a smile, and his eyes never left his grandfather's.

"Wuz her name?"

"Shakenna," he whispered. "Her grandmamma know you too."

Hammer was impressed, but he shrugged it off. Before he left the boy's room, Hammer said, "Well maybe we need to take them both out to dinner. I'm a people person."

Corleone snatched the covers back and dug his feet into the mattress until he was in an upright position, a broad smile stretched all over his face. "Shakeena is in the *Romeo and Juliet* play with me. Her grandmamma rich, too, like us."

Hammer grinned and said, "Long as you know."

Corleone wasn't about to let him leave.

"What does her grandmamma look like?" Hammer asked.

"She real pretty, Granddaddy, wit' long, wavy hair like an Indian. She keep two body guards wit' her too."

"You sure know a lot about her." He stood up again, anxiously making his way to the door. He stopped and turned. "You tell Shakeena that I need to meet her grandmother," he said seriously, and then he left.

Nearly a week passed, and Hammer had finally arranged a private dinner date with the so-called star-studded grandmother. Hammer and Corleone rode in the rear of a luxurious stretch limousine. Three of Hammer's goon associates rode in the back with them as well. The artist Mossberg was flowing through the speakers and had everybody's head bobbing in unison. The limousine came to a halt and in front of an exclusive restaurant somewhere in Buckhead.

No more than fifteen minutes later, Hammer and Corleone were being escorted to a private seating area arranged with oversized leather furniture and prestigious marble tables covered in linen cloths. It didn't take Hammer long to take to his surroundings, and the closer they got to their table, the more eager Hammer became when his eyes locked onto this beautiful, long-legged woman with flawless skin. Her hair was long, but she wore it pinned up. Her neck sparkled with diamonds. There were four rows of them, and it looked to be worth more than a million dollars. She wore a strapless black dress and matching heels. Shakeena stood next to her. Her young smile was just as beautiful as her grandmother's. She ran and hugged Corleone, and Hammer introduced himself to the lady with his huge hand extended. She extended her hand to him; her fingers were long, with manicured nails. They shook hands, and Hammer realized she had soft, delicate skin—a real woman's touch. They stared into one another's eyes.

"Nice to meet you," she said proudly. She didn't look a tad bit over thirty, but over the phone, she'd told him she was fifty-one years old. Hammer couldn't believe it. She was extraordinarily beautiful.

He gave her a good-hearted smile and locked his eyes into hers. He was actually lost for words for a moment. Then he said, "I've been waiting over forty years for this." He was still holding her hand.

She smiled even more with a million-dollar grill. Her teeth were white, pretty, and even. Her name was Atiya, which meant "gift." She was a rich Arab woman who was about to be swept off her feet.

The four sat down. Hammer and Atiya jumped straight into a long conversation concerning the kids and the *Romeo and Juliet* play. A well-dressed waiter arrived and they all ordered and talked more. They were feeling one another for sure.

They ate Cajun chicken Alfredo with tomatoes, green onions, and classic Alfredo sauce. Hammer told her about his businesses, and she told him about hers. Between her and her two Arab brothers, they owned over twenty BP and Texaco gas stations throughout the South. She had trucking companies and oil tankers in Texas. Hammer was impressed by all of this, and the words that came to him were, *Arab money*.

The next day, Hammer met with her again. They went to a classical restaurant that played live jazz. Atiya hadn't experienced anything like it before. They talked more, neither one of them lying to each other. That night, Hammer got his first kiss from her. He was progressing, and that was what he needed.

Two weeks later, she and Hammer flew to Paris on a leased jet for lunch. They were back in Atlanta the same night. She enjoyed Hammer and his adventurous stories. She adored his swagger too. The way he moved spoke with so much confidence.

# CHAPTER 59

The tattoo gun the Mexican used wasn't homemade. Young Hollywood was in his cell sitting on the toilet facing the wall while Jose covered his entire back with free world ink. Huge, exotic lettering spelled out "Young Hollywood, Zone 1 Certified." He had two AK-47s crossing one another. Two more of his homeboys were in the room as well. Clouds of marijuana smoke filled the air with T.I. bumping in the background. Young Hollywood was definitely feeling himself now. A knock came from outside the door.

The Mexican removed the needles from his back as one of the other guys went to the door. He pushed the towel to the side.

"Tell Wood he got a visit," the guy said from the other side.

Young Hollywood looked toward the door; he wasn't expecting a visit—not today anyhow. "Jose, we finish when I come back." He stood up and then added, "Wash me up."

It was nearly thirty minutes later before Young Hollywood stepped inside the visitation room. The area was crowded, and people laughed with their incarcerated family members. Young Hollywood stood at the desk scanning the crowd. A female officer pointed him in the direction of his daddy. He saw Hammer sitting at a small table in a cocaine-white three-piece suit and white silk tie, his left leg crossed over his right. On his left pinky finger was a seven-carat diamond set in a mountain of platinum. When Young Hollywood approached Hammer, he stood up, and they embraced one another.

"How you doin'?" Hammer asked.

"I'm coolin'," Young Hollywood responded back. They sat down across from one another. Then Young Hollywood asked, "Why you didn't let me know you were comin'?"

"I just happen to be in the area."

"What's the occasion?"

Hammer shrugged and said, "Sasha say you goin' against the grain."

Young Hollywood sucked his teeth and replied, "You came all da way down here to tell me dat shit?"

"No. I came all the way down here to tell you that I put in a lot of hard work and spent a lot of money to get this bitch in position for you. Understand me?" Hammer didn't raise his voice; however, he did give Young Hollywood an almost deadly look that spoke for itself. They knew one another from head to toe, their weakness and their strengths. It was definitely hereditary.

Young Hollywood took a deep breath. "It's hard fa me to fake kick it. Dat cCHAPTER ain't in my book."

"You need to wake up, Wood, and realize your position. Shit like this just doesn't happen to the average Joe. Don't let your emotions get in the way and fuck up what we got going. Understand me?"

Young Hollywood nodded his head in total agreement.

They sat in silence for a few more minutes. Then Hammer said, "I got good news."

Young Hollywood paused, his eyes fixed dead on Hammer. "What we got?"

"My lady friend, she's Arab and down by law. Believe me." He paused, looked around the visitation room, and waved at a younger kid who was waving at him. He looked back at his son. "Anyway, we've been kickin' it real strong, and she's plugged in with a lot of big people."

"Like who?"

"Like the judge who sentenced you," he said. "She also knows Michael Myers, the DA."

LC woke up with a headache and removed himself from the comfortable hotel bed and ordered breakfast. After that, he showered and left. He drove the aqua-blue Aston Martin at the speed limit. He wasn't about showing off. He knew the Black Cartel family rules. He was in East Atlanta, Zone Six, driving down the busy Second Avenue. He pulled in front of a huge old house with chipped paint and a three-legged dog hopping in front of an old Chevy being held up by bricks. He parked his Aston Martin. The front yard was surrounded by a four-foot chain-link fence. He flipped up the latch and walked up the short concrete walkway and upon the front porch.

A speeding ambulance passed by, the sirens screaming. LC turned around and watched it pass before knocking. When he finally knocked, an old lady's voice shouted, "Come in!" LC opened the screen door and walked into the living room. It was neatly arranged with a two-piece plaid sofa set, a wooden coffee table in the middle, sitting on an oriental throw rug. In the recliner sat a chubby lady. She was dark skinned with silver hair pulled back into a tight ponytail. She was clad in a powder-blue housecoat, and her leather-bound Bible rested in her lap. Her eyes were closed.

LC walked over to her and placed his hand on her shoulder. "How you doin', Miss Daisy?" he asked her.

She never opened her eyes, but her response was, "I'm jus' prayin' everything gon' be all right and we get betta days 'round her'. I jus' know Jesus gon' fix it." Her words flowed off of her tongue in rhythm as if she'd practiced the phrase several times.

LC had heard it several times before. He dug in his pocket and removed a knot of money held together by a thick rubber band. He tapped her shoulder with it.

Her eyes sprung open. They stretched even wider when she saw the money.

LC handed her the money. "Buy yo'self something nice," he told her.

A wide smile spread across her face. "God bless you, baby," she said.

Inside the kitchen, a short and wide dark-skinned guy was standing over the stove. He had a yellow box of Arm & Hammer baking soda in one hand. Staring into it, the steam from the boiling water had him pouring sweat.

LC was leaning against the door seal, his eyes focused on his younger homeboy as he watched him water-whip his crack. He wasn't aware of LC being behind him. The guy that slaved over the hot stove took a fork and began whipping the cocaine and talking to himself. "Lord, please let it take," he said. "Please, Lord—"

"Ain't no need in prayin' now," LC finally said, his arms folded across his chest.

The guy's name was Boobie. He turned and faced LC with the glass beaker and fork still in his hand, beads of sweat popping and forming down his face and neck. His wife-beater was drenched. "How long you been here, shawty?" Boobie asked. He was whipping uncontrollably now, then he finally realized the cocaine he'd just bought was nothing but re-rock. He set the fork in the glass beaker and roughly set the glass on the countertop.

"Nigga don' gotcha on da work, ain't it, pimp?" LC said as he moved toward Boobie and gave him some dap.

"Nigga jus' got me fa fo' and a baby." His eyes were bloodshot red and the palms of his hands were sweaty. "I'ma kill dat fuck nigga, and dat's on my mama."

LC knew Boobie wasn't just talking; he definitely had a track record for robbing and killing. He'd inherited it from his uncle and brothers, who were all either dead or in prison. LC placed his hand on Boobie's shoulder. "I'm plugged in myself now, shawty, and I need you on my team."

"What I got to do?" Boobie asked anxiously.

"You know dat nigga Mossberg dat be rappin'?" LC asked.

Boobie nodded, his eyes drifting off.

"Can you dome him?"

Boobie placed his hands behind his back. He thought long and hard. Then his eyes cut up at LC. "You know, shawty roll deep wit' dem Pittsburg niggas."

LC shrugged his shoulders. "Black Cartel roll deep also. I'm backing you trust my work shawty." He paused and then added, "We got big shit lined up. You can get down wit' dis shit or you can sell breakdowns fo' da rest you life."

"Fuck it." He fired up his last Newport. He inhaled, and then he allowed the smoke to casually seep from his mouth. He looked back to LC and asked, "Who da fuck is da Black Cartel?"

There was a long pause. LC then removed the beaker from the table and held it in his hand. He stared at it for nearly a minute and then dropped it in the trash. His eyes went to Boobie. "Da hardest robbin' crew da city will eva see," he said.

# CHAPTER 60

Atiya and Hammer sat next to one another on the front row in the Fox Theater. The stage was well lit and decorated in an 1800s setting. The audience was silent; over 300 guests came out to see the play. Corleone played Romeo, and Sheekena had the role of Juliet. Other kids performed as well, and the play was a smash hit. The Atlanta Symphony produced the best music.

Dramatically, Hammer looked at Atiya, and her hand reached out for his. A grave little smile spread across her face. He wedged his fingers between hers. Hammer had never felt anything like this before. Affection and love are sometimes unexplainable. Atiya had the same type of feelings; they accepted one another in the most natural way.

After the play was over, everybody escaped to the Egyptian Ballroom and the Grand Salon, which were lavishly decorated with sweeping columns and ornamentation creating the perfect setting. A party was being held for the kids, and toys were given away. Gift certificates were being handed out like candy. Caterers offered some of the best food money could buy.

Out on the Grand Terrace, Hammer and Atiya held on to each other. It was romantically lit, and a lovely breeze blew through their clothing. Her hands were casually on his shoulders, and his were at the small of her back, and when they kissed it was more breathtaking than anything. Her eyes were closed, and her mouth was soft and wet. She tasted good to Hammer. He kissed her on the neck, and she tensed up a little. The feeling was overwhelming.

She rocked side to side, easing herself further into Hammer arms. Then she rested her head on his shoulder. She whispered, "I just want to be loved." She raked her nails through Hammer's hair and across the back of his neck.

Her words made him hold her tighter. He nibbled on her right earlobe, and she felt her panties soaking between her legs. She pressed her thighs together, and then Hammer allowed his tongue to slide inside her ear. "No man will love you better than me," he whispered. His hands fell down below her waist and palmed her ass cheeks. She was soft back there. He waited for her to come with a negative response.

She never did.

He squeezed her tighter, and she smiled even more. Her eyes were penetrating into his. "I'm... I'm lost for words," she whispered in his ear.

They snuggled together and slow-danced in one another's arms. Their heartbeats were ticking in rhythm.

"You're the type of man I've been looking for all of my life," she said.

"I'm a gangsta, Atiya," he shot back. "Is that what you want?"

"Apparently," she replied as she raked her fingers through his hair again. Then she slid her tongue inside his mouth again. The soft, elegant music was playing far in the background. The tone was set, and the night sky was beautiful. Atiya lifted her head.

Hammer kissed her neck, kissed her diamonds. Then he asked, "What's on the agenda for tonight?"

"It doesn't matter, Rufus. I'm under your command." She smiled up at him.

Later that night, Hammer and Atiya walked inside a hotel suite somewhere downtown. Atiya filled the Jacuzzi with hot, sudsy water. She began undressing, allowing her formal dress to slide from her body. Her breasts were firm, and her nipples were hard.

A soft knock came from the door. She opened it, and Hammer walked in. His eyes searched her beautiful naked body. Her stomach was tight and flat, her hips were curvy, and her pubic area looked as if it had been waxed. She bent over and removed her heels; her toenails were painted a bright red.

Hammer began undressing himself, and moments later, he was naked and standing at full attention. Atiya couldn't resist his hard, stiff manhood. She eased her way toward him and grabbed his throbbing, hot penis. She couldn't wait for their bath. They went back into the bedroom. She pushed Hammer onto the bed and climbed on top of him. Her vagina was tight and gripping. Her eyes stretched as she slid down further. His huge hands palmed her soft, naked ass. He took her left breast in his mouth, casually sucking on her nipple. Her eyes rolled to the back of her head. "Ohhh God," she moaned.

Hammer worked his hips, pushing further inside of her.

She grinded her body in unison, then she whispered "It's soo good." She came quietly, but her body jerked violently.

He spun her around. Her hands were gripping his ankles, and she dropped down on him.

"You're a freak," Hammer said playfully.

She looked back at him with a smile.

At 2:35 a.m., A-Town Studios was crowded and buzzing with activity as if it were normal working hours. A guy by the name of Zoë, an up-and-coming producer, was controlling the boards and console. Mossberg was standing over him, kenning his ear into the beat, with a glass of Patron in one hand and a cigarillo rolled blunt of purp in the other. He stared in the air, his dreadlocks bouncing every time he bobbed his head to the slow, mellow beat. Mossberg was twenty years old, raised in Pittsburg project, hustling coke and marijuana. He was the youngest of five brothers. They loved him and spoiled him to death when he was younger. Now he was in position, a certified breadwinner. His four older brothers were in the studio with him. Everybody was armed to the T. Altogether, there were a dozen cats, all of them there to protect their up-and-coming millionaire homeboy. Zoë, the producer, pressed a button and found another sound, something coming from a symphony. Mossberg paused, and the sound caught his ear. He puffed the blunt, but to his surprise, the fire had gone out. He looked to another unknown guy who was engineering over some buttons. "Give me a light," he demanded.

The guy did.

Mossberg puffed, and the smoke enveloped his face. He then shook his long wicks away from his eyes. His mind was on a journey. Thirty minutes earlier, he'd been fighting sleep, but now he was alive and energetic.

One of his brothers looked at him. "Take ya time, shawty," he said.

Mossberg sipped the Patron from his plastic cup, and his eyes narrowed. Then he said, "Dat be me, Zone Three, ridin' through da city in a stolen Grand Prix... all my bitches pop ecstasy, Jonesboro South cop weed from me."

Outside the studio, Boobie was parked across the street in a stolen Yukon with slightly tinted windows. The driver was behind the wheel, and another guy was in the passenger's seat.

Boobie was in the rear with a thirty-thirty rifle attached to a tripod with an infrared beam aimed directly at the front entrance of the studio. His patience was growing short. He took a deep breath and asked, "Shawty, fire me a cigarette."

The guy in the front passenger's seat handed him a pack of Newports. Boobie removed one and lit it up with a lighter. The flame highlighted his face from behind the tint.

It was no more than a split second, but still somebody else saw it, a member of Hammer's crew.

# CHAPTER 61

LC and Big Low pulled up to a ranch-style home in Aiken, South Carolina in a rented Dodge Ram pickup truck. They rode down a winding driveway that led them toward the garage of the house. There were two white guys standing in front of a Chevy Suburban, both of them clad in tight jeans, boots, and Harley Davidson T-shirts. LC put the car in park, and the taller white guy approached the driver's side. LC pressed the button on the door panel to quickly open his window. The big white guy smelled of wintergreen chewing tobacco. LC noticed the huge .357 strapped on his waist inside a brown leather holster.

The guy extended a hand, and LC shook it. "From Atlanta, right?" the big white guy asked. His eyes scanned the inside of the truck.

Big Low had a half-full Corona bottle between his legs. He looked over across LC at the white guy and asked, "Where can I take a leak at?"

The white guy pointed toward a dense line of trees and said, "Over there."

Big Low bounced from the front seat of the truck.

Then LC got out and stood beside the white guy. "You da guy I talked to on da phone?" LC asked.

"Our drug-sniffing canines cost a pretty penny, and we train for government officials only—"

LC cut him off. "I didn't come all the way down her' to play no games. I brought $100K cash fa ten of them. Take it or leave it."

The big white guy looked at LC, examining him thoroughly. The offer was on the table, too big to refuse. "Hold tight for a second," he said to LC and walked over toward the other white guy. They stood in a two-man huddle for nearly ten minutes.

By then, Big Low had relieved himself and walked from the bushes. He stood next to LC, his arms folded across his chest and his compact .45 concealed in his waistline. "What dem crackas talkin' 'bout?"

"Hopefully good business," he said, staring in the direction of the two men.

The white guys began heading toward LC and Big Low. They walked in stride beside one another, dust forming underneath their feet at every step, leaving a cloud behind as they came, like some scene straight out of a Western movie.

"How soon will you need these canines?" the other guy asked as he looked directly into LC's eyes.

"Today if possible," LC shot back.

"Man dees dog's ain't gon' turn on us, is they?" Big Low asked in a serious tone of voice.

Both of the white guys smiled at the same time. The bigger one pulled a Marlboro from the pack. He lit it up instantly. Then he said, "These canines will be trained on your voice command, or we can have one trained for each of you."

"Can they sniff out drugs?" Big Low asked anxiously.

The big white guy spread his huge hands and commented, "I can promise you this... For a hundred grand, I'll make them motherfuckers play a piano."

Later that night, LC and Big Low had two handsome German Shepherds on the bed of the truck, each in his own separate cage. They drove to a red brick two-bedroom home in the Decatur suburb area. They backed the truck into a paved driveway. The motion lights in the yard came on. LC backed further alongside the house, deep enough into the driveway until the truck couldn't be seen by neighbors or by passers.

They parked, removed the canines from the rear of the truck, and walked them inside the house through the back door. It took them through the kitchen. LC removed the chain from the dog he had and stood next to him. The dog never left LC's side. Then LC said in an assuring manner, "Go getta." The dog took off around the empty house, his nose sniffing every crack and crevice. He went into another room, disappearing away from LC, Big Low, and the other dog they called Yayo.

Nearly three minutes later, they heard barking coming from the front room. LC walked through the house and switched on the lights. In the living room, G Getta was scratchin' at the bottom of a La-Z-Boy recliner chair, the same chair where LC and Big Low had left an ounce of cocaine the night before. LC was more than satisfied; that gave them assurance. They repeated the same process with Yayo. Each of them was highly trained. Yayo was a success also, and all they needed was the perfect lick to get their money from the six-figure investment.

LC went back into the kitchen. He wanted to hear about the murder on Mossberg, detail for detail. He damn sure knew Boobie wouldn't leave anything out. He removed his cell phone from his pocket and punched a speed dial number, but to his surprise, Boobie didn't get answer. A bewildered look appeared across his face as he looked at Big Low.

"Wuz up, shawty?" he asked, recognizing the unfamiliar look in his comrade's eyes.

There was a short pause. Then LC said, "I don' know why pimp ain't answerin' his cell. Dat ain't like him."

"Call him again," Big Low said, his eyebrows bunched together as a confused look spread across his face.

LC dialed the number again. There was still no answer, only the voicemail. He shook his head.

Seven hours earlier, Hammer was called on his cell phone while relaxing in Atiya's arms at the hotel. He read Kangoma's number on the screen and didn't waste any time answering. "Yeah?"

"I'm at the ranch," was all he said. Then he hung up.

Now Hammer was confused. He was tired, but he was a businessman. When Kangoma called and said he was at the ranch and that it was a life-or-death situation, he sat up in bed and dressed quickly.

Atiya was lying on her side, facing him. "What is it?" she asked him. Sleep was still in her eyes.

Hammer looked back at her, one of his eyebrows arched. "I got a small situation that must be handled tonight."

"I'm flying to Seattle at noon," she whispered.

"I'll be back before you leave."

"Is that a promise?" she asked.

Hammer leaned down and kissed her mouth and then her cheek. "Trust me, baby," he said in a confident manner.

"I do," she whispered.

When Hammer arrived at the ranch, he drove around to a huge garage warehouse. He then pulled into the wide, spacious garage in his glossy black Phantom and got out.

Kangoma approached the vehicle and greeted Hammer with a handshake.

Hammer held on to his hand and looked him square in the eyes, "What's the problem?"

Kangoma, with his deadly yellowish eyes, stared back into Hammer's, and then he pointed to the far end corner of the 100,000-square-foot warehouse. Hammer turned his head and followed the direction of Kangoma's pointed finger. From the distance, Hammer noticed three human figures sitting on the floor. He began walking into the direction where the men were, his hard-bottom gators clicking against the concrete floor.

Kangoma walked in stride next to him. "There's three of 'em," he said. "They were parked outside the studio in a Yukon with several weapons."

"Are they talking?" Hammer asked. His voice was calm. He'd been in situations like this before, and normally it always turned out in his favor.

"Neither one of them," Kangoma responded.

They were near them now. An armed henchman stood over them with a mini-assault rifle. There were two metal folding chairs sitting in front of Boobie and the other two unknown goons.

Hammer scanned the three faces; he didn't recognize any of them. Hammer pulled up one of the folding chairs and sat directly in the face of Boobie, who was duct taped and cuffed with plastic bands. "Take the tape from his mouth," Hammer insisted.

Kangoma eased toward Boobie and snatched the tape from his mouth. He stood next to him and never took his eyes off of them.

Hammer cleared his throat. "What were your intentions?"

Boobie looked Hammer square in the eyes and didn't utter a word; he kept his face twisted angrily.

Hammer had to smile; he actually laughed a light chuckle. Then he asked one more question. "Do you know who I am?'

Still, Boobie sat with his hands bound behind his back. His cold stare was still on Hammer.

Without hesitation, Hammer stood. "My time is very valuable," he said as he looked at Kangoma and shrugged his shoulders with a smirk on his face. "Chop their heads off." He pointed toward Boobie. "His first."

Kangoma bowed his head in an obedient fashion, then he went to his pants and came up with a stainless steel machete.

"Okay, okay!" Boobie said.

Kangoma grabbed him by his hair, yanking his head back. He looked back at Hammer to see if he wanted to hear what he had to say.

Hammer shook his head; it was too late for any negotiations.

Kangoma turned his attention back toward Boobie, whose eyes stretched wide with fear when he saw the long, razor-sharp blade looming above his head. Kangoma swung and chopped him inches below his Adam apple. Blood splattered everywhere. Kangoma chopped at his neck again, and his head was severed from his body. He held the detached head by his dreads.

Hammer turned and began walking back toward his Phantom. "Make all three of them disappear, Kangoma," he said. *Wasting my motha'fuckin' time,* he thought and shook his head.

# CHAPTER 62

Scooter was on a mission, getting beside himself. In the last forty-six days, he'd moved to the west side of the prison to keep up with a female officer who had just gotten to the prison. She was slim, petite, and dark chocolate. Scooter kept her with the latest hairdos; he bought her jewelry and new shoes. Last week, he had her bring in two ounces of cocaine. He made $10K off of it and told her to buy herself a car. There was a Toyota Avalon in the parking lot with a paper tag, courtesy of ATL's finest if you let him tell it.

That morning, Officer Harris, the female he was dealing with, was working L building. She was standing out front of the dorm when Scooter approached her. He was carrying a store net bag slung across his shoulders. Miss Harris flashed him a smile. She knew she couldn't get too loose in the public eye. Nearly the entire west side of the compound had heard about the relationship, but nobody dared utter a word about Scooter and Miss Harris. He and Young Hollywood had the entire prison on lock with a respect level out the roof.

"Wuz up, shawty?" Scooter said.

Officer Harris couldn't control herself. She liked Scooter just as much as he liked her. She smiled, and her teeth were wrapped in metal braces.

Scooter could've kissed her there, but he decided against it quickly.

Then she asked, "Where you goin'?" Her accent was country as all outdoors. She was from Americus, Georgia.

Scooter didn't stand too close to her, maybe two feet away. He sat the net bag on the ground. It was filled with ramen noodles, honey buns, and a variety of Little Debbie snack cakes. Also, there was nearly a pound of reefer stuffed inside one of the boxes and four ounces of cocaine in another. And last but not least, he had seventy-five different colors of x-pills. He was arrogant and thought he was untouchable. Scooter was selling dope in the prison as if he was on the street. "I came by ta see you," he finally said. Then he asked, "Why you ain't workin' G building?"

"I'ma be ova there tamorrow." Her eyes were dancing all over Scooter. She looked at his waist and the lump in his pants. "You gon' be ready fa me?"

He laughed. "Won't miss it fa da world," he said. Then he stared out toward the walk. The yard was filled with other prisoners wearing a sea of blue and white clothing. There, beyond the prisoners, he noticed a circle of black clothing. The cert team popped in his head. He saw them from nearly 100 yards. He grabbed his bag and slung it across his shoulder and began heading toward his dorm building. "Tomorrow," was all he said and blended in with the other prisoners as if he was coming from the store.

When he got to his building he tapped the window for the officer to let him in. The officer pressed a button, and he pulled the door handle to go inside the sally port. When he stepped inside, another inmate was in there with him. Scooter looked at him; the guy was a peon. Then he wondered why the officer hadn't popped the door to let him inside the dormitory. He looked in the control booth and banged on the window with his nub. "Open da do'!" he yelled. The older white officer looked at Scooter and then turned his back to him. That made Scooter furious, and his eyes turned red instantly. He thought for a mere second and removed the store bag from his shoulder. He looked at the peon again. Then he tapped him on the shoulder. "Take my sto' bag in da dorm. Get ya them two packs of cigarettes out of there for yo' trouble."

The guy took the bag and set it in front of him.

Scooter went back to the exit door. He was looking for the cert team, but he didn't see them. Then, to his surprise, the entire squad appeared in front of the entrance door.

A huge black cert team officer who stood nearly six-five had his hand on the outside door handle. The officer in the control booth popped the door, and the officer said, "Come out here, Mosley."

Scooter didn't look worried or anything. He moved back outside where he was surrounded by the entire cert team. They put him against the wall and patted him down.

Then the officer from the control booth came out. "He gave the other guy the sto' bag."

Scooter frowned and looked back toward one of the cert team

officers. "I ain't had no sto' bag."

The big guy went inside the sally port and retrieved the store bag from the unknown inmate.

Other prisoners were standing around now. They knew something was up. That was part of prison. Everybody—or at least somebody—saw something.

The cert team officer didn't search the bag. He looked at the team and said, "Cuff him. Let's go."

"Cuff me up fa what?" Scooter asked. He spun around quickly. Now he was facing them, his eyes searching every officer.

"Calm down, Mosley," one officer said. "Cuff up."

"Cuff up fa what? I ain't did shit."

"Pending investigation, we gotta take you to the hole."

"Get da warden down here then." He defenselessly backed up against the wall, ready to fire off on whomever. He folded his arms across his chest.

The officers had already heard about Scooter, and they knew he was dangerous. It was in his file.

Nearly fifteen minutes later, the head warden and captain appeared. Then two LTs and several more other officers showed up. Scooter and the warden stepped to the side and spoke amongst themselves. Five minutes later, they were escorting Scooter to the hole without handcuffs. When they got him inside J building, they thoroughly searched his property and the store bag. They placed him in a cell by himself, and he was written up for possession of unauthorized contraband. He sat down and wrote the warden a note, two pages. He had to; he couldn't leave Miss Harris. He refused to let another prisoner get her, and that was just that. He sat down on the edge of his bunk. He was in his selfish mode again. His face begin popping beads of sweat. He thought hard and serious about Young Hollywood and everything he was doing for him: the lawyer and the account he had his daddy to set up for him. He was loyal to his comrade, a one-of-a-kind soldier. Scooter fell back on his bunk and began thinking about Miss Harris. He needed his bitch.

# CHAPTER 63

The next evening, Young Hollywood was sitting in the back on one of the blue chairs at a bottled-down square table covered with a sheet. He smoked on a Black & Mild; four other cats were at the table as well. Cards were being dealt.

The white guy who was dealing said in an even tone, "Dis is five card stud. You get three draws, and you can draw three cards each time. Mandatory bet five all da way down and ten on da end."

Young Hollywood had on a pair shades. They were cheap, but he made them look expensive and fancy. His eyes couldn't be seen, and he was high out of his mind, passing time, giving the unfortunate convicts a chance to get some money. He had money to spend, blow, and give away. Young Hollywood pulled on his Black & Mild cigar. The smoke curled up around his unshaved face. His eyes darted around the table, and he was seriously trying to read everybody who sat at the table with him.

Then out of nowhere, somebody yelled out, "Hollywood!"

Without hesitation, he snapped his head backwards toward the window. A guy was standing outside in front of his dorm, motioning his arm for him to come to the window.

"I'm gambling, shawty," he said.

"It's an emergency. I got something fo' you, pimp."

Young Hollywood flipped his shades up on top of his head. "Y'all hold ya hands," he said. He removed himself from the table, walking with a high-caliber swagger that was unexplainable. He went to the row of windows across the front of the dorm. The vents were just below it. "Wuz up, shawty?" he asked the guy through the vent.

The guy on the outside was clean shaved and wore a nice haircut. "I got a letter from Boogaloo. He says it's urgent."

"Where at?"

The guy reached in his back pocket and removed a small folded piece of paper. He moved down toward the emergency exit door and slid it through the crack.

Young Hollywood got it and unfolded it right there. He began reading the few lines that were on the page: "What it is, pimp? This Boogaloo. You know I'm in the hole. I caught a jack charge. Anyway, how have you been? Me? I'm coolin'. I'm dropping you these few lines to put you up on the game. You know Scooter just came back here yesterday. They say he got caught with an ass-load of work. I know they came and got him this morning. I'm assuming he went to security. Just watch yo'self, pimp. That nigga snitching."

Young Hollywood tore the letter in small pieces and dropped his shades back over his eyes. He knew Scooter was too tough for anything like that. However, being himself and the caliber of person he was, he still had to investigate the situation. He removed himself from the card game and allowed someone else to take his seat. When he went inside his cell, he threw his towel on his door and locked himself inside. He sat on the desk and relit his Black & Mild. He was in deep thought now, his eyes down. His mind was sharper than a razor. Then his eyes flashed in surprise. He bounced from the desk and retrieved his cell phone as if the best idea in the world had just come to his mind. He knew Scooter's number by heart, and he punched it in and listened while it rang.

No answer.

He still wasn't defeated, and he didn't seem angry. He knew Scooter was the only person besides him that knew when Sasha was going to make a drop, and the next day, she was gonna bring in three pounds and twenty cell phones. Young Hollywood called her on her cell.

She answered, "Yes?"

"Hey, wuz up. Don't talk, jus' listen. I don't want you or the LT to bring nothing in tomorrow. As a matter of fact, nothing don't come in non' dis week. Tell ol' girl if Scooter call her, to go ahead with everything he asks, but neither one of you should bring nothing. You got dat?"

"Yeah," she responded. Then she asked, "Are you all right?"

"I'm good. Jus' do as I say, okay?"

"All right.'

Young Hollywood hung up his phone and immediately called Scooter's cell number again. Still no answer. He pressed the end button and held the phone in his hand. He was undecided now. He sat back on top of the desk and scratched his head. *Why da fuck dis nigga ain't answering?* he wondered. He jumped up from the desk again when he heard a bunch of screaming and commotion out in the dorm. He was at his cell door with his phone in one hand. He pushed the towel to the side with the other, and before his eyes, cert team was gathered around his door. He turned immediately and dropped the phone in the toilet and pressed the silver flush button. Young Hollywood was furious now. His cell door popped open, and three of the cert team officers rushed in.

Young Hollywood was forced up against the wall in a rough manner, and then they cuffed him. "I think he jus' flushed the phone," one officer said.

"Check the cell, everything. Take the goddamn walls down if you have to," the sergeant growled, his hand pasted on his hips as he stared at Young Hollywood angrily.

He gave him the same stare back, and then he smiled at him. "Da payroll always open," Young Hollywood said.

"I don't need yo' fuckin' money."

"We found a cigarette lighter," one of the cert officers said.

The sergeant leaned against the door. His eyes wouldn't leave Young Hollywood for anything.

"I already know who sent you, Sarge." He shrugged. Then he said, "Things don't always be what it seems. Now if you'll wanna do some work, I'ma give ya'll some work to do."

"I take dat as a threat."

"It'll be in yo' best interest to take it as a promise," Young Hollywood said casually. Then he showed him his grill.

"You sellin' drugs in my chain-gang?"

"Don't have to." He gave a grin. "Dis *my* chain-gang."

"What about cell phones?"

"You makin' my stomach hurt, and then you workin' ya officers fa nothing." Young Hollywood faked a yawn, funny as an actor.

Then another officer yelled, "Bingo!"

The sergeant craned his neck and stretched his eyes at the same time. "What cha got?'

"Cash money, about $6K."

When Young Hollywood got to the entrance of J building, there were a few inmates in the sally port waiting to come out. Young

Hollywood was standing to the side in handcuffs with two of the cert team officers on each side of him. The sally port door swung open, and four inmates poured out. Among the four was Scooter, who looked Young Hollywood in his eyes.

"What cha did, shawty?" Scooter asked.

Young Hollywood wouldn't even look at him; Scooter didn't exist to him anymore. He pretended not to hear him after he called his name several times. Young Hollywood was escorted inside the sally port. He turned and watched Scooter fade from his eyesight. He knew he did it.

# CHAPTER 64

Richard Myers had plenty of time to think things out. He'd received a call last week from one of Hammer's attorneys. The phone call was to let him know he'd been invited to dinner and to disclose the amount or fee that would be brought to the table for an overturned conviction in is son's case. Richard Myers was living a good life. Some said he was modest, while others said he was the dirtiest district attorney Atlanta had ever seen.

The entire black community knew him, or at least had heard of him. His name was stamped on every indictment that had been handed down in the last ten years. Richard Myers stood in front of his wall mirror examining himself in a cream-colored tailored suit.

His wife was beautiful with long, elegant black hair. Her high cheekbones enhanced her beauty. There was a dimple in her chin, and her body was toned. She wore a strapless dress and brown leather heels. "How do I look, honey?" she asked him. She was more elegant than ever.

Richard Myers turned and faced his wife; his eyes went to her breast cleavage. He thought she was revealing too much, even though she was charming. This meant nothing to him. There was more than a million dollars on the line, and he could be worth that by next week. He'd heard so many wonderful things about Hammer. The mayor had given him the key to the city. He'd paid college tuitions for unfortunate kids and sponsored free concerts with top-notch artists like T.I., Luda, Da Brat, and OutKast. Richard Myers had definitely heard about the great Hammer and the twenty years he'd served for a double-murder.

"Honey?" his wife said again.

He snapped out of his trance and focused his attention back to his lovely wife. Her eyes were soft and innocent as a child. Richard finally gave her a smile. "Fabulous," he said. "Now let's go before we're late."

Kangoma had an expensive tri-level four-bedroom house somewhere deep in the Buckhead area. He and hammer sat next to one another in recliner chairs with thick cushions. There was a floor-to-ceiling glass window that overlooked a small pond and a manicured golf course. The ceilings were high, built in a dome shape with one huge chandelier. The floor was covered and stretched out with imported colorful marble. A soccer game was being played on a huge projector screen. The volume was on mute, and the room was dimly lit.

"You know, Africa is much different than here," Kangoma broke the silence.

"Different as in how?" Hammer asked. His rough ,thick fingers twirled a Cuban cigar.

"Different as in killers. In the United States, your soldiers aren't really soldiers. Jus' in Uganda alone, we have over 10,000 child soldiers that are certified trained killers, assassins at twelve years old."

Hammer listened carefully, he soaked up every word. His eyes were fixed on the projector screen. He said, "Right here in da city, I got at least fifty killers on the payroll. Some of them are adolescents and very skilled with an AK. So see, our countries are pretty much the same, and still, niggas sleepin' in Atlanta."

"We need child soldiers here. Eye trickery. Our enemies will never see them coming," Kangoma said.

"You think too hard, Kangoma. Sometimes you get a little farfetched." Hammer exhaled a stream of smoke from his mouth.

"That's why our countries are very much different. Things happen over there you wouldn't believe."

They were interrupted by the sounds of the doorbell.

Hammer stood from his chair. "I'll reason with anybody first." He spoke in the most ordinary voice. He moved toward the living room and disappeared from Kangoma's eyesight.

Kangoma just shook his head. He stood to his feet as well, his lean body covered in linen pants. He wore a cream-colored dress shirt tucked inside his alligator-skin belt, and he had matching shoes. He followed casually behind Hammer, through the living and dining room areas, and toward the front door. By the time he got there, Hammer had already opened the door and was greeting Richard Myers with a firm handshake.

His wife came inside also, and she was staring at the fourteen-foot ceilings and the tailored living room as if she hadn't seen such a well put together house. "This is beautiful," she commented. Her eyes scanned quickly. Then she set her eyes on Kangoma; he was handsome. Her eyes said it all. She greeted him and Hammer.

An hour later, they were all sitting around a long marble dining table covered in a white linen. An array of special dishes was spread from one end of the table to the other. Hammer sat at the head of the table, and Atiya was next to him. She was beautiful as usual, casually dressed but neatly decorated with expensive jewelry. Richard Myers and his wife occupied the next two chairs, and Kangoma and his wife occupied the other end.

An old lady served them as ordered. Her hair was white and her face was chubby. She had a wide nose and wore a dark-colored dress and a white apron.

After Hammer said the prayer, the maid was told to have a seat as well. She sat down on the opposite side of Richard Myers. The old lady didn't smile and tried her damnedest not to make eye contact with anyone around the table. She bowed her head and said a silent prayer to herself. Hammer waited for to finish. When she raised her head, she had tears in her eyes. Kangoma stood and walked around the table to where she was. He gave her a silk handkerchief, and she wiped her eyes. Then he leaned down and mumbled something in her ear. An assuring smile spread across her face, and she patted Kangoma's hand.

After the wonderful meal, Hammer and Richard Myers walked outside. There was a Cadillac golf cart parked around side of the house. Hammer got behind the wheel. "Take a ride with me," he told the DA Richard Myers.

The DA didn't see any harm in it. He got in, and Hammer started the fancy golf cart and pulled out onto the beautiful manicured lawn. Their ride was smooth and quiet for a moment until Hammer broke the silence. "I brought you out here so we could talk one on one." Hammer pulled the golf cart under a huge tree that gave a lot of shade. He looked over at Richard Myers and said, "The street's got your name fucked up all over Atlanta."

"Been that way for years. What can I say? Both of my kids have graduated from college, Spelman and Morehouse," Richard Myers said.

"So I'm assuming you've been eating good?" Hammer asked.

"It could be better. There's always room on my plate, not for just any average Joe though." He folded his arms across his chest, and his eyes wandered out across the golf course. Two white guys were teeing off about fifty yards away. "I'm 'bout ready to retire now. That's the only reason I'm taking you up on the offer."

"What exactly is it that you have for me?"

"Your son's trial transcripts. I've gone through them and outlined every mistake the judge and I made. This is another reason I'm retiring. This could put my career on the line, and for two million, I'll even testify in your son's favor."

"What about the witnesses?" Hammer asked, squinting.

There was a short pause. Then Richard Myers said, "That'll be something you'll have to deal with yourself." His eyes darted nervously side to side, as if to be giving Hammer some sort of sign.

Hammer got the message loud and clear. In a very casual manner, he reached in his pocket and removed a cigar and an engraved lighter. He lit the Cuban and puffed until the tip was bright red. He then squinted against the smoke. "And how will I find these witnesses?" Hammer asked.

"Any names and addresses are inside the transcripts. For this type of money, I can assure you that you won't be disappointed."

# BOOK VII

# CHAPTER 65

Nearly five months had passed, and another year had come. Kelly, one of the key witnesses in Young Hollywood's trial, was walking out of the Publix grocery store on Cascade Road. He pushed a grocery buggy filled with food and drinks. His girlfriend was next to him carrying an infant boy in her arms. Kelly had a head full of dreads now and wore black Chanel shades over his eyes. The wheels from the buggy were rattling against the paved parking lot.

Kelly watched the parking lot with keen, trained eyes. High on x-pills and exotic marijuana, he couldn't wait to get home. A line of cars and SUVs were entering and exiting the parking lot. To some people, Kelly was a feared man, but he was wanted by a few petty dope boys he'd robbed in the past and even killed for as much as two ounces of crack and $600 in cash. Kelly, his girlfriend, and his infant baby squeezed between a row of parked cars. He pushed the grocery cart up to the rear of a black '02 Lincoln four-door. He removed the keys from his pocket and disarmed the car alarm. The car chirped, and the lights flashed two quick times. He opened the trunk and began loading it with bags of groceries.

His girlfriend was in the backseat. She carefully strapped their little boy inside the car seat and reached for a bottle of milk. Then, a split second later, there were over a dozen shots fired from somewhere. She screamed and covered her baby. The shots were close, and her little boy began screaming at the top of his lungs. She didn't have a clue what happened; it was so fast. When she finally crawled from the car and checked on Kelly, he was lying face down on the pavement in a pool of blood. His shirt was filled with holes, and so were his dreads. Three locks had been detached from his head. The high-caliber bullets had ripped him and his dreads apart. She looked up and noticed a forest-green Lexus LS with tinted windows parked a few feet away.

The guy behind the steering wheel gave her a deadly stare. He raised his index finger up to his lips and whispered, "Shhhhh," and then he pulled off.

She fell to her knees and picked her boyfriend's head up and placed it in her chest. She began rocking back and forth with him as tears flowed down her cheeks.

Across town, a light drizzle fell to the ground and sprinkled across the windows of the park cars that lined a one-way street in a quiet area in Midtown. The restaurant was a nice, elegant spot where a woman in her mid thirties by the name of Caroline ate bread sticks and chicken fingers. Caroline was a registered nurse. A few years ago, she had worked as a paramedic and drove ambulances for Grady. She was on the scene when Ghost was brutally killed, another witness who testified against Young Hollywood in trial. Caroline didn't have the slightest idea that she was being followed by two certified hit men who sat across the restaurant from her in a booth. They wore dresses and disguised as homosexuals with thick make-up and long weaves, colored contact lenses, and rubber-bottom boots. The two men watched Caroline as she ate. She flirted with a guy who sat next to her. He appeared to be waiting on a beer.

The two hit men finally stood together. "I'm hungry, girl," one of them said in the most annoying voice.

"Child, please! You jus' ate a steak."

They walked through a sea of tables occupied by singles and couples. An aisle led them toward the bar. They followed one behind the other, approaching Caroline to their left. The undercover hit man that walked in front had carefully removed a black .380 with a screw-on silencer from his Dooney & Bourke purse and then, as they passed Caroline, he put three bullets in the back of her head. She slumped over face first to the bar, and neither hit man broke their stride. A simple walk by, and they exited the front door without being noticed. They jumped into a waiting Navigator and slowly pulled off. The light, misty rain was beginning to turn into a pour.

It was the wedding day of Paul and Sandra Hickman, a perfect couple that had been together for nearly four years. Paul Hickman, a college graduate, young and handsome, stood six-one with a strong, solid build. He was blond and evenly tan. His bride Sandra had just enrolled in Emory University with a bright and promising future ahead of herself. Paul had met her a little while after he'd testified against Young Hollywood and Scooter in the murder trail. He was the ambulance driver they pulled over that night. Sandra was dressed in a long, beautiful wedding gown. Paul was with her, in his tuxedo. A crowd of people poured out to of the church and applauded the couple as they headed to a stretch limousine that was parked in front of the church. A sign was on both sides of the limousine that read "Just Married." A group of women huddled up, and when Sandra tossed the bouquet of flowers over her head, the women went wild. One of them caught it. Sandra and Paul waved goodbye as they loaded inside the waiting limousine to head off to their honeymoon.

The driver, a handsome and well-dressed black guy that looked as if he'd just graduated from high school, closed the door for them. He went around to the driver's side and climbed in the front. The driver started the limousine and eased out into traffic.

The weather was beautiful, and the sky was blue. Paul pressed a button, and the sunroof slid open. He hugged his wife and kissed her passionately on her lips. His hands slipped underneath her gown, and she spread her legs. She was a hot little something. Two of his fingers inserted her bald vagina. She moaned and squirmed, but then tragedy struck.

The limousine driver stopped in the middle of the street and threw the car in park. Four masked men came out of nowhere and riddled the entire limousine with assault rifles. Paul and Sandra never had a chance. A cocktail was dropped in the sunroof, and the fire erupted instantly.

# CHAPTER 66

Hammer was in a tailored Armani suit, apricot-colored gators, and a platinum-and-diamond watch that cost nearly $200K. Atiya stepped out the passenger's side of the Phantom. She wore a cream-colored two-piece linen suit and matching stilettos with gold studs. Her neck was fluttered with the same expensive diamond-and-platinum necklace. When she reached back inside the car to retrieve a simple leather Coach purse, Hammer said, "You can't take no pocketbooks or cell phones inside." He closed the driver's side door and stuffed the keys in his pocket. Today would be Atiya's first time meeting Young Hollywood. They walked together up to the front entrance of Macon State Prison. They held hands; their relationship had grown closer, and together they had a net worth well over a billion dollars. Hammer was one lucky son-of-a-bitch.

Inside, Hammer told the lady behind the desk that he was there to see Terry Keys. She picked up the phone, and Hammer and Atiya were escorted through a set of doors and led into the visitation area.

Young Hollywood was back on compound. This time he was in E building, the same building where he started when he first got here. Female officers weren't allowed to work the floor on the east side, but that morning, Young Hollywood had convinced the male floor officer to let the chubby-faced white female officer who worked the control booth make a round in the dorm. When she came inside the dorm, it was ten minutes after nine. Young Hollywood was standing in the mop closet with the door slightly ajar. The white girl walked straight toward the door and opened it. There Young Hollywood stood with his hard, throbbing penis in his hand. The officer looked down and it and turned pink in the face. He waved her in.

The white girl was overwhelmed because she had never been so close to a black man before. "You gon' get me in trouble," she said and eased toward him. She gripped his penis with one hand and slightly bent at the waist. She nervously looked back at the door. "Ain't nobody gon' come in here, is it?"

Young Hollywood said, "Jus' come on and suck dis dick."

She closed her pink lips around the head of his penis and quickly deep-throated his entire nine-inch pole. She was into it now and dropped to her knees. She licked his balls and sucked him for nearly three minutes until someone came over the intercom.

"Terry Keys, report to visitation," someone said.

She paused and slid his shiny wet penis from her mouth and asked, "That you, ain't it?"

He grabbed the back of her head without saying a word. This wasn't a love affair for sure. He guided her mouth back to his hard penis.

She giggled and started on him again, this time faster; she wanted him to cum.

His fingers entwined in her sandy-red hair.

The door came open. A guy peeped his head in and saw Young Hollywood on his tiptoes. He threw up the peace sign and disappeared.

"I'm cummin'" Young Hollywood said, his eyes staring down at her.

"Umhmm," was all she could say. She sucked harder and faster until he came in her mouth. She swallowed and looked up at him with her dreamy-looking eyes. "How was it?" she asked, his penis still in her mouth.

He shrugged his shoulders and gave her a look as if he didn't have a care in the world.

She recognized his demeanor and stood to her feet. "I guess it wasn't good huh?"

"Practice make perfect." He moved toward the door.

She wiped her mouth with the back of her hand and wiped her pants off at her knees.

He gave her a folded one-hundred-dollar bill.

She looked at it as if she was insulted.

He laughed. "You ain't shit," he said before he walked out of the closet.

In the visitation room, Hammer checked his watch. Thirty minutes had passed, and Young Hollywood still hadn't shown up. Just as he was about to stand up to leave, he noticed his son coming through the gray metal door.

Young Hollywood handed his ID card to a lady officer, who was sitting at a long wooden table with metal folding legs. She looked up at him and flashed her teeth, which were covered with braces. Her hair was in tiny micro-braids and pulled to the back. "Mr. Celebrity," she said, her eyes examining him from head to toe.

Young Hollywood threw his head up, "Where my people?"

She pointed toward the third row, nearly the eighth table down.

He moved in that direction, walking with an extraordinary swagger that couldn't be imitated. He'd had the coolest demeanor you'd ever want to see. His walk alone made nearly the entire visitation room stare in his direction. Other cats were calling his name, and he occasionally threw them the peace sign. If they were close enough, he'd stop and dap them up. When he approached the table where his father and up-and-coming stepmother were sitting, they both rose from their seats.

Hammer embraced him first. "You lookin' good," Hammer said, and then he turned to Atiya. "This is Atiya."

Young Hollywood, being the gentleman and gangster he was, knew how to turn on his charm when it was needed. "Can I call you mama?" he asked. Then he hugged her.

"I don't have a problem with that," she said.

They separated, and the three of them sat down around the round wooden table.

Young Hollywood looked at Hammer. "Why you won't never let me know ahead of time when you comin'?"

"We just stopped by while we were down here checkin' on some property," Hammer said.

Young Hollywood nodded and gave his daddy a devious grin, as if he knew Hammer wasn't telling the complete truth. When he showed up unannounced, he always had something to share with him.

Atiya flashed an overwhelming smile, then patted the back of Hammer's hand. "Go ahead, Rufus. Tell him," she insisted.

Hammer's eyes sparkled with joy when he looked at Atiya. Only love could make a man feel that way. An electric bolt of energy was running through him. He looked away from Atiya and stared at Young Hollywood. He couldn't hide his emotions if he wanted to. His eyes turned teary, and they were tears of joy. He finally whispered, "You'll be comin' home in the next fourteen months."

He couldn't believe it, but he didn't want to question his daddy as to how it happened. He wanted to know, and deep down inside he knew he'd have to sit down and talk with him one on one in the near future. Young Hollywood leaned closer to Hammer. "What about Scooter?" he whispered.

Hammer silently shook his head. He was hurt on the inside, and the grieving pain was shown all over his face. "He died," Hammer whispered.

Young Hollywood didn't feel any remorse, but he didn't want to appear heartless and ruthless in front of his new mother. He raised his hand toward his forehead with two fingers pressed tight together.

Approximately thirty-nine days ago, Scooter was transferred to Augusta Medical State Prison by ambulance. It was rumored that he'd died twice and was brought back to life by a machine. Actually, after Young Hollywood had ordered the hit out against him, he was stabbed over fourteen times, from his head down to his calves. He'd been beaten in his head with combination locks and dumped over the upstairs railing in the prison dorm. As a result, his spine was pinched, and he was paralyzed from the waist down. All the karate in the world couldn't stop the goons that nearly ended his life. For a while, he lived off a machine that kept his heart pumping. Scooter was a dying man, and he was in torturous pain. He nearly felt death just to breath. His lungs burned, and one of them was punctured, which caused massive internal bleeding.

When Hammer and his attorney went to visit with Scooter, they saw a man whose body had wasted away to nothing more than a skeleton. His head was shaved bald, and his facial bone structure was disfigured. In his private hospital room, he was attached to enough machines to run the entire prison.

A nurse was standing over him mopping his grotesque face with a damp washcloth. She looked up at Hammer and the attorney when they entered. Her face was shaped in the form of a teardrop, and she wore heavy make-up. She was in her early fifties and wore a white nursing uniform with cheap plastic shoes. She raised her finger to her lips, telling them to be quiet.

Hammer pulled her away from the attorney. He extended his hand out to her, and she shook it. "I'm his uncle, Rufus Hayes," he said, staring at her with intense eyes. He'd lied through his teeth, but he did have paperwork declaring such a fib, not to mention a trust fund for him.

"Truthfully?" the nurse asked nervously.

"I'm a powerful man. I can handle the truth." His words were delivered more like a message than a statement.

Her eyes quickly searched his. "He's not gonna make it past next week. The administration doesn't allow us to give out information like this because the majority of the families can't handle reality."

He nodded. "I understand," he said. There was a short pause, and then he gave her a hint to leave them alone. When she left the room, Hammer pulled up a chair to Scooter's elevated bedside. His eyes were closed, and the only sounds that could be heard were the beeping noises coming from one of the machines and another machine that breathed for him. Hammer clutched his boney fingers inside his fleshy hands. Caressing Scooter's hand as if he was a woman, Hammer then whispered, "If you can hear me, Scooter, move your fingers against my hand. I'm not a stranger. This is Hammer. Can you hear me?"

Scooter wiggled his fingers inside of Hammer's hands.

Hammer eyes cut to the attorney that stood over him.

The attorney nodded his head and whispered, "Go ahead."

"Do you know why you're on your deathbed?" Hammer asked.

Scooter's eyes slowly blinked open; Hammer's word forced him to open his eyes.

The attorney's eyes even opened wide at the type of question he asked.

"I was born a killer," Scooter managed to whisper, "and I know Wood is responsible fa doin' me like dis." His sentence was barely heard.

"Was he wrong?" Hammer asked as his eyes narrowed, his lips and teeth pressed together.

"He feared me, and he had every reason to. You make sho you tell him I said that." Scooter's eyes were filled with water. He then closed them and left them closed. Tears streaked his boney face.

Hammer was still caressing his tiny fingers. He was staring hard at Scooter's face. "Wuz wrong?" Hammer asked. His head cocked to the side. "Speak your heart."

"Come closer," Scooter said, barely a whisper.

Hammer leaned his ear toward Scooter's mouth.

Scooter then began whispering, "Tell Wood I robbed him. I was the one with the flashlight and the other arm behind my back. I was da reason yo' grandson was placed in da microwave..." His voice trailed off, and he turned his head and grinned.

Hammer nodded and moved his mouth to Scooter's jaw. He kissed him on his cheek. Then he covered his mouth and nose with both hands. Moments later, Scooter was flat-lined.

The emergency alarm buzzed and alerted the nurses' station. The door came open, and two nurses rushed in and went to Scooter's aid. Hammer and the attorney were standing next to one another. They stared on as if they were in shock. A doctor entered and went to the bed. They were checking vital signs, but there were none to check. Scooter was gone.

The doctor turned to Hammer. He was short and wore a bald head and a white overcoat on top of a nice suit. Hammer glanced at his wristwatch, an expensive Rolex. Hammer was impressed. Then he glanced down at the doctor's feet and noticed expensive Gators with a gold tip. Hammer shook the doctor's hand.

"I'm sorry about everything," the doctor said.

Hammer turned and walked away with the attorney right behind him. Hammer always liked his employees in nice alligator-skin shoes. He was beginning to build his own secret society.

# CHAPTER 67

On the first day of Six Nine's trial, there was an entourage of TV reporters huddled together outside the courthouse on Pryor Street, even though they were there to interview the attorney he'd hired. He was from California, and his track record for beating jury trials stretched from the West Coast to the East Coast. His name was Peter Desoto, a short man with jet-black hair slicked to the back. His skin was pale olive, and he had handsome features with bright blue eyes. He was the type of man who made his attire look good instead of the other way around.

It was rumored that he had requested three million dollars to represent Six Nine. LC and some members of the crew had hit a lick and took the attorney $700K in cash. Peter Desoto was feared by prosecutors, and judges from all over recognized his name. That alone had sparked the Black Cartel's interest in hiring him. LC had heard about him in a *XXL* magazine, how he'd beaten murder cases in Los Angeles, Chicago, Detroit, Miami, and even against the Feds—cases ranging from low-level criminals who were sponsored by some type of Mafia or secret organization to high-paid celebs. Today, Peter Desoto was in Atlanta, Georgia, sitting in a jammed packed courtroom with his legs crossed. In his hand was a nail file; he was toying around with his manicured nails. Next to him was Six Nine in a triple-black tux with a black silk tie neatly tucked inside his vest. He looked like a professional athlete and wore medicated rimless wood-framed Cartier glasses on his face. His face was shaved, and he wore his mustache trimmed. He'd cut off all of his hair and wore a close-shaved haircut.

The attorney looked over toward his left. The jury box was filled with people who wanted to hear an excited case. Six were black, two were Latino, and four were white.

Six Nine didn't wanna stare too long. He knew jurors like to try to read the facial expressions of some defendants. He shifted his attention to the huge black bailiff who stood on the front left corner. An American flag was next to him. Then Six Nine's eyes shifted around a little. He didn't have one friend or family member there to support him. He grinned to himself and slowly faced the front. Six Nine had the most intelligent look across his face: a look he'd never possessed in his life. This was part of the expensive attorney strategy. Six Nine adjusted his tie and the collar on his shirt.

His mind flashed somewhere else, far away from the Fulton County courtroom. He had a vision of a row of expensive cars, all driven off the showroom floor. A smile nearly spread across his face. He saw himself and his crew pulling up in front of the most extravagant nightclub in Atlanta. The line was long, but the Black Cartel wouldn't have to wait. He thought about BMF and the night he saw them at Magic City. He remembered how they pulled up, stepped out, and guarded the parking lot. He envisioned himself in that position, with enough goons to rotate three shifts. There was more than enough work around the city to keep them all busy.

He knew the trial started at nine a.m., and he was getting bored. Then, he saw an extravagant female in a skirt and blouse and a soft leather briefcase stroll pass him and his attorney. His eyes followed her to the DA's table.

Even Peter Desoto had to take a look at her. He nudged Six Nine with his right elbow and asked, "She's hot, isn't she?"

Six Nine held his composure. He nodded his head, but he sharply cut his eyes away from her.

"She's the appointed," Peter Desoto said. "She's never tried a murder case nowhere. We'll eat her alive."

Five minutes had passed, and it was now ten minutes until nine. Suddenly, mumbled chattering was growing louder from the audience. Everyone in the courtroom craned their necks or turned their heads around to see what all the commotion was about. Six Nine had nearly spun around in his seat. He saw LC come in first, wearing a pinstriped suit, crocodile shoes, and a black fedora. He led the way for a group of nearly a dozen goons. They were all dressed alike: same suit, same shoes, and same fedoras. They lined the back wall at the rear of the courtroom. Six Nine turned and faced the front again. He knew the jurors were watching him now. He kept his eyes away from them to keep a genuine confident look across his face.

When the clock struck nine, the big black bailiff stepped toward the side door. "All rise!" he shouted. He opened the door and held it for the judge.

When the judge stepped inside the courtroom, the first thing he noticed was twelve men lined the back wall. Each of them had their fedoras pressed against their chest. Every last one of them had their heads bowed and their eyes closed, as if they were silently praying. He couldn't believe it. He casually climbed up to his bench. He looked over his courtroom again. "You may be seated," he said.

Everyone sat down, all except the dozen men who lined the wall of the courtroom. They never raised their heads and never removed the hats from their chests.

Court was in session.

Six Nine glanced at the clock again. It was now 9:01 a.m., time for the first real lick from the Black Cartel.

Lil' Willie's stopwatch on his wrist also said it was 9:01. He studied the parking and the front entrance of the Federal Bank in Marietta, Georgia. The morning was breezy. A light rain had come down last night, and even though it had stopped, the streets were still wet. At that moment, five armed goons, dressed in jeans, vests, fatigue overcoats, and high-tech boots rolled their Pepé Le Pew ski masks down over their faces in a parked Suburban. They rolled from the SUV as it pulled up in front of the bank, armed to the T with mini-assault rifles and nylon backpacks and black spray paint for the cameras. When they entered, they began spraying pepper spray, blinding the civilians. People began screaming for their lives.

"Everybody down!" one of the goons yelled. He jumped up on the counter with his assault rifle aimed at them.

The other goons spread out, moving like trained Marines. The guns were aimed at the many faces of the bank workers. The vault was opened. The bank manager knew he was facing his Maker if he didn't comply.

Back in the parking lot, Lil' Willie was now listening on the police scanner. The silent alarm had been pressed, and the call had just gone across the radio. The five goons were filing out one at a time. The last man chained the doors from the outside. When the SUV pulled off, Lil' Willie got out of the parked station wagon. He pulled on a brown

Chic-fil-A cap and dialed 911 from his cell phone.

The dispatcher answered.

"Yes, I would like to report a bank robbery." He already had his lie prepared.

# CHAPTER 68

Later that night, Peter Desoto waited downstairs in the lobby of Ritz Carlton Hotel. He was surrounded by total elegance, a magnificent layout with a huge burning fireplace. He sat in a comfortable cushioned chair with a laptop computer on his thigh. His cell phone rang, and he answered it. "Hello. May I help you?"

"Hey, Mr. Desoto," the voice said from the other end.

"Yes. Speaking."

"I'm parked out front in da yellow cab. Come out. I got something fa ya."

"Well, I hope it's not a bullet."

"Jus a payment," the voice said.

Peter Desoto got up and left his computer in his seat. He was sure nobody would steal it there. When he walked outside, the night air rushed his face.

The cab was there. Two guys were sitting in the front seat, and another guy waited in the back. The backseat passenger leaned down and motioned his hand for Mr. Desoto to get in.

Mr. Desoto pulled the door open and got in and sat down. He sensed something was wrong by the way his flesh crawled.

Lil' Willie pulled up a nylon duffel bag from the floor and politely handed it to the attorney. "Here's $300K. This will make our tab an even two million. By Thursday night this time, you'll be paid in full, and if that's the last day of the trial, I'll be eating dinner with Six Nine and the rest of you guys."

The attorney stuck his hand out, and Lil' Willie shook it. Mr. Desoto got out of the cab and carefully moved back through the electric doors and vanished as the cab pulled off.

The second day of the trial, the mother of the midget was called to take the stand. She was a midget herself. They caller her Ruth, and she stood four-three. Ruth was forty-six years old and dressed in nothing but Baby Phat and Nikes and still partied as if she was in her early twenties. She wore her hair in fishbone braids. She moved quickly when they called her to the stand, and she waved out at people as if she was in a Morris Brown parade. When she was finally seated, her eyes darted around the courtroom. It was jam-packed, and she saw the ten men in pinstriped suits lining the back wall. They stood the same way with their hats pressed against their chests and their heads bowed.

When the female district attorney took the floor in a casual two-piece skirt suit, the courtroom fell silent. She carried in her hand a manila envelope stuffed with black-and-white photos of every victim who was killed by Six Nine. "Good morning, Miss Bartow," the DA said cheerfully.

Ruth leaned into the microphone. Her chair was equipped with three encyclopedias for her to sit on so she could reach it. "Hey, y'all," was all she said, but her words were loud and boomed all through the courtroom.

Six Nine and Peter Desoto listened patiently as the DA hit her with several question. Not one time did Peter object, nor did he raise an eyebrow. He leaned over toward Six Nine and whispered in his ear, "I hate when prosecutors try to use witnesses of the family to get a conviction."

Six Nine could only nod his head, because he didn't know the law, and he damn sure wasn't trying to learn it then.

"No more questions, Your Honor," the DA said. She turned on her heels with swiftness and took a swallow of water from a glass. She sat it back down and slightly cut her eyes over to Peter and Six Nine.

"Any question from the defense?" the judge asked.

Peter Desoto sprung to his feet and turned and looked toward the many faces of the courtroom. He was poised and standing full erect. He moved toward the jury box, allowing his hands to rub the wooden rail that caged them in. He looked in the eyes of each and every juror. "Good morning, ladies and gentlemen of the jury."

They all spoke back, and a few women blushed, but he didn't pay any attention to them—or at least he didn't show it.

He turned his attention to Ruth Bartow, stared at her in her eyes. He moved toward the witness stand and turned the microphone toward him and said, "Your Honor, I would like to ask the court if we could all bow our heads and say a prayer for each and every last one of those innocent people who were killed in that apartment."

The judge gave a confused look, his eyes nearly squinting. He couldn't refuse a man who wanted to pray. He thought of himself as a God-fearing man. He agreed.

Peter spoke in to the microphone, "Will everyone please bow their heads?"

The courtroom loomed in total silence.

Peter looked around. Every head was bowed, and eyes were closed. He made eye contact with the lady prosecutor. She gave him the most evil stare before dropping her head also. Peter started, "Dear Father God, our Christ and Savior..." All the deceased names were called. Peter then called out Six Nine's real name, Bernard Reese. That alone made the prosecutor come out of prayer and object, and when she did, chaos erupted in the entire courtroom. It was exactly what Peter Desoto wanted.

Across town in Alpharetta, Georgia, a street just east of Georgia 400 was lined with million-dollar houses. Fifteen members of the Black Cartel, including LC, pulled up to the front of one of those estates in a stolen service truck. A U-haul truck followed that one, and they also had a white commercial van loaded with hydraulic jacks, sledgehammers, metal detectors, lock busters, and their two drug-sniffing dogs.

Big Low was the tail. He was driving a burgundy and gray Chevy TrailBlazer. He was dressed in jeans, boots, a crisp white clean button-down shirt, and a yellow construction hard hat on top of his head. Each of the vehicles pulled into the long brick driveway. LC got out first, dressed like a construction worker with the bright yellow hard hat also. He carried a piece of long, wide cardboard rolled and tucked underneath his arm. Big Low followed in stride, and they climbed the red brick steps together. The front entrance was twin white French doors. LC pressed the doorbell. According to their sources, nobody would be here. The house belonged to an old-school drug kingpin from Seattle, Washington that had been living in Atlanta for nearly a year. He had revealed his hand to the wrong female.

He pressed the doorbell again, and they waited patiently for another three minutes or so. They looked at each other for a brief moment, as if to be giving each other the go-ahead. Big Low turned around and motioned his arm. The rear doors of the white van flew open, and two slender guys hopped out. They wore gray coveralls and carried the quiet whisper lock buster. When they got up to the red bricks they popped the door lock with a hydraulic pump. LC entered first and stood in the foyer. No alarm came on. They held scanners to their ears waiting for a call to come across the airwaves. Five minutes, and there was still nothing. By the time fifteen minutes had passed, all fifteen members were inside the beautiful, spacious estate. They'd taken up every piece of furniture in the living room; it was now loaded onto the trucks. The living room floors were made of gold and white marble. Three of them spread out with a sledgehammer and eye protecting goggles. They began busting the marble tile, looking for one of two safes that were supposed to be built into the living room floor.

Upstairs, the master bedroom was equipped with expensive drapes and a king-sized bed with mahogany dressers. LC walked Go Getta through the room and into the huge walk-in closet. There was a row of garment bags hanging in there, along with a few mink jackets. The dog didn't detect anything. "Take the carpet up," he told one of the younger goons. He immediately went to work around the edges of the room. LC went back inside the closet and began snatching every piece of clothing and jewelry and throwing it out. After he emptied it, he eased around the walls and knocked in certain spots. The left side of his face was pressed against the wall. He knocked every few inches until he made it all the way around to the door again. He stopped, his head turning side to side. Then something told him to look up. The closet ceiling didn't look right. He clicked the light switch on the wall. The closet lights blinked off and on. Then he noticed another switch at the rear of the closet, he went to it and flipped the switch, and then suddenly the entire ceiling slid back. LC looked up in amazement and said in a low voice, "I be damned."

An hour and fifteen minutes later, they'd gotten away with $1.7 million in cash and every piece of furniture, clothes, expensive artwork and décor, and whatever else they could get. This was just the second day of trial, and they had pulled off their biggest lick yet.

Later that night, LC met with Peter Desoto. He copped a suite in the Ritz Carlton himself. When Peter came to LC's room he gave him an extra large duffel bag that was stuffed with bundles of money that equaled up to $700K in clean cash. Peter Desoto was impressed with the way the crew conducted business, and he'd remember that.

When he left the room, LC got on the phone. He called Lil' Willie to see was everything set up for tomorrow. It was all confirmed. Afterwards, he phoned several comrades. Everybody was giving him the same response: It was good on their end.

# CHAPTER 69

It was Wednesday morning, approximately 8:37, the third day of trail, which would probably be the most heckled one. Six Nine was dressed in Polo lined pants and a collarless shirt. His physique was well defined in what he had on. His posture, along with his attitude and swagger, said more than enough. His powerful attorney was sharing major game with him, and that alone had made him feel more superior. He had a lot of influence over the rest of the Black Cartel. It was a powerful statement that was made, and even more were about to be made.

He crossed his legs and cleared his throat in a most professional manner. This would be the day he would test himself. He would use the most polite voice, which he'd practiced for the last four months. He hoped he wouldn't insult the beautiful prosecutor's intelligence. Then again, he didn't give a fuck about her feelings. *This bitch wanna send me to prison fa da rest of my life,* he thought. He slightly cut her eyes over toward her. "Fuck yo' feelin's," he mumbled.

Peter shot toward him and patted Six Nine's shoulder. "Just relax. It'll be a breeze," he said. Then he looked toward the prosecuting table at the assistant, a blond-haired white guy with broad shoulders. He stood about five-eleven and was very handsome. When 8:53 a.m. rolled around, Peter looked back to examine the courtroom. The goons in black weren't there. He looked back toward Six Nine and said in a whisper, "Your crew isn't coming in this morning?'

Six Nine flexed his long fingers. He was feeling exhilarated and began glancing around involuntarily. He actually got a couple of thumbs-up from the audience. Then, in a low, raspy drawl, he said, "Very, very big day." He removed his glasses from his face and rubbed the bridge of his nose.

"What are you guys into?" Peter Desoto asked. He didn't want to raise any suspicion toward his client.

Before Six Nine could answer, the judge entered the courtroom.

The big black bailiff yelled out, "All rise!"

The entire courtroom shuffled to their feet.

Six Nine was nearly the last person to stand, and when he looked back over his shoulder, he noticed four members of the Black Cartel, all dressed in black three-piece Ralph Lauren Purple Label suits and handcrafted crocodile-skin shoes. A smile nearly appeared across Six Nine's face, and he slightly nudged Peter Desoto with his elbow. "It feel good to have goons on yo' team, certified, loyal. And you know da best part about it?"

"What?" the attorney replied.

"I don't even know these niggas back here," Six Nine said.

They sat after the judge gave them all the green light.

"I'll be recognized through every zone all over da city in a lil' while."

Peter Desoto laughed and asked, "Why not all over the world?"

There was a short pause. Six Nine really had something to think about. Then he said, "A-Town, dis is my world."

Court was in session.

On the same time schedule, just a few blocks away almost, a guy by the name of Aaron Allen, who was a casual dresser and business owner who stood nearly six feet tall, got into the shower quick, brushed his teeth, and dressed even quicker. Aaron lived downtown in an expensive apartment building—a high-rise, equipped with two penthouses, valet parking, and more than one bellboy. Inside his state-of-the-art kitchen, he went to the fridge and removed a container of Tropicana orange juice and cracked open two eggs. He separated the whites from the yokes and downed the orange juice and the protein in one shot. When his doorbell rang, he raised his head, bunching his eyebrows together in pure curiosity. *Who could that be?* he wondered.

He walked through the hallway and into his spacious living room. He quickly flipped his wrist and checked his watch. It was only sixteen minutes after nine. When he got to the front door, he looked out through the peephole. In the hallway were two Fulton County police officers standing nonchalantly. Aaron's heart nearly fell to the bottom of his stomach. He was desperately wondering what he'd done now. He thought about the young girl he picked up last week. *That bitch said she was eighteen.* He gritted his teeth and took a deep breath. He unchained the door handle.

The two goons rushed inside, and one of them caught Aaron square across the bridge of his nose with a right hand that was covered by a pair of brass knuckles. Blood splattered in seconds.

Aaron grabbed his face and stumbled backwards and fell across the glass living room table, which shattered into several tiny pieces. His vision became blurry within seconds. He couldn't even make out a face.

"You got five minutes," one of the officers said.

"For what?" he barely yelled out, his hands and face covered in blood.

Another powerful blow came to his midsection.

He balled up and grabbed his stomach, and vomit erupted from his mouth.

"Keys to the jewelry store. Combination to the vault and safes," the officer said.

Aaron Allen couldn't believe his ears. He thought maybe he wasn't hearing them correctly. Then again, he knew these guys didn't come to play games either. He quickly decided to give them what they wanted. Before they left, they hogtied him buck naked and left him there across his king-sized bed. They took photos of him with a vibrator wedged between his ass cheeks.

In the parking lot of a shopping plaza on Gresham Road, there was another jewelry store owned by a Chinese couple that catered to the black community, mostly dope boys and their girlfriends. The store had been open for a couple of hours when a Dodge Ram pickup truck came crashing through the entire front window, muscling its way in. Another SUV pulled up to the curb, and six young goons dressed in black hopped out and ran into the store. They moved swiftly, breaking the glass shelves with hammers and cleaning out every piece of jewelry in sight. They took diamonds and rubies form the safe and got away with nearly $70K in cash.

Another bank was hit right after lunch break was over. The only thing eyewitnesses saw were five women. A security officer was shot, and still nobody was caught. The Black Cartel had their shit together, and it was still the third day of trial.

# CHAPTER 70

The moment Six Nine took the stand, he jumped out of the gate with his version of the story. The jury was anxious to hear him speak his side. Even the Fulton County officers and the remainder of the people in the courtroom thought his should be an interesting testimony. Six Nine held his composure as his eyes swept across the courtroom, glancing at several unknown faces. Members of his clique now occupied the last two pews on either side. To his left was a professional artist, feverishly drawing pictures of him.

Six Nine's mind flashed back a few months ago, with a broad and vivid imagination. It was the second time Peter Desoto had visited Six Nine on Rice Street. They sat in the small, private room, one across from one another, a screen of glass and chicken wire separating them.

On that day, Peter Desoto was clad in a beige two-piece suit and hard-bottom shoes. He flipped open his expensive briefcase and leafed through several pieces of paper, occasionally cutting his eyes up toward Six Nine. "I get paid to beat cases, and I charge a lot of money to make my clients look good—more than good actually," the attorney said.

There was a short pause. Six Nine was covered with perspiration. He looked down his nose at Peter Desoto. He looked like a caged madman. "I feel dat," he nearly growled.

"Do you really?"

Now they were making eye contact. Six Nine had a deadly stare in his eyes. He didn't really understand where the attorney was coming from, but he agreed anyway.

Peter Desoto went on. "So do you wanna go hard or go home?"

Six Nine smiled, his teeth gleaming. "I'm hard, pimp, but I damn sho wanna go home."

Peter Desoto nodded and looked down at more paperwork. Then he cut his eyes up to Six Nine and back toward the paperwork. "Did you do it?" Peter Desoto asked him in a casual manner.

"Naw. You know who did dat shit."

Another pause.

"I'm charging you three million dollars to create the best damn lie that the courts would want to hear. I'm a high-priced professional liar," he said. "Don't you know I can tell when someone is lying to me?" Then he added, "Now do you wanna go hard or go home?"

"Why da fuck do you keep askin' me dat shit? I wanna go motha' fuckin' home!" Six Nine yelled.

Peter Desoto stared at him long and hard. His eyes didn't blink. He knew Six Nine was guilty as a son-of-a-bitch, and it was written all over his face. He sat back and folded his arms across his chest. Leaning back on the two back legs of the chair, he commented, "We gonna have to put you at the scene of the crime, because it's evident that you were there. Now, how good you are at telling a story that'll convince a judge and a jury?"

"I don't know," Six Nine said, "but I damn sho can practice."

Peter Desoto smiled. "We'll start as if you're the leading actor in a movie. Have you ever seen *Training Day*?"

Six Nine nodded.

"Well, when you get on that stand, I want you to perform like Denzel Washington." He pointed an expensive fountain pen toward Six Nine. "Let me hear your side of the story."

Six Nine fired rapidly with his words. The female who answered the front door was someone he knew. As for the midget, he'd had sex with her two times in the past. That would be good also. He was there to see them. He asked Peter, "Any eyewitnesses against me?"

"Not one. You're the only witness. Everybody else is dead. Come on, Denzel. Don't let me down."

Six Nine grinned ear to ear. He was beginning to get his swag back. He leaned slightly in his seat. With his left arm dangling and his head cocked, he could really be arrogant at times. Then he asked, "Can you let me know what kind of food was in the house?"

Peter Desoto was impressed at that, and he pointed the pen his way again. "Good point." He began leafing and fumbling through his paperwork. Moments later he said, "Pizza Hut, three empty boxes and one meat lovers with four slices left."

"Me and shawty was fuckin' earlier when everybody else came."

"I'm gonna need you to learn those guys' names—at least nicknames. You can't mess this up, Denzel."

Now it was time for Six Nine to perform. He'd either get an Oscar award or an EF number and a one-man cell in Jackson State Prison.

Peter Desoto took the floor, ready to costar in the movie alongside Six Nine. He went up to the stand and whispered, "Don't mess this up, Denzel."

Six Nine nodded with pure confidence. Bernard Reese was on his way to stardom. The *Atlanta Journal Constitution* would have loved to take the article. Fox Five wouldn't let it slide either, not with Peter Desoto behind him.

Later that night LC, Big Low, Lil' Willie, and ten more goons were all gathered in plush, comfortable chairs and sofas in the pool suite at the Renaissance Atlanta downtown, surrounded by pure elegance. A long dining room table was covered from one end to the other with cash money. Cigars and cigarillo rolled blunts of purple exotic weed were being passed around by a naked female in six-inch heels. Another female, a hired stripper from Strokers, paraded around naked and in heels also; she carried a tray of poured champagne. This was a corporate event for them. They'd pulled off a lick that was worth nearly two million dollars, including the flawless diamond, rubies, emeralds, several strings of pearls, and enough gold to build a twenty-foot solid statue. In the last three days, they had wreaked havoc all over the city while banks and jewelry stores were losing tremendous revenue. The Black Cartel was gaining big numbers by the hour. Their goal was to cripple the city of Atlanta in one week, lay low for a few months, and hit them all over again.

When a knock came from the door, every available hand in the hotel room clutched a weapon of some sort. LC got up from the table with an unlit cigar hanging from his mouth. A fifty-caliber Desert Eagle was snuggled in the palm of his huge hand. When he noticed Peter Desoto on the other side, he tucked the big gun in the small of his back. Then he fanned his hand at the rest of the crew for them to put heir guns away, at least out of eyesight.

He opened the door, and Peter walked inside, dressed in a gray jogging suit and New Balance running shoes. LC greeted him with a powerful handshake and a pat on the back. Peter Desoto's eyes swept across the room, and the stacks of money caught his attention. He was nearly finding it hard to breath at the sight of all the money. And all he could say was, "The jury is deliberating. I'm sure we'll get a not guilty verdict. He's a good actor."

# CHAPTER 71

Two weeks before, Big Low was in the Blue Flame Strip Club on Bankhead. He wore Sean John sweatpants, a wife-beater, and a pair of retro Jordans. He'd had a couple of lady friends that danced at the club and provided him information on any new licks around town. He caught up with a high yellow girl they called Cream. Cream was classy. Despite being from the Bluff, she possessed an outstanding and well-shaped body. She wore a honey-blonde wig, gold lipstick, and matching paint on her toe and fingernails. She exited the club in jeans and a halter top, pulling a rolling luggage bag.

Big Low stalked the parking lot from behind the steering wheel of a black souped-up '96 Chevy Impala with tinted windows. Cream went to the driver's side door of an Infinity and disabled her car alarm. It chirped. Big Low flashed his high beams, and she turned and looked in his direction. He flashed her again, and she walked over to the car.

Not recognizing him or the car, she finally saw his face. A smile spread across hers. She moved swiftly to his side, the window fell, and she hugged him. "Nigga, where you been? I got some real good news fa you."

He kept it cool, reached in the visor above his head, and removed two white sealed envelopes stuffed with cash. "Accurate information or hearsay?" he asked.

"Oh, baby, dis shit accurate. I'm always on point. Bitch like me always got to stay two steps ahead of the game. Only one thang though."

"What?" he asked with a bewildered look across his face.

"I don't know an accurate date." Her eyes became anxious. She was praying Big Low could use the information, and he did.

Two days later, he found two white guys, both crack smokers but in good heath. It took him three days to clean them up. They both liked the proposition that was laid on the table for them. It was free money.

It was now the forth and final day of trial, and Six Nine was sitting on pins and needles, hoping like hell he'd be sipping on some expensive champagne and in the ass club by midnight. He was in a tailored Armani suit. His hairline was sharp, and his beard was trimmed and connected. The courtroom was still slightly empty, and he had enough time to think to himself. It was a million-dollar robbing crew. Just the thought of that nearly made him smile. Six Nine wasn't into keeping up with the Joneses. He *was* the Joneses. He envisioned himself through his third eye in this big spacious, state-of-the art high-priced strip club with a gym, kitchen, game room, a spiral staircase, and flowing marble everywhere. He loved the women and definitely had an eye for taste.

He'd get back to that though. He was lost in thought again. This time he could see Hammer bowing down to him. He'd read newspaper and magazine articles about him. He studied everything about him, and the man fascinated him. He still had some unfinished beef with Hammer. Who wouldn't? Hammer was the reason he was sitting in that courtroom fighting for his life. He folded his arms across his chest in a stubborn manner. He had a relentless state of mind. Then he smiled and envisioned himself in the back of a Maybach geeked up on x-pills and his favorite drink, promethazine-codeine cough syrup, and Tupac bumping in the background. Television reporters would be asking him questions, and magazines publishers would want to do segments on him. He would be the new leader of the Black Cartel.

Down in Jonesboro, Georgia, the rain was falling and the sky was dark gray. Three dump trucks rolled in a line. They were filled with dirt and covered with thick plastic tarps, strapped down with bungee cords and hooks. They moved at the speed limit, and each driver was damn good at what he was doing: trafficking cocaine and heroin. The work was coming from Miami but picked up from the Port of Savannah, Georgia.

Then out of nowhere, a row of black SUVs and Crown Victorias emerged, nearly surrounding the dump trucks on the expressway. The driver of the last truck noticed the bold letters that said "DEA." Then there was the K-9 unit, then the blue lights. They forced the three dump trucks to the side of the road. Nearly a dozen men in jeans and blue DEA jackets emerged from the SUVs, weapons drawn. LC and Big Low led the way. The two white guys played their role also. They "arrested" the three drivers and loaded them up in the rear of one of the SUVs. It didn't take them ten minutes to hijack the trucks. They took them to Atlanta, somewhere on the Westside, where they'd located

500 keys of cocaine and 22 keys of china-white heroin.

By 3:30 p.m., the jury had come from the jury room and were taking their seats in the jury box. The foreman remained standing.

The judge looked at him and asked, “Have you reached a decision?”

The foreman nodded his head and kept a serious face, and then he unfolded the paper. “We, the jury, find the defendant not guilty on count one. We, the jury, find the defendant not guilty on count two. We, the jury, find the defendant guilty on count three. We, the jury, find the defendant not guilty on count four.”

The courtroom went into an uproar as the judge banged his gavel and frowned. He stared out into the sea of people, including a bevy of news reporters, and everybody was making all types of noises. Cameras were flashing, and some cheers and whistles rang out also.

Six Nine didn’t smile, nor did he look toward the jury box or the judge. He turned around and saw ten goons in suits, fedoras pressed against their chests, their heads still bowed.

“This court is dismissed,” the judge said. He stood as if he was mad. He went to the jury box and shook each of the jurors’ hands and thanked them all.

Six Nine stood, and Peter Desoto did the same. He looked up at his client. “How you feel?’

Six Nine turned his neck from one side to the other as if he was developing a crook. “I need me a motha’ fuckin’ Newport,” he said in a deep Southern drawl.

Peter Desoto grinned and patted his shoulder. Together, they moved toward the rear of the courtroom where they were escorted by the ten-man entourage. Six Nine acknowledged each and every last one of them with hugs and handshakes. Outside, Six Nine paused briefly on the Fulton County Courthouse steps. He glanced around. The sights and sounds of freedom was displayed before him.

Three triple-black limousines pulled up and stopped. Lil’ Willie bounced out of one of them.

Six Nine went down the steps, and somebody handed him a fresh pack of Newports. He popped one out. Lil’ Willie gave him a light, and he closed his eyes for a moment and allowed the menthol to fill his lungs. After he separated from Peter Desoto with promises to keep in touch, he hugged Lil' Willie. They got in the rear of the middle limo and relaxed in the comfortable leather seats. The first thing he did was demand a phone. He punched in the phone number of A-Town Records and Studios. A secretary answered on the other end.

"Yes, I would like to speak with Mr. Rufus Hamma Hayes please," Six Nine demanded.

"May I ask who's speaking?" she asked in a very professional manner.

Six Nine pulled on his cigarette; the smoke circled his face. Just tell him it's the CEO of Black Cartel Records.

"Just one moment please," she replied.

Moments later, Hammer's voice came through the phone. "Yes? How may I help you?" he answered.

"Yeah, fuck nigga, guess who back!" He hung up the phone in Hammer's face.

The limousines left the courthouse parking lot, and Six Nine was ready to reclaim the city...and this time, there would be no games in A-Town.

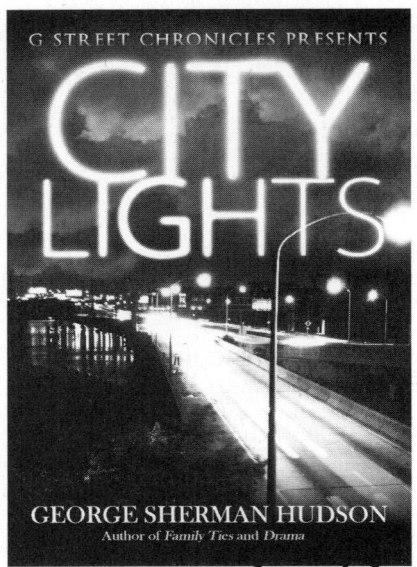

Visit www.gstreetchronicles.com to view all our titles

Join us on Facebook G Street Chronicles Fan Page

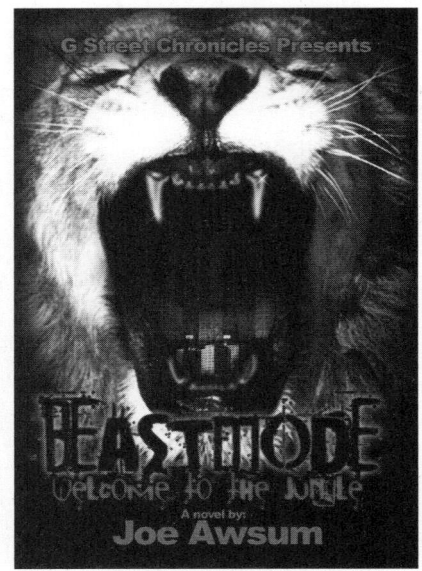

Other titles from G STREET CHRONICLES

City Lights
Beastmode
Executive Mistress
Essence of a Bad Girl
Two Face
Dealt the Wrong Hand
Dope, Death & Deception
Family Ties
Blocked In
Drama

The Love, Lust & Lies Series by Mz. Robinson

Married to His Lies

What We Won't Do for Love

"Coming Fall 2011"

The Lies We Tell for Love (part 3 of Mz. Robinson's Love, Lust & Lies Series)

Still Deceiving
(part 2 of India's Dope, Death & Deception)

"Coming 2012"

Trap House
Drama II

Name:						
Address:			8 s	2		
City/State:						
Zip:				1		

ALL BOOKS ARE \$10 EACH

QTY	TITLE	PRICE
1 1 1 1 1 1 1 1 1 1 1 1 1 1 1 1 1 1 1	A-Town Veteran	
	City Lights	
	Beastmode	
1)	Executive Mistress	
	Essence of a Bad Girl	,
	Dope, Death and Deception	
	Dealt the Wrong Hand	
	Married to His Lies	9 6
	What We Won't Do for Love	
	Two Face	
	Family Ties	
	· Blocked In	
	Drama	
	Shipping & Handling (\$4 per book)	

TOTAL \$

To order online visit

www.gstreetchronicles.com

Send cashiers check or money order to:

G Street Chronicles P.O. Box 490082 College Park, GA 30349